I0672030

THE NEIGHBORHOOD

A NOVEL OF BROOKLYN

&

Some of the People

Who Made It Famous

Alfred J. Faragasso

THE NEIGHBORHOOD

By Alfred J. Faragasso

Published in the United States of America

ISBN 978-1-7354497-0-8 (paperback)
978-1-7354497-1-5 (ebook)

FIRST EDITION

"If you are lucky enough to have lived
in Paris as a young man, then wherever you
go for the rest of your life, it stays with you,
for Paris is a moveable feast."

–Ernest Hemingway to a friend, 1950

"If you are lucky enough to have lived in
Brooklyn as a young man, then wherever you
go for the rest of your life, it stays with you,
for Brooklyn, as with Paris, is a moveable feast."

–Alfred J. Faragasso to himself

PROLOGUE

The story presented herein is a work of pure fiction—for the most part, anyway. To better explain the essence of this novel, the author cites a disclaimer of sorts written by Ernest Hemingway in the preface to his timeless novel A Moveable Feast. It is included here for the very same reasons that Mr. Hemingway included it in his own work.

"If the reader prefers, this book may be regarded as fiction. But there is always the chance that such a book of fiction may throw some light on what has been written as fact."

–Ernest Hemingway
San Francisco de Paula, Cuba
1960

The neighborhood where this story takes place really existed, and the street names and some of the structures still stand to this day. Each character that you encounter is a fictionalized amalgam of many different persons involved in varied incidents wrought from the author's memory. Thus, situations and incidents involving Carmine Della Rocca are recollections drawn from a series of events occurring over many years and involving several different real-life persons. The fact is that the only Carmine the author ever knew was a brilliant student and a perfect gentleman—not much at all like the fictionalized Carmine presented within these pages. The same approach holds for all of the other characters as well.

The author has used first and last names that were common in the neighborhood, but has carefully avoided linking fictional situations with the names of real persons known to the author. In fact, except in two instances, the author has avoided using complete names of any person who actually lived in the neighborhood. One character, Frankie Famiglietti, was a real person and a good friend of the author for many years until his death in April, 2002. The author has sought to memorialize Frankie by using his name for a fictional character who, like the real Frankie, was beloved by many in the neighborhood. The other character with a real-world name is Joe Weintrauben, a high school and college chum of the author. The real Joe became an engineer far outside the world of television.

Whereas all of the events related have happened at one time or another and can be verified by many of the persons who lived in and around the neighborhood, the presentation compresses time as a tool for the storyteller. Many stories involving interesting persons and events have been left out of this book for reasons known only to the author.

Brooklyn was a magical place in which to live and is revered even today for its character and wonder and the fierce loyalty it inspires from its denizens. Yes, Brooklyn was a magical place; in the following pages, I hope you too will experience some of the magic and enjoy a few short days in the life of the neighborhood.

The author (age 6) and his father, out . . .

. . . in the neighborhood

THE NEIGHBORHOOD:
(SOME OF) ITS CHARACTERS

Marie Gargano is a typical long-suffering wife and mother in a neighborhood where many residents struggle to survive. Despite the abusive nature of her marriage, she is committed to her household and her son. With little support from her spouse and insufficient funds for expenses, she does what many other women in the city do: she plans and scrimps and chooses to serve.

Angelo Gargano may not be the perfect archetype of the neighborhood husband and father, but he does represent many men of his era who worked hard at dead-end jobs. Barely earning enough to satisfy his family's needs, he spent freely on his personal needs and leisure time.

Donny represents a lifestyle where selfishness and greed are a part of someone else's life. Naive among his peers, he could not see what was; he saw only incompletely. Honest, ethical, moral, he put others' needs before his own. He took one day at a time without hidden agendas. *Donny's Lament* questions the undermining effects of the looming new order in his neighborhood and in society overall. Changes already disrupt the status quo, but is chaos inevitable? Donny, typically frightened of the unknown, realizes, finally, that family, love, and friendship are essential to the overall welfare and safety of one's self, one's family . . . and one's neighborhood . . . wherever that happens to be.

Robby is a harbinger of positive change. As a youth, he gratified his personal wants regardless of the impact on others. He, like America at that time, was confronted with many issues of ethics and morality. Unable to solve his own problems, he required others to help promote his maturity into polite society. His tenacity is the strength required to satisfy his personal goals amid obstacles presented by an impersonal society.

Nick is a fine example of the American dream. He grew up with little in the way of advantages, yet drove himself and those close to him to major successes. His story should stand as a model for others who feel put down or left behind. He worked hard, studied, asked the right questions, and helped others to share in his growth.

Carmine. *The Neighborhood* may just be the story of how an average guy made his way despite being born into a "What's in it for me?" society. Carmine had little chance for success while living in the neighborhood. His role models taught him to cheat and scheme and use people for his own purposes. His opportunity came when he was struck by cupid's arrow. Love brought about Carmine's transition from loser to lover and then to businessman. His story highlights the miraculous power of love over indifference and greed.

Al is by far the most complex person in the neighborhood: he has money, education, a good job, and a loving wife. Yet, he supports society's passion to use people selfishly. His affair stems from greed and disrespect for his wife and her commitment to their marriage. He risked his stable home to satisfy life's most primal urges. Selfish. Foolish. Greedy.

Al's Soliloquy departs from his straight-forward business style. He questions the superficial nature of societal norms and the value of truth versus myth. He ponders the extent to which our life choices are manipulated by others and the role reality plays in our homes, our businesses, our hearts.

Laine Powers August is a myth that symbolizes the American dream for many: well educated, successful, sophisticated, self affirmed. She succeeds in the high-pressure corporate world of power, wealth, and accommodation. Her private life appeals to one's most narcissistic needs. Proficient in her ability to manipulate men, her goal is self-gratification when she lures Al into her life. He, unwilling to resist her advances, becomes slave to his own ego. Laine transports him from his "humdrum" life of marriage and family into her world, rife with episodes of hedonistic adventure. The superficial nature her lifestyle is devoid of life's essentials . . . love, trust, friendship, honor. She exists in an alternate cosmos that mimics the predatory nature of society in general.

Donna-Marie, though not stereotypical of women and wives of the 1950's, is a caring, generous, and trusting, well-off woman in a neighborhood of persons with mixed means of support. She is committed completely to her husband, and trusts him in all things. As with some neighboring wives, she may have had insights into his activities, but chose to ignore them. She was lucky; he never beat her nor withheld money for household essentials. Her loving family comforted her whenever she felt alone. It was her trusting nature that let her down. In the end, however, her abiding, unselfish love sustained her and won out.

Ellen is one of society's casualties. Her early life contravenes her ability to love or be open to accepting love from another. She disputes the concept that anyone could love her for herself. Untrusting of men and wary of most friendships, she makes her way in society alone, bereft of companionship, depending on herself and her efforts. Her world is fraught with misgivings, fear and doubt: anything good that befalls her must be tainted. When she permits herself to love, she is betrayed.

THE BEGINNINGS

I

It was just an ordinary address: 920 Dean Street, Brooklyn 16, New York. (The 16 was later changed to 38 when the Post Office underwent monumental changes in an attempt to upgrade mail handling and launch itself into the twentieth century—which was already half gone by the time they started.) Located between Classon Avenue on the east and Grand Avenue on the west, Dean Street was bounded on the north by Pacific Street and Bergen Street on the south. Dean Street was a microcosm of Brooklyn itself and, in the life of Donny Gargano, 920 Dean Street and the dozen or so houses bordering it were his entire world. In the days of Donny's youth, not many persons ever ventured far from home—even those who eventually were allowed to cross streets alone. The reality was that most persons lived out their entire lives in the neighborhood, even marrying someone within walking distance of their own residence. Not until the late 1950's did the average person buy a car or venture beyond the Brooklyn or Manhattan corridor. In fact, persons from boroughs other than Brooklyn or Manhattan were rarely seen in Donny's neighborhood. And the relative who lived in New Jersey was considered exotic especially when they spoke with that unfamiliar "twang" that said to everyone, "I ain't from around here."

Donny's family moved into the six-family, wood-frame tenement when he was barely one year old, and his earliest recollection of living there was the day his mother (he called her Ma) wheeled him in his second-hand stroller the few dozen steps along Dean Street and around the corner to Classon Avenue. He was about four years old then, which placed him smack in the middle of the beginnings of WWII—December 1941. Of course Donny's only world was centered around his mom and dad, their four-room cold-water flat, and the stroller in which he traveled. The war, as it turned out, was a blessing to the Gargano's, since Donny's dad, Angelo, finally got some steady work.

Since their marriage in 1936, Angelo and Marie Gargano struggled, as did many of their contemporaries, since work was scarce since the Great Depression. People wondered whether president Roosevelt got the USA into the war with Germany to help stimulate the economy and help put an end to the depression. When Donny was born in 1937, Marie scrimped to buy one egg a week to give him—at a time when eggs were six cents a dozen. Milk was another commodity that by today's standards seemed relatively cheap—about four cents a quart. But Marie Gargano, consistent with so many other mothers of that era, chose to nurse Donny until he was almost three years old. The common folk of the late thirties apparently believed that mother's milk was better than store bought—and besides, it was free.

Smoking was a problem for the Gargano's—they both smoked—and they pinched pennies to buy loose cigarettes, 'loosies' they were called, once a week from the candy store around the corner. When Donny was about six years old, they trusted him to go around the corner with a nickel to buy ten cigarettes for Marie and Angelo. He liked going to the candy store to buy the loosies because it gave him an opportunity to look into the display case with its many different kinds of candies and to savor the exotic aroma of milk chocolate chunks that were sold by the ounce to anyone who had the few pennies it cost.

Moving into 920 Dean Street was not something the Garganos chose to do, nor would they have wanted to move anywhere at all at that time, except that the landlord of their Prospect Place apartment wanted their rooms for his daughter. Maybe he thought it was glamorous for his daughter to live above a drug store. So after only eighteen months in their apartment and with a newborn son, the Garganos left Prospect Place to move onto Dean Street, three blocks north, past St. Marks Avenue and Bergen Street. In moving three blocks further north, they moved out of an all-white neighborhood that had some measure of respectability and into a mixed ghetto-type of setting that was common in the Brooklyn of the 40's. 920 Dean Street housed six families—at that time, all Italian. Attached to it on the left was number 918, another six-family tenement of roughly the same style and age, but infinitely more beautiful in appearance since it was newly refaced with a type of artificial material that was popular in Brooklyn homes in those days. This was also populated by six Italian families. On its right side was an ice house, a single-story structure that was run by the Pillechio family from Bari, Italy. (Most New York City ice men were from Bari, it seemed.) The Pillechio's lived adjacent to the ice house in a three-family house that was 18 feet wide, four stories high, with a three-foot-high wrought iron fence guarding it. They were the "wealthy" people in the neighborhood, which was obvious since they had a car, a truck, and a business and traveled to Italy every year. There weren't too many cars around in those days, and if you had one, you were thought to be rich or, at least, very well off.

Across the street were three attached four-story buildings, each housing twelve families. Some apartments faced Dean Street, while others faced the back yards of the homes on Pacific Street further to the north. These larger buildings were rather plain and would not have stood out from the surrounding buildings except for the huge fire escapes hung on the building fronts. These buildings were exclusively populated by black families. A tiny 'grocery-type' store was located in the lower level of one of these buildings, and everyone who lived within a hundred yards in either direction shopped there for milk or candy or a package of Kool Aid. Thelma Jones owned the store and lived in the back, and whenever you went in, it smelled of good things—foreign things to be sure (that is, things not Italian).

Of interest on this street was the way that everyone got along, though Italians lived in all-Italian buildings, Blacks lived in all-Black buildings, and down a few doors three Jews lived in an all-Jewish building. But everyone in this area of the neighborhood knew everyone else, and all the children played together: White, Black, Jew, Irish. (The Irish lived around the corner and south two blocks.)

II

Marie Gargano made it a point to take Donny out for a walk every day because it was good for him. Although they had barely enough money to pay their rent, which was $12.00 a month in 1941, she managed to keep her apartment and her son scrupulously clean. She was a very proud woman and she would never allow dirt to remain for too long on her son's body or clothes. And so as they strolled up and down Dean Street each day, Marie Gargano, poor and struggling, held her head high knowing that her son was polished shiny from his face to his shoes, as were the chrome fenders on his weathered stroller. Marie Gargano felt like a queen; in turn, she treated Donny like a prince.

Life in Brooklyn in the early forties was peaceful with little concern about the war 'over there.' The war movies were mostly propaganda types that played directly to America's nationalism. Many families saved war stamps; those lucky enough to have adequate cash also bought war bonds. Almost every downtown area had a recruitment center and a platform from which bonds were hawked during the popular rallies that were held almost weekly. Al Jolson once appeared at a band rally set up downtown near the Brooklyn Paramount theater right off the Flatbush Avenue Extension. He sang a couple of his most popular songs, knelt down once or twice, and then urged everyone to "buy bonds." And they did! Marie Gargano hoped one day that she too could afford to buy some bonds and put them away for Donny's education.

As he grew older, Donny became familiar with Marie's weekly routine and looked forward to his ride on the Bergen Street trolley car. He would always kneel down on the rattan-covered window seat and happily watch the shops go by as the trolley approached Flatbush Avenue and a free transfer point. Donny began to notice young boys who hitched rides on the back of trolley cars and jumped off a few feet before the trolley stopped to pick up more passengers. The boys thought they were fooling the motorman who easily saw them in his mirror and tried to slow the trolley gently so as to lessen their chances of falling off and getting hurt. When Marie noticed that Donny laughed at the boys holding onto their precarious perch, she admonished him, "Don't you ever do that; only bad boys do that. If they ever fall off they'll die! Promise?" And Donny always promised that he would never hitch on the back of a trolley car. "Wow! What fun it must be to do that," he thought. He thought about it, but never did it.

The Flatbush Avenue trolley took them downtown to Livingston Street where it made a left turn and headed west toward Brooklyn's Borough Hall. They would get off several blocks before that because Marie liked to shop in Namm's, which was one of the less-expensive places to shop. It was also desirable to shop there because Angelo had opened a charge account years before when he was single and when money was more plentiful. Marie used the charge primarily for Donny's clothes, which were usually irregulars or 'specially marked down.' Marie had dreams about someday being able to shop at A&S or Loeser's, but they were the upscale stores, and for now she could only window-shop their lovely displays. At Christmas time she brought Donny down to see the various displays—especially the life-size Santa who rocked back and forth laughing in Loeser's front window. Donny always banged on the window as if to get Santa's attention, but Santa just kept on rocking and laughing while the wars waged on in Europe and Asia. Perhaps Marie tried to suppress the war effort from her thoughts, knowing that someday her son might also be called to serve in far-away places. She prayed for peace every day.

Marie and Angelo decided to have only one child, and Donny soon learned the joys of being an only child. When he was about six years old, he realized that other families with three or four children were always strapped for space. Their children's toys were scattered all over, and the brothers and sisters would often battle one another over some seemingly insignificant issue. Donny loved having 'his' toys and 'his' bed and being able to do all of the helping that his ma or dad needed. Donny especially liked helping when Marie made homemade bread or fresh ravioli or 'home mades', the long, thin, flat, soft macaroni that persons today refer to as fettuccini. Donny still calls them 'home mades much to his own embarrassment.

III

When the war ended, Angelo began working more regularly, but Marie continued making the most of the money they had by baking her own cakes or making home-made 'something.' Donny loved to help roll out freshly made pasta dough, though only Marie could use the knife to cut it into strips. Donny learned to seal the raviolis that Marie made using a fork around the edges of the ricotta-filled pouches. He always did it twice, because, "We don't want the filling to escape while it cooks in the boiling water." Donny always said that no one anywhere could cook as well as Marie or make things as tasty—except when she prepared escarole and beans or liver or . . . fried flounder filet (on Fridays). Marie was special to Donny, and remained so for as long as she lived.

As good a cook as Marie was, Donny had a difficult time with some of her dishes, especially when it was time for liver . . . or fish, which was every Friday. He rebelled often about how much he hated fish, so that Marie reluctantly prepared pasta fagioli on Fridays. But when it came to liver, Donny could only think and say, "Yuchk!" Not only did the smell of the liver cooking make him sick, the taste made him upchuck more than once.

And so Marie, like many of her stay-at-home sisters, devised methods of tricking her offspring into eating tidbits of whatever dishes he hated. When it was liver night, she sliced the liver into tiny little slivers and try to fork-feed him. "Take just one bite," she would cajole. But Donny prevailed causing Marie to worry that he would shrivel up and die if he did not eat his liver each week.

When it came to him eating carrots, she developed a scheme whereby she made extra-creamy mashed potatoes and then ground up the carrots and mixed them into the potatoes. These Donny could eat—but it took Marie a long period of trial and error to figure it out. The fish issue was more difficult because it was traditional to eat fish each Friday . . . or else die under the pain of mortal sin . . . even if you were at Nathan's in Coney Island and forgot that it was Friday until after you had already eaten half a hot dog. So when the budget allowed, Marie bought shrimp as a substitute for the forbidden meat. Some substitute! Donny, early on, decided that he liked shrimp . . . and pasta fagioli.

IV

After the war ended and with a larger household income, Marie responded to a long-suppressed desire to stretch her wings by seeking out some leisure things to do—apart from cooking, cleaning or shopping for household essentials. Here again, though, she never strayed too far from Dean Street. One of her favorite things to do was to spend an afternoon at the movies; the theater she visited most frequently was the National Theater on Washington Avenue, a short six-block walk from home. Donny loved to go to the movies on Saturday with Marie, since he was entertained during the four or five hours it took to see a double feature, a newsreel, perhaps a weekly Batman or Superman 'serial,' and two or three cartoons. He also anticipated the fantastic lunch that Marie prepared for them to eat . . . during the show. 'Going to the show' meant bringing food, soda, candy or anything else into the theater with you; inside the theater, candy was vended from machines and was expensive. Popcorn came prepackaged in small containers and was overly salty; the average person could make the stuff at home for pennies.

On the Saturdays when she took Donny to the movies, Marie would stop at Sidney's delicatessen at the intersection of St. Marks and Washington Avenues. Sidney's was a mini-market before the term was invented. It was one of those very special shops that ultimately disappeared from Brooklyn neighborhoods never to be seen again. Sidney and his dad, Jewish immigrants, spoke fluent Italian including three or four of the local neighborhood dialects. Local women felt comfortable shopping there for the friendly, personal attention and the product quality. Women agreed, "If you want the finest in Italian foods or spices or imported delicacies in this neighborhood, shop in one place: Sidney's." (Unlike Manhattan and the Bronx, Brooklyn did not have its own 'Little Italy' section except for a tiny enclave in Williamsburg.)

Sidney's store was about twelve feet wide and forty feet deep. The aisles were narrow and the floor-to-ceiling shelves were crammed with a vast array of neighborhood-specific foodstuffs and essential household items. The store was not of the self-service type. Upon entering, customers waited their turn and told Sidney, or his father, what they wanted, and Sidney and a helper went through the store gathering each item and taking them to the front counter. If items were stored on the high shelves, Sidney used his five-foot wooden 'grabber' wand to reach up and topple down a can or box into his hand. This was years before supermarkets.

If you wanted cold cuts, Sidney would slice them up for you. When all the dry foods and canned goods were gathered up front and he finished slicing up your cheese and salami and ham (Marie always had him slice the ham wafer thin since it had 'a much better taste that way'), he tallied the cost. Cash registers were uncommon in the typical neighborhood grocery store in those days, so Sidney and other market owners tallied the cost by hand on a paper bag using a #2 pencil stub kept on the right ear. Sidney never made a mistake adding in all the years that Marie shopped there, though she always checked his addition as soon as she got home. She never saw that pencil fall off his ear either. There were no coupons.

V

A Saturday afternoon trip to the movie theater meant that Marie stopped at Sidney's and bought the 'large' loaf of Italian bread, the kind with the huge crack down the middle and the deliciously crispy crust. She also bought a half pound of Genoa salami, a quarter pound of domestic Swiss cheese, and one pepperoni stick (sliced very thin). Then, she and Donny walked to the movie house with their package carefully tucked under Marie's arm; inside her ample purse was a small jar of Gulden's mustard, a sharp knife and two cloth napkins.

Admission was ten cents plus a two-cent luxury tax (loge seats, three aisles closer to the screen, cost thirteen cents plus tax). So for twelve cents, parents could get themselves or their kids out of the house for most of the day. Parents now had a rare opportunity to be alone. Tenement living did not always ensure that all bedrooms had the luxury of a privacy door; thus, this lifestyle was not conducive to conjugal quiet time. Indeed, many couples looked forward to movie days when there was some certainty that children would be out of the apartment for specified periods of time. Under these common conditions, one wonders how so many large families came from the tenements.

Parents were happy that their kids could be entertained on Saturdays with other neighborhood children also there—

some with sandwiches, others with candy bars or an orange or sarsaparilla soda.

Once seated in her favorite section of the movie theater—usually in the balcony a few seats behind the more expensive loge seats—Marie waited until the appropriate time (how she knew when that was is still a mystery, but it probably had something to do with when the ushers or matrons stopped patrolling her area) before beginning her well-rehearsed ritual. She carefully removed the loaf of crusty Italian bread from the paper bag (trying not to make too much noise) and laid it on one of the napkins on her lap. She removed the small knife from her purse, sliced the loaf lengthwise and laid it open. She then opened the remaining waxed-paper-wrapped packages and doled out the salami, cheese, and pepperoni, making one monstrous and delicious-smelling sandwich (in the Bronx, these sandwiches were called 'sang-weeches'; they weren't called heroes then). Interestingly enough, no one complained about this practice, and patrons throughout the theater did something very similar. As the final act to this gustatorial delight, she applied Gulden's brown mustard—never French's yellow—to both sides of the entire loaf of bread. When done, she cut it in two, giving Donny a slightly smaller piece than her own; then, they feasted while watching the giant screen. If heaven was anything like this . . . Ahhhh.

Going to the movies was an activity that everyone enjoyed, for where else could one go and, for twelve cents, spend so much free and uninterrupted time? Some of the upscale theaters in the downtown area of Brooklyn offered movies plus vaudeville acts. The admission to these theaters was expensive compared with the price of admission at the National. For two movies and vaudeville, it might cost twenty-five cents—a fee that was often beyond the means of persons like Marie Gargano. Nevertheless, there were times when she and Donny would get to see vaudeville performed on stage at the Brooklyn Paramount or the Fox of any of several other theaters on Livingston Street or Fulton Street. It was such a thrill for Donny to see live people perform on stage in colorful costumes and makeup in contrast to the dull and scarred black and white images projected on the aged and torn screen in the National.

Multi-colored spotlights highlighted the colorful vaudeville costumes and stimulated audiences to sit up and cheer for even mediocre acts. Much has been written about vaudeville, but nothing can describe the excitement Donny felt when he saw real people singing and dancing and juggling and telling jokes—some of which were even a bit risqué, but that was OK; it was vaudeville. Vaudeville was great, but for Marie it was just more make-believe. The reality for her was centered about 920 Dean Street; she was household manager and held the purse strings tightly. Though vaudeville was entertaining, she preferred going to the National Theater especially when, twice a year on Tuesday nights, she could see a show and receive a piece of free dinnerware.

It was going on all over Brooklyn during the post-war years: women flocked to the local move house, usually on Tuesday nights, and handed their ticket stubs to the ticket taker in exchange for a free piece of 'fine china.' One week might offer a cup and saucer while the next might be a soup bowl. Over the years, Marie and her neighbors built up several collections of good china this way. With money always scarce and having lived through the Depression, it was a practical thing to do: see a show and get a dish.

This attitude pervaded her way of thinking even when she chose a brand of jelly for Donny's frequent lunches of peanut butter & jelly sandwiches. Why spend money for jelly that came in an 'ordinary' jar when you could buy jelly that came in a jar that could also be used as a glass? Many contemporaries of the Garganos were known to scold children who broke one of their 'good' jelly glasses. In fact, most families had a dozen or so of these glasses, which were always used at family meals and given to children of guests.

VI

Often, when Marie took Donny to the movies, the duration of the day's entertainment somehow precisely coincided with the time it took for their ice box to overflow. In Marie's kitchen stood a small wooden box almost two feet square and just barely four feet high. There were two doors. The top one opened to reveal a chamber of sheet galvanized steel with its bottom lined with corrugated steel upon which rested a solid block of ice. The size of the block depended on several factors: First, how much money you had available for ice that day—a typical ten-cent piece would last about a day and a half, and this is what the Garganos usually purchased. On payday, Marie would sometimes call for a fifteen-cent piece, and the neighbors would know that Angelo got paid. The really poor families across the street got five-cent pieces, since they didn't have the cash reserves that Marie or her contemporaries had. The second determining factor was the size of one's ice box—the more affluent you were, the larger your ice box. Many professionals, like those who lived along Eastern Parkway, owned ice boxes that looked a lot like today's refrigerators: five or six feet high and plenty wide. These boxes could hold half a cake of ice (a piece five-feet long by eighteen inches wide). It was cut into several smaller pieces and then placed into the upper compartment onto the same type of corrugated galvanized steel base.

Sturdy hinges held both doors of the ice box, which were secured by heavy-duty locking handles that clunked shut when the doors were slammed hard. Sadly, it was not uncommon for children to play and hide inside discarded ice boxes and suffocate when the doors slammed shut on them. Their muffled cries went unnoticed amid the din of city traffic. Marie told Donny never to play with or near a discarded ice box. He never did.

Some ice box hinges were ornate (not on the Gargano's ice box); indeed some ice boxes themselves were wonderful pieces of furniture made of oak and carved with elaborate designs. The lower compartment held the food that needed cooling, Unfortunately, though, spoilage rates were high since ice boxes were not efficient. People often stuffed the more perishable items on top of or on the side of the block of ice in an attempt to stall spoilage. What that usually did, though, was either freeze some foods or cause the ice to melt more rapidly. In any event, people shopped quite differently in those days in accordance with the refrigeration available to them.

Ice melts: invariable—inexorably—undeniably, and especially quickly when subjected to temperatures between 40 and 45 degrees F which was about the coldest it ever got inside an ice box.

The water that developed from the melting ice flowed toward the back of the upper compartment along the corrugated ridges of galvanized metal and into a hole connected to a galvanized metal tube that passed through the back of the lower compartment and, usually, into a pail or pan on the floor. A moveable flap at the ie box bottom hid the pail from view. The design of the box and the size of the pail consorted to defy even the most alert homemaker, for the pail often either overflowed or was so full that one invariably spilled water all over the floor in an attempt to remove it from under the ice box and carry it to the bathroom and pour it down the toilet. (For moviegoers who forgot to empty their pails before leaving for a Saturday matinee, there was the inevitable puddle slithering along the kitchen floor as if to greet them as they walked in the apartment door.)

VII

In 1944, Marie decided to send Donny to St. Teresa of Avila parochial elementary school on St. John's Place. Contrary to the established policy of starting him in kindergarten, she chose to start him off in first grade. "Kindergarten is such a waste," she would say. "All they do is play; they can't make the transition to first grade when they get there. All they want to do is play!" Marie could have sent Donny to the local public school, but she knew that the education there was mediocre. "Those kids can't even spell their own names," she was often heard to say about the children who attended P.S. 42 on Classon Avenue and Prospect Place. And she was generally correct in her assessment of the situation in this typical, low-income neighborhood school. Many of the neighborhood children who attended P.S. 42 did not know how to spell their first or last names even though they were in second and third grade. In sharp contrast were those children who attended St. Teresa School and other local Jewish or Christian parochial schools.

These children were generally better trained and educated than their counterparts in the neighborhood public schools, especially throughout the poorer sections of Brooklyn. Although most of the parochial schools did not have shop classes or gymnasiums, the high level of teaching attracted persons of all faiths. As with all decisions that Marie made concerning Donny, she chose the best among the choices available to her. St. Teresa did not charge tuition for its parishioners, so it was clear that Donny would begin his grammar school education there. And he would start in first grade—not kindergarten—since St. Teresa didn't have kindergarten classes. (This confirmed her opinion about the wasteful nature of 'just playing in school.')

The process of enrolling a child in St. Teresa School involved sitting down with the principal, Brother Artemus, CFX. The letters following his name stood to confuse just about all newcomers to the school, until he himself announced that he was a Franciscan and was in absolute control of discipline and education (in that order) at St. Teresa School. The fact that he was personally responsible to the parish pastor didn't seem to lessen his own belief that he was really in charge. Many parents supposed that he really was—until he encountered Marie Gargano.

St. Teresa School consisted of two four-story buildings about 100-feet apart. Between them was an open concrete area divided in half, each half surrounded by an 8-foot high chain-link fence. The chain-link fence provided a permanent barrier between the separate and distinct school buildings: one for boys and one for girls. The open concrete area also provided separate play areas, so that at no time during the school day could boys and girls commingle except to speak to one another through the fence at recess or lunch time. This practice sat well with Marie, who believed that Donny should spend his time on school work anyway rather than getting involved with the opposite sex at such an early age.

The first few days of school began with clear, sunlit mornings filled with excitement all through the neighborhood as mothers walked their first and second-grade children to school. For Marie it was imperative that she escort Donny since they lived eight blocks away and had to cross seven streets. This was also relatively unfamiliar territory to Donny, who had only visited this area of the neighborhood once or twice before to attend Mass with Marie and Angelo. They often went to Mass at St. Joseph's parish on Pacific Street near Underhill Avenue because it was closer to Grandma Gargano's house on Atlantic Avenue; they could head toward Grandma's and attend Mass on the way.

On the morning of the first day, there was chaos at the school, people were running all over the two school yards trying to establish some kind of order among the returning children and two hundred or so mothers of the incoming first graders who kept asking questions but got no answers that made any sense. Nuns in habits and Brothers in cassocks rushed to and fro seemingly without much purpose to what they were doing, when suddenly— at precisely 8:30 A.M.—a loud whistle blew. It was a police whistle, the loudest one Marie had ever heard. Concurrent with the shriek of the whistle, all motion and sound ceased! Not a soul moved except for the first graders and their mothers who were struck dumb with awe. After four or five seconds, a black-clad figure was seen strutting through the mass of children gathered in the boys' yard. "That's Brother Artemus," someone whispered. "He's checking to see if everyone is frozen."

Being 'frozen' is what Brother Artemus expected from everyone when he blew his whistle. If you were throwing a ball and his whistle blew, the ball just kept going—even if it meant you might lose it. If you were kneeling on the ground trying to get up, you froze midway up. No matter what you were doing: when the whistle blew, you froze!

And then, the whistle blew a second time and children scurried to positions somehow mysteriously defined on the schoolyard floor. Groups lined up as if by magic, yet all was silent. Brothers and nuns also assembled in front of a specific line of children, and it became obvious that they were the teachers of the groups before them. When all were settled, Brother Artemus called to the first graders, "In here, all of you!" Some mothers attempted to accompany their charges, but he stopped them cold. "Not you, only the child!" he growled, and pointed his finger in the desired direction of retreat.

He struck fear into everyone, and sadly, he enjoyed it too. Into everyone except Marie Gargano. She walked with Donny right up to brother Artemus, and demanded to know what was going on.

"Where is he going? What line does my son go on?" she confronted him.

"You're not allowed in here," he scowled.

"I'm not leaving until I know where he's going and who's going to watch him."

He could feel her strength, and he did not want to waste time in a confrontation—yet. He backed down and explained that Sister Mary Steven was Donny's teacher, and she would take care of everything. Marie, too, backed down, but not before telling him, "My son is not accustomed to crowds; he's an only child."

The first-grade class of boys—one-hundred and six of them—lined up two by two from the smallest to the tallest. Donny, relatively tall for his age stood near the back of the line. Marie was so proud, for she had not realized just how special he was:

"God even made him taller than just about everyone his age." She felt extremely proud of her son.

When she straightened out the line, Sister Mary Steven gave the boys some instructions, all the time with her index finger pressed tightly against her lips to indicate 'SILENCE.' She was tall, and, in her black habit, presented an imposing figure to the new first graders, many of whom had not gone to kindergarten either. Sister began to lead the boys toward the school and stopped only momentarily to address the mothers.

"Lunch break is 11:30; line up again at 12:45."

Off she went like a mother hen with her hands folded inside her habit and her brood of young following dutifully along. Marie couldn't wait for the time to pass, and arrived back at school long before 11:30 and found others waiting there already.

Back and forth they went—each day racing home eight blocks one way for lunch and then racing back eight blocks before the whistle blew to freeze everyone once again. At the 3:30 dismissal bell, the school emptied in an orderly fashion, from the top down, eighth graders first and first graders last. Marie waited amid the group of other mothers until Donny burst through the doorway. "Hi, Ma. It was great!" He was beaming. She smiled and said, "Good, I'm glad." And then to herself sighed, "Thank God."

On the way home, she asked a hundred questions, and got an unbroken stream of answers and opinions and exaggerations. Donny seemed happy with school, and this also made Marie happy. Most important was the fact that her son was happy; nothing else ever mattered . . . ever.

The next morning was filled with excitement as Marie and Donny scurried through the tiny apartment preparing for the second day of school. Maybe today he'll get some books, she thought, and I can help him with his homework. She was at peace, even though she had not yet spoken to Angelo who was sound asleep, having come in only a few hours before from his night job on the New York Central Railroad and a brief, three-hour stop at Tony's Bar and Grill on Grand Avenue.

VIII

Angelo worked the 4 to 12 shift for the railroad during the war, since it was the only work available at that time. He enjoyed night work and chose it every time he had an option—much to the dismay of Marie and, later, Donny. Angelo enjoyed stopping off at Tony's on the way home at about 1:00 A.M., since he could drink as much as he wanted without bothering anyone and then walk the block and a half home and go right to sleep. This did not trouble Marie much since she was free to do as she chose most of the time and could act independently and without being second guessed too often. It was also good that he fell asleep right away—on most occasions anyway—and did not 'bother' her too often. The major issue was that Angelo drank a lot, about fifty cents worth of 5¢ beer each night not including an occasional boilermaker. On a salary of $15.00 per week, his habit ate up a substantial portion of their income. Marie could have used the money he spent on drinking, but she realized it was futile to pursue it further. She had argued with him about it before Donny was born, and he had shoved her against a wall so hard that she banged her the back of her skull and passed out. It was better to let him drink, she thought, just as long as he leaves me alone and doesn't bother me too much. Angelo did leave her alone most of the time; life together was not always pleasurable for either of them. And that's the sad part because they were so much in love before. One wonders whether Donny's arrival caused a rift in their relationship or whether it happened naturally. Regardless, their life together was one of tolerance, very often like two ships passing in the night, each going its own way, self-centered and self-gratifying at best—and generally incomplete.

Marie was scrupulous about cleanliness especially when it came to Donny. Each morning, she bathed him from head to toe at the kitchen sink. She scrubbed with a wash cloth of the coarsest type, all the while Donny standing on a towel so the linoleum floor didn't get too wet. This routine continued each day until Donny realized that boys should get in the shower and bathe alone as quickly as possible. One day he overheard his friends speak about Timmy whose mother still washed him. Donny didn't want to be like 'him' so he announced his independence early one morning by racing into the shower before Marie quite knew what was happening.

"How come you went into the shower this morning?" she asked.

"Oh Ma," he replied, "all the boys take showers."

Marie understood. Donny had decided to assert his independence from her. It was expected, but not so soon. She wondered just how far he would move—and she felt alone.

When he was dressed, she had to ask, "Did you wash—did you wash everything?"

"Oh Ma!" he responded. "Come on—awright? I know what to do."

And she offered still another prayer.

IX

One day, they arrived in the school yard to find the familiar bustle of activity with children running here and there, apparently doing nothing but running, while others played basketball or ring-a-leav-e-o. And then, as on every other day: the whistle blew.

Everyone froze as Brother Artemus gazed from one end of the school yard to the other; everyone was frozen-solid. "Good," he said to himself, and blew the whistle a second time. Everyone scurried to their assigned places trying to remember exactly where and how they should line up. Most had no problem; the first graders were a bit confused, and tried their best to line up in silence. Donny found his place, but realized that the boy in front of him wasn't the same boy as yesterday.

"You have to move up one more," he whispered. "You're in the wrong spot." Pointing to the boy two places in front, he said, "He belongs in front of me."

From out of nowhere came the raging body of Brother Artemus, with flailing arms and his cassock swinging wildly around his legs. When he reached Donny, he grabbed him by the shoulders and started shaking him and tossing him like a little rag doll. All this time, he was screaming out loud, "Don't you ever speak after the first whistle! I'll punish you so you'll never sit down all day!"

Donny began to cry.

"What the . . ." In an instant, Marie had flown across the school yard and almost tore the shoulder off Brother Artemus as she spun him around. "Just who do you think you are?? What do you mean by shaking my child like that? Nobody touches him but me! Do you understand?"

Marie was enraged, and eyeballed Brother Artemus with a ferocity he had never experienced from a parent before. In fact, no one had ever challenged him or his authority before. That was before Marie Gargano.

Brother Artemus had conducted himself brutishly with the children on many previous occasions; however, even though a few parents spoke to him about his conduct, no one had dared to confront him as fiercely as did Marie. In fact, most parents were actually afraid of him as much as their children were. But not today. Indeed, today, every mother watched incredulously as Marie went toe to toe with him, and all secretly wished that they had the guts to do the same.

Marie must have broken his spirit, because Brother Artemus never finished out the semester; he was 'recalled' to the main house in Boston and was never heard from again. This incident served to cement the bond that already existed between Donny and Marie, and though she didn't know it, rather than seek more independence from her, Donny only grew to love her more, knowing that she would go to any lengths for him. He hoped that he, too, could react in the same way for her if it ever became necessary. One day he did.

Marie always believed, as many women do, that her child was special—more special than any other child in the world. She knew that he was destined for greatness and that he would make her proud. And because Marie believed all these things, she did all that she could to help him along on his road to success.

Toward this end, she would read to him each day from the moment she was able to set him down and let him hold a book. Reading is the most important thing, she thought. Donny must learn to read as soon as possible so he can learn. And he did read early. At first, he memorized the words of children's books and easily fooled people when he moved his eyes from one page to the next or turned a page at precisely the right word. Donny and Marie knew that this was only a game, but it amazed all the relatives and gave them a taste of the pride that Marie felt.

Nevertheless, Marie insisted that Donny read soon. She never let up. By the time Donny entered St. Teresa School, he could easily read the daily comics, many simple children's books, and all the required books in first grade. Marie was pleased, and Donny, who didn't mind her attention, took everything in stride. He had a great deal of confidence in himself. In fact, when Donny entered the classroom on the very first day of school, he watched everyone scurry for a seat next to their 'special' friends. Amid this commotion, he just stood there. Sister Mary Steven approached him.

"Don't you want to take a seat, young man?"

"Yes, Sister," he smiled.

"Well go ahead; don't be bashful," she prodded.

"I'm not bashful, Sister. I want to sit next to Robby," he pointed, "the kid with the nice face, but someone else is sitting there."

Sister Mary Steven walked over to where Donny pointed and asked the boy sitting next to Robby to move over.

Donny looked into her face and smiled. "Thank . . you . . Sis . . ter," he said in the same sing-song fashion he had heard others use.

X

The American economy grew and Marie found that she could put meat on the table more frequently. Angelo's uncle owned a butcher shop on Washington Avenue, but he catered to a more-upscale clientele. Marie never shopped there. Donny visited the shop often on his way to Grandma Gargano's, and always anticipated eating lunch in the back room where a full kitchen awaited. His hope was that Uncle Jim would take out some of his homemade pepperoni from the kitchen table drawer and hack off big chunks for Donny; it was a memorable treat especially with the crispy loaf that was ever present! One day while munching on some pepperoni and bread, Donny chomped down on a hard, yellow substance. His manners told him to bring his napkin to his mouth and spit it out. Uncle Jim, who was also eating the pepperoni, asked, "What's a matta, Donny?" When Donny showed him the yellow clump, Uncle Jim scoffed saying, "It's-a nutting—just some chicken feet I put in for the color. Mangia! Eat!" Donny swore off pepperoni for life then and there.

Marie and many of her women friends from the neighborhood rarely bought meat at Gemeiner's butcher shop on St. John's Place. The reason being that it was owned and operated by the genus Thief, subgenus Crook. Scales in butcher shops were large, but they had tiny, hard-to-read numbers on the display. They were, inconveniently—for the shopper—placed above eye level on top of the showcase, which made it practically impossible for a shopper to read the numbers. This butcher had the habit of tossing the meat on the scale and almost simultaneously calling out the weight before the customer could see it. The average shoppers just accepted the fact that they had no control over the process. Some butchers had heavy thumbs, which also added a few ounces to every sale.

Butchers were not alone in using scales for their ill-gotten advantage. Indeed, Sleven Bros, a city-wide fresh fruits and vegetables chain, insisted that all their clerks leave three or four string beans or radishes at the bottom of every scale pan. Because nothing ever weighed in at precisely one or two pounds,

Sleven Bros accountants calculated that five cents be charged for each additional ounce of fruit or vegetable that sold for sixty-nine cents per pound. Thus, every additional ounce was billed at eighty-cents per pound; the string beans only added to the theft. Sleven Bros disappeared when supermarkets arrived.

Hoping to economize, Marie joined others in the neighborhood by shopping for meats at the Brooklyn Fort Greene Meat Consortium—more commonly known as the Fort Greene Meat Market. The Fort Greene Meat Market was located on Fort Greene place just off Fulton Street in downtown Brooklyn a few blocks south of Brooklyn Technical High School. It was not one butcher shop, but rather a series of loosely affiliated butcher shops that did business under the same name. Prices were set independently by each shop owner, and customer loyalty was fierce. Strangely, one could often hear the women shoppers talk about 'their' butcher and how his meat was always more tender than the others. It was no secret that the meat was delivered by the same trucks—they unloaded each morning for all to see—and there seemed to be no pattern to how the meat was selected and routed to each butcher shop. The reality was that the meat was the same meat and only the prices and the butchers varied. (Admittedly, some butchers were younger and better looking than others!)

On Saturday mornings, Marie headed out for the meat market at about 7 A.M. and walked the fourteen blocks to buy whatever meat products she needed for the coming week. More often than not, she walked back home juggling her bundles to save the five-cent, one-way trolley fare. It was probably faster to walk anyway since the trolley ride required two transfers and she wasn't always guaranteed a seat. Marie carried the heavy parcels in her arms the entire way, shifting the load dozens of times en route home, stopping often to catch her breath while resting her bundles on one of the front-yard wrought-iron gates protecting the brownstones she passed along the way. Other times, Marie might meet a neighbor with a rolling metal shopping cart that they shared; Marie put some of her bags in the cart— and they both dragged it home. Regardless of how she traveled, Marie made the trek in all kinds of weather: winter and summer, rain or shine, snow or sleet. During some of the coldest winters of the century, Marie remained undaunted in her goal to save the fare whenever she could and so she walked with her long, heavy cotton coat and a hand-knitted scarf and cap to keep her warm; many times, her fingers almost got frostbite when her woolen mittens became sodden with sleet and little balls of ice formed around each finger as she clung tightly to her packages. And through all this, she never once asked Donny to get out of bed and help her carry her heavy burden; it was better that he sleep late on Saturday—he worked hard in school all week. It was only when Donny was about fourteen years old that he became acutely aware of Marie's Saturday morning efforts in keeping the household stocked with food; before this, he somehow thought the meat magically materialized on the kitchen table. He made no association between his mother's regular absence every Saturday and the effort it took in getting to and from the market. After a while, he also realized the toll being taken on his mother by her solo shopping trips so he made it a point to accompany her—whenever she allowed him to. But whenever the weather was icy or sleeting, she would sneak out of the apartment alone, before Donny awoke. Her need for Angelo never surfaced during these times.

Sometime around 1952, many American women began using the mesh shopping bags so popular in Europe for large purchases, but Marie felt that it was time for her to purchase a shopping cart of her own; they cost seventy-five cents. She was getting too old to be carrying heavy bundles without some assistance.

ROBBY

I

Robby Ventura lived in a three-story walkup on Classon Avenue above Lowe's tailor shop. Mr. Lowe, a diminutive black man with thick, silver hair, operated a successful tailor shop and dry cleaning business in this mostly white Italian enclave of several dozen stores and apartment houses that made up this small part of the neighborhood. Mr. Lowe was well respected by whites and blacks for many reasons, probably because he was successful and also because he was tough. No one—black, white, or other—got away with anything out of the way anywhere near Mr. Lowe's shop; he insisted that nobody loiter in front of his shop and could often be seen waving a broom at those who were a bit too slow to move along when he urged them on. The Italians in the neighborhood respected Mr. Lowe for his work ethic and how he treated people. They loved how his store was clean and the sidewalk in front of his place was always swept clean and free from litter. Yes, Mr. Lowe was a model citizen, but he wasn't Italian.

One day, Vincent Speranza, age seventeen, was in a mischievous mood and decided to make his mark in the neighborhood. He had stopped of in the hardware store on Washington Avenue and bought a can of Bon Ami window cleaner. Women of the day used this paste-type rub-on cleanser on their kitchen windows when they were especially dirty. It was a fine product, but when left on too long before wiping off—well it required serious elbow grease to remove.

Vincent Speranza, also known as "Vinny The Bull" because he was so stupid and charged into situations and people without too

29

much thought, wiped Bon Ami all over Mr. Lowe's windows late one night. The result was that the windows were completely white and opaque to light. Abandoned stores also wiped Bon Ami on the windows to shield the inside from view. Coating the windows wasn't all that bad a prank since Mr. Lowe could have easily washed the product off and gotten back to work once it was done in the morning. Unfortunately, "Vinny The Bull," couldn't be satisfied with the prank as it was. As he stood back admiring his handiwork, he decided to write some unpleasant words in the white powder that covered the window. They were racial slurs that were spoken only quietly and in small groups around the neighborhood; these words were never said out loud or ever written on walls or on the sidewalk along with the other expressions of youthful exuberance. Nevertheless, writing these words on Mr. Lowe's window made Vinny feel like a real tough guy—especially since nobody saw him do it. He thought.

He jumped, startled by the voice that seemed to come from nowhere. "Hey, Vinny, what-cha do-in?" the heavily accented Brooklyn voice said. Vinny turned and saw Frankie, 'The Boy,' Famiglietti standing about two feet away with his hands on his hips and a sardonic smile on his face as he rocked slowly back and forth on his heels. Vinny felt a bit more at ease since he and Frankie lived in the same apartment house. Unfortunately, they were not friends and did not move in the same circles. Vinny was known for always just getting out of trouble whereas Frankie was known as a peaceful kid who always tried to do the right thing and keep peace in the neighborhood.

"Hey, man, you scared me," Vinny said as he ambled closer to Frankie.

"Whatta you doin' here, Vinny? Mr. Lowe is a nice guy and he didn't do nutthin' to you. He's been a good guy all these years.

Why're you writin' that stuff on his window for?"

"Just havin' some fun, man. It don't mean nutthin'.'"

"Well, it means somethin' to me!" Frankie was visibly upset and Vinny took two steps back toward the wall.

Vinny didn't want any trouble with Frankie even though Frankie was younger and shorter than Vinny. Vinny was a tough kid, and had been in lots of fights around town, but he and Frankie seemed to steer clear of each other—it just happened that way. Frankie never started a fight in his life, but he never lost one either. And at sixteen and only five-foot five, Frankie commanded a respect among his peers and many others that was unusual. Perhaps it was that Frankie didn't fear any thing or any one. It may have also been that Frankie was blessed with a body that was rock hard as though he had lifted weights for years. But what really struck fear into those who knew Frankie well was his hands.

Frankie had hands that people referred to as "catcher's mitts." His fingers were short and thick, but his palms were huge—reminiscent of Michelangelo's David. And even though he didn't drink beer, he would show off against the older guys in the neighborhood by crushing the steel Rheingold or Schaefer beer cans with one hand. Most of the men in the neighborhood who could crush a beer can required two hands and pushed the can into their belly for leverage. Not Frankie. Maybe that's how he got the name, "Frankie the Boy." Maybe. Anyway, it was a simple fact of life in the neighborhood that "nobody messed with Frankie The Boy." EVER!!

So Vinny didn't know how to respond to Frankie's statement, which actually sounded more like a command to "Wipe the stuff off the window before I break your legs!" Sort of.

And then another voice was heard as "Buster" Sperato bounced around the corner and greeted the two figures before him. "Hey guys, what's happenin'?" he asked. Vinny took the opportunity to walk toward Buster so as to solidify his own position a bit. Vinny could feel his confidence returning and said to Buster in the slowest and most accentuated way he could, "Frank-ee- The-Boy- here- wants- me- to- clean- off- Mr.- Lowe's- window." And then pointing his finger directly at Frankie, he added, "Ain't that right, Frankie Boy?"

Vinny was itching to get it on with Frankie especially since he knew Buster would take his side against the younger boy. But Vinny was clever enough to believe that he would need some help with Frankie—and Buster had come along just in time. Vinny grabbed hold of Buster's arm and pulled him toward himself as he inched closer to Frankie in an obvious attempt to intimidate Frankie and to back him down. But Vinny, stupid Vinny, miscalculated again. Frankie was not only book smart—he was also street-smart and would not have even gone over to Vinny in the first place if he weren't certain that he could easily dispatch him along with one or two of Vinny's friends.

But Vinny slowly continued to inch closer to Frankie sort of looking down his nose at him and egging Buster on as well. Vinny was about to say, "You wanna make me clean this window, Frankie boy?" But as his face came within six inches of Frankie's face, Frankie's massive hands flew from his side and clamped down simultaneously on Vinny's and Buster's throats. His vice-like grip, though seemingly uncontrolled, exerted sufficient pressure to cause the other boys to gasp for air. Though Frankie could have easily broken their windpipes, he was satisfied to force them to their knees and make them crawl into the gutter.

Before he let go he asked, "Had enough?" but whereas Buster shook his head in a back and forth motion indicating, "Yes," Vinny struggled futilely to get up and continue the battle. What battle? Vinny had lost all face and would be laughed out of the neighborhood once Buster told everyone what Frankie had done. But Vinny continued to struggle all the more.

Frankie let go of Buster's throat and ordered him to stay right there in the gutter on his knees. And he did. Frankie then asked Vinny if he had enough once more. Even though Vinny shook off the question one more time, Frankie decided to loosen his grip and let Vinny breathe a bit easier. As he did, Vinny exploded off his knees and threw a punch at Frankie's groin. Frankie easily sidestepped it and smashed Vinny on the back of his neck with a clenched fist and sent him sprawling on his face and into a puddle at the curb. Vinny was unconscious for about thirty seconds, and when he came to, he whimpered, "Enough." He was wheezing and coughing and would have a real headache for the next couple of days. But Frankie wasn't finished yet.

"I want you guys to clean that window before I let you go; got it?" he said to both of them—but only Buster assented. He repeated to Vinny, "You gonna clean that window?" Vinny coughed again and then finally said, "Yeah." When they were finished wiping away the words that Vinny had scrawled, Frankie said, "Now I want the both of you to crawl all the way down to the corner on your hands and knees before you get up. YOU GOT THAT?" There was a ferocity in his voice that frightened Frankie himself, as he felt the veins in his neck throbbing. But both Vinny and Buster dutifully crawled to the corner on their hands and knees before they got up and went home. "Man, he's some mean son-bitch!" Buster said when they finally turned the corner. "You shouldn't be doin' that kinda stuff in the neighborhood, Vinny!!" Vinny merely nodded his head and barely muttered, "Mmm" as he reached for the pack of cigarettes he had rolled up in the sleeve of his tee-shirt.

II

"The smell of cleaning fluid often invaded the apartments above Mr. Lowe's shop, and sometimes it was strong to overcome the myriad aromas of the Italian cooking that seemingly went on constantly. Hallways always had the hovering presence of some type of lingering aroma, whether from the remnants of a recent scrubbing with a pine cleaner or from someone cooking fish like bacala—the salted dried codfish popular among Sicilians and Calabrese—or from homemade bread, freshly baked. Hallways reflected the seasons, too, in Italian tenements, when women would create the special regional dishes of their ancestral villages. At Easter, for example, one could always detect the aroma of egg-breads and cakes so very important to that holiday. In March, for the feast of St. Joseph, special crullers were made (Zeppoli di San Giuseppe); at Christmas, little honey balls sprinkled with candy nonpareils (Strufoli) were found everywhere. In slummier Brooklyn neighborhoods, hallways often had their own special aromas, like urine from derelicts or feces from animals that claimed the darkness as their private domain.

But Robby was fortunate: his grandmother had owned the house at 606 Classon Avenue, and when she died, it became the sole possession of Robby's mother, Carla. (His father, Vito, being a life-long lover of good whiskey, wasn't too much trusted by his mother-in-law in matters financial.) Carla had an income from the rental of the other apartment and from the tailor shop downstairs. Though meager, the rents put the Ventura family in a better position than most of their friends or other neighborhood families. Robby assumed that his life style was the norm, never having experienced any other style of living. He was one of the first children in the neighborhood to have a two-wheeler (with training wheels, of course), and was in the height of childhood fashion when Carla bought him a pair of twenty dollar cowboy boots that fit him perfectly. How lucky he was, for when most parents bought shoes for their growing children, it was assumed that the child would "grow into" each pair—that is, they bought shoes at least a half-size larger so that the child would never 'outgrow' his shoes, and by the time they were destroyed, sufficient use would have been had. Cowboy boots were considered a true luxury for children in the 40's, since they certainly would be outgrown before they were worn out. But what did Robby know? He did his best to wear them out anyway.

III

Jenny's candy store was four doors away from Robby's apartment building, and was the local hangout for neighborhood kids and teenagers. In Brooklyn, in those days, every local neighborhood was strictly defined by some unwritten geographic formula that included streets, trolley stops, various shops and, always, a hangout; and to be included within the neighborhood, the overall area had to be within easy walking distance of the hangout. Some neighborhoods were large enough to accommodate two or even three hangouts. The confines of the neighborhood were so well defined and protected that one could always hear someone say, "Hey, that kid's not from around here," when a stranger walked onto the very closely guarded region also known as "our turf." The turf was protected in many ways, and those who came home late at night knew that they were always safe after entering their own neighborhood turf. It was almost unheard of that anyone living within the neighborhood would ever harm or steal from anyone else within the confines of the neighborhood. Of course, this excluded the almost daily fist-fights and arguments that were de-facto exclusions of the "in neighborhood" policy. But strangely, there were hardly ever any reprisals due to lost battles or arguments. The neighborhood was truly a family wherein residents needed one another to help protect the turf; for that reason alone, altercations were quickly forgotten so as not to interfere with choosing up sides for the next day's stick ball game or getting your favorite partner for a pinochle game at the hangout. It was always nice being in the neighborhood.

IV

A hangout could be a candy store, luncheonette, ice cream parlor, tavern, pool room, barber shop, or even a bake shop, the kind where one could buy a piece of pastry and sit for a half hour at wrought-iron tables drinking espresso from tiny cups.

The hangout could also be a storefront like some Italians used for hosting birthday parties, the (illegal) Italian lottery organization, or late-night gambling, also illegal. These particular hangouts often operated under the guise of organizing the various feasts in honor of a venerated saint from a specific hometown in Italy. Any hangout, regardless of its purpose, was also one of the few places where the rules of neighborhood protocol were relaxed— as such, each hangout had its own specific rules.

As an example, if a luncheonette or an ice cream parlor were a hangout, the allowable level of noise was always higher than in a pastry shop, as might be expected. In the barber shop when young boys were absent, language was rough and sex was the preeminent subject—but hardly ever when youngsters were present. Since Playboy had not yet been published yet, the barber shop had its own inventory of "girlie" magazines such as The Police Gazette and Esquire. The Police Gazette was noted for its pictorials of oversized women clad in fishnet stockings and what we would call today "teddies." Nudity in print was practically unknown except for the occasional French Postcard or a deck of imported playing cards with fifty-two fully naked ladies that found its way into the back room of the barber shop and caused a stir among the adult male patrons and regular hang outs. One of the most popular kids in the neighborhood was the boy whose elder brother pocketed one of the French playing cards and let his brother borrow it to show off at 'the corner.' When Esquire published a photograph of Sophia Loren topless in 1951, sales skyrocketed and every barber shop in America had its own archival copy.

The pool hall (always called the pool room) was the most notorious hangout in the neighborhood. Mothers cautioned their sons, "Don't go near the pool room," and their daughters to, "Stay away from boys who hang out there!" The language heard while passing by the pool room was hardly the king's English, and there was always a debate among those who knew where you could hear the most cuss words in the shortest period of time: the pool room or the barber shop.

The mysterious goings on inside the dimly lit pool hall were the stuff of legends among the denizens of the neighborhood. It was thought that anyone who picked up a pool cue was, by definition, a low life and anyone who hung out in a pool room was a gangster. While this may have been true of some pool rooms in Brooklyn, throughout the nation, it was a different story. Pool was fast becoming a family sport and pool tables eventually found their way into the YMCA and church recreation halls. But not in Brooklyn. In Brooklyn, gangsters did hang out in pool rooms as did the organizers of the numerous, illegal, lottery games—especially the Italian numbers. (Funny thing: the Irish Sweepstakes was allowed openly everywhere in New York City.) Bookmakers were always on the phone or near the phone in the pool room, and, though off-track betting was illegal, anyone could place a bet on any race at any time, anywhere in the world; just walk over to the pool room and look for the guy with a rumpled fedora and a cigarette hanging from his lower lip. He usually stood near the large, coin-operated telephone that hung on the wall.

V

The neighborhood was truly a village within a city and each had its own distinctive characteristics. Beyond the neighborhood were other entities that neatly fit into the same type of geo-political structure found in neighborhoods. For example, several local neighborhoods consisting of perhaps 100 square blocks made up geographically defined areas such as Park Slope, Crown Heights, South Brooklyn, Williamsburg, Greenpoint, etc. In the '40's, it was not uncommon that residents of Park Slope would never have visited Williamsburg or South Brooklyn unless some special mission drew them there—like buying illegal fireworks for the Fourth of July.. More than likely though, they lived, shopped, played, and were waked very close to home.

VI

When Robby was about eight years old, he was allowed to go into Jenny's alone and buy a candy bar or a Mel-O-Roll, a frozen cylinder of ice cream wrapped in a paper container that had to be unwrapped and then placed into a tasteless cake cone. Carla exhorted him to be very careful, making sure that he counted his change and came 'right back home.' Robby became quickly enamored of the goings-on in Jenny's. Young boys and girls sitting at one of the three tables drinking Coke from a bottle (Carla told him to always use a glass or a straw), smoking (they seemed so young to smoke), and listening to Glen Miller on the juke box. Robby loved going into Jenny's and soon managed to become a regular himself. Instead of playing with his toys or listening to Jack Armstrong or the Green Hornet on the radio, he would go over to Jenny's and just hang out. His first real step beyond his childhood came when he was almost ten years old and he spotted a young girl that he recognized from school. She walked into Jenny's and was evaluating the vast array of candy on display in the showcase. Much of what was sold was not wrapped; it was loose and sold for a penny or two-for-a-penny. Candy bars were becoming popular, but they cost five or ten cents—much too expensive for an eight-year old. Robby felt a sudden urge to meet this young lady, and so he kind of eased himself next to her as she peered into the candy showcase.

"Hi," he said.

"Hello," she replied.

"I'm Robby Ventura from Brother Joseph's class."

"Yes, I know. I've seen you in the schoolyard. My name's Eileen."

"Hi!"

"Hi."

Robby got all flustered and tried to control his racing mind.

"Would you like to share a soda?" he tried.

"Sure. I like Coke." She was so friendly.

"OK; I'll get us one. You get two straws."

Robby tried to be "cool" as he headed for the coffin-like soda box that was loaded with a variety of soda bottles covered with large chunks of chopped ice. He stood on tip toes, lifted up the heavy cover with his left hand and plunged his right arm deep into the near-freezing mixture. He pulled out bottle after bottle until he found a Coke. He used the bottle opener clumsily and walked to the table where Eileen waited. She had already removed the paper from two straws and placed them into the bottle of Coke when he set it down between them.

"You got your sleeve wet," she offered, trying to hide a gentle smile.

"I know, I forgot to roll it up."

This first 'date' for Robby was the beginning of a long line of encounters with women that would one day bring him to his knees in despair.

VII

Robby's involvement with girls proceeded at a rapid rate, and he soon had a reputation in and out of the neighborhood—though all of it was merely hype: he did nothing more than sneak a kiss or two from his youthful counterparts. Of course, his parents never knew about this. Robby's first, real physical encounter occurred when he was eleven years old. He had overheard some of the older boys in the candy store talking about their previous night's escapades in Prospect Park, and he wanted to experience some of these forbidden carnal delights himself—even though he could only guess at what it was all about. He didn't know what to expect when he asked Sally Benson to go for a walk with him, but he proceeded nevertheless with a calm, confident manner that made him appear debonair to girls.

Sally was only thirteen and had been to the park often—sometimes for quarters or half dollars, so she was aware of why she was being asked to accompany Robby. His youthful heart pounded as they entered the park and searched for a lonely place under a tree, unseen by anyone. Unfamiliar though he was, Robby knew enough to kiss Sally who responded willingly. Within a few seconds, he was all over her, his hands groping, touching, feeling; he never felt such a complete release of inhibitions before. And then . . . Sally touched him in a way no woman had ever touched him before . . . not with sophistication or teasing—just a simple . . . touch. Almost instantly, his body reacted uncontrollably, and—he spent his manhood—without consent and all over his boxer shorts. Sally, really inexperienced herself in the art of lovemaking, had been through this scene before with other young, inexperienced boys of the neighborhood but never with one who so quickly reacted to her touch. Mostly it took a minute or so to get them to this point, and the boys were a bit more prepared for what happened. After their first time, the boys also learned how to make themselves last a bit longer and enjoy more of Sally herself. With Robby, Sally found herself trying to stifle a laugh, as she watched him trying to hide his embarrassment. He looked at her with a sort of shrug and said, "It was so fast!" She just smiled at him and said, "It usually is." She realized that this was his 'first-ever' experience, and tried her best as a thirteen year-old to make him feel at ease with his magnificent spontaneous explosion. After he caught his breath and began to feel less self-conscious, they spent a few minutes together laughing about Robby's first time. "Maybe you should get out of those shorts," she advised; "they're gonna get real messy in a while."

He walked a few steps away where she couldn't see him and quickly removed his pants and threw his shorts under a bush. When he returned, Sally was applying a fresh coat of lipstick thinking they would be leaving now. But since Robby was not one to miss out on any opportunity open to him, he persuaded her to give him another chance. And she did. And so after a half hour in the park with Sally Benson, Robby had become a man, never again to think or act as a child again. He tasted, and enjoyed; he experienced, and learned; his goals regarding women were clear.

There were plenty of 'those' girls around, and Robby periodically availed himself of their services. Only once while still in grammar school did he have some doubts about his actions regarding girls. Arlene D'Arcy was NOT one of 'those girls'; in fact, she was one of the sweetest girls in the entire school and everyone knew it. She was pretty with blonde hair and the bluest of eyes, and was always dressed nicely in starched dresses and highly polished shoes. Arlene was a beautiful girl and a model student. She was respectful of her elders and a favorite of the nuns whom she helped often after school. She was a serious seventh grader, and many believed that she had a vocation and would enter the convent after completing grammar school. The boys labeled her as a nice girl.

And so it was difficult for her friends to understand why she was so smitten with Robby Ventura. For some strange reason, Arlene liked Robby and followed him around whenever she saw him near her house or around the school grounds on weekends. When the eighth grade senior class sponsored a dance in the school auditorium, Arlene asked Robby if he would take her, since he was a senior and she was in seventh grade. Robby refused on the grounds that he should be seen with some girl from the eighth grade and not with someone as young as Arlene. This did not deter Arlene, and she kept asking him to her house to listen to records and play Monopoly or just hang out on the steps to her apartment building. But Robby refused her imprecations, though over time, he admitted to himself that she sure was pretty for a seventh grader.

It was during a school break for the Easter holidays that Robby relented and decided to take up Arlene on her request for a 'date. Early one afternoon, he stopped by her building and rang the bell to her apartment. When Arlene's father buzzed him into the first-floor vestibule, Robby heard the familiar shout of, "Who is it?" echo down from the D'Arcy's third floor apartment. Robby responded telling Arlene's father who he was and asked if Arlene could come down to the vestibule for a few minutes. Mr. D'Arcy's reputation as a strict disciplinarian was well known throughout the neighborhood, and Robby was just a bit apprehensive about calling for Arlene. When Mr. D'Arcy shouted down that Arlene went to Washington, D.C. with the nuns and some of the other boys and girls from St. Teresa's, Robby was relieved; he thanked Mr. D'Arcy and exited quickly.

The next time Robby saw Arlene, instead of avoiding her as he had been doing all along, he spoke with her but she seemed somehow different toward him. Eventually, Robby forgot about her and pursued his usual interests, though whenever he saw her, he wondered what had happened to cool off the interest she previously had in him. When Arlene dropped out of the seventh grade class a few months later because of her developing pregnancy, Robby understood. But he often thought that if he had been more interested in her himself—maybe she wouldn't have gotten into this predicament; everyone knew that you didn't get nice girls pregnant—everyone knew, except the eighth-grade father of Arlene D'Arcy's baby.

Robby eventually graduated and went off to high school where he left behind any further interest in nice girls; instead, he worked hard to embellish his "rep" as a ladies man, hardly ever being seen without a girl on his arm or in his car. (He worked hard to earn enough money to buy a car and be free to explore other regions of Brooklyn.) Naturally, his school work suffered, and—much to the dismay of his parents—he graduated near the bottom of his high school class. Although others in the neighborhood had begun to go to some of the free city colleges, Robby would not have such an opportunity afforded him—his grades were too low.

NICK TOSCANO

I

Nick Toscano lived on Bergen Street near Washington Avenue. Tall for his age, muscular and well developed, he was one of the first boys in the neighborhood to work out each day lifting weights and punching the heavy bag. He was rather shy around people, though he let his hair grow long and sported a thin mustache at fifteen. When black leather jackets became the vogue, Nick had one: he stole it from Cooper's dry goods store on Washington Avenue when the owner went into the back room to get something for one of Nick's friends. Nick did not consider himself a thief—in his circle, you took what you wanted if you couldn't afford it. This street code was widely accepted in the 40's as long as no one got hurt, and neither Nick nor his friends had yet resorted to violence.

It wasn't long before Nick and his friends realized that the world would soon pass them by if they didn't obtain a source of steady income. Now 1952, the country was moving again, people were buying cars, big bands were appearing all over, the city was on the move. Nick was eighteen, and had just graduated from Lafayelle High School. Although he was bright enough to get into Brooklyn Technical High School, he intentionally failed the entrance exam so that he wouldn't be thought of as a fag by his friends. He tried his hand at being an auto mechanic, did well, but disliked the grease under his nails and the way his hair got messed. Something better had to come along.

II

Nick was sitting in Jenny's one day guzzling a Coke from a bottle when he heard a disturbance coming from the room in the back of the store. He recognized Jenny's voice screaming, "Stop, you'll kill him!" Nick tore open the curtain that divided the dingy back room from the front of the store and saw two men beating up a teenager who looked vaguely familiar, though his face was bloodied.

"Hey man," he said, trying to sound as intimidating as possible, "what's go-in down?"

"Beat it creep," he was told "or I'll beat in your head too!"

Nick realized that he knew the teenager from the neighborhood and from his excursions in Prospect Park, but he didn't recognize the two men. The pounding of the young man had stopped momentarily while the two interlopers assessed Nick's presence and whether he posed a threat to them.

"Hey Jenny, what's happening here?" Nick asked Jenny.

When Jenny saw Nick enter the back room, she rushed over to him and clung to him with all her strength. She trembled uncontrollably. "Oh Nick, they want to break his legs because he fooled around with one of their girlfriends; they're animals. Get the police!" "We don't need no police, Jenny," he said as he unbuckled his wide garrison belt and wrapped it around his right fist.

Jenny seized the moment to grab the battered young man and almost drag him out of the store and onto the sidewalk.

Meanwhile, Nick stood at his full height, breathing deeply, and began to tense his muscles and then relax them as he had done so many other times when he had to defend himself. Slowly he began to pound his left palm with his right, which was tightly wound with his black leather belt. His icy stare bore into the eyes of one goon and then the other. And then one of them began to laugh.

"You gonna take us on pretty boy?" he said. "Why don't you just walk away and let us finish what we started; this ain't none of your business." Nick just kept pounding one fist into the other, waiting and planning. "OK then, big shot," the goon continued, unsure of why Nick would even want to get involved in someone else's problem, "you want it one at a time, or both of us together?

"You call it man," Nick replied feeling his entire body fill with a strange, raging excitement.

Almost simultaneously and without warning the two goons lunged at Nick, but he side stepped one and tripped the other and then threw his falling body head first into the cement block wall at one end of the room. Almost instantly, Nick lunged after the other goon and pounded the base of his skull with his belt-wrapped fist. He went unconscious immediately. The other picked himself off the floor and drunkenly pulled a switch blade knife from his back pocket and thrust it at Nick who blocked it with his forearm and then kicked him in the groin. As this one doubled over, Nick drove his knee into the man's nose and heard it crunch as he fell immobile.

As they both lay unconscious, Nick went outside where a crowd had been gathering since Jenny had first screamed. It seemed as though people from all over the neighborhood had suddenly appeared, and when Nick first appeared in the doorway, some were saying, "Go, Nick!" and , "All right, Nick!" and "Who the hell do they think they are anyway coming around here?" As Nick strode out onto the sidewalk, he said to himself with a deep sense of pride and only the barest hint of a smile upon his lips,

"Nick Toscano, this is your turf; these are your people." He then glanced over toward the battered teenager being cradled in Jenny's arms, and after a few moments went over and knelt beside him. The teenager was bloodied, but Nick had seen people look a lot worse from a beating. The teenager was crying but looked up at Nick and began to speak, but Nick interrupted him.

"You all right guy?" Nick said.

"Yeah, I guess. Thanks," came the forced reply and more tears.

"Don't you know messing around with women can get you into trouble?" Nick said.

After a brief pause, the teenager wiped his eyes and said through his tears trying to force a smile, "It seemed like a good idea at the time. She's got great legs."

He caught Nick's eye and both of them broke out into uncontrolled laughter.

"What's your name anyway, kid?" Nick asked almost gasping for air himself now convulsed in laughter.

"Robby . . . .Robby Ventura."

Nick helped him to his feet and then turned to face the crowd. "C'mon," Nick ordered to the crowd in general, "some of youse guys help me get those creeps out of the back room before the cops come and we gotta answer a lot of questions."

Within seconds, several boys raced into the back room and helped Nick to toss the two goons out onto the curb and help them make a quick exit from the scene, shouting obscenities after them. In just a few more seconds, Nick, Robby, and most of the crowd had hastily retreated into the darkness of nearby hallways and into other stores along the street, which became suddenly quiet and normal as though nothing had happened.

In fact, nothing really did happen that was of interest to anyone outside of the neighborhood anyway. The neighborhood could take care of itself without the help of outsiders—and the police were definitely outsiders. In the distance, the sound of a police siren could be heard, but no one would be around to tell them what had happened or who had called them in the first place. Jenny was already back inside the store closing the curtain to the back room as people began to come back in and sit at tables. Someone put a nickel in the juke box and pushed a button. A metal arm searched the stack of 78-rpm records that stood on edge at the back of the machine, made its selection, clamped onto the record and dropped it onto the already-spinning turntable. The Glenn Miller Band began to play. The neighborhood once again was at peace. And there would be no reprisals either; it just didn't happen that way.

III

During the summer of 1950, Nick worked hard at Pete's Gas, a filling station and auto repair shop a few doors away from his rundown three-family tenement. Pete Kelly was an affable fellow who was a top-notch mechanic and honest in all his business activities. He was trusted by everyone—and he guaranteed his work. Nick had gained Pete's trust and was given the keys so that he could open the garage at 6 A.M.and pump gas for the early morning customers. Nick didn't mind getting up early, since it made it possible for him to get off early and hang out in the afternoons or, on nice days, go to the beach.

As a young man, Nick's father, Rocco never had the luxury of swimming at any of the magnificent beaches available to the residents of New York City; no, during the heat of the summer he swam inn the East River just a half block from the building he lived in with his parents, which was located almost directly under the roadbed of the Brooklyn Bridge. One of the City's really poor, Rocco was one of nine children born to Salvatore and Rose Toscano who came to this country from their little village of Coscenza in southern Italy. The few run-down homes left standing after the construction of the bridge formed a tiny enclave that attracted the poorest of the city's poor. This neighborhood was constantly in the shadows because the bridge roadway completely obliterated the sun. The din of the trains was almost constant as the "E" train rumbled overhead all day long and only less frequently during the night. It was here that Salvatore and Rose Toscano came to raise their children—the only neighborhood in which they could afford to live—on the east bank of the East River. Strangely, New York City's East River happens not to be a river at all, but a tidal estuary of Long Island Sound that flows south around the north end of Brooklyn until it joins the Hudson River and continues out into Jamaica Bay and the Atlantic Ocean. Who 'woulda' thought? Only in Brooklyn.

Rocco Toscano and the few children that lived in this dark, decaying neighborhood at the turn of the twentieth century walked the half block under the gloomy shadow of the bridge to the river front and jumped off rotting pilings into the murky water as their recreation. Oblivious to the rats that swam alongside them and the garbage that floated by, they frolicked and learned how to float on their backs and tread water. On shore, they learned how to smoke hand-rolled cigarettes and Italian stogies that scorched their young throats until they were raw. Before they reached their teen years, sexual activity among them was as common as breathing. There was nothing for the children to do, no place for them to play and no one to watch over them. They were the poorest of the poor and open to any opportunity to make a buck. It was from among these people that the notorious group known as Brooklyn's 'Murder Incorporated' sprang.

But that was then and this was now. Rocco was fortunate that his parents instilled in him the desire to work hard in this land of opportunity, though Salvatore wondered when his opportunity was coming. He made Rocco aware of the ease with which he could wind up floating in the river with the rats and garbage if he allowed the criminal element to work its way with him. And so Rocco heeded his father's pleas and became determined not to succumb to the call of the easy buck or the few quarters offered by some local hood to break someone's legs for not paying off a gambling debt.

Rocco burned with a desire to move out of these squalid surroundings and, forsaking formal schooling, he worked at whatever jobs he could get to earn a few pennies each day. From running errands for local merchants, Rocco earned a reputation for honesty and dependability. The local merchants always called upon him when they needed someone to pick up a package across town or in Manhattan. He worked hard at these menial tasks and supplemented his income on weekends by shining shoes from morning to night on street corners in some of the adjoining, 'more' affluent neighborhoods. Before the depression began, he was recommended to a New York City alderman as someone who had many friends and who could get them all to vote for the Democrat Party candidates. Rocco knew where the power base was at that time, and as long as he did not break the law, he counseled his friends and family to vote for the Democrats on election day. For his loyalty, Rocco was ultimately hired on as a full-time New York City sanitation worker—a garbage man. First, as a street sweeper pushing a broom along the avenues of Manhattan, Rocco eventually became a driver of one of the City's large garbage trucks. This was the prestige job among the many immigrants who were classified as 'Sanitation Worker.' Driving a truck meant that he went to work clean and came home the same way. He was proud of himself and vowed to do whatever he had to do to make life better for his son, Nick.

Rocco worked hard and saved almost every dollar he earned. Within two years, he saved enough money to move his family into a clean apartment in a run-down building on Bergen Street, where they lived now. His ultimate goal in moving was to get the family out of the old neighborhood and into this one, which was surrounded by many nice homes and lots of shops and a movie house. There were good grammar schools and even a library within easy walking distance. Perhaps one day, Rocco thought, I can buy this building and fix it up into something nice. It was from these humble beginnings that Nick Toscano rose.

Neither Nick nor many other Brooklynites these days had ever swum in the East River, especially since swimming in the river was no longer permitted. Instead, Nick's contemporaries had a multitude of clean and safe beaches from which to choose. Nick Toscano and his friends settled on two primary choices: Riis Park or Coney Island.

If someone had a car available to them, they would all pile in and ride out to Riis Park in Flatbush; if a car was not available, Nick would hitch a ride by himself all the way out and meet the others there. Nick hated the long subway ride out to the beach, but his friends chose that route because they were frightened to hitch a ride in a stranger's car.

Riis Park was known for its free-wheeling drinking places that never checked ID's as much as for its sandy beaches. Nick shied away from those whose only reason for going to the beach was to guzzle beer until they fell down drunk and were forcibly ejected from the saloons before they got sick outside in the parking lot. When Nick was alone and felt the need for a beach fix, more often than not, he took the Franklin Avenue "El" to Coney Island and walked along Surf Avenue to Nathan's where he devoured a half dozen of the world's most 'famous'—and delicious—hot dogs, a bag of greasy french fries, and a frothy root-beer. He skipped the buttery corn-on-the-cob since it would stick in his teeth and, possibly, lessen his 'cool' look as a quintessential male sex machine. Then, once on the boardwalk, he would get a Coney Island custard at Kohr Brothers Famous Custard, a shop just a few feet from the surf and sand. Of course, though he had sated his primeval need for food, he never for one instant forgot his main objective—the primary reason he came to the beach: to check out the chicks on the beach. He had several well-practiced moves for meeting girls and setting up a heavy-duty make-out session under the boardwalk as soon as it got dark.

One morning, Nick arrived at Pete's at 6 A.M. and fumbled with the keys opening the door. As he turned on the lights, he saw the ever-present cockroaches scurry into their daytime hiding places. "Just like home," he thought: "turn on the lights and away they go." He pulled at the cardboard container of coffee he bought at the deli and began to straighten and sweep up the debris from the previous day's work. The area around the lifts was usually littered with broken parts, cotter pins, spark plugs, etc., and Nick wanted it clean before Pete arrived. Nick was a fanatic when it came to cleanliness.

At around 9 A.M. a car pulled up to the front door and two men got out. They had suits on, but they looked somehow different from the usual customers Nick saw. "Maybe it's their eyes," he thought.

"Hey you," the driver called to Nick.

"Yea?" he replied.

"You the mechanic?"

"No; he'll be here in a few minutes. I pump gas and do grease jobs and oil changes. Pete's the mechanic. You got a problem with your car?"

He ignored Nick as though he weren't there and waited until Pete arrived; both men then went immediately to him.

"You Kelly?"

Pete said, "Yep. What's up?"

The driver said, "Look, my name is Carmine. I need some 'special' work on a car; we gotta hop it up. I hear you're real good."

"This the car?" Pete asked.

"Nah. I got a '48 Packard for ya; it's a big muttha."

Pete Kelly was anxious to get this type of work because he enjoyed the challenge of reworking an engine to get maximum output from a Detroit creation. Besides, tune-up and brake jobs were becoming boring. The Packard was to be brought in that afternoon, and Pete would estimate the job, tell the driver what he could expect, and then agree on a price.

At about 3 P.M., two cars pulled into the station; the Packard and another car driven by the young man from the morning. Nick observed the discussion as Pete and Carmine went over the details of the deal. As the men left in the second car, Nick went over to Pete and said,

"Those guys look like hoods."

"I think you're right," Pete Kelly responded. "They want me to soup up the Packard; it's got a V-8."

CARMINE

I

Carmine Della Rocca was an enigma to his parents and to many who knew him. Born in 1930, he was old enough in 1952 to realize that he just wouldn't make it as a numbers runner for the Italian lottery. Many within the vast lottery organization were earning large sums and spending it freely. Carmine, however, made three or four dollars from his route each week collecting policy slips from older Italian men and women and a handful of Irish gamblers around the neighborhood. He delivered his slips and the money each Wednesday evening to someone known to him only as 'Al.' Al lived in one of the luxurious brownstones on Lincoln Place, just five blocks away from Carmine's six-family tenement at 495 Park Place. The brownstones on Al's block were not actually luxurious or expensive—except to those who couldn't afford to live in them—like Carmine.

Each week when Carmine arrived at Al's, he was greeted by a meticulously groomed man about five years older than himself. Whereas Carmine sought the look of a business man by wearing a double-breasted suit each day, he never achieved the desired result. He had the popular 'greaser' look of the day with slicked-down hair and a poorly trimmed mustache. His image was that of a cheap hood. Which he was.

Carmine's Park Place apartment was situated directly across from an empty lot in which a week-long carnival was staged each year. The local residents disliked the carnival since it was run by 'outsiders'—Amer-i-gans, people who did not live or work in the neighborhood. For Carmine and his friends, it was a time to pick a few pockets and fool around with the girls who visited from other neighborhoods.

Fooling around with neighborhood girls was forbidden by the neighborhood code, and any young man who violated the code was certain to 'earn' a broken nose or a fractured arm gratuitously provided by the girl's older brother and his friends—or others who chose to maintain the sanctity of the code. Not every neighborhood girl was pleased by this policy; it was just a bit more difficult for those who chose to violate it.

Carmine's rise to prominence (as he might say) occurred two years earlier in 1950, when he led a group of eight neighborhood teenagers in a successful attempt at climbing the greased pole at the feast of Saint Sebastian. The feast of Saint Sebastian was sponsored by the Societa di San Sebastiano, a group formed for the specific purpose of honoring the patron saint of several small villages surrounding Coscenza, Italy. A large contingent of immigrants from that area had settled here and in nearby neighborhoods. As was their custom in Italy, they formed committees and elected officers in preparation of conducting an annual festival in the saint's honor. They rented a local storefront and made signs and hung various flags and banners to clearly define and identify who they were and what they were all about.

It was the custom each year for the president of the society to pick his own daughter to be queen of the feast. This year, Carmine's sister, Anna, was chosen queen. Her job was to select two best friends as ladies in waiting to join her riding in an open car during the parade that heralded the feast's opening. The purpose of this ritual was as much to show off your daughters to the neighbors as to the eligible young men in the neighborhood. Anna, at fourteen, was lovely, and had never been accorded such attention before. Carmine worried that he would have to keep his eyes open to ensure that none of the wrong boys came calling.

Anna and her ladies in waiting rode in the open car behind the rented, gaily uniformed, rag-tag band that marched up and down each street in the neighborhood. The band played melodies familiar to the Italian immigrants; the sightseers enjoyed the gay tunes for their entertainment value. Anna smiled genuinely, as did the other girls, and waved continuously from her perch atop the folded-down convertible top of someone's year-old Pontiac Chieftan.

Close behind the slow-moving vehicle was a throng of men and women on foot who tried unsuccessfully to control the dozens of young children parading with them who struggled to 'get away' and play with other children on the sidewalk. Following them were older men dressed in black suits with white cotton shirts with skinny black ties; their only purpose seemed to be to wear sashes of red, white, and green—the colors of the Italian flag—with the word COMMITTEE stamped in four-inch-high gold letters. Behind them was another group of men wearing large, brightly colored buttons on wide red ribbons, proclaiming PRESIDENT, PAST-PRESIDENT, TREASURER, etc. Every man in the parade seemed to have either a sash or a button. It was a truly democratic organization.

Trailing the marchers at the end of the parade was a group of younger men straining to carry on their shoulders a heavy, six-foot-square wooden platform supporting a larger-than-life-sized statue of Saint Sebastian. These men rocked to and fro as they performed a ritualistic dance while the procession slithered through the narrow, steamy city streets. Onlookers strained to see the procession waiting for the patron saint to be ushered over to their side of the street. Designated women (who wore no sashes or buttons) responded to calls from women at open windows in the upper floors who tossed dollar bills down. The designated women gathered up the floating bills and pinned them to one of the many colored streamers attached to the statue. Everyone in the neighborhood enjoyed the procession. It was a good thing to do each year; it cemented community relations in ways now long gone.

III

The procession always took place on a Saturday, and, as it snaked its way through some of the city's narrowest streets, it grew in length and breadth as onlookers left their perches on stoops or in front of stores along the route to join the committeemen and women marchers. Inevitably, there was always a handful of rascally youths that followed the marchers mimicking the way they walked or talked. Happily, it was always harmless fun. People cheered and prayed openly as the saint passed their location; the community enjoyed itself, and a joyful spirit pervaded the air as anticipation grew for a few nights of fun and games at the feast.

Those eager to join in the festival spirit showed up at the street venue earlier in the week to watch as vendors set up booths and stalls from which to hawk their sausage and pepper sandwiches or great blocks of Torrone—the imported hard nougat candy that had to be chopped with a meat cleaver and a hammer. One could almost taste some of the more popular delicacies being readied for nighttime sale: ricotta & mozzarella calzones that were deep fried in hot oil; tripe, rolled up pork skin and tomato sauce; and other regional favorites from the old world.

Festivities usually began about 2 P.M. with a pie-eating contest where young men would vie to see who could devour a blueberry pie the fastest. One year there was a cannoli eating contest, but the young men who participated ate so many that the cost became too much. As always though, the highlight on Saturday, and the activity that drew the most attention, was the climbing of the greased pole.

In 1950, Carmine Della Rocca, then 20 years old, knew that he would win the pole climb with his team of hand-picked youths. Having failed two years in a row to reach the preserved meats and cheeses atop the greased pole, Carmine schemed all year to ensure success. At the very top of the pole was a large metal ring from which dangled the prizes. Today, the prizes that brought out the lusty young men were soppressata, the spiciest of the large Italian sausages; various lengths of Genoa salamis; pepperonis; and two huge wheels of Parmigiana grating cheese.

Several teams of eight shirtless young men came forward and knelt before a local priest who prayed for their success and safety. The pole—a 32-foot high telephone pole adapted for use in back yards to anchor clothes lines for the hundreds of neighborhood apartment dwellers—was anchored in place and slathered with hundreds of pounds of auto grease by members of the local fire department using ladder trucks. Once greased, the pole had to be scaled without ladders or ropes, though burlap bags were permitted as an aid in removing as much grease as possible and aiding in gripping the slippery pole. The gamble was this: The first team chosen had to deal with a 32-foot pole covered with about two inches of grease from the bottom all the way to the top. Going first was bad. Going last would be better since much of the grease would have been wiped away. Going last had its own issues:

you could get beat by someone who went before you. Carmine figured that going third was the safest—so he bribed the committee man who pulled the team names out of a hat.

The previous day Carmine and two of his henchmen had taken their ten burlap sacks to Coney Island and rolled them in the surf until they were impregnated with sand and salt water. This was his calculated advantage. And it worked! After a few false starts, his team had built a human pyramid at the bottom of the pole so that Carmine could climb over their bodies and get as high as possible before shinnying up toward the top using the sand-infused burlap sacks. When he reached the pinnacle, he tore at one of the huge Genoa salamis above his head, bit off a piece and held it high as the crowd roared.

IV

It was two years since Carmine had cheated his way to prominence among his peers. Now, an area numbers runner at 22 years, he was doing a favor for Al Zito who had asked him to soup up the '48 Packard. He prayed that Pete Kelly really knew what he was doing. Carmine figured something crooked was up, but he knew better than to ask any questions. People who knew too much—or even sounded like they knew too much—often wound up rotting atop one of the reeking, methane-spewing mounds of garbage in any of the many Staten Island landfills.

AL

I

Al Zito was twenty-seven years old in 1952; he was also the focal point for the Italian numbers racket covering the borough of Brooklyn. The numbers runners worked for him; they were men or trusted youths who collected the nickels, dimes and quarters from Italian bettors, brought their policy slips and money to Al each Wednesday, and picked up any winnings on Friday. A steady stream of men arrived at his first-floor apartment in the two-story Lincoln Place brownstone; each was met personally, by Al, himself.

Al was a handsome man and tall for a first-generation Italian, standing almost six feet two. He weighed just under two hundred pounds, but carried no noticeable fat. He had a magnificent set of teeth that sparkled when he smiled—which he did often, making his usual demeanor nonthreatening and pleasant. He had a broad forehead and charcoal black eyes. His upper lip sported a meticulously groomed pencil-thin mustache in the style of male Hollywood movie stars such as David Niven. Al Zito cut a handsome figure and caused many hearts to break when he married Donna-Marie Capasso two years earlier.

Al graduated from Brooklyn College in 1947 with a degree in Accounting. He had expected to go to work in a bank, but was offered a better job working as an accountant / tax adviser for the Della Croce Produce Company, one of Brooklyn's largest importers and employers. It didn't take him long to discover that the business was a front for the Carducci gang's illegal gambling operations. Al's education, demeanor, insightful accounting practices, and consistently flawless output brought him to the attention of Sevvi Carducci, the president of Della Croce Produce. Carducci, an astute businessman himself, had a gift of making matters seem better than they really were, and he used these powers to persuade Al to transition from corporate accountant to heading the vast numbers operation for the Carducci crime family. Al wasn't fearful of the job since people would always gamble whether it was legal or not, and, besides, what harm could come to him? He was an accountant.

Al agreed to Sevvi's request and rented himself an apartment on the first floor in a brownstone owned by one of Carducci's cousins. After about six months, he realized that too much attention was being drawn to himself with the runners coming and going twice a week. Besides, he was married, and it was troubling that his wife had to be disturbed every time the doorbell rang. He thought of leaving the job, but was too deeply involved; besides, he knew where the bodies were buried so it was virtually impossible to extricate himself.

II

The July day began as usual for Al. He rose at 6 A.M., did his regular morning exercises, which consisted of sit-ups, pushups, running in place, and ten minutes of dynamic tension, a program designed by Charles Atlas and advertised on the back page of many men's magazines. He then went into the back yard, which was about forty feet wide and 150 feet long. A cement walkway ran straight down the middle separating the yard into two equal halves. On the right side, which was sunnier, Al had planted a garden that consisted of plum tomatoes, zucchini, lettuce, radishes, and other summer vegetables. At the far end, there were four fig trees, and this year was the first time that they would bear fruit.

The left side of the yard was totally dedicated to rose bushes. Al loved roses and sought out only the most beautiful and exotic types available. He worked in the garden each morning for an hour before showering and having a light breakfast of espresso and one of several light biscotti that Donna-Marie brought in from the local pastry shop. Al enjoyed all that he had, and at twenty-seven, he had plenty.

At 10 A.M. the telephone rang. The voice from work said that he should get to the main office on Henry Street right away. Al sensed that something was wrong, but didn't give any indication to Donna-Marie as he left.

"Sevvi wants to see me," he said. "I'll take the car."

Al drove downtown to the Della Croce main office on Henry Street, which took about twenty minutes since the traffic on Flatbush Avenue and Livingston Street was unusually heavy in the Brooklyn downtown shopping area. He parked his car and climbed the stairs to the glassed-in office at the end of the hall. Eight men were already there. When Al walked in, one of the men punched the intercom and said, "Tell Mister Carducci that everyone is here."

Sevvi Carducci walked into the office from an adjoining room. Compared to those gathered there, he presented a pitiful figure. Once powerfully built, he was now obese with jowls and hardly any neck. His nose was red and swollen, and he wheezed as he spoke. But no one doubted the power that he wielded; Sevvi Carducci, even today, was capable of incredible evil, and tolerated no intrusion into any activity that he claimed was rightfully his. He was the cliche of the typical gangster as he chewed on a black cigar and commanded the 'respect' of his subordinates.

"We got trouble," he said, and began a litany of ills that had erupted seemingly overnight. He went on to describe how a rival gang from South Brooklyn had begun moving in on some of his bookmaking business. Al listened, but really couldn't get too excited since, as an accountant, he knew that he would be safe from any warfare and also that Della Croce Produce had plenty of money to withstand any losses.

Carducci went on to describe that if they didn't respond to this overt attack on their operation immediately, they could be out of business in six months—or worse, all dead. One by one Carducci led his men into the adjoining room and gave them specific instructions, which were unknown to the others. One by one they went in, and one by one each left with a solemn look going his own way to carry out his Sevvi's assignment. Al was the last to be ushered into the back room, and wondered what he could possibly be called upon to do. "After all," he thought, "I'm not a combatant!"

III

"Hello, Hon," Donna-Marie greeted Al as he returned home with his assignment from Sevvi Carducci.

"Hi," he muttered.

"What's wrong, lover? Big boss grumble at you? She said this in a sort of mocking tone with her voice lowered several octaves.

"Nah."

"Come on; you can tell me."

"I can't; just drop it. OK? It doesn't involve you. I'm fine."

Donna-Marie was a happy person, and in her presence others caught her joy. Now, however, she sensed fear—a darkness—in her husband. "Look," he partially ordered her, "just leave me alone right now for about a half-hour. All right?"

Speaking to Donna-Marie in such a manner was completely out of character for Al; she shivered as fear consumed her.

Al climbed the stairs two at a time and practically slammed the bedroom door. He paused momentarily, then padded across the carpeted floor and into the bathroom while removing his double-breasted jacket. Looking at himself in the full-length mirror behind the door, Al was frightened as his eyes sighted the slightly used Beretta model 948 pistol in the small holster clipped onto the waistband of his suit pants.

Al was unfamiliar with the use of firearms, and felt uncomfortable bringing one into his home, but Sevvi insisted that everyone who worked for him from now on had to be armed. The Beretta was a small weapon, designed specifically to be carried concealed in a vest pocket of a suit jacket or in a holster attached to one's waistband, as was Al's. This particular Beretta model was manufactured in Italy and designed to be lightweight—though deadly; it fired a .22 caliber cartridge.

When Al had examined the box of bullets that Sevvi gave him, he wondered how such a small cartridge could do much damage. What Al did not know was that the gun and the cartridges would be completely ineffective against the massive warfare that Sevvi feared was imminent. Handguns like the Beretta or handguns of larger caliber would be useless against Tommy guns, high-powered rifles or dynamite. Sevvi exhorted Al to keep the Beretta loaded, on his person, at all times . . . just in case!!

Al undressed quickly and hid the gun and the box of bullets under the mattress; where else could he hide it to make it safe while he was home? Slipping on just his silk bathrobe, he tried to be casual as he came down the stairs and returned to the kitchen. Donna-Marie was washing escarole salad leaves in the sink. She did not speak.

Al wanted to calm her and restore peace to his home; he needed the joyful spirit his wife generated. As nonchalantly as he could, he padded over to the stove and sniffed deeply of the amazing aroma rising like ambrosia from Donna-Marie's huge sauce pot. Momentarily, he forgot about the Beretta. He tore off one end of a crusty loaf of Italian Bread and dunked it into the bubbling sauce.

Donna-Marie spied him out of the corner of her eye doing what he had always done since he was a little boy. In an instant her fear subsided, and she thought, "Thank God; he's OK." She turned toward him and mocked, "Al! Stop that right now! You'll burn the roof of your mouth!" She admonished him again, but he ignored her well-intentioned warning and chomped on the steaming, sauce-laden piece of bread. He was hoping his actions would allay any remaining hurts he had brought into his household; inside, he was sick to his stomach with fear of the potential war.

Al walked snuggled over to her while chewing the bread, gulping air so as to cool his scorching mouth. He drew her close and squeezed her rear with his free hand while pressing her hard into him. He nuzzled her as he continued to eat.

"You are the weirdest person I know, Al Zito. You walk in here all gloom and doom two minutes ago, and now you're happy and relaxed and getting the hots." The Beretta under the mattress was back in his mind's eye again. He faked at being his usual self.

"When I'm with you, I can only think good things," he chuckled. "Good food, clean house, great woman! Let's go upstairs—wanna fool around?"

Madly in love with her man, Donna-Marie hardly had to think before she tore herself away from him and ran into the hallway that led to the staircase, flinging her clothes at him as she raced up the stairs and toward the bedroom. Suddenly she stopped! Al caught up with her at the entrance to the bedroom; she put her hands directly in his face, halting him in his tracks. "What's wrong?" he said. He was puzzled, as he enveloped her in his powerful arms. "What's the matter?" he asked again.

Wearing a huge, child-like smile and opening her eyes as wide as possible, she implored him speaking the baby talk he loved to hear from her, "I forgot to shut off the sauce! You better let me go; it's gonna burn!"

Al smiled right back at her before whispering, "No worries, my love; we won't be that long," and he swept her up and inside.

"I'll bet you won't!" she laughed at the man she loved so intensely. Al and Donna-Marie were very good together.

IV

When the Korean War ended, Al Zito returned to his home on Lincoln Place a different person from when he left home a year before. His connections at the draft board were able to keep him out of the conflict for just so long. Ultimately, he was called up and spent eleven months in the mud and slime of the Korean wilderness trying to stay alive. But Al was a survivor, and he came home with a radically different philosophy on life. The fifty-five thousand American soldiers who died on foreign soil left a lasting impression on him; he began to understand what a precious gift life really was. Once home, he remained haunted by the memories of July 1952 and the gangland massacre orchestrated by Sevvi Carducci. Although Al's role had been purely administrative, he did arrange for the getaway car, which made him an accessory before the fact and eligible for a prison term if convicted. During the days preceding the massacre, he was physically sick anticipating the senseless killings that were an integral part of each crime family's operation; Sevvi's goal had been to eliminate anyone or any group that he sensed was a threat to his 'family.' Al ached at the realization that crime families were no different from any country or political group that resorted to murder to maintain their own position of power and special interests. His stint in Korea was, in one way, a blessing since it shielded him from his former gangland associates and further developed his distaste for fighting and killing. Now twenty-eight years old, he resolved to make something of himself—apart from Sevvi Carducci and the Della Croce Produce Company. After weeks of doing nothing at home and seeing no one, Al announced to Donna-Marie that they were going to move into Manhattan.

"Manhattan; why? How come?" She was bewildered by the sudden and unusual finality of his proclamation. She couldn't remember ever questioning his decisions like this before.

"We can't stay here anymore. Things will be the same for us just like before if I don't get away. Sevvi got along without me while I was in Korea, so now's a good time to split. Besides, I . . . we need to break out of this neighborhood; we'll wind up just like everyone else around here if we don't leave. Look, we gotta go. OK? Everything will work out."

Donna-Marie may have been a bit naive about the lifestyle she and Al shared on Lincoln Place probably because he isolated her from much of what went on with his job at Della Croce Produce; she became adept at avoiding questioning him. But she could not comprehend his sudden urgency to leave the neighborhood; what exactly was wrong with living here?

She appreciated all the benefits derived from Al's former job; the money afforded her many benefits, and she knew that. She also played little mind games with herself whenever she began to see too much or suspect things—never believing that he was in any danger. But leaving the neighborhood was more than she bargained for. Growing up here had filled her life with many wonderful, lasting memories, and the thought of living in Manhattan—taking a subway or a bus or both—would isolate her from her roots; she was not happy.

V

She remembered the first time she saw Al in Otto's ice cream parlor on Underhill Avenue. It was April, 1947 and she was with her girl friend, Eileen McGill.

"Who's the handsome boy, the tall one in the booth all alone?" she asked Eileen as they entered through the front door surveying the entire place as usual.

"I've seen him here once or twice before. I've heard some of the guy's call him Al. He's a senior in Brooklyn College."

"I'd really like to meet him. Whatta you think?" she giggled.

Al noticed Donna-Marie immediately when she and Eileen walked into Otto's. She's something special, he thought. Donna-Marie was taller and prettier than Eileen with a posture that reminded him of models who walked in that 'special' way, exhibiting a charm and grace not found in so many women with bad posture. Al wanted to meet her, so he put the wheels in motion.

Eileen and Donna-Marie sat in the booth directly across from Al's and ordered cherry Cokes. Al had been drinking coffee, and when the waiter took the girls' order, Al motioned him over.

"What's the short girl's name?" he asked in a whisper.

"The short one? She's Eileen McGill; I don't know the other one."

"That's OK. Thanks. Bring me another coffee."

While the waiter went to get the cherry Cokes and coffee, Al emptied the contents of the sugar bowl into his jacket pocket. When his coffee arrived, Al pretended to murmur to himself, then looked over to the two girls who were sipping their drinks.

"Excuse me," he said. "My sugar bowl is empty; may I borrow yours?" Donna-Marie's pulse quickened as Al leaned over to take the sugar bowl that Eileen eagerly offered him.

"Here goes nothing," Al murmured to himself. "Aren't you Eileen McGill? I recognize you from the neighborhood." He felt his pulse quicken.

"Yes, I am; this is my girl friend, Donna-Marie."

Their relationship was always good during their courtship and grew better even up to the present. Al had always stressed the importance of fidelity to Donna-Marie even though he himself had been the target of many 'friendly' takeover attempts while they were dating. Both Al and Donna-Marie had deep family ties and often talked about the family they would raise someday.

VI

"How do you like this one, Hon?" Al asked Donna-Marie as they walked through the high-ceilinged rooms of a three-family walkup on West Fifty-Fourth Street near Ninth Avenue.

"It's beautiful, Al, but it's so far from home. It's two trains and a bus to get back home . . . I mean . . . back to the neighborhood." She fought back tears, but she knew that Al had made up his mind.

"Look," he said, "it's got a fireplace, a big bathtub AND a shower. There's a skylight too! Oh honey, c'mon; let's take it."

She knew it was useless to avoid the inevitable, so she smiled back at him approvingly and nodded her acceptance.

"Great! We'll have the entire family here for Christmas." Al could hardly contain his excitement as he raced through the rooms measuring everything with his hands as he moved from room to room.

"Al," she called.

"Yes, Hon?"

"I know we'll pay cash for this house, but there's something we should talk about."

"What?"

"You need to get a job."

Al walked into the front room and peered out onto Fifty-Fourth Street. "Sevvi Carducci," he thought, "I've finally done it; I'm free! Free? What do I do next?" He put off those thoughts when he heard Donna-Marie slipping into the room behind him. He turned to greet her with an enormous smile, swept her off the floor and into his arms, gave her a passionate kiss and said, "Let's do it!" "You gotta be kidding me! Here? Where? Now? I can't!"

She began laughing hysterically as she tried to extricate herself from his love crunch. "The sales agent is downstairs."

"You can't blame a guy for trying, can you?" he retorted semi-seriously, setting her gently on the floor and kissing her hard.

She prayed silently that all would go well. She was still afraid. "I love you, Al!" "Me too."

It was Monday of the week of Thanksgiving when Al returned to his new home singing and bouncing up the front steps. "Honey!" he shouted as he threw open the front door.

Donna-Marie called to him from the kitchen, "In here, Al."

He could hardly control himself as he held her shoulders and stammered, "Listen; I've got news! Great news!" He drew a deep breath and continued. "Some of the guys I went to school with are setting up a television show—they call it a 'special'—for the Christmas holidays. They want me to invest and help them out."

He could hardly contain himself as he danced them both around the kitchen. His excitement was contagious, and Donna-Marie found herself rapidly being caught up in Al's exuberance.

"Television?" She could hardly speak since Al was waltzing her about leaving her breathless. She interjected a few words as she caught her breath, "What do you know about TV?"

"Nothing!" he almost shouted, setting her down. "Nothing at all, but—I've got cash. I've got cash, and they need it!"

He helped Donna-Marie to a chair, and they both sat down eyeball to eyeball. "These guys need my money, and if it goes over—and I know it will—we can make our money back a hundred times over! A hundred times over!" To himself, he added, "And it's legal!"

He leaped up from the chair as though his legs were springs. He paused, looking toward Donna-Marie for confirmation. She cracked a smile and queried, "Is it risky, Al?"

He walked over to her, and she rose to meet him, locking her arms around his neck. He calmed himself, sensing here anxiety; looking deeply into her eyes he smiled his most comforting smile trying to help her relax.

He whispered, "Honey, don't worry; everything will be all right. Those guys have connections—and besides, it's honest!"

"I know, I know. You've been looking for something ever since we left Brooklyn." She felt more at ease and asked, "Tell me about it."

Al explained that some of his college friends had been working the theater district behind the scenes since 1947. During those years, Al had kept in telephone contact with them, but saw them only infrequently while he was involved as an 'accountant' with Sevvi. They had already backed a few minor Broadway shows, and were now anxious to produce a television show for Christmas starring an unknown black calypso singer. They felt that America was ready for the entrée' of a black leading man on TV, and a special at Christmastime seemed the ideal vehicle at the right time. They had convinced a major network about the merits of the show, but they needed thirty thousand dollars cash for pre-production expenses. They asked Al to put up ten thousand; they would put up the rest.

The following months saw Al becoming more and more deeply involved in the working of the TV show. He attacked his work with a passion he had heretofore never known was possible. Quite literally, he loved all that he was doing, and he learned quickly. In fact, Al—having been trained to operate in high-risk areas by Sevvi Carducci—was comfortable dealing with the dozens of network personnel who constantly bombarded him with problems.

One day, a senior network vice-president stopped by to see Al.

"Al Zito?"

"Yes, how do you do?" Al said matter-of-factly.

"Al, my name is Joe Weintrauben; I'm the network exec in charge of production for your Christmas special. I'd like to speak to you if I may."

Joe Weintrauben was about the same age as Al, though he was already a network vice-president. He had a slight paunch and smoked incessantly. Compared to Al Zito, Joe Weintrauben appeared sloppy and unkempt, a second-rate hustler who should have been selling ties on Delancey Street. But something told Al that Weintrauben didn't just happen to become a VP at twenty-eight. He must have had plenty of smarts to be successful in the highly competitive world of commercial television.

Weintrauben ushered Al into a quiet corner of the recording studio.

"Al, I've heard a lot of good things about you," he began.

"I really enjoy this work," Al replied. "It's fascinating—so dynamic; it's great!" Al exhibited the enthusiasm that he had been carrying around with him since his involvement with the show a few short weeks ago.

"It's obvious that you enjoy your work," Weintrauben continued, "but there is much more about you that sets you apart from so many others working here."

"What's that?" Al asked, looking at Weintrauben quizzically.

"You move people well; you arrange things like a big-time Hollywood producer. Word has gotten to the big boys upstairs. Some of us would like to talk to you after the show airs at Christmas; we've got some ideas that might be of interest to you. It could be good for you and us."

"Sure; I'll look you up first of the year." Al put all of this in the back of his mind and went back to work.

Christmas 1953 was on a Friday; the network had scheduled the special to air on Wednesday, December 23. Television spot announcements promoting the show began on the weekend of the 12th, and newspaper adds followed on the 19th and continued daily until air time. Sponsorship was excellent with major funding coming from national American manufacturers who used the air time to stimulate Christmas sales. Now that all of the available commercial air time had been sold and Al and his partners were guaranteed a financial success, Al's main interest had become acutely focused on the television industry itself as a vehicle for his personal future growth.

Television was primarily a live medium in 1953, which meant that a full-dress rehearsal was necessary; it was scheduled for 2 P.M. on December 23. Al woke early that morning, showered and dressed casually. He took a dark blue suit from his closet and hung it in a garment bag with a clean shirt, tie, and black shoes.

"Honey, I'm going to skip breakfast today. I'll get something at the commissary," he said to Donna-Marie as he put on his dark-blue woolen overcoat.

"What time shall I meet you tonight?" she asked.

"The show goes on at eight-thirty, so be at the studio near seven; take a cab, and don't be afraid. We'll have a light supper with the boys and then sit in the control room during the show."

"Great."

Al bent over and kissed her only lightly, which was usual for him; he was filled with excitement and was eager to begin his day. When he approached the front door, Donna-Marie reminded him of her doctor's appointment later that morning. He left only half hearing her, racing down the steps and across the street; her words trailed off into air. She offered a silent prayer for both her husband and her marriage; she felt uncertain of the world in which he was now involved. She also prayed that the doctor's visit would work out OK.

LAINE POWERS AUGUST

I

Al Zito walked into the studio that day, and out of habit sat in his usual chair. Off to his right, silently weaving past cameras, wiring, poster board, and an array of lighting fixtures, Al saw a shadowy figure approaching the seating area. As his gaze became more focused, the figure morphed into one of the most beautiful women he had ever seen. He fought the impulse to stare, but barely was able to look away. As she grew closer, he pretended not to notice, but the voices of the crew made it impossible for him to maintain the charade: male voices seemingly from nowhere resounded, "Hello, Miss August; how are you today? Miss August, do you need anything? Miss August, can I get you some coffee? Miss August . . . Miss August . . . " over and over.

Laine Powers August was Joe Weintrauben's executive staff assistant. Laine Powers August was a sophisticated, sexy, delightful-to-look-at, get-anything-done, knows-everybody, super-secretary—that's what she was. Laine Powers August was the only person Joe Weintrauben trusted to get important things done—and done right the first time. Make no mistake, Laine Powers August was a force to be reckoned with! And she knew it all too well.

II

Miss August, a statuesque, thirty-two-year-old female whose imposing presence often intimidated men and women, commanded attention wherever she went. In business and in social settings, Miss August was a person whose words demanded

79

attention; some might even say—respect. Everything about her was impressive: her wispy, yet strong, voice, her intellect, her confidence, the subtle poise—all packaged in a breathtaking presence five-feet-eight-inches tall in stocking feet. Today, she presented a vision of elegance in bright-red, four-inch-high, Coco Chanel sling-back pumps. Her stunning super-model figure sported a taut, slender waist, gently curved hips, adequate bust and long willowy legs that seemed to reach upward endlessly. Her measured gait drew eyes from everywhere.

The natural arch of her eyebrows complemented the mystery harbored beneath her sultry countenance. Her lips were full and perfectly defined, colored this afternoon with the most subtle shade of calming pink; they were warm and welcoming. When she smiled, her teeth sparkled like deep sea pearls. Two hazel-green eyes, seductive for certain, perfectly augmented her gorgeous face, which was crowned by a head of full, thick, auburn hair that fell softly in highlighted waves to her shoulders.

Truly a natural beauty, she used the slightest hint of makeup to complement her already flawless skin. Her high cheekbones needed no rouge for they blushed naturally from within. Her eyelashes, long and lush, enriched imperceptibly from the deftly applied mascara; it was difficult to improve on perfection. The eyebrows, simply arched, required no enhancement from a pencil or tweezing. By any measure, Laine Powers August was blessed with singular natural beauty; truthfully, she was stunning by anyone's measure. Her demeanor and grace complemented her physical beauty perfectly; any man . . . or woman . . . was instantly comfortable in her presence. Today, strangely, she appeared somewhat aloof: desirable yet beyond reach; passionate but controlled.

Potential suitors experienced a contrasting side of Laine Powers August. Her smile gave them pause as if projecting her innate fortitude that spoke silent words to their hearts: "Pursue me, if you will, but know that I am in control . . . you are a pawn in my personal game of chess." This aspect of hers spoke to the single life she chose . . . single though never lonely. Her private life was amply augmented with a pastiche of short-term affairs that sated her most elemental needs. Close friends and a scant number of business acquaintances furtively asserted that she could unapologetically sabotage anyone who got in her way—male or female. Laine Powers August was one of the highest paid women in New York City.

III

Her perfume reached him before she did; then, once there and leaning so that her ample bosoms were at his eye level, she practically sighed, "Hello, Mr. Zito; my name . . . ." Al clumsily stood up, tripping over his own feet, awed at the striking presence before him. At full height now and with a knowing grin on her face, she caught his eyes and held out her hand repeating, "Hello, Mr. Zito. My name is Laine. Laine . . . Powers . . . August. Mr. Weintrauben's executive staff assistant."

She spoke with a softness in her voice that belied the obvious strength and confidence she possessed and her position at the station. Having a Master's degree in market research from Barnard College didn't hurt her confidence at all.

Struggling to catch his breath, Al stammered, "Hello." He was momentarily out of control, and tried desperately to regain his composure without seeming too obvious. "You seem to have me at a disadvantage, Miss August. I . . . ah; I don't believe I've seen you around the studio before."

"No, you haven't; but please call me Laine—everyone does."

"Sure. And you can drop the Mr. Zito. It's Al."

"OK, ... Al." Her eyelashes did flutter when she responded, and her face bore the merest of hint of a smile while they were speaking; she never diverted the hazel-green eyes that seemed to pierce his soul. (He thought, "She can read my mind.") Eventually, a broader, more obvious smile filled her countenance, and her eyes appeared even more intriguing. She did know what Al was thinking, and, more importantly, what he was feeling. Al knew that she knew.

"Let's sit, shall we?" she suggested; to Al, it was a command.

"Of course. Of course," he said, again grasping for a breath.

IV

They sat in their respective chairs, and Al sensed his pulse quicken when he ogled her each time she slowly and sensuously crossed and uncrossed her legs. "Did women practice doing that?" he wondered. "They probably do." Eventually, she turned toward him, and her short skirt rode up revealing more thigh than necessary and a hint of bare skin where her stocking was secured by a black garter. The fragrance of her perfume played tricks with his mind such that he momentarily forgot about the ongoing rehearsal. His thoughts wandered . . ..

(For years Al always had a pleasing reaction when he sensed a quality perfume worn by a quality woman. His response to Laine's perfume required no active participation from him whatsoever; it worked its magic without his consent.

Today, as on so many other occasions, he mused on why women chose to use perfumes (it was always a conscious decision) and the rationale that drove them to change from their natural hair color to something different (how do they figure out which color looks best on them? They always make the right choice.) And then there is the almost universal female predilection for eye makeup, rouge, false eyelashes, lipstick . . . cosmetics in general.

You can't smell perfume on yourself after a few minutes, so maybe women wear perfume to attract men. That must be it. But why the other makeup? Probably for the same reasons, though Donna-Marie says she uses makeup because she looks 'washed out' without some color on her face. And what about eye shadow and mascara? Nail polish? Earrings?" Then he considered, "Maybe women went through the effort of selecting from the innumerable shades and tints and textures because of other women; maybe they wanted to say, 'Hey, look what I can do with a little powder puff, a pencil and a lipstick . . . !' Maybe they even thought, 'I can do this better than you!'

That was probably a reasonable guess, he surmised, ever since a woman stopped Donna-Marie a few weeks ago as she was exiting a local green-grocer. The woman walked right up to Donna-Marie and, with the boldness of a sideshow hawker, told her how lovely her 'makeup' was. She never said how lovely Donna-Marie looked, but only that her 'makeup' was lovely. Like a coat of wax on a car: what is it we admire? The wax job, the paint or the car? Then again, a car does look much nicer with a fresh coat of wax. Hmm.

Al knew many women who frequently wore one shade of lipstick in the morning and a different shade in the afternoon or at night; they rationalized that, "One never wears pink at night—it isn't done!" Even if women chose to use cosmetics because other women did so, then what about older women? They're not looking for men. Are they? Maybe they are. Perhaps after years of wearing makeup, older women use cosmetics because they think they can make themselves look the way they once looked, or the way they think other women would want them to look.

He had often chuckled to himself pondering why so many not-so-pretty-women (both young and old) used cosmetics, often to excess and not always successfully, to make-over—or, in some cases—radically change their . . . faces. Once he had the opportunity to view before-and-after photos of such women; only very infrequently, by his judgment, was their effort actually worth it.

His nose reeked as a boy when his mother and aunts used the 'Ladies' Depilatory Creme' to remove 'unwanted hair of the lips and chin.' The entire kitchen area stank from the gooey cream they applied to their upper lips and chin to remove one or two wisps of black hairs that popped up every so often. They were firmly committed to removing these 'ugly' facial intrusions! He was thankful that Donna-Marie had no need for that smelly goo.

It was dizzying trying to puzzle these 'deep' thoughts; he was happy that he met Donna-Marie long before she succumbed to the world of high fashion and cosmetics. He always said that he fell in love with her 'inner' beauty and not for stuff she patted on her face or smeared on her lips. Privately, he was overjoyed that Donna-Marie had such great legs that kind of knocked him off his feet—even to this day! Soon after they married though, he spied her using a nighttime moisturizing cream on her face and a special 'tightening' cream on her legs. "She looks the same to me," he always said. He did like it when she wore perfume. A lot.

Maybe someone ought to write a book on all this . . . maybe not. He came back into the moment recognizing that he did not mind at all how women 'fixed themselves up'; it was none of his business anyway—he knew that. He resolved to celebrate the 'difference' as the French said. It was ironic that he actually enjoyed the company of women, especially those who knew how to apply cosmetics properly. He knew the other kind too.

He decided that since he had no actual control over anything concerned with women's makeup or hair color or styles, that he was going to enjoy the efforts that they put into making themselves 'pretty'. Didn't matter for whom they did it.)

When the calypso music began, Al was attentive . . . though . . . her perfume lingered; he wanted this woman! "What??"

He was convinced that she was aware of everything that he was thinking and feeling, and he flushed with embarrassment, hoping that she did not notice. He tried unsuccessfully to maintain a business-like attitude during the dress rehearsal, but it was only when Joe Weintrauben arrived that he felt himself relax, freed from Laine's paralyzing attraction. "I wish Donna-Marie were here," he heard himself murmur, realizing that he sounded like a teenager who needed the protection of someone older and stronger. "This is crazy," he thought. "I love my wife. She's wonderful. I've got to get hold of myself."

V

The rest of the day passed in a flash and Donna-Marie arrived right on schedule at five minutes to seven. She looked beautiful in the new dress that she bought especially for tonight. Al hugged her, and as he did he suddenly felt guilty—as though he had somehow cheated on his wife. "Holy --," he thought. "Why do I feel like this?"

Following a light supper with the partners, Al, Donna-Marie, and the entourage entered a special glass-enclosed soundproof room from which they would view the special. Joe Weintrauben was already there and welcomed Al and Donna-Marie indicating that they should sit next to him. Donna-Marie sat on Al's left so that he could be next to Mr. Weintrauben. The room was quite cool since the air-conditioning had been on for several hours to compensate for the tremendous heat generated by the studio cameras, lights, and other equipment. As the room lights dimmed, the stage lights came on full, and an announcer pranced onto center stage ready to begin the now-common pre-show studio audience warm-up.

The large, overhead clock ticked off the time remaining till show time: sixty seconds—thirty seconds—twenty seconds—. Al heard an almost imperceptible click and glanced over his shoulder to see Laine ease herself into the room. Joe Weintrauben rose from his seat and moved to his right and motioned for Laine to sit between himself and Al. Al warmed in her presence as her perfume worked its magic on him once again.

Al got hold of himself quickly and remembered his manners; he leaned back in his chair and whispered, "Laine, this is my wife, Donna-Marie." Compulsory smiles were quickly exchanged and everyone settled back to watch the opening credits rolling on monitors; the orchestra began; silence. Donna-Marie glanced over at Laine more than once in the following minutes, wondering WHY this . . . woman was in the booth . . . with them . . . sitting next to her husband. It was obvious that she wasn't the wife of anyone there. She wasn't dressed or made up like any wife she knew; Donna-Marie was intimidated by Laine's commanding presence, the style and quality of her clothing, and especially her makeup; yes, by just about everything to do with Laine. Uncharacteristically, Donna-Marie was . . . jealous!

Al, too, was having a hard time keeping his eyes off Laine, who had changed from the afternoon's short skirt into an elegant, billowy, ankle-length, crimson-red-crepe skirt. On top she sported a white satin blouse with matched pearl buttons at the wrists and all the way up the back. The blouse was tight at the neck and tied in an oversized bow of the same luxurious white satin. "What a woman! What class!" Al thought. "Wow!"

In the silence of the semi-darkened room, he found himself stealing glances at Laine's bosom, which rose and fell seductively in cadence with each breath that she took. At one point, he noticed that her nipples had firmed and were prominently outlined, expressing themselves against the exquisite satin of her fitted blouse. She sensed his focus and smiled seductively as if to acknowledge his gaze; she placed her lips close to his ear, and barely whispered for only him to hear, "It's getting cold in here." As she backed onto her seat, Al's eyes remained focussed as before; he was certain that her nipples had stiffened further and grown even larger, causing him to wonder whether she had the power to control them too.

"Y . . . Y . . . Yes, yes it is," he stammered. He sat further back in his chair, but moments later, his eyes darted back and forth between Donna-Marie and Laine, wondering why Donna-Marie's nipples hadn't reacted to the air-conditioning the same way as Laine's. He questioned his apparent obsession with bosoms tonight. Then it struck him. "Ahh! Good grief," he stifled his words, "Laine is . . . Laine is bra-less!" Al excused himself and fumbled his way out of the booth. It was 1953.

AL / DONNA-MARIE

I

The show was hailed as an artistic as well as a financial success for the network, and Al considered his payback huge compared with what was, for him, a modest ten-thousand dollar investment. It had to be criminal, he thought, to make all this money while having so much fun; there just had to be a catch—something was bound to go wrong.

The day after the show was Christmas Eve, and, while lying next to Al in bed, Donna-Marie could only think of the preparations that lay ahead of her this day to prepare for her first real 'family' dinner. She knew that Al expected this meal to be something extra special, having bragged of the sumptuous holiday feasts he experienced at his home or at his grandparent's from when he was a boy. He reminded her often of the Sundays that his parents took him over to Gran-Ma and Gran-Pa's house on Atlantic Avenue to eat on Sunday. Gran-Ma Zito always made everything from scratch, even grinding her own veal and pork for her special 'casalinga' meatballs, which were incomparable.

Al rejoiced in telling Donna-Marie how Gran-Ma, with help from her two daughters who shared the house with her, would begin the sauce at 7 A.M. every Sunday morning. And it would never be ready until almost 1 P.M. when Al and his parents arrived with a box of awesome pastries from LaViteri Pasticceria right around the corner. Al loved to share how the women were in absolute control of the kitchen, and the men were relegated to any of the other rooms in the house just as long as they stayed out of the kitchen while the meal was being prepared.

And then, always at the same time each week, everyone returned to the kitchen to find the table set and ready to go as soon as Gran-Pa sat down in his chair and said grace. The macaroni was dispensed from a huge bowl in the center of the table, and only Gran-Ma could do it properly—so no one even offered to help her. When she had finished doling out the macaroni, she passed the bowl of steaming 'extra' sauce and the ancient, rusting, knuckle-grinding, cheese grater together with a wedge of rock-hard sheep's milk Romano cheese—Locatelli brand only! And, just about when everyone had finished off their plate of macaroni, she passed out steaming bowls piled high with meatballs and sausages while someone retrieved the two wicker baskets from the closet and filled them with warm, crusty Italian bread that had been warmed in the oven. Then came clean dishes and the huge bowl of salad. Red wine flowed continuously throughout the meal, and the children sipped small amounts of wine mixed either with cream or sarsaparilla sodas.

When everyone was stuffed to capacity, the men disappeared into adjoining rooms either to catch a few winks on the couch or to sit in one of the overstuffed chairs and read the paper while listening to the large, cabinet-sized radio that might be playing *The Shadow* on WJZ or operatic music on WQXR. This was also a signal for the children to go outside and play while the women cleaned up and prepared black coffee and pastry. After an hour or so, the men returned for the remainder of the meal after which, typically, was followed by the men-only, nickel-and-dime pinochle game in the parlor. And this is how it went week after week, month after month; it was expected; it was planned; it was well-orchestrated without drama or stress. It was a happy time for many of the families in the neighborhood, and memories were built. It was the essence of dreams in 'the old days.' Al's dream was that he and Donna-Marie could replicate the essence of this tradition in his new home; he prayed that his family would recognize his attempt at sustaining the 'tradition' and sanctity of 'La Famiglia.'

Of course on this day, Donna-Marie's parents, Rafaela and Sal Capasso would be coming early to help their daughter and to put her more at ease. Also invited were Al's mother, Rosa, his older brother, Manny, and Manny's wife, Cathy, and Donna-Marie's two sisters, Marcella and Elena, their husbands, Joe and Lou, and their respective children. In all, Donna-Marie and Al would be entertaining sixteen people for the traditional Christmas Eve fish dinner.

II

Donna-Marie, always in control of herself, was the slightest bit anxious as she reviewed over and over again the menu and the endless tasks that had to be done prior to everyone's coming that evening. Donna-Marie also wanted to set aside time to tell Al that the doctor had found her to be about seven-weeks pregnant, and that she should expect to deliver her child about the third week in July. She had tried to tell him the previous night before dinner, but he was so obviously excited about the show, she knew that it was the wrong time. During the show in the darkened control room, she had even thought about telling him, but then he mysteriously excused himself until the show was over.

No time like the present, she thought, smiling impishly as she rolled over on top of him. "Al," she said nuzzling him and gently biting his ear.

"Ummm," he half growled not realizing that she was lying fully on top of him.

"Al, wake up," she persisted while slowly kissing him all over his face. "We're going to have a baby!"

"He wasn't fully awake, but when he heard 'baby,' his attention focused. "What?"

"I said, we're going to have a baby!"

When he tried to move, he was aware that Donna-Marie had pinned him down with the full weight of her body. She kept nuzzling him and did not allow him to move.

"You're pregnant?" He hardly had sufficient air with which to speak.

"Yes," she smiled as she allowed him to gently roll her over on her back so that he could look deeply into her now laughing and extremely joyful eyes.

"You can't be pregnant!" he said quite dumbfounded.

"Why not?"

"Because . . . I don't know—just because."

Al's look was one of joyful disbelief. He was in a state of semi-shock, and looked at his wife wide-eyed. She, now jubilant that she had been able to share her news with him, simply replied, "Well—I am!"

It took a few moments before he became infected with the joyous feeling his wife conveyed and to absorb the wonder and reality of the moment. Ever so slowly, a grand smile grew upon his face lighting up even his still sleepy and somewhat crusty eyes. She knew finally that he felt his rightful pride in becoming a father-to-be.

She kept kissing him all over until he began to giggle, and she interjected, "Wanna celebrate, daddy?"

Their lovemaking was always good, for they shared a oneness that was honest as well as open. Yet somehow, as they made love today, Al couldn't help recalling the night before and the magnificent vision of Laine Powers August that continued to haunt him even as he caressed his now-pregnant wife.

III

Donna-Marie had to finish some last-minute food shopping so when their love-making was over she dressed quickly and walked down Ninth Avenue to below Forty-First Street into 'Hell's Kitchen,'which was known for the excellence and wide variety of foodstuffs available—all within a few short blocks. Donna-Marie shopped quickly, and enjoyed walking in the crisp air on this sunny Christmas Eve. She sought out six different kinds of seafood as she developed the menu for the traditional Christmas Eve fish feast and had to wait on some long lines as other last-minute shoppers joined in the search for precisely the right items and the freshest as well. She already had the salted bacala soaking at home, so she bought jumbo shrimp, lobster tails, scungilli, octopus, clams, and mussels. It was to be the first time that she would be doing all this alone, and she wanted it to be extra special. When she returned home, she found that Al had already vacuumed the entire house, and had begun to wash the stemware all the while singing out loud for the neighbors to hear. They spent the entire day cutting up fish for salad, cleaning shrimp, and cooking bacala. The house smelled—actually, it stank, but this was to be expected. Several bottles of Airwick would take care of it easily.

Dinner was going well as both families relaxed and allowed the holiday mood to embrace them. Donna-Marie's cooking was praised by everyone, but it was not until Al's mother nodded her head and said, "You make-a good-a meal, Donna-Marie," that Donna-Marie finally relaxed, satisfied that she had passed her first real test as a housewife and cook. "Now," she thought, "Al and I must tell them I'm pregnant." But before she could, Rafaela looked across the table at her and said, loudly enough for all to hear, "Donna-Marie, is there something going on that I should know about?" She had early on noticed how her daughter clung coyly to her husband as if sharing some special secret.

Donna-Marie flushed and squeezed Al's hand in a vise-like crush. "Well," she stammered looking toward Al and smiling school-girlishly, "We're going to have a baby . . . in July."

Everyone rose immediately, and hugs and kisses were shared joyously, since this was—in fact—a family event. Everyone congratulated everyone else and the men all patted Al on the back as though he alone were responsible for Donna-Marie's pregnancy. After everyone settled down to continue the meal, Al's brother, Manny, clinked his wine glass with a butter knife and stood as all eyes focused on him. He reached down and grasped his wife's trembling hand momentarily.

IV

"You all know," he began somewhat abashed, "that Cathy . . . and I . . . haven't been able . . . to have any children . . . yet. And so—I speak for both of us—I want to tell you all just how happy I am, I mean how happy we are—for Donna-Marie being pregnant—and also for what we have here tonight: a real family—something that Pop would've been proud of if he was alive."

"We share a special gift that many people only read about—dream about. You know what I'm saying—we've got a loving family that comes together and shares not only the spirit of the season, but the warmth of each other. I'm so proud of Al and what he has achieved." Then, holding his hand to the side of his mouth, he whispered aloud for all to hear and said, only half-jokingly, "We sometimes wondered whether he would be wearing a pair of cement overshoes one day. No-one laughed. The immediate silence spoke to the truth of Manny's words.

Somehow, with his voice quaking, Manny continued. "I'm not good at this, but I just want to say a few things. You know, it's kinda corny to speak about love and stuff, but if we don't have love in our lives, most of what we talk about is garbage; it don't mean nothin'. Even if a guy makes a pile of money, if he don't have a family that loves him, he's never gonna be really happy. Remember what Pop used to always say? 'Some of the most important things in life—we can't even see or touch them—like love and trust and respect.' These things are real important. Sure, we all make sacrifices, but the pain and worry we go through mean nothing unless we do it because we love our family."

"Some of us kill ourselves at jobs we hate just to make ends meet, but without Cathy—I know I couldn't keep going; it wouldn't be worth it. I'm so lucky we have each other." He paused and motioned his hand slowly toward each one at the table, pausing purposely at each of the children. "We have to try—and I mean me too—to be more patient when one of us screws up; we should try to be a bit more gentle in our dealings with each other because we are family. Ya know—some of the silly fights we have? They gotta stop. Right? And we can't keep holding grudges either."

"I don't know if I'm saying this right, but I want you all to understand what I mean: I love each of you, and I want to tell you how sorry I am for all the times I haven't done the right thing." He was visibly crying and his words were slurring. "Please help me to remember that—because we are a family; we gotta forgive one another instead of being mad and then feeling funny when we get together." He paused and composed himself. "I feel like I'm in confession now, but I am so happy for Al and Donna-Marie; I'm gonna be an Uncle!! In this room, we have what most people only dream about: a loving family—a real, loving, caring family that is always there to help us out. Believe me, nobody can be depended upon like the family when the chips are down. I know . . . friends are great, and they're important in our lives, but when it really matters, blood is always thicker than water."

V

(Then—in the barest instant of time—Manny's thoughts returned to the early days of his youth when he and Al played together, frolicking carefree in their Brooklyn apartment and on the sidewalks of the neighborhood. They were friends then, good buddies, and no one could or would ever come between them. Manny wondered what had caused the relationship to deteriorate over the years to the point where, even today as grown men, they felt the slightest bit uncomfortable in each other's presence. He thought then of their teenage years when they learned how to tease one another even though the teasing itself had become an annoyance to their parents who failed at lessening it. Shouting had grown to become commonplace whenever the brothers were together for more than a few moments. He remembered how as young men the sassing and bickering had degenerated into outright insults as they strained to cast the most crude and demeaning brickbats at each other.

Sibling rivalry it is called today, but to Manny and to Al it was one of the most painful periods in their lives.)

(He recalled the numerous holidays when the family came together to renew itself by sharing sumptuous meals and gifts, and how especially painful it was for his mother, who was often found hiding her tears from the others, and his father, who felt shame because he had failed to convey the vital importance of each family member's dignity to the well being of all. Indeed, it was the lack of respect that Manny and Al showed for themselves that cast a pall over every group encounter for so many years. It was the memory of all this and the desire to strike off in a new and better direction that prompted Manny's boldness this day. He prayed that today could be the milestone that his parents had longed for where mutual respect and admiration for one another— at least within the family—could become the reality sought for and desired by everyone.)

Manny looked over to Al and spoke slowly with a deliberately soft voice, "Al, a man is no good unless he places his family first. Now that Donna-Marie is pregnant, you must reevaluate your life once again; you're gonna have your own family to take care of. Keep your eyes open and don't be fooled by what's out there, Al. Family first, and then everything else works out. In the old days, it was easier since everyone lived close, and we could walk a few blocks and visit. Today—oh, it's so hard now to stay close. And I guess I'm a little saddened to see so many families moving away from their roots. Anyway, I have only one more thing to say: whether you're a man or a woman—you're NOTHING unless you put your family first. Enough now!" Manny lifted his wine glass high in front of him, sighed deeply, and repeated the familiar Italian toast, "Alla famiglia! To the family!"

Everyone lifted their glasses—even the children with their water glasses filled with cream soda and a splash of red wine—and joined in with one voice, "Alla famiglia!"

When Manny had begun to speak, Al initially felt resentment toward him. Who was Manny to speak out like this in Al's house? But Manny's words struck deeply into Al's heart, and he avowed what his life could have been, compared with now. His mind raced, believing in the truth of Manny's hard-fought speech, yet he ached with guilt. In the midst of this family celebration, he could not rein in the clandestine feelings he had for Laine; though his eyes moistened, everyone mistook the cause. "These are only feelings," he thought, "they will pass. "

Donna-Marie's glow was infectious, and the guests all shared in the jubilation of the moment. She held tightly to Al's arm and noticed that his eyes had filled up with tears. She also assumed that he was caught up in the emotion wrought by Manny's words. Manny bravely proclaimed what many Italian men felt but were too macho to verbalize. She wondered whether Al felt as strongly. She glanced once again at her husband not certain why the tears flowed; it was not the last time that she would see him cry.

VI

The holiday season passed like a blur, and the entire city seemed to wind down simultaneously with the fading December days. Donna-Marie and Al stayed home for New Year's Eve, watching the Times Square mob on their television set. They spent New Year's Day with Donna-Marie's parents in the old neighborhood in Brooklyn. Strangely, it now seemed run down to them, though they had been gone only a few short months.

January 4, 1954 was a cold and snowy day in New York City, and Al Zito did not want to move from under the heavy comforter when the telephone rang at 7:30 A.M. It rang three times before Donna-Marie's urgings got Al to reach out and bring the receiver to his ear, which was submerged under the heavy bed clothes.

"Hello." He was barely audible, but the caller knew Al's voice though it was heavily muffled by the comforter.

"You have a meeting in Joe Weintrauben's office at eleven," came the crisp response. "Can you make it?"

As Al's mind cleared, he remembered what Weintrauben said to him several weeks before. He sat upright in bed, now fully alert, with Donna-Marie gazing over at him from under the covers.

"Yes, yes . . . I'll be there. 11 A.M. Goodbye." He hung up and immediately went into the shower.

He arrived at the studio at 10:30 A.M. and ordered a cup of black coffee in the commissary. It was very hot, and Al almost burned his mouth as he gulped it down trying to settle himself before meeting with Weintrauben. Just before eleven, he walked toward Joe Weintrauben's office. The secretary motioned for him to go directly in.

"Good morning, Al."

Al froze in his steps as he focused on the person before him. He felt the pulse in his neck quicken, and he wondered if it were possible for someone to hear the thumping in his chest. He cleared his throat, and spoke. "Good morning, Laine." He then closed the door slowly behind him.

LAINE

I

Joe Weintrauben asked Laine to familiarize Al with the inner sanctum of television broadcasting. Her goal was to ensure that his future involved becoming a network producer of 'special programs' similar to the recent Christmas music special. Toward that end, Laine's priority was to answer his questions, explain the intricacies of being a producer at the network, and, in general, offer oversight into the mysterious world of television broadcasting. Weintrauben stressed the importance of securing his approval of the lucrative personal service contract they were preparing to offer him. For the next few weeks, Laine's responsibility was to win him over.

The relationship began innocently—at least on the surface—but Al sensed his involvement with Laine moving beyond a professional business relationship. He repeatedly warned himself not to become involved with her, but he was smitten. Compared with Laine, he viewed Donna-Marie as an innocent school girl in pigtails and jeans. Laine's style and freedom in what she said and how she reacted in front of people coupled with her self affirmation made her all the more desirable to him. For several weeks he had been struggling with his hidden passion for her, fending off the desire to take the relationship to another level. During their daily business lunches, he couldn't keep his eyes off her, often admiring her hair and the way it was fixed or the way she now used makeup. Mysteriously, Laine's appearance had become more striking than ever, and Al was drawn in by each nuance of her endless self iterations. He focused on her use of eye shadow and eyeliner, cosmetics that Donna-Marie used only on rare occasions when she was going to a wedding or a special dance. He never realized how much of a turn-on eye makeup could be until he had studied Laine's face. Her makeup, applied discretely and flawlessly, enhanced her overall beauty and heightened the mystery and sensuality of her eyes.

She was acutely aware that his fascination with her breasts and generously exposed cleavage diverted his attention from documents she had prepared for his perusal. She laughed at how easy it was to predict—- and manipulate—- some men's reactions.

When he felt himself becoming vulnerable in her presence, he would scoff at himself by pretending that Laine was in total control of herself and the present situation. He often wondered, though, whether he was wrong about her having a slight interest in him. Perhaps he was merely courting a boyish fantasy, and Laine was actually the dedicated network executive intent on doing only her job. Somehow, he was unable to resolve these thoughts, and wondered whether she might really be a tease, intent on seeing just how far she could push him. Regardless of these mixed emotions, he tried desperately to focus on the tasks at hand, but found himself, nevertheless, envisioning himself in a relationship with her. Throughout all of this, Al's deep feelings for Donna-Marie and his unborn child hardly lessened the blatant passion he felt while in Laine's company. He was two distinctly separate men in this regard.

Laine had spent many days with Al trying to ease his mind about signing a contract with the network. He feared that being locked into an agreement would negate other business opportunities that might come along. Laine assured him that Weingarten could structure the contract to allay any misgivings he might have. Al waited.

When she thought the timing was right, Laine arranged a meeting at her apartment where Al could discuss specifics about the contract with Joe Weintrauben and other key network executives. She felt it best to arrange a social setting wherein she could present him with the contract and he could ask the right people his 'hard' questions. Laine provided drinks and light snacks; the evening was generally relaxed but in an elegant style. Al was impressed with how well he was being treated. "They must think highly of me," he thought.

As the evening evolved, Weintrauben and Laine presented some of the broad details of the contract, which stimulated further discussion. Later, Weintrauben conferred with Al over his plans for an upcoming special that they wanted Al to produce. They had brought preliminary storyboards that they hoped would persuade him to produce the show, while hoping that he would also sign the contract. Al's genuine excitement signaled that Laine and Weintrauben had done their work well, and they were ecstatic when he agreed to produce the show; he would review the contract over the weekend and discuss the details with his wife.

Al's response was what they had hoped for, so Weintrauben signaled for everyone to say their good-byes, lest Al feel continued pressure; he really liked Al. As Laine helped everyone find their coats, she eased Al's to the bottom of the pile on her bed.

When it was just Laine and Al, she casually asked, "Would you mind staying a while longer to help me clean up a bit? I'm kind of worn out."

"No . . . not at all." Al's response was mildly tentative, but he quickly acknowledged that up to this point, it had been only he who had the sexual fantasy. If anything, he rationalized, Laine may have been a tease, but hardly anything more. And—since he had already expressed a desire to produce the show and was probably going to sign the contract anyway—he began to laugh at himself discounting any planned seduction on Laine's part.

As they began to place the dishes and glasses into the dishwasher, he heard her exclaim, "Clumsy!"

"What's wrong?" he asked, turning toward her.

"Oh—I just splashed some wine onto my suit. Would you mind while I change out of this outfit and try to clean it? If I don't, It'll ruin for sure."

"No problem. Go right ahead." Al continued gathering ashtrays and adjusting chair cushions, assuming that Laine would return in jeans and a cotton western shirt, the kind of outfit she favored when dressing down or doing housework.

Momentarily, she padded silently across the carpet, her freshly applied perfume wafting invisibly before her. He turned and stared, watching as she flowed across the room, her silken robe a tease, hardly concealing her milky, alabaster flesh. Watching her move ever closer, there was no decision for him to make—Laine had made it, and somehow . . . he was relieved. She loosened the sash that cinched her robe and let it fall carelessly to the floor. Al's mind slammed shut allowing primitive instincts to drive him; carefully, he lifted her, joining her lips in passionate kisses as he ushered her into the bedroom. He never noticed that she kicked off her jeweled, high-heeled slippers.

II

What followed was neither pretty nor romantic; rightly defined, it was unbounded, animal lust. Hours of unbridled passion continued unabated. Al, unprepared for Laine's animal energy, was nevertheless consumed by her prowess, which enraptured him totally. It was her aggressiveness that struck him most, and how it heightened his own delight. He was the pawn in her chess game, in which she challenged him continuously, urging him onward. He was a mere babe in her learned, capable hands.

Al acknowledged that Laine was in a different league from him . . . she was well studied in her approach—sometimes aggressive seeking to tantalize—then submissive allowing him to explore and learn. He discerned no limits to what Laine could do—or would do . . . and he didn't care; she had transported him to heretofore unknown heights of pleasure. Her experience was vast leaving her knowledgeable and proficient. Later, he was so physically spent and completely taken by Laine that if she had not mentioned Donna-Marie's name, he probably would have remained there all night, oblivious of his wife or home.

"Donna-Marie will be worried sick waiting for you. You should be leaving now," she whispered to him as they lay naked, exhausted from the unbroken hours of lovemaking. But, to Laine, this was not lovemaking—not at all. She had never deluded herself into believing that what they shared was love. Indeed, every moment they shared was anything but love. Her desire was to possess him and the strength he brought to her. She wanted from him what few men could give, and Al's endurance as a partner was stimulating. She reveled in delight that his hunger matched hers precisely and, for the first time in her adult life—she felt sated.

"Donna-Marie? Good grief," he cried out loud. "I forgot about her completely. She'll be worried sick! What time is it anyway?"

Laine glanced over at the clock radio and said, "Two-thirty A.M."

She then rose from the bed, picking up her silken robe from the floor where it lay, and, dragging it behind her, strode into the bathroom.

The interjection of Donna-Marie's name into this hedonistic drama seemed incongruous to Al, and he broke out in a cold sweat. He was confused—more confused than ever before—he was unable to reconcile what he felt for Laine with what he owed Donna-Marie. Owed?

"What's come over me?" he thought as he paced the luxurious bedroom. "I love Donna-Marie. She's my wife. She's pregnant with MY child—our child. But . . . but . . . Laine . . . is . . . fantastic! I never knew how fabulous . . . . Sure . . . what Donna-Marie and I share is good . . . , but . . . ."

III

Al returned to the moment when Laine re-entered the bedroom, her hair brushed a bit, and her robe loosely wrapped though barely shielding her voluptuousness. When he saw her again, thoughts of Donna-Marie vaporized. He walked slowly toward her, cupping her face in his hands as she backed up feigning a retreat from his advance. As she reached the wall, he held himself hard against her, and kissed her lightly all over her face until his passion filled him once again.

"No more, Al," she protested softly.

"Why not?" He kept kissing her face and neck, hoping to arouse her too.

"Well, for one reason, I've got to go to work tomorrow morning—in just a few hours, that is. I do have an important job, you know."

She was speaking semiseriously, though never moving an inch from him or offering the slightest refusal to his physical advance. It did seem, though, that her respiration had increased significantly and her breasts had firmed as she breathed deeper and more fully, responding in kind to his renewed arousal.

"Once more for the road?" he smiled.

She looked at him, incredulous, and said, "What the hell—why not?"

IV

During the next few months, Al grew increasingly creative in formulating excuses for his frequent late-night meetings with 'network executives.' Donna-Marie—being Donna-Marie—trusted him implicitly, though she was somewhat concerned with his diminished need for the pleasures of their marriage bed. She rationalized that he was probably being careful with her since the pregnancy was not going as well as it should, and he was afraid of hurting her or the baby. She was content to know that he was happy with the contract he signed and that he was successful at what he had done for the network thus far. And, since he called her twice a day, she had no reason to be suspicious. She therefore devoted herself to knitting baby things and preparing the nursery.

But Al was becoming involved with Laine in a way that he tried doggedly to refute: he had fallen in love with her. They were good together—just like it was with Donna-Marie—only with Laine, things were . . . different. She would come on to him as often as he to her. Donna-Marie had never done that in all the years he knew her; indeed, she would never do that. Oh, he thought, she might hint at having a need, but she would never actually solicit him or express any genuine passion for sex. Once Al initiated a move, however, she became a different person, anxious for whatever Al had in store for them—within reason, of course.

Laine on the other hand, was an explosive, dynamic person, exciting both as a sex partner and as a business woman. "Is it possible to love two women?" he wondered, ignorant of the countless problems implicit in continuing such a relationship. One nagging question tormented him: "How long can I survive in this dual existence before I am found out or required by Laine to become more open about what we are sharing?" In spite of endless self recriminations, he never missed an opportunity to spend an evening in Laine's bed.

DONNA-MARIE

I

Winter faded quickly, and the spring of 1954 brought with it the continuing evolution of Donna-Marie's pregnancy. By the end of May she had already gained thirty-five pounds, not unusual according to her obstetrician. But she had been experiencing constant back pains for several weeks, and nothing she did seemed to help. Her mother scoffed and pronounced that pains at this time in her pregnancy were normal. Al's mother told her that when she was pregnant with Al, her pains were even worse than when she was pregnant with Manny, so, "Don't worry." But Donna-Marie did worry. She was afraid.

She recalled girlfriends who had babies and never felt as poorly during their own pregnancies. It wasn't merely the pain in her back that worried Donna-Marie as much as the fact that she did not feel well overall. She had experienced pain in one place or another at various times during this pregnancy, but she had never felt as poorly before. And, yet, no one seemed to share her concern. With Al out of the house so often and keeping very late hours, she felt obliged to keep her worries to herself rather than to place him under any undue stress—he had enough to worry about with his new job. "Right?"

One afternoon very late in Donna-Marie's pregnancy, the pains became so severe that she called Manny's wife, Cathy. When Cathy answered the phone, there was no immediate response. "Hello, hello; is anyone there?" She repeated it several times, shouting into the mouthpiece louder each time. And then she thought she heard a whisper at the other end. She shouted anew, "Hello! Who is this?"

Mustering every last bit of strength she had within her, Donna-Marie managed a weak response saying, "Cathy, it's Donna-Marie! Help me!"

Cathy could barely make out the words except for help me and Donna-Marie.

"Donna-Marie, what's wrong? Are you all right?" Cathy panicked. "Answer me!" she screamed into the receiver, but there was silence at the other end.

The police arrived at about 1:30 P.M. and had to break in the front door when there was no response to their banging. Donna-Marie was lying on the floor in the living room, the telephone receiver next to her. A few moments later, Cathy arrived in a cab and raced up the front steps screaming out Donna-Marie's name.

"We found her lying here, ma'am," one policeman said.

"I'm her sister-in-law. Did you call an ambulance yet?" she demanded.

"Yes, we phoned it in on the police radio. I hear the siren now."

"I'll call her doctor; tell the ambulance driver to take her to New York Hospital for Women on First Avenue and ninety-Second Street."

"Yes, Ma'am."

Everything happened with blinding speed after that. Cathy called both mothers and Manny, and by 3:30 P.M. all had gathered outside of Cathy's hospital room awaiting the diagnosis of the doctor. Manny had tried unsuccessfully to locate Al who had gone to a staff meeting somewhere downtown according to the person who picked up the phone in Al's office at 4:15 P.M. No one seemed to know exactly where he was, though Manny worked his way through every key executive at the network via the switchboard operator.

Just before five o'clock, Manny remembered the name Joe Weintrauben.

"Try his office," he told the harried operator.

"Yes, sir," came the frustrated response.

"Hello, Weintrauben here," came the response when Joe Weintrauben picked up his own phone.

"Mr. Weintrauben? This is Manny Zito, Al's brother. I've been trying to locate him for almost an hour. He's supposed to be at a meeting somewhere, but no one seems to know exactly where."

Weintrauben hesitated a moment before responding. "Well what exactly is the problem?"

"His wife is in trouble; she's pregnant, and we're all here with her at the hospital; the doctors don't know what's wrong; I gotta get a-hold of Al."

Weintrauben, sensing the gravity of the situation from Manny's voice, responded immediately, "Try Ulster 7-7102; you should be able to track him down from there." Weintrauben already knew what many at the network had merely suspected.

"Thanks, Mr. Weintrauben!"

II

The phone in Laine's apartment had rung seven or eight times before she slid open the door to her brand-new, ultra-modern stall shower and hastily wrapped a bath towel around her lower body. Leaving a trail of wet footsteps behind on her plush carpet, she darted for the phone. Still dripping, she picked up the receiver while tossing her hair and set it against her ear; in a somewhat breathless voice she muttered, "Hello, Laine August speaking."

"Miss August, this is Manny Zito. Is Al there?"

111

An icy chill ran through her damp and now chilled body as she sensed the apprehension in his voice. Laine excused herself and returned to the shower where Al was smiling up at the shower head as it poured down streams of steaming water on his face. As he waited anxiously for Laine's return, he promised himself that he would get one of these stall showers for his own home—they were great and a lot safer than climbing in and out of a slippery bathtub. Fleetingly, his thoughts turned to Donna-Marie and how he watched her struggle getting in and out of the tub during these late months of her pregnancy.

"Who was it?" he asked tugging at Laine's towel when she returned to the steamy bathroom.

Laine's face had taken on a seriousness that Al hadn't seen before. "It's your brother, Manny."

"Manny? How did he know I was here?" Suddenly, his mood changed and he became enraged. "What's he want anyway?" he screamed as he raced to the phone naked, never stopping to grab a towel. He shouted into the phone all the while dripping water onto Laine's expensive carpeting, "What the hell's going on? I'm at a meeting. Couldn't you leave a message with . . . ." Somehow, even though he was shouting, he managed to hear Manny shouting back at him and words like 'sick' and 'hospital.'

"What are you talking about? Who's in the hospital."

"Al," he implored, "shut up and listen to me. It's Donna-Marie; she's really sick. Something's wrong!" He tried not to transmit the total gravity of the situation until he could speak to Al at the hospital. "She's in New York Hospital for Women—on First Avenue at Ninety-Second Street."

"What is it?" Al interrupted. "Is it the baby? Tell me!" he demanded.

"Al, we don't know; there are three doctors with her now. We just don't know yet. Please hurry—Room 902."

"I know where it is, I'll take a cab and be there as fast as I can."

As he hung up he turned to find Laine standing at his side. She was solicitous as she asked, "It's Donna-Marie isn't it?"

Al nodded as he reached for the towel she offered. Suddenly aware of his nakedness, he excused himself and went into the bedroom, closing the door behind him. When he came out fully dressed a few moments later, he found Laine standing exactly where he had left her; her eyes were wet.

"Laine . . . " he stammered walking toward her, "I . . . I."

"I understand, Al. Go. Hurry now. Your place is with her."

As she spoke, he looked deeply into her eyes, but could say nothing; he put his head down, turned away and raced out of her apartment.

It was almost 6:20 P.M. when the cab carrying Al squealed to a halt in front of the hospital. Al had given the driver a fifty dollar bill as an incentive to ignore all red lights and stop signs. Still, with all the cross-town traffic, it took an unbearable amount of time to get there from Laine's apartment.

III

He took the steps to the entrance of the hospital two at a time, quickly scanned the lobby for the elevators, and punched the service buttons of all the elevators as he paced waiting for one to open its doors. When the doors opened at the ninth floor, he scanned the hallway and saw Manny and the others at the end of the long corridor gathered outside Donna-Marie's room. Both mothers were crying as Cathy tried unsuccessfully to console them.

"How is she Manny?" Al asked frantic with concern.

"The obstetrician called in a surgeon to consult. They both just left a few minutes ago; they're going to run some tests tonight."

"I'm going in."

He eased the door open and in the darkened room saw his wife's face contorted in pain. The low moans that came from her mouth broke him down immediately, and he began to cry. At the sight of him she gathered all her energy and spoke his name in what was hardly more than a whisper, "Al." She moved her arm, reaching out to him, but it barely came off the bed. He knelt beside the bed, tears streaming down his face. "Al . . . " Her voice was fainter now.

"Don't speak, honey; just rest." But she did struggle to speak as though these were to be her last words. "Al . . . Al . . . make sure that nothing . . ." She was gasping for breath now as Al buried his face against her. " . . . make sure that nothing happens to the baby. If I die . . . it's OK. Just make sure they don't do anything to hurt the baby . . . our baby. I . . . love . . . you . . . so . . . much."

Her breathing was labored and shallow, but Al couldn't hear her breathing: he was sobbing uncontrollably calling her name: Donna-Marie—Donna-Marie.

The next five days were no different, for Donna-Marie's condition remained unchanged. Neither the obstetrician nor the surgeon had come up with anything positive from the tests they had given her. The painkillers had little effect; she continued to suffer excruciating pains. The dared not administer large doses or more powerful medication since they feared damage to the fetus.

They finally told Al that they would need his permission to do an exploratory operation in a day or two if her condition didn't improve. They couldn't risk waiting any longer since her strength was leaving her so rapidly. Her obstetrician told Al that if they didn't reverse her condition quickly, she could possibly go into a coma. Both doctors agreed that they could not wait much longer. Al had discussed the possibility of the operation with Donna-Marie and she had screamed, "No! I will not have them hurt our baby!" Al cried his eyes out every time he thought of how courageous she was and how much she was willing to endure to give their child a chance to live. He tried to reason with her that if something weren't done to improve her condition, it would be just as dangerous for the baby. But nothing could sway her; she would not jeopardize her baby's life by having them open her up.

She repeated the words to him over and over, "It's ours, Al; it's our love that gives life to this baby. It doesn't matter if I die." The pains continued.

Now in its seventh month, the fetus presented a major obstacle to the medical team observing Donna-Marie's condition. Procedures that would have been considered normal were too dangerous to attempt on a woman that was seven months pregnant. Ultimately, the medical team decided to ask a urologist to join them in their search for the source of Donna-Marie's pain. Since their own blood tests showed no evidence of appendicitis, it was possible, they thought, that Donna-Marie was suffering from some type of renal failure. After examining Donna-Marie, the urologist said that his suspicions led him to believe that the kidneys were the primary source of the pain—there was general sensitivity when he probed there and, if he had to guess, he would suspect that Donna-Marie was suffering from a kidney stone. But since he had no prior experience with a late-term pregnancy, it was impossible to make a precise diagnosis. Even though he believed himself to have made a valid diagnosis, the many blood tests he had ordered had all came back negative and failed to confirm his suspicions.

The urologist then recommended that a set of X-rays be taken of Donna-Marie's kidneys. The IVP was a common procedure performed by injecting a dye into a vein and then shooting a detailed set of X-rays. Urologists used this procedure to examine the kidneys and check for the presence of stones. Potential side effects of this test included convulsions and high blood pressure from the chemical cocktail used; lesser issues included severe vomiting and stomach cramps. The obstetrician balked at the idea of the test even though he agreed that the procedure could be useful in other persons. He knew that severe vomiting could possibly bring on early labor, but he was more concerned about radiation poisoning from the extensive use of X-rays which could be extremely hazardous for the fetus. The three doctors then held a conference to review the options open to them. They finally concurred that the least risky option was an exploratory operation. They would then be able to rule out several major concerns such as ruptured appendix, gall bladder, twisted bowel, etc. Yes, an exploratory operation was essential if Donna-Marie's life and the life of her unborn child were to be saved.

After the other doctors left, the obstetrician called Al aside and gave him the options in the order that he recommended: perform an exploratory operation to try and discover what was wrong inside; do the IVP, but risk exposing the fetus to an excessive amount of x-rays or cause the early onset of labor; do nothing and see what happened.

IV

Al was not a religious man; far from it. When he agreed to work for Sevvi, he knew full well that he was helping to promote an underworld empire of crime that was responsible for murders, extortion, prostitution, and terror all over New York City. He fooled himself into believing that since he was 'only an accountant' he wasn't really guilty of any crimes. He fooled himself then, but he wasn't fooling himself now. In his heart of hearts, he believed that God was punishing Donna-Marie and him for his affair with Laine Powers August. It was his fault that she was suffering so intensely. It was up to him to give the obstetrician an answer, but he did not know what to decide. He reasoned that if God were punishing them, then maybe God could provide the right guidance he sought if he could plead his case directly: he would go to church.

It was about 9 P.M. when he headed south on First Avenue scanning the tops of buildings along the side streets. A few blocks into his walk, he spied the object of his search: high above the flat roofs and naked brick chimneys of the surrounding tenements and shops, a spire topped by a shimmering golden cross soared upward into the sky. It was one of many community churches open all night for the benefit of the area's many swing-shift printers working locally.

Located on Sixty-Third Street about a hundred feet west of First Avenue, this church was built early in the twentieth century by local artisans. The entryway was narrow consistent with the style for neighborhood churches. Statues of Saints and holy pictures welcomed visitors to the Church of Our Lady of Sorrows. An appropriate name, considering. Al pushed at the heavy, carved entry door; he could smell the presence of ancient incense hanging heavy in the air. Slowly, he walked down the well-worn mosaic center aisle toward the altar rail guarding the white-marble altar beneath a huge crucifix. Even though it had been a very long time, Al did not feel all that uncomfortable inside this holy place. The church was quietly empty except for two elderly women kneeling side by side in the first row before the life-size statue of Our Lady of Sorrows, murmuring to themselves as they gingerly fingered their rosary beads. Later tonight, a midnight mass would be celebrated for about one hundred shift workers who attended regularly. Suddenly wary of being here amid holy objects and dedicated believers, he paused as a young priest entered the church from a side door and sat in one of the front pews at the far right.

Al, filled with an overwhelming sense of hypocrisy, felt compelled to kneel at the altar rail, though consciously averting his eyes from the huge corpus hanging in front of him. Eventually, he bowed his head and closed his eyes, locking his fingers; he remained so for about five minutes in silence. Tears came freely to him and he did his best to daub them with a clean pocket handkerchief.

When he looked up eventually, he noticed a metal cart to the left of the altar which was filled with flickering candles in red glass holders. He walked slowly over to the cart, found an unlit candle, lit it with a taper, and placed a five dollar bill in the slot provided for donations. Most visitors put in nickels and dimes when they lit candles, and Al hated himself for thinking that five dollars would buy him a better response than the nickels and dimes from everyone else. He knelt down again and put his head on his hands and almost immediately began to sob uncontrollably just as he had in Donna-Marie's hospital room.

"Oh God," he prayed (it was a prayer), "please don't let Donna-Marie suffer any more; don't let her die. She's such a beautiful person, always giving and serving others. I'm the one who should be punished." He lifted his head and felt his eyes being drawn to the crucifix and the image of Jesus; he reflected on the suffering that Jesus endured . . . for us? For him? He hoped. He felt hope. He was transfixed on that image. "You know what pain is," he sobbed. He had begun a dialogue with his savior. He continued, "Please don't let her suffer any more! I'm the selfish one, not her. I'll change; I promise; I promise." His voice trailed off. "Please . . . please . . . "

He cried freely for several more minutes before he felt a presence—something was happening to him; he felt a warmth in his body, a sensation coursing through every blood vessel within him; a tingling all over. He felt suddenly peaceful—and then—a gentle touch on his arm.

"May I be of some help? I'm Father Michael."

Al turned to see the young priest he had noticed before. Standing up, he said, "I'm sorry, Father," displaying the merest hint of a smile. "You know, Father, It's really funny calling someone younger than me, Father."

"It happens all the time; I'm used to it. Would you like to talk?"

Al got up and walked outside, escorted by the young priest; he explained about Donna-Marie's condition. "She's in so much pain, Father," he began.

"Call me Michael; it's OK, really."

. . . "Al, Al Zito. You know, Michael." He hesitated after calling this priest by his first name. "You know," he began again "it's really all my fault."

"Why?"

"Why?" How could Al explain?

"Why is it your fault, Al?" Father Michael was gentle as he asked, yet persistent and genuinely concerned enough to deserve an honest answer.

"God is punishing us for what I did," he offered, shrugging his shoulders and waving his arms in space.

"God doesn't punish us, Al. He loves us." Father Michael knew this was not the time to preach. He continued, "We don't really know why bad things happen, Al. All we know is that Jesus went to the cross for each of us as the supreme act of His love."

"I believe that now, Michael, but all this is still my fault."

"How could that be?" Father Michael sensed that he was losing ground, and silently prayed that he would be divinely inspired to come up with the right words for Al to hear.

Al thought about telling him, but quickly set it aside. "I just know it is."

"You know, if there's something that's troubling you, maybe it would be better to get it out in the open."

"I just can't discuss it; I haven't been a good husband."

"We all sin, Al."

"Not like me, Father; Not like me!" Al began to cry again.

"Would you like some coffee? Why don't we go around the corner and grab a cup?" He already had his arm around Al's shoulder.

"Sure, why not."

They walked over to Second Avenue and found an open coffee shop. Climbing into a booth, Father Michael pursued his query. "You want to tell me about it?"

Al nodded, "I can't."

"Could you tell a priest in Confession?"

"Probably, if I ever got into the Confessional. I haven't gone for years."

"Why don't we just pretend we're in church and you're in the little box hiding your face behind a screen. I am a priest, remember? My lips are sealed—forever."

Al seemed to readily absorb the gentle spirit of peace emanating from Michael; he then spent the next hour in 'confession.' Surrounded by a half-dozen other patrons sipping coffee and munching donuts, Al related to Father Michael details of his secret life with Sevvy and then his affair with Laine. Nothing Al said seemed to faze this young priest.

"Is that all, Al?"

"Isn't that enough?" Al managed to smile but was impressed with the maturity of this young man / priest.

"Now listen. I'm going to give you absolution . . . "

"Here?" Al was incredulous.

The priest smiled, "Yes! Here; it's a sacrament—it brings grace. Bow your head and try to look inconspicuous."

The priest joked but then became serious very quickly. Al remembered the words: the almost forgotten phrases that he first heard in Saint Teresa's Church so many years ago . . . "Ego te absolvo. In nomine patrie, et filii, et spiritui sancti. Amen."

Al responded from memory, "Amen. So let it be done!"

And so it was done. Al had confessed in a coffee shop and felt . . . better. Somehow, deep inside, he believed—he knew—that Donna-Marie would recover—and soon. He didn't know why he felt so strongly; he just did.

V

Al found a cab at the hack stand across the street from the coffee shop. As he neared, he heard the cabbie strumming a guitar and singing along; Al got in. The cabbie asked, "Where to, Mac?" On their way to the hospital, Al inquired about the song remarking on its lovely melody. The cabbie handed him the sheet music with hand written pencil notes and lyrics. "It's something my friends and I have I have been working on for a while. Trying to get some country singers to hear it." Al told him that he was working in TV, and that maybe he could help out. They shared names and addresses, and Al folded the sheet music and put it in his coat pocket.

He returned to the ninth floor just after 1:00 A.M. only to hear incredibly loud shrieking down the hall where Donna-Marie's room was located. He raced toward her door to find two nurses forcibly restraining his flailing wife; Donna-Marie was screaming and writhing in pain. He felt utterly helpless watching the nurses attempting to control her to prevent her from banging her head or falling off the bed. And then . . . suddenly . . . unexpectedly . . . Donna-Marie was silent, relaxed, limp; her breathing was not labored but came easily; she opened her eyes. Color slowly flushed back into her face, she seemed somehow . . . different, better. Al watched incredulously from the doorway—totally useless not knowing what was happening.

One nurse placed cold compresses on her forehead while the other sought to remove the bed pan; moments before during the struggle she thought she heard an almost imperceptible 'ding.' She examined the bedpan and gasped, holding her hand to her mouth. "Look-ee here!" she burst out. "Look at what we have here!! I don't believe it --. Alleluia!"

The other nurse turned. "What?"

"A kidney stone; one gigantic, son-of-a-gun kidney stone—she passed a kidney stone!"

"Praise the Lord! She's gonna be OK!"

Al stood there dumbfounded glancing back and forth between the nurses and his wife whose sweat-soaked face had what seemed to be the glimmer of a smile forming.

"Al . . . Al," she called to him. "The pain; the pain—it's better—it's over! Oh, God; it's better!"

"Thank God." Al heard himself say it again, "Thank You, God."

Nurses had swarmed into the room when the screaming began, and now were happily changing Donna-Marie's bed linen, combing her hair, and replacing her nightgown. One nurse offered her fresh makeup and lipstick, but she refused . . . she wanted to be alone with her husband. The only thing she wanted was her husband. The others waited outside so they could be alone.

He padded over to her slowly as though walking on eggs. Their eyes locked and he fell to his knees beside her. Even though salty tears covered both faces, they began kissing one another. Momentarily, they paused and looked into each other's eyes and smiled; she felt her body calm as she melted into the familiar comfort of her husband's powerful arms . . . arms that had been absent so often recently. She began to weep anew knowing that her unborn child was safe, and that she could return to her normal life soon. They cuddled silently like newly weds. Moments passed and somewhere off in the distance, somehow, Al heard the faint echo of the words spoken to him by the young priest from the parish of Our lady of Sorrows, "Ego te absolvo . . . I forgive you."

Al had already decided to stay overnight at the hospital with Donna-Marie, so some aides set him up at her bedside with a recliner-type chair. Throughout the long nighttime hours, he watched the rise and fall of her body as she slept. "How beautiful she is; how peaceful—now." His own attempts at sleep were peppered with conflicted thoughts of how he had failed her as a husband and as a man; he wasn't always there for her, and he had no excuse. He knew right from wrong and still made bad choices. He could never undo what had been done, but he resolved to change himself and his approach to life. He had been so blessed all his life; what took him so long to come to this point of decision? What could he do to become a better person . . . a better husband . . . a good father? He tried prayer, but his mind was conflicted; his thoughts always returned to Donna-Marie and how lucky he was to have her as his wife . . . and the soon-to-be-mother of his child.

The priest's words of forgiveness droned on in his head; he would never forget the words Father Michael expressed during his confession. Father Michael exhorted him that even though God forgives us, we must forgive . . . not only others, but ourselves. He knew that Father Michael was right when he counseled, "If you can't get to the point where you can forgive yourself, you will never attain the fullness of your ability to love Donna-Marie, your children, or anyone else." Al would need lots of time before he could ever forgive himself.

Through the long, fitful night, peace came to him sporadically upon recalling the cab driver's haunting melody and soulful words. His hands reached for his coat pocket and the sheet music. He smoothed the crumpled sheet and focussed on the title words. Through tear-filled eyes he read: 'You are always on My Mind; You are always on my mind.' He wept ceaselessly.

CARMINE

I

When Al Zito had asked Carmine Della Rocca to drive the 1948 Packard over to Pete Kelly's, there was just the slightest trace of apprehension that Carmine detected in Al's voice. "What could be so wrong about doing an errand for Al?" Carmine thought. Besides, he wanted to make a good impression—one never knew what good could come from doing a favor for 'Big Al' Zito. It was only later when Carmine heard about the gangland massacre of July 1952 that he felt sick to his stomach and stayed in his apartment for two weeks without speaking to anyone. He had never been so scared in his life before, believing that someone would soon be looking for him—to eliminate any

witnesses or potential stool pigeons. Carmine went to a lot of gangster movies and was half frightened to death of what might happen to him. But nothing did happen, and when Al Zito was drafted in September 1952, Carmine gave up his business of running numbers for the Italian lottery. "A guy could get killed in this business," he was often heard to say or, "I'm too young to die."

And yet, when Carmine tried legitimate work, he found himself choking on the miserable salary that he was earning. When running numbers, he kept every penny he earned plus the tips he inveigled from the winners. When he tried legitimate work, he found his check depleted by federal taxes, state taxes, social security taxes and the various other deductions that honest laborers endure. Carmine, who bought lunch each day rather than bring something from home, found that he was taking home less than fifty percent of the meager salary he grossed at the jobs he tried.

One day while sitting on the steps of the United Tire Valve Company on Atlantic Avenue in downtown Brooklyn eating his lunch among several coworkers, he noticed two young men skulking about the empty lot directly across from where he was sitting.

Talking with his mouth full of an overstuffed meatball sandwich, Carmine queried the man sitting next to him, "What's wit dose guys, Johnny?"

Johnny Wenofski was five years older than Carmine and a well-paid machinist. He enjoyed having lunch with Carmine because he liked to hear the stories that Carmine always managed to tell. Carmine was a marvelous storyteller, and Johnny really didn't care whether the stories were true or not. Carmine's manner was amusing, and the diversion was a welcomed reprieve from the noise of the shop. Johnny, well built and extremely muscular, was lighter skinned than Carmine and had thick, dark-blond hair. Sitting together, one could not help but notice the stark contrast between these two. Carmine, always looking sleazy, adamantly refused to wash his hair more than once a week, instead using a cream-oil to give himself the long out-of-style plastered-down look.

Johnny, crew cut and clean shaven, often admonished Carmine, "How come you don't shave more often?" Carmine's only response was, "Man, them blue blades is rough on my skin; I got baby skin—ya know, real tender; good for the girls when they stroke my face on Saturday night."

Johnny and Carmine both laughed at Carmine's references to romance, which were solely restricted to 'quickies' in the deep shadows of the Flatbush Avenue drive-in or bare bottom on the damp grass in Prospect Park at night. They enjoyed each other's company greatly, though never spending time together other than during work hours: they came from different worlds.

When Carmine queried Johnny about the two men in the empty lot, he noticed that everyone else's eyes were focused on them as well. "Somethin' strange with dem guys," he thought.

"Don't you know what they're doing?" Johnny asked, half disbelieving that Carmine could at the same time be so worldly and yet so naive.

"Nah; what's wit 'em?"

"They've been doing marijuana in the back of the lot."

"Marijuana? Shoot . . . where'd dey get that stuff?"

"Hey, Carmine; where've you been? You can get whatever you want these days."

"Yeah, I bet," he said still incredulous. "You ever try it, Johnny?"

"You crazy or something? I drink scotch; it costs less and it's better for you; stimulates the heart."

For the remainder of that afternoon, Carmine's mind was riveted on the two figures that had used marijuana in the empty lot. He thought about what he had heard in the neighborhood and about how narcotics was becoming a big business with some of the local crime bosses. He made up his mind to discover as much as possible about "dope" as he could, to see if there were a quick buck in it for him. His memory of the brief association with Sevvi Carducci seemed to have faded, as he once again looked for a way to make some easy money.

Toward that end, he watched carefully each day to see whether the two men would return to the lot. Sneaking glances out of a window near his workstation on the eleventh floor, Carmine hadn't seen them when they entered the lot. However, during lunch times, he did notice the same two men emerge once or twice. He had intended to sneak up on them when no one else was around while they were smoking and, maybe, scare them into giving him information. After several weeks of waiting, he spotted the two of them walk into the empty lot at about 11:15 A.M.and hide among the overgrown milkweed and brambles. Carmine raced over to Johnny's lathe and said, "Cover for me; I've got to run out for a few minutes."

He raced down the fire stairs, cautiously avoiding the elevator used by supervisors and foremen during working hours and by workers only to come and go in the morning and evening and at lunchtime. As he approached the two men hidden well among the brush, he could hear them speaking in muffled tones. Slowly he removed the switchblade knife he always carried in his pants pocket and opened it quietly. Pretending to clean his nails with the knife, he practically leaped onto the two men who, upon seeing this figure, coughed loudly almost choking on the smoke they had just inhaled. They started to get up and run, but Carmine blocked their way by casually, yet menacingly, holding up his knife. Just looking at carmine was a scary scene, and with him holding a knife, well . . . They froze in their tracks, one of them stomping out the single cigarette that they had been sharing.

"We ain't doin' nuttin! Whatta you want anyway?" They were scared, but managed to bluff at arrogance.

"Hey guys, be cool. I just wanna talk; like you know what I mean? Huh? Just talk."

They uttered some curses, but Carmine continued the pretense of cleaning his nails with his switchblade. "Let's just sit for a few minutes; OK?" Carmine, only twenty-three, figured that the two men before him couldn't have been more than eighteen or nineteen, though from across the street he had thought they were much older.

They seemed to relax, believing that if he were going to harm them, he would have done so already. "Whatta you wanna know?" the first one said.

Carmine smiled slyly. "Where you get your smokes? I'm interested in gettin' some for myself."

The young men simultaneously breathed a deep sigh of relief. The second one spoke, "Is that all you wanna know? Damn! You scared us half to death. You want reefers, man? Just go down to the depot on Atlantic Avenue and Flatbush Avenue Extension. Some dude deals outside the Long Island Railroad terminal about eight each night. Wears a Brooklyn Dodger baseball cap. Can we go now?"

Carmine just smiled at them, and the closing of his switchblade gave them the assent they sought. Their departure was instantaneous. Almost simultaneously, Carmine heard the noon whistle blow, signaling the beginning of the lunch period. He never saw those two young men again.

II

At a quarter to eight that evening, Carmine stepped off the Flatbush Avenue bus in front of the Long Island Railroad Depot. He went into Bickford's and bought a cup of coffee, adding three teaspoons of sugar but did not stir; he never did. Seating himself at a table near the window, he sipped his coffee and waited for the man with the Brooklyn Dodger baseball cap to arrive. A few minutes before eight, a two-door 1949 Ford pulled up to the curb and a man in his mid-thirties stepped out and onto the sidewalk.

The car sped away. The man, good looking, about five-feet six inches tall with an average build, wore a pair of war-surplus combat boots under a pair of Levi's blue-denim jeans; the pants legs were folded up in the style of the day. Settling himself in a nearby doorway, he removed a baseball cap from his back pocket and pulled it onto his head.

Carmine's heart raced. He swallowed hard and walked out onto the sidewalk, easing himself slowly toward the figure in the doorway, his mind retracing his former days running numbers, wondering if now were the time he would break out of the rat race and become somebody important—and not be just another face in the crowded Brooklyn streets—someone better, someone able to move up to Eastern Parkway and have a dog and a wife with a maid to clean up. Maybe now was the time . . . maybe . . . maybe. He hoped.

Carmine continued his 'stealthy' approach to the figure in the Brooklyn Dodger baseball cap, convincing himself that the man was totally nonthreatening—he's a guy, just an ordinary guy. Standing two feet away, he found it at first difficult to speak, though the man's eyes were locked onto his own. " . . . Excuse me . . . ah, I was told . . . ." The man turned and headed away. Carmine, sensing a missed opportunity and ignoring every human instinct to remain calm, jogged after him, blurting out, "Hey, man; you da guy dat's got the reefers cigarettes?" He repeated himself more loudly as the man in the hat tried to elude this loudmouth goon.

The Long Island Rail Road depot area was already teeming with people, and normally would have been a perfect cover for any clandestine activities that Brooklyn natives chose to pursue. Not today! Carmine's ridiculous outburst not only brought attention to himself but forced the man off the street, into the station and down the nearest stairway trying to escape Carmine and any cop stationed nearby. Comical as it already was, Carmine speeded up his pursuit of what he had figured would be his ticket 'up the ladder.' Once inside the huge, poorly lit rotunda of the dingy station, he spied the man racing down the steep flight of stairs and onto the narrow, almost completely dark platform. Commuters were everywhere; Carmine was oblivious to their presence. He just pushed and twisted his way deeper into the crowd along the lengthy platform and began whispering—rather loudly—into the blackness of the station, "Hey man, where are you? Huh? I only wanna buy a couple a reefers; I got cash; I ain't no cop or nuthin. Where you at, man?" Nothing but leers from anyone close enough to hear him.

He slowed his walk and increased his probing looks under each stairwell finding sleeping drunks and bags of stinking garbage left by slovenly passengers too lazy to wait for trash bins elsewhere. He paused momentarily by one of the most dimly lit stairwells straining to see and calling out to his unknown contact when the glint of cold steel caught his eye seconds before the point of a seven-inch Buck knife was thrust up and into the fleshy part of Carmine's throat. He knew the feeling well, and froze silently as the pressure on the knife increased just enough to break the skin and cause one or two drops of blood to appear.

Carmine passed out, falling to the floor in a swoon. He awoke several minutes later in a pool of his own sweat and chilled to the bone. Realizing he was still alive, he staggered to get up. "Sheeet," he said wiping the perspiration from his face with his sleeve. "Sheeet!! Dese guys is crazy . . . sheeet!"

The very next day, true to form, Carmine was back on the job at the United Tire Valve Company sharing his tale of adventure with anyone who would listen. He concocted a really exciting adventure of how he and one of New York's biggest drug dealers had almost gone into business together. Of course, he omitted the part about his passing out and how a seven-inch Bowie-style hunting knife almost ended his young life. Strangely, though, he kept keep fingering the spot under his chin all day long; no one seemed to notice or care! Carmine would not forget last night too quickly. "Sheeet!"

"Tenacious Carmine" could have been his name. He was fixated on the idea of getting rich on narcotics, though the thought of dealing with pushers was the furthest thing from his mind now. What to do? What to do?

One night while he was sitting alone in the balcony of the National Theater watching a double feature of B-movies, he smelled something different from among the wide variety of smells in this now semi-run down theater. Turning to his right, he saw two teenagers puffing on a hand-rolled cigarette. "Damn," he said and slithered over the intervening seats toward them; he determined NOT to repeat the fiasco of a few weeks ago. "Hey fellas," he whispered in the darkness, "You—you got a light?"

They looked at him strangely before offering a book of matches.

"Thanks," Carmine said and lit his own cigarette, returning the match book. He waited a few moments before asking, "You got any more . . . stuff? I'm all out—ya know what I mean?" he said, assuming 'they knew that he knew' what they were up to.

There was a slight hesitation before one of the boys said, "Cost ya a buck."

"No problem." Carmine handed over a dollar bill and carefully pocketed the funny-looking, hand-rolled cigarette and left the theater quickly and straight for his apartment.

It was two days before Carmine looked at the cigarette he had stashed under his underwear in his top dresser drawer. He inspected his purchase for several minutes before realizing that there wasn't very much inside the wrapper. "Sheeet," he muttered to himself, "this better pack some wallop for a buck." Then, instead of smoking it, he decided to unwrap it. More careful than he had ever done anything before, Carmine gingerly unrolled the cigarette and placed the contents onto a sheet of newspaper on his bed. He gazed and gazed, mesmerized by the entire episode and the absurdity of paying one dollar for this! For this! "Ya know," he thought, "these dried marijuana leaves look just like some pipe tobaccos I've seen; what they really look like is tea leaves . . . tea leaves!"

III

The next day Carmine bought a cigarette rolling machine—it wasn't really a machine, merely a simple mechanism into which an edge-moistened cigarette paper was placed, tobacco laid on top, a handle pulled and—presto! A cigarette rolled out: crude-looking but smokable. During the war, many smokers bought and used these machines since 'ready-mades' were scarce. Carmine went to work. He bought several different kinds of loose tea from the neighborhood A&P, inspecting each one until he was able to concoct a mixture that closely matched the contents of his single marijuana cigarette. Each night he would carefully roll several dozen of his newly invented 'Tijuana Tea' cigarettes, until he had about three hundred. He was eager to complete this undertaking since a carnival was scheduled to open in the empty lot on Park Place in just two days—on Friday evening—and he wanted to be well prepared for his new business venture: "Carmine Della Rocca: Cut-Rate Reefers." He had decided to sell his home-brew smokes for fifty cents and thus corner the market in this as-yet untapped neighborhood. "Hell," he thought, "these neighborhood kids won't know the difference between this and the real stuff anyway. Besides, what should they expect for fifty cents?"

All day Thursday at work Carmine let it be known that someone was going to be selling marijuana cigarettes 'real cheap' at the carnival; they should look for someone wearing a Yankee baseball cap. When Friday came, he took the day off, opting instead to cruise the neighborhood and advertise. By evening, as the carnival drew its crowds from many adjoining Brooklyn neighborhoods, Carmine was as high as if he had been smoking the real thing, anticipating a real killing in the local marijuana market. He sauntered through the carnival for about fifteen minutes regretting that he would miss some of the fun with the girls who 'did it,' but more intent on making his first sale. He pulled the crushed Yankee cap from his back pocket and was almost immediately accosted by a tall Black man whom he had noticed following him. "You got some stuff, man?" he asked with a heavy drawl.

Excitement filled Carmine as he reached into his jacket pocket saying, "Sure; fifty cents a piece." The man handed Carmine fifty cents, took the cigarette and said, "Thank you," but now the drawl was gone, surprisingly. Reaching into his hip pocket, he produced a badge, showed it to Carmine and said, "Take it easy now; you're under arrest!" Two other plainclothes policemen quickly joined him and led Carmine, handcuffed, to the 80th precinct station house a half-block away.

Carmine fought them every inch of the way there screaming out loud, "It's only tea; it's only tea!"

NICK

I

When the Korean War began in September 1952, Nick Toscano was among the first to volunteer. At eighteen years of age, he was worldly enough to realize that his life was destined to be limited to living in roach-infested Brooklyn tenements and working in gas stations like Pete Kelly's unless he made a major break from the patterns into which he found himself becoming locked. Military service presented itself to him as one viable alternative to his current way of life. Since his graduation from Lafayette High School, he had many regrets, and wished that he had worked harder and pursued a more career-oriented curriculum. On the first Monday in October, he presented himself to the Navy recruiting officer located in a store front on Joralemon Street in downtown Brooklyn near the main shopping district... Nick was going to be a swabbie.

Nick's experiences in Navy boot camp only amplified his desire to make something of himself. Surrounded by hundreds of enlisted men, Nick realized that only a mere handful of them measured up to his own physical and intellectual powers. He had never fully realized how bright he was, since most of his friends from the neighborhood were equally bright and did well in school. His choice of refusing to enter Brooklyn Technical High School was now looked upon by him as a colossal blunder, since his days at Lafayette were spent just hanging out and learning how to act tough. At Brooklyn Tech, the discipline would have served him well and forced him to study, which in turn would have allowed him the opportunities he needed to break out of the life style that he now felt was smothering him. Now, in the Navy, he began to recognize his own capabilities and just how much more he was able to grasp when compared with the average seaman.

After six weeks of basic training, Nick felt physically strong whereas many of his companions suffered from bouts of almost total exhaustion. On the obstacle course, Nick always performed in a superior way, encouraging others to move faster and strive harder. On the firing range, he was surprisingly adept and won every sharpshooter medal available. He became an assistant instructor, which motivated him further to achieve higher goals. When aptitude testing was scheduled, Nick became nervous and apprehensive, ready to question his own mental abilities. The men from cities like Boston, Philadelphia, Hartford or New Haven seemed more confident than he, though, when the scores were posted, he held his own, producing grades consistently in the 95th percentile. The overall result of his first six weeks away from home had done more for Nick's self esteem than all the fights he had won and all the women he had conquered. He was growing up, and this man's navy had helped him to see his own potential and, further, to convince him of the innate power within each human to reach out beyond self to achieve success. He believed in his heart that he was capable of great things, and when he was chosen for electronics technician school, he was certain.

To Nick, being selected as a candidate for electronics school was like being given a second chance at life. This was his opportunity to dig in and produce for himself all that he desired: a real education that would ultimately lead to a good job.

II

Nick's first day in class found him seated next to a sandy-haired young man called Phil Ryan; Phil struck up conversation with Nick immediately while the class awaited the arrival of the instructor. Phil's appearance reminded Nick of Pete Kelly who was also light skinned with steel-grey eyes. Phil was slimmer than Pete who had already developed a beer belly at thirty years of age and wore his pants low on his waist so that he could tell everyone that he still wore size 34. Phil, by contrast, was neat, well polished and affable.

"Hi," he said as he smiled, offering his hand to Nick.

"How ya doin? Nice to meet-cha," Nick responded in the jargon and drawl of the old neighborhood.

"I'm Phil Ryan, from Jersey—Jersey City." He continued smiling at Nick while pumping his hand with a manly grip.

"Nick . . . Nick Toscano; Brooklyn."

"I know . . . I could tell . . . that you came from Brooklyn . . . I mean."

They both laughed at the friendly jibe about Nick's unmistakable Brooklyn accent.

"Did you go to a technical high school," Phil queried.

Nah. I went to a good school, but kind of dogged it. Ya know. Didn't really have any incentive to do well . . . I could have; well I guess I really blew it. This is a good chance for me to begin again."

"Yes it is," Phil replied realizing that Nick must have excellent potential or the training director wouldn't have recommended him for the electronics school.

"I'm really good at math," Nick told him "though I sort of wasted my time by only studying enough to get by in high school."

"You must have done well on the aptitude tests though."

"Yeah. Ninety-fifth percentile!" Nick was happy to offer that information.

"That's great, Nick. You're going to love this stuff. It's what's coming along now. Electronics will change the way things are being done all over the world."

"I don't know much about it . . . really."

"My dad works for Jersey Power and Light, and he says that before long vacuum tubes will be gone and transistors will be used exclusively. He says that they're even working on devices smaller than transistors that will permit us to have radios that will fit in the palm of our hand. He said his boss told him that one transistor the size of a thumb nail can do the work of a dozen vacuum tubes. They're even speculating that some day computers like the gigantic Sperry UNIVAC will become obsolete, and that every office will have a computer of its own."

Nick could feel his own self image begin to collapse once more as Phil began to speak of things that he had never even heard about. His only knowledge of electronics came from the Dick Tracy comic strip, where he read about the famous fictional detective wearing a magical wrist-radio. Everyone joked how only in the comic strips could people dream about things like that. He felt intimidated by Phil and wondered whether his broad base of knowledge would make him do better in school than everyone else.

"Whatta you do for fun, Phil?" Nick asked, trying to change the subject.

"Nothing much," he responded. "I read a bit. Have you read *From Here to Eternity* yet?"

"No." Nick flinched and pretended at stretching his neck in mock exercise, hoping once again to change the conversation. Nick read only the Daily News and the Sunday comics.

The instructor came in, and Nick sighed in relief that he no longer felt the need to joust with Phil. The instructor, a lieutenant, was rather short, with crew-cut blond hair. Nick looked at him carefully, noting his scrubbed-clean look and erect posture. "Definitely ain't from the old neighborhood," he thought. Nick was right; he was from Tucson, Arizona—wherever the hell that was, he wondered.

Surprisingly, Nick did well at the introductory course in basic electronics. He learned about Ohm's law and electrons and what made batteries work. He studied simple circuits and switches. He learned about resistance, capacitance, and inductance. It was easy! Nick was overjoyed as he aced every examination and received an 'A' in the course. The next course began immediately after the basic course concluded, and this was touted to be even more difficult. But Nick also did well in basic circuits, superheterodyne receivers, principles of radio transmission, etc. He was a natural!

After six months, Nick received a diploma as an electronics technician, third class. His job would be to repair 'black boxes' on Navy ships, an assignment that immediately pleased him. He was also pleased to learn that he and Phil Ryan would be working together; they had been assigned to the Oregon, an aircraft carrier presently stationed in Tokyo, but scheduled for duty off the Korean Coast. It was an important job, a job that would enable Nick and Phil to learn about radar systems, fire-control devices, aircraft landing systems, and other exotic and highly sophisticated devices. Nick was joyous for he saw himself returning home and opening a TV repair shop. It would be great!

Phil Ryan had other ideas. He was going to enter college and become an engineer. The excitement was not in repairing these black boxes—but in designing them. He and Nick spent many hours planning for the time when their Navy careers would end.

"You really want to go to college, Phil?" Nick asked one day.

"Yes, I do. My dad knows several engineers who are working with him, and they tell him that the work we're doing is way beyond anything they've ever heard of. Nick, we are at the forefront of technology, and I want to be a part of it."

Nick was impressed, but he really couldn't see much beyond being a TV repairman. He wanted to be his own boss, set his own hours, own his own place. He would make more money than he did working for Pete Kelly, and he would never even dirty his nails.

III

One day while on liberty in Japan, Phil and Nick were walking along the Ginza taking in the sights. They paused as they noticed several Japanese queuing up on a sidewalk outside a large department store and watched as the Japanese put coins into a box-like device attached to the building.

"What the hell is going on here?" Nick asked of Phil who was just as wide eyed.

"Don't know; looks like a vending machine of some sort."

As they drew closer to more clearly observe the process, they observed a Japanese man drop a coin into this machine, push a button, and wait a few seconds after which the machine dispensed a small packet of cleansing tissues at its bottom.

"Well wadda ya know!" Nick was awestruck. "They're buying packs of tissues right here on the street rather than going into the store."

It was common knowledge that Japanese never used handkerchiefs: they chose instead to use tissues, which they disposed of immediately in the ever-present trash containers on all Japanese streets, thus avoiding carrying around in their pockets a germ-laden cloth—as was the custom with most Americans. Nick could not get over the vending concept: bring the goods to the people right here on the street—Wow!

Nick's time in the Navy went quickly: he learned much and matured quickly, eventually becoming an instructor himself after only ten months. He enjoyed the teaching even more than the work he had been doing because it gave him an opportunity to grow and continue to learn. His free time was spent in the ship library where he devoured the latest magazines and newspapers, forcing himself to keep up with what was going on back home. He did not want to return home when he was discharged only to find himself out of the main stream as did his uncles after World War II. No, he would come home ready to begin a career path that would be exciting. Somehow, the idea of being a TV repairman was rapidly fading from his mind.

Nick, was discharged from active duty in October 1954, five days before having served two full years in the Navy. He saved practically every penny he had earned—which wasn't a lot anyway—about $1500. His first stop after disembarking at the Brooklyn Navy Yard was Pete Kelly's garage.

"Hey, Nicky!" Pete shouted as Nick picked him up and twirled him around. "You look great, kid. How ya doin?"

"I'm just great, Pete," Nick said laughing and beaming from one ear to the other as he gently set Pete back down. "Just great!"

Pete held Nick at arm's length and checked him over carefully. "Did you grow while you were away, Nicky babe?"

"I think so, Pete. I'm almost six foot two now . . . weigh about 190."

Pete beamed at the sight of his former employee who now stood before him: tall, well-built and handsome, especially in his Navy uniform. "You want some coffee, kid? I've got some on the hot plate inside."

Nick gestured "No," but ushered Pete inside and motioned for him to sit down at the familiar shoddy desk that seemed to be cluttered with the same type of old and new repair bills, tire patches, cigarette butts, and other miscellaneous litter.

Pete sat at the desk on the three-legged, rickety old arm-chair that had been there from long before the time when Nick started working for him; it still squeaked every time Pete sat down in it or rocked even a little bit. Clearing a spot on top of the desk, Nick sat down and became very serious, speaking softly and very deliberately to his old boss.

"Pete," he began, "do you trust me?"

"Of course," came the puzzled response. "Why?"

"Pete," Nick was looking deeply into Pete's eyes now, "when I was in Tokyo, I saw people all over the city buying small packs of tissues from sidewalk vending machines."

"So?" Pete said matter of factly.

"So? Do you realize that the only vending machines in the United States today are in subways and the only things you can buy are gum, penny chocolates, and cigarettes?

Again Pete looked at Nick quizzically. "So what, Nick?"

"Listen. If I want a soda. Where can I get one?"

"You want to drink it now? I mean you want it cold?"

"Yes." Nick patiently played out the scene with his former boss.

Pete pondered and then continued, "The only place to get a cold soda in a bottle is at Sidney's market two blocks over or at the ice cream parlor—but the ice cream parlor don't sell bottles, only by the glass."

Nick interjected, "Now suppose . . . just suppose that you had a vending machine that would dispense bottles of cold soda and that this vending machine was standing outside of this office. How many bottles of soda do you think you would sell in a day?"

"Nicky . . . what are you getting at? . . . a vending machine that sells soda?

How would you keep it cold? You can't be serious." Pete started to get up, reaching out to Nick. He put his arm around him, smiling broadly and said, "C'mon. I'll buy you soda at Sidney's. I need a break anyway." He yelled over to Sal, the curly-haired young man he hired when Nick joined the Navy, "I'll be back in about an hour; take over, OK?" "It's funny, he pondered, how Sal, like Nick, hates getting his hands dirty. Whatta they expect? They're working in a gas station." Sal, was, if possible, even more fastidious than Nick: on the advice of his sister, a nurse, he rubbed Vaseline under his nails each morning before coming to work to make removing the grease easier at the end of the day. He did that in lieu of wearing the surgical gloves she recommended; he thought that was a bit much—but he thought about it, he really thought about it.

"No," Nick interrupted, "let's walk up Underhill Avenue to Otto's Ice Cream Parlor . . . I want to point out a few things along the way."

Nick knew that Pete was a good businessman and that by providing good service and standing behind his work, he had developed a growing number of steady customers. What many people didn't know was that Pete had a fifty-percent interest in

Allied Brake Repairs and also totally owned Park Slope Towing Service. Pete was a wise businessman who was not afraid to risk some capital . . . but before he did, he had to be fully convinced of the profitability potential. Nick knew this as he carefully led Pete up Underhill Avenue. As they passed Allied Brake Repairs, they paused allowing Pete to chat with his partner, Ben Harris.

When Ben saw Nick in his uniform, he walked directly up to him and pumped his hand hard. "You look great, Nick! You out for good?" He was genuinely happy for he had always liked Nick.

"Yeah; I was discharged this morning at the Brooklyn Navy Yard." Nick paused a moment and then asked, "How many cars do you handle each day here?"

"Well we've got three bays and the average brake job takes about an hour . . . I guess we do about twenty cars a day on the average. Why? You lookin' to open up a place of your own?" He joked knowing Nick hated grease and grime.

"Nope," Nick replied laughing.

Pete and Nick continued walking, and after a few minutes Pete asked, "What was that all about . . . back there?"

Nick carefully presented his idea, trying at first to be as dispassionate as possible. "You've got customers coming into your gas station all day long . . . sometimes about two hundred just for gas. You work on ten or twelve car repairs too. Right?" Pete nodded his agreement.

Nick continued, "You also do oil changes too. Right?" Pete continued walking and nodding yes. Nick continued, "All by yourself, Pete you handle almost two-hundred and fifty customers and workers each day. These people are all potential customers for soda . . . cold soda . . . in a machine that is conveniently located in your—he stressed YOUR—places of business."

Pete began to catch on to Nick's train of thought. He added, "I suppose we could charge a premium too, a few cents over what a deli would charge . . . "

"Of course!" Nick knew that Pete's mind was now in high gear.

" . . . but refrigeration—that's a prob—"

Nick interrupted, "No! Refrigeration isn't a problem. When I was aboard ship, we had the latest types of refrigeration units; they were compact, quiet and very reliable. The only thing I haven't solved is how—or where—to get data on the vending process itself. It's all new technology, but it shouldn't be too difficult for an M.E.—that's a mechanical engineer—to work out."

"Boy," Pete interrupted, smiling in admiration, you've come a long way since you left to join the Navy."

"Do you think it's possible Pete? Can it really work?"

"I think so . . . I think so . . . "

They continued their walk up Underhill Avenue on their way to Otto's. Passing a grocery store, Pete indicated that he wanted to stop off for a minute and pick up a pound of coffee for the garage.

"I'm almost out of coffee; the deli charges twenty cents a cup in the morning—it's getting too expensive. I'm gonna make my own in the morning now too" . . . Suddenly he paused, looked off into space and then said to Nick, "Do you suppose?"

Both men stared at each other and simultaneously blurted out, "A coffee vending machine too . . . ? Nah!"

IV

The walk that Nick had conned Pete into taking had accomplished its purpose. Up and down the avenue, people were shopping in stores, walking, and visiting the various establishments along the way. Each one offered a unique opportunity for some type of automated vending machine. Pete and Nick exchanged ideas in rapid-fire delight, recognizing the tremendous business opportunities. As they passed the fire station, Pete addressed one of the firemen who was sitting on the front steps.

"Hi, Larry."

"Hi, Pete. How's it go these days?"

"Great. Say, let me ask you a question. Would you firemen have a need for a vending machine that would have bottled soda—ice cold?"

"Sure, we have a refrigerator, but it's usually full of food for our meals; we forget things like soda all the time—besides, the guys are lazy. Yeah, sounds great. You selling one?"

"Not yet, but I've got some ideas. Take care; see you later."

When Pete and Nick turned the corner of St. Mark's Place, they were confronted with the lunchtime exodus of workers from the Knox Hat Factory. "Must be three hundred fifty people work there; right Pete?"

"Yes."

"One bottle of Coke or Pepsi at lunch time, one more at break time . . . "

"Coffee . . . tea . . . "

"Soup sandwiches . . . " Nick's mind raced.

"Soup? Sandwiches? From a vending machine? Now let's not get carried away."

"Yeah, right."

When they arrived at Otto's, the afternoon lunch crowd had already jammed the place. People were eating freshly made sandwiches, drinking coffee or cherry Cokes, or munching on ice cream in deliciously crunchy sugar cones.

They sat at the counter and ordered tuna salad on rye toast with pickles and cole slaw. Pete ordered a cherry Coke while Nick ordered a chocolate malted. Otto, himself, served them, deftly creating both sandwiches with hands that moved rapidly with the confidence of many years of experience. When finished with the sandwiches, he took a large glass and pumped the cola syrup into it followed by two quick shots of cherry syrup. In one smooth motion, he went from the syrup dispenser to the seltzer fountain, moving the handle first backward for a powerful blast then forward for the remainder of the seltzer to fill the glass. He stirred just enough to allow the bubbles to overflow slightly. He was an expert to be sure.

"You back home for good, Nicky?" he asked of Nick.

"Yes, Otto, It's good to be home again."

"You met a lot of nice ladies there I bet," he said in his heavily accented German/English accent, smiling and winking with a knowing eye.

"They call it poontang over there, Otto."

"We call it some-ting else in Germany. Still good stuff. Ya?"

"Ya!"

The three friends laughed as Otto brought Nick up to date on the goings on that he had missed. After a while, Nick asked him, "Wouldn't you like something that would hold fifty or sixty bottles of cold soda so you wouldn't have to keep spritzing syrup and seltzer all day?"

"That would be good. My cooler up here only holds a few bottles. But a big refrigerated cabinet that holds a lot of bottles would be better. I keep cleaning the fountain, refilling syrup . . . you know."

Nick thought for a moment, and added, "The best thing would be to devise a system where both the syrup and the seltzer could come out of the same spout."

"That would save me a lot of work—for sure."

Both Pete and Nick finished their lunch and walked through Otto's, greeting old friends and acquaintances. Nick paused at the Juke box, staring at it contemplatively. "You know, Pete," he began "we had a juke box on board ship in the lounge. But in the maintenance shop, we would record important data on a wire recorder. Maybe someday someone will figure how to put records on wire so that you can carry around a dozen or so in your pocket."

Pete confirmed Nick's assessment by adding, "Those new 45-RPM records are now being made in extended pay—four songs on one record!"

"No kidding? Wow!"

The next few weeks found Nick spending lots of time on the phone with his Navy buddy, Phil Ryan. They discussed the engineering problems implicit in developing a vending machine that would be adequately refrigerated and virtually tamper proof. Phil's father had introduced Nick to a mechanical engineer he knew who had designed some small parts used in bottling plants in Jersey City. The problem itself was not terribly difficult to solve unless you wanted the soda cold too—or you wanted the box tamper proof—or you wanted a machine that would . . . . He joked with Nick, realizing that there would be the need for some financial backing before an assignment of this magnitude could begin. "How about going to the Coca Cola people themselves?" Nick asked. The engineer nodded his head and said only, "Hmmm."

Nick knew enough now to realize that neither he nor Pete could attempt this on their own; there just wasn't enough money to do this independently. "What should we do, Pete?"

Pete realized the financial merits of their ideas, but was stumped when it came to the next step. "I don't know, Nick; I just don't know."

"Can we go to Coca Cola directly?"

"Suppose they steal our ideas?"

"What other choices do we have?"

"None," Nick sighed, regretting that he was born so poor, and was doomed to remain so unless some quirk of fate played an important part in his life real soon.

CARMINE / NICK / AL

I

Carmine spent the night in jail—wailing all the while: "It's only tea . . . !" When the laboratory report came in on Saturday afternoon, the round-faced desk sergeant practically threw Carmine down the front steps of the police station.

"You dumb jerk!" he screamed after him, "You got nothing better to do than waste our time? You *@ % $ # * Idiot!"

Carmine was glad to be out of jail, but couldn't resist one final comment as he looked up at the ferocious officer. He cupped his hands to his mouth and whispered, "I told you, you beer-belly jerk; it's only tea!" He ran all the way home.

After showering and shaving, Carmine realized—once again—that he had failed in an attempt at making a quick buck. He got locked up, scared half to death, and—worse—was the laughing stock of the entire neighborhood. He vowed never again to listen to himself when he had one of these wild ideas. As dusk settled, he remembered the carnival and put on a pair of clean jeans and went out. When he got there, he immediately bought a hot dog and a Coke from a vendor and walked in and out of the various pathways that led to the attractions and rides. He was a changed man, he told himself, and tried hard to ignore the lovely ladies that roamed the carnival in groups of twos and threes. No more trouble, he told himself.

Absentmindedly, he ate his hot dog and drank his soda, not paying attention to the sailor who was backing away from the shooting gallery in front of him. The collision knocked Carmine to the ground causing the remaining soda to spill all over him.

The sailor reached down to help him up, saying, "Gee, I'm really sorry. I . . . I wasn't looking. Are you OK?"

Carmine recognized the sailor. "Don't you . . . didn't you work at Pete's garage?"

"I did. About two years ago. I joined the Navy."

As Carmine stood up, he did his best to brush off the dirt and dry himself with his handkerchief. He looked directly at Nick, "It's really my fault; I wasn't looking."

"It's really both our faults. Can I buy you another soda?"

"Sure—thanks."

This was a strange association: Nick and Carmine—emerging class and slime—tall versus short—clean-cut and—. Whatever the attraction, these two hit it off right away. Carmine told Nick how he hated his job making tire valves. Nick confided that he had some plans but needed a financial backer.

"You know, Nick," Carmine offered, "I used to run numbers for a guy. There was some trouble and—well now he's legit. Maybe he'd help somebody from the old neighborhood. He moved to Manhattan a while ago, but I saw him a couple of weeks ago. His wife had a baby in July, and they came back to show it off to the old gang."

"If you think he'd talk to me."

"Hey, hey—what're friends for?"

The next day Nick arrived at Pete Kelly's garage dressed in a pair of new jeans, cowboy boots and a denim jacket over a pullover ski sweater.

"You look like you never left, kid," Pete said, admiring the new strength he saw in Nick and how well he carried himself. "I'm really proud of you, Nick. You've come a long way since you worked here in the garage."

Nick, though not normally shy, felt a bit embarrassed at what his friend said, though he realized that what Pete said was true. "I guess the Navy agreed with me. By the way, I ran into one of the neighborhood guys at the carnival last night," he began, "and he said he might know someone who might be interested in financing some of what we talked about."

"I don't know," Nick. Pete seemed hesitant now, whereas previously he had seemed enthusiastic and eager to move into this venture with Nick.

Nick felt a bit disappointed with his friend, but realized that the way things were developing, it was becoming a totally speculative venture. Pete, with a good solid business base already in place, didn't want to risk investing in some dream that might never bear fruit.

"Pete . . . I understand if you want out." Nick expressed genuine concern for his friend's feelings.

"Nick . . . it's just that it sounds like big money is needed. I'm too old for adventure. You understand . . . ."

"Sure." Nick felt a strange relief that at least his idea seemed to have merit. He could trust Pete's instincts. Now it was up to him to either pursue it or not, which was, of course, totally dependent on obtaining funds from some backer.

Nick spent the remainder of the day renewing old acquaintances, stopping off at Otto's for another sandwich—generally cruising the old neighborhood just to make himself feel at home. At about 3 P.M., he stopped in at Dorman's Bar and Grill and had a short beer; it tasted fine, but no one in the place seemed to recognize him nor he them.

II

The old black and white Dumont TV that used to be propped up on a makeshift stand hanging from the ceiling by wires had been replaced by a Sony color set that was neatly cradled on a chrome-plated stand that was securely anchored to the wall. "Be careful," he said to the bartender "or the Japanese will take over everything." Everyone chuckled, but paid no attention to Nick's outlandish prophetic comment. He had two more quick beers then left to continue his cruising. Somehow the traffic seemed a bit heavier than when he had left, though the streets in the old neighborhood were still rather quiet.

"Hey Nick!" Nick looked across the street and noticed Carmine waving at him. Nick signaled to him to wait while he crossed over to meet him. "What's happening babe?" Carmine asked.

"Oh, just trying to renew my old ties with the neighborhood. Things have changed—strange."

"You said it," Carmine retorted. "Hey look! I got the name of this dude I told you 'bout in New York."

Carmine said "Noo Yawk," which was like music to Nick's ears. "How come," he wondered, "the whole country speaks funny and only those of us from Brooklyn speak right?"

Nick tried for several hours to reach Al Zito at his Manhattan home, but it wasn't until 7:30 P.M. that a soft voice responded to the ringing.

"Hello?"

"Good evening," Nick said, struggling to sound relaxed while feigning a business-like demeanor, "I was told that I could reach Al Zito at this number."

"Yes, you can. May I tell him who's calling please?"

When Donna-Marie realized that the party on the other end

of the line was extremely nervous, she attempted to put him at ease immediately—as was her way. When she finally handed the telephone to Al she said, "It sounds like someone really young—he mentioned someone named Carmine, from the old neighborhood."

Al's memory recalled vividly the numbers runners of the old days, and a Carmine in particular. He feared that events of days long gone would return to haunt him. The nightmares of Sevvi Carducci resurrected themselves and threatened to destroy all that Al had built for himself and for his family.

He took the receiver from Donna-Marie and responded tensely, "Hello; this is Al Zito speaking."

Nick spoke in an unbroken stream for five minutes, explaining all the events that led up to his belief that there was a market for automated soda vending machines. He sounded so sincere, so honest, that Al agreed to meet with him the following day in a small mid-town restaurant. When the two men met they were both visibly impressed with one another, noting the striking similarities that they shared. Al and Nick both stood at about six feet two inches in height, though Al was more powerfully built. Nick, slightly leaner, carried himself erect seemingly adding to his stature by his excellent posture. They greeted one another with a hearty handshake and deep reciprocal smiles. Nick, noting that Al was dressed in a conservative, dark blue, one-button-lounge suit, felt awkward about his own casual dress. He apologized, saying that he had just gotten discharged and hadn't a job yet nor had he done any shopping for clothes.

"I guess I grew a bit in the Navy," he said shyly; "nothing fits."

Al put him at ease immediately—now that he had allayed the fears he held that Nick might have been sent as an emissary from members of Sevvi's old gang.

"Would you like a drink? . . . expense account."

"Sure . . . ah . . . just a beer. OK?"

"Sure." Al nodded to the approaching waiter and held up two fingers mouthing, "Two Rheinglod drafts."

The waiter dutifully went off to get the drinks.

As they drank and began to pick at their lunch, Nick felt more at ease with Al, seeing him as somewhat of a former acquaintance from the old neighborhood rather than a threat. Al gave the impression that he was sincerely interested in what Nick had to say, and listened intently asking questions along the way. Nick realized that, in Al Zito, he had come upon a bright and articulate businessman. Al's grasp of what Nick had to say confirmed immediately what Nick had hoped: that someone with insight would be able to channel his dream for this new business venture. When Nick was finished, Al meticulously explained what he saw as potential problems in developing this idea. There were many obstacles—though that in itself didn't mean that they couldn't be worked out—and solutions needed to be addressed. Al continued to explain to Nick that several key factors needed to be investigated after which a formal business plan would be developed. He described market potential, return on investment, payback, a distribution network—things that Nick had not ever understood—and frankly didn't care to understand now. He felt weary when Al concluded his evaluation of Nick's idea supplemented by the brief exercise in macro-economics.

Nick glumly looked at Al and said, "So I guess I should forget about it, huh? I'm in over my head . . . ." He slid back in his chair and was about to thank Al for his time when Al interrupted him.

" . . . Oh no! I don't think we should forget about it at all. I think your idea has merit. It sounds like a concept whose time has come. There are just a lot of details that need to be worked out . . . ."

"Well what does it mean . . . ?"

"What it means is that I've got to get some people together and see what needs to be done. There's refrigeration, electronics, automation, site selection—lots of things. But—I think it bears a good hard look."

Nick felt excitement building within himself as he listened intently to Al. His eyes bored into Al now and he began to really trust this man whom he had just met. Al was the prototypical businessman, he thought; he looks the part and speaks with a confidence that makes one trust what he has to say. He did not pretend that this scheme was foolproof or that it would ultimately turn a profit. But if it were approached in a strict business manner, one would know quickly whether the potential for success was real or not. Al had taken charge, and Nick felt in awe of his new friend.

"We need to set up an office, someplace for you to work."

Nick was taken aback as he was drawn back to reality. "An office . . . for me?"

"Sure. If we're going to do this, we've got to do it right; I can't spend the time necessary to do the up-front research and planning. We'll need a place for you to operate from, to meet the engineers, distribution people—you know. Are you still interested?"

"Well—ah—sure. Me?" Nick suddenly felt the weight of Al's high-powered business acumen. Up to this point, Al's approach had been slow, methodical and tutorial. Suddenly he seemed to change, setting wheels into motion.

"You do want to pursue this don't you?" Al asked quizzically.

"Of course—yes. But I'm not a businessman. I've just got an idea—several ideas."

"Nick, listen carefully to me." Al looked at him intently, smiling gently, his eyes glistening. "You came to me with an idea. I think it's a good idea. The next step is to plan a strategy, get some experts involved and go from there. We'll never know whether this whole thing is feasible until we examine it closely. You've got to be the focal point of this venture. I'll handle everything nontechnical—finance, contracts, whatever. But someone needs to establish a firm foothold from which we can jump off. And that's got to be you." Al stuck out his hand. "Besides, who else can I trust . . . partner?"

III

Nick couldn't believe how quickly events unfolded after that. Al had rented a small office, brought in some desks and a phone, and hung a sign on the door: ADISCO. it stood for Automatic Dispensing Company. He liked the sound: ADISCO; it had a . . . successful sound to it. Al had laid out several assignments for Nick, including contacting several well-known mechanical engineers at the network. He didn't want to solicit them himself since he was still on contract as a producer. Next he had Nick look up a patent attorney and have him research the files for potential conflicts related to design concepts. Then he had Nick personally canvass as many stores and shops as possible to determine their feelings about having an ADISCO machine on their premises.

Nick was continually impressed with the precision with which Al moved. Everything seemed to fall into place, and questions were resolved quickly. He spoke to Al only at night via telephone but had dinner with him at least once on every weekend. And things continued to develop rapidly.

Shopkeepers thought the idea had merit, as they likened it to a juke box—only it was silent. "You mean a box full of soda that plugs into the wall and people put money into it and a bottle comes out, and I get a percentage of the net?" It all seemed wonderfully exciting, but as the weeks evolved into months Nick realized that he was not earning an income on his own; no, he felt totally dependent on Al Zito for money and a livelihood. It was not a good feeling, and he was not satisfied at the prospects of being penniless if this entire concept should fall flat on its face.

That Saturday evening, Nick was having dinner with Al and Donna-Marie. he appeared a bit nervous—a situation that did not go unnoticed by Al—as he ran over the events of the past week.

"You OK?" Al asked, trying to make light of Nick's obvious anxiety.

"Yea . . . well. I've got something to tell you."

"Shoot."

"I . . . I've . . . Al, you may think I'm not committed to our business anymore, but I've got to . . . ah . . . I've got to think of my future."

" . . . Of course, but—."

"Please let me finish." Nick had stood up and began to pace, trying to say what he had to say without hurting Al. "Look, I've enrolled in Cooper Union—in the electrical engineering program— at night. I begin with the January session." He sighed deeply, relieved.

A smile came to both Al and Donna-Marie's faces as they put their arms around him and wished him well.

"Why are you guys smiling? You seem so happy—I thought you'd be upset."

Donna-Marie spoke first, "Nick, you've become like family to us. Al has told me how diligently you worked so far on this project and how well you've dealt with the engineers and others. And we've . . . " Donna-Marie looked at Al and let him continue.

" . . . and we've been waiting for you to discover just how important an education is in today's business world. We figured that you'd sign up for school sooner or later."

Nick smiled back at them both, realizing just how much these two really cared about him.

Al lifted a glass of wine, "To our new engineer!"

Donna-Marie responded, "Hear, hear!"

The months raced by, and in January of 1955 ADISCO had a working prototype of a bottle-dispensing device. Minor difficulties occurred not in the refrigeration end or in the bottle-release mechanism, but in the coin receiver. Nick had discovered during his interviews that the shopkeepers themselves wanted control of the price of each bottle. Where the audience was captive—like in a theater or a department store cafeteria—they wanted to charge a premium. Gas station operators, for example, were content to make a lesser profit.

The problem with the coin mechanism was that it had to be made adjustable—for the various locations as well as, they discovered, for future price increases. An adjustable mechanism was favored since it also eliminated the necessity of replacing a major mechanical component when price or location changed. As it turned out, a key-way was developed to permit a different mixture of coins to be accepted prior to releasing one bottle of soda. This resolved, Al Zito set the wheels in motion to file the necessary patents and develop a distribution network. Nick had previously established contact with the local bottling distributors, and needed only ten days lead time for them to begin regular deliveries. On February 7, 1955 the very first ADISCO bottle-vending machine was installed outside of Pete Kelly's garage. The entire neighborhood was there, not only to cheer Nick's new venture but also out of a sense of curiosity.

Pete Kelly put in the first dime. The box clunked a few times as the coin activated an electromechanical switch. Pete opened the long vertical door and grasped the neck of the bottle. He hesitated a moment as everyone waited anxiously, squeezed the bottle harder feigning a struggle, then gently eased out his selection—the machine clunking once more to prevent another selection until another coin was deposited.

Pete popped the cap on the opener mounted on the side of the machine and sipped his ice cold soda to the delight of the crowd, which immediately converged on the soda machine pouring dimes into it until it ran out of bottles. Pete turned to Nick and said, "Nick, me lad, I think you've done it."

How well he had done wouldn't really be known for a while: that is, until the concept of chilled soda in bottles caught on. But the ADISCO name became well known literally overnight by all the major bottlers who wanted machines of their own. Being a shrewd businessman, Al Zito realized that he could not stifle the tide that he had been instrumental in creating. The choices he had were: (1) continue to distribute and stock his own soda machines or (2) permit the major bottlers to take on the distribution and lease units to them to be located wherever they chose. The first choice would net a profit, to be sure, but required a continuing marketing strategy. It was also highly probable that the major bottlers would be able to quickly develop machines of their own with the potential of shutting out ADISCO completely, as soon as they could develop their own technology.

The second choice offered the only viable option: ADISCO would continue to manufacture the boxes and lease them to anyone who wanted them. Thus, Al and Nick could concentrate their own interests in the research and development of new products. Following one of their weekend dinners, Al and Nick had agreed to a meeting with representatives of the major bottling companies to apprise them of the decision to lease.

Nick rented a suite of rooms at the Waldorf Astoria, and catered a light luncheon. About twenty persons arrived representing the three largest soda companies in the New York metropolitan area. As Nick began to relate the details of ADISCO's decision to continue the manufacturing process of the boxes while permitting lease/rental agreements, he was interrupted by one of the attorneys present.

Robert Jarvis, a portly gentleman about fifty years old, represented New York's largest supplier of soda and syrup. "Mr. Toscano," he began, puffing on a long, black cigar, "we fully realize that you intend to retain the manufacturing rights to these boxes. My organization is prepared to absorb the manufacturing process and compensate your firm with a royalty whose value we can work out."

Nick was unsure of what was being proposed, and nodded to his own lawyer to pay strict attention to what was transpiring.

Nick responded, "Do you mean that you want to manufacture the ADISCO box under some kind of licensing arrangement with us?"

Jarvis leaned back in his chair nodding as he puffed heavily on his cigar, "Exactly! Besides, you must admit, Mr. Toscano, that your box is ugly."

Nick reeled at Jarvis' words, but noticed that the others seemed to agree. He peered at Jarvis, giving no indication of how he really felt or what he was thinking.

Jarvis continued, "The reality of the situation is this: ADISCO has cornered the market on automated bottle-vending machines—for a while, anyway." Jarvis had a sardonic smile on his face, which Nick interpreted as a veiled threat to do exactly as he suggests or get run out of town on a rail. Nick also realized that he was playing in a game that could go either way: his way or down the sewer. There was real power gathered here and he discovered for the first time that big business was something not to be trifled with. Jarvis added, "Our own patent office had researched the files and determined that with today's technology, there is no way that we could make a box as good as yours in a timely way without stealing your ideas. As a result, we are willing to pay ADISCO substantial royalties so that we can manufacture our own boxes, and we'll even make 'em a little prettier at the same time!" He laughed a sneaky kind of laugh looking around to see who agreed with him.

When Jarvis finished, there was a general consensus among the others that they, too, preferred a licensing agreement that would permit them to use the "guts" of the ADISCO box while modifying the exterior. What it turned out to be was a desire for a proprietary box selling only one company's products.

Nick's attorney was quick to point out that by having the major bottlers pay ADISCO a royalty, the profits could be astronomical considering their own nationwide distribution networks and advertising exposure. ADISCO could never compete with these bottlers once they decided to manufacture something—their resources were too vast. And it was only a matter of time before their own engineers would design new and better boxes under their own patents. It was a lucky break that ADISCO had the patents for the current machine so tightly locked up—or was it luck?

Immediately at the conclusion of the meeting, Nick called Al at the network, something he rarely did, and explained to him what had transpired. Nick could visualize Al's broad smile at the other end and wondered just how much he had really planned for.

"Do you have all the numbers, Nick?" he asked excitedly.

"Yes. If I can believe what I hear, these guys expect to manufacture OUR boxes in thousands of units each year—at least until they can develop new technology and design newer, proprietary boxes of their own. They sort of have us over a barrel—a nice barrel though. With a minimum royalty of $100 per box, ADISCO could net a half a million dollars—for doing nothing!" He was so excited he was practically screaming into the phone, "For nothing Al—a half a million bucks!!"

Al was trying to restrain himself as best he could, but when he heard Nick bellowing into the phone, he burst out in guffaws. It was too good to be true. "Nick!", he interrupted, "bring our lawyer over for dinner tonight. We'll work some numbers.""OK . . . OK." Nick was as high as a kite, hardly able to control himself, but gratified that everything seemed to positive. "Hey, Nick," he heard Al say into the receiver.

"Yeah?"

"You did good, kid; you did really good!"

The twenty-one year old was pleased with himself for he had done well—really well.

ROBBY

I

Robby was not a quick study. Eventually, he 'decided' to grow up, and made three major resolutions: (1) never fool around with someone else's woman—unless he wanted to risk a sustained pounding to the head , (2) study really hard right before an exam so that he could pass even though he hadn't studied up to that point because his nights were spent with girls and, (3) most recently—work at a job he really liked rather than something dead ended—like most people. This latest decision had its genesis early in his life when he saw how hard his father, Vito, worked and how he truly hated what he did. Robby remembered the many nights that Vito sat at the kitchen table in a tank-top undershirt drinking glass after glass of Four Roses whiskey from a tiny shot glass until he was so drunk he could hardly make it into bed. Indeed, sometimes he fell asleep at the kitchen table only to be awakened by Carla barely in time to shower and get dressed for another day at work. Robby's image of this scene was burned deeply into his mind, and, perhaps, that is why he sought out the carnal pleasures of life so early: he saw life as dead-ended—so why not take what you could whenever you could from whomever was fool enough to let you?

Life in the Ventura household was not unlike that of other middle class working families in this section of Brooklyn except that there was a bit more money available here. The Venturas were by no means wealthy, but did have sufficient income from the rental of the tailor shop to make them reasonably comfortable when others in the neighborhood were still pinched for money to buy eggs and milk. When WW II ended, Vito lost his job in the machine shop that subcontracted work from the larger defense contractors. A skilled machinist, Vito could have become a lead man or foreman, but he hated what he did and cursed himself every day for not having gone into the fuel oil business with his brother, Jabbo. Jabbo opened a fuel oil business in 1942 and made a fortune dealing in black market OPA stamps—stamps that every American needed to present when purchasing fuel oil and gasoline during the war. Vito, a basically honest man, didn't want any part of the crooked racket at that time, so he took the job in the machine shop. With the war ended, however, Vito saw his brother's business continue to grow while his own life turned bitterly sour, especially now that he worked only three or four days each week as a freelancer. Solace came to him only from the ever-present bottle of Four Roses.

One could imagine that Carla Ventura's days would have been as horrible as Vito's, but such was not the case. Whereas Vito was physically unkempt and outspoken in his condemnation of the role dealt to him by society, Carla, petite and neat as a pin, was joyful most of the time. It was an apparent mismatch with Vito squat, hairy, and grumpy and Carla thin, impeccable, and pleasant. One might shudder to think of the sex life they shared, since the two of them just didn't seem to be the least bit compatible. Robby shuddered each time the thought of them in bed together—for whatever reason.

Carla and most of her neighborhood contemporaries did not work outside of the home, but her time at home was truly prime time work. Her oaken floors were polished to a mirror finish, brought to that condition by many long hours on her knees. Her furniture, of average quality, was polished regularly and gave off a deep lustrous sheen. Her kitchen was spotless at all times, even during the height of the various holiday seasons when the kitchen became the center of all family activity. Somehow she managed to mix cakes, roll out dough, make pasta and breads, bottle tomatoes and do all the other chores essential for the 'good life' in Brooklyn without messing up her kitchen. She was efficient at her work and enjoyed all that she had and all that she did. Her life was devoted to her son and her home—though not always necessarily in that order.

When Robby's grades began to slip in grammar school, it was Carla who rebuked him and tried to get him to mend his ways. Robby, affable always, nodded agreement but chose his own path. When it came to selecting a high school, Carla knew beforehand that it would not be possible for him to enter one of the more prestigious technical schools that her friends had talked about. No, he would be destined to attend either a city high school like Lafayette, Boys High, or Manual Training or one of the parochial high schools such as Bishop Loughlin.

She convinced Vito to let Robby go to Bishop Loughlin even though there was a monthly tuition. "Why couldn't he have studied harder?" she thought to herself often—"Then he could have gone to a really good public high school or even gotten a scholarship." Well, it was too late; fortunately, Carla could afford the tuition and a small allowance for Robby.

It wasn't long before Robby 'found' himself and got a part-time job playing drums at local gin mills on weekends. He hadn't had formal training on the drums, but his innate musical ability and good 'ear' served him well. Each weekend from the beginning of his sophomore year in high school, he played drums with friends who had a rag-tag band that consisted of a saxophone, trumpet, guitar, and drums. The fact that Robby was only sixteen years old at the time seemed to have gone unnoticed by everyone including the proprietors of the clubs in which he played.

Playing the drums afforded him two distinct pleasures: first, he met lots of older women—women in their twenties—who lived the fantasy that drummers were persons to be idolized; next, he saw himself as a celebrity—someone who could break out of the old neighborhood and be somebody—really be somebody. Robby's timely meeting with Nick Toscano in Jenny's back room solidified his belief that one had to get out of the neighborhood: otherwise you were destined to run into local punks who would think nothing of jumping you for making time with their girl. He had to get out of the neighborhood, and he knew that the drums were his best, and probably only, ticket out.

When he graduated from high school in 1955, Robby felt free as a bird, expecting to conquer the world as quickly as possible. His high school years had proven to be a great training ground for him for he had become expert at two major occupations: women and drums, and he played hard with both incessantly, caring not at all when something broke—regardless of whether it was a drumstick . . . or a heart. At nineteen years old, Robby felt like many of his peers; he would conquer the world.

Unfortunately, the world had quite a different plan for him as he awakened to the harsh reality that bands were literally a dime a dozen in 1955, and a 'good' drummer could be found on just about any street corner, and a black drummer was more in vogue than a young, white drummer. Nonetheless, he practiced daily at his drums, but even as he improved, the money he made barely kept him going from one weekend to the next. He played the several small clubs in Queens, and those that dotted Flatbush Avenue in

Brooklyn on the way to Reis Park. It was a bitter intellectual struggle for him too, since he really believed that what he was doing was more right for him than working at a job he hated and then coming home each night and sitting at the kitchen table drinking Four Roses from a shot glass. He really believed it. He really did.

As each day unfolded, it turned out to be the same as previous ones: he woke close to noon, had black coffee and buttered toast, didn't shave until the weekend (when he worked), and presented a rather grisly image to anyone visiting his parent's apartment or anyone who saw him swagger through the neighborhood. Carla had given up on him almost totally, and became numb pleading with him about his appearance and his health and the continual arguments and shouting matches when he was home. Vito, seemingly oblivious to the entire affair, went his own way content to spend his nights listening to Fibber M'Gee and Molly or anything else that the radio had to offer so long as it was followed by a whiskey chaser (or two).

As uncommon as it was for a neighborhood boy in those days, Robby had decided to move out: he would leave Brooklyn and take an apartment in Manhattan (after all, he was a musician and musicians needed to be where the action was). "Brooklyn is only stifling me," he fooled himself thinking; "I'll have more of a chance in Manhattan where all the agents are and auditions are held."

Robby bought the latest copies of Variety, Down Beat, and the Village Voice, poring over their pages looking for a cheap apartment to rent. After several weeks of intensive searching, he found a tiny studio apartment on the fringe of Greenwich Village. Though dark and gloomy with only one grimy window that opened half way, it cost forty-five dollars a month—relatively inexpensive when compared with other Manhattan apartments in some of the better, surrounding, neighborhoods. The price, though affordable by many, would really strap Robby since his income ranged from thirty to fifty dollars a week depending on how many gigs he worked. He took the apartment anyway, trusting his destiny to lead him to better things soon.

He continued practicing diligently on his drum pad and eventually secured steady work in Queens and Brooklyn clubs; periodically, he got called to the small girlie strip joints on Fifty-Second Street in Manhattan. His reputation grew, and being physically attractive caused small groups of devoted female night-clubbers to follow him wherever he happened to be playing. He reveled in this attention, and felt comfortable dreaming of himself as another Gene Krupa, Buddy Rich, or even jazz great, Cozy Cole.

He was approached one evening at a Flatbush Avenue club by a middle aged man dressed in a garish blue pin-stripe suit with a black shirt and white tie. He seemed familiar to Robby, though he wasn't sure where he might have seen him before.

"Hi ya, kid," the man said as he approached the band stand during a ten-minute break. "My name is Ziggy Lune—it rhymes with tune! Hey that's a joke . . . and I don't smoke; you're supposed to laugh at that!!"

Robby was taken aback by the strangely forward mannerisms of the odd-looking man. He merely nodded and said, "Hi."

"Look kid, I'm a talent agent, and I've been interested in your act for several weeks now. You may have seen me at some of your gigs in the city." As he spoke he chomped unceasingly on two sticks of spearmint gum, cracking it at every second chew. He appeared like a caricature from a 'B' movie as he handed Robbie his business card and followed him to an empty table near the kitchen.

Robbie looked at the inscription on the card and smiled as he read: LUNE TUNES—MUSICAL TALENT—Ziggy Lune: AGENT.

"It's corny, but it kinda sticks with ya, don't cha think?" He chewed and cracked until it became obviously intrusive, causing Robby to wince in anticipation of every crack of Ziggy's gum.

"What do you want with me?" he asked suddenly wary of the rodent-like person with the red and purple bulbous nose seated across from him.

"Well, Louis Prima's comin' to town for a couple of weeks, and his drummer's wife just had a baby in Canton, Ohio. I've been asked to find a young, good-looking drummer to fill in."

"Are you on the level?" Robby's heart began to race, sensing that if this suited-up rodent-like creature were in fact sincere, then this could be the break of a lifetime.

"Yeah, of course," Ziggy responded. "You think I'd drag myself all the way out her to the end of the world if I wasn't on the up and up?"

"Hot damm!"

When the Prima band arrived in town during the middle of the following week, Robby was escorted to a rehearsal hall located in the basement of the New York Paramount Theater on the corner of Forty-Second Street and Broadway; it was here that he would audition for the job. Nervous, though still very much in control, at nineteen, he was too inexperienced to be intimidated easily—after all, he thought, he was 'only' going to play the drums.

The band director asked him to run through standard drum exercises using a full set of drums. "Piece of cake," he thought until one of the sticks slipped through his fingers and flew through the air. Undaunted, he picked up another stick and continued—now playing with an intensity he had never exhibited before.

When he was done there was gentle clapping and murmurs of "OK, man," and "sweet licks," terms of approval spoken only by pros when they are truly impressed. He got the job.

Robby turned in one outstanding performance after another for the five shows a day. There seemed to be a natural affinity between Robby and the audience who cheered and screamed in delight when he concluded one of his two-and-a-half-minute drum solos. The musicians liked him too since his timing was good—though not perfect—and he performed with a deep respect and appreciation for the other musicians. At the end of the week when the men in the orchestra lined up for their pay, he couldn't believe that he didn't even know how much he was going to be paid—he forgot to ask! All the more was his surprise when he was handed five fifty-dollar bills—two hundred and fifty dollars a week! He couldn't believe it—especially when he realized that all his meals had been free—part of the band's contract with the theater—the drums were in place already, and the audience was always friendly (and never drunk!).

When the band concluded its second week at the Paramount, Robby was given a five-hundred dollar bonus as a special thanks from the band itself. He had performed admirably, and, as always with musicians, they were truly appreciative and showed it. Robby, too, was ecstatic for now he considered himself a real professional, having performed with one of America's leading bands. For two weeks. Anyway, it would look great on his resume!

Robby visited the offices of Ziggy Lune on the Monday after the band left town. He wanted to thank Ziggy and also see what other work was available for him—now that he was a 'star' and had some cash to put aside.

Ziggy Lune had a tiny one-room office not unlike so many others in lower Manhattan that were rented by small businessmen. He had a secretary, several second-hand file cabinets, and two phones each with five pushbuttons; Robby had never seen phones like those. As an agent, Lune was moderately successful and could have become really big time had he altered his style and body language. People didn't feel comfortable in his presence, and business sometimes suffered as a result. Of course, when a top-notch musician was needed, Ziggy was always called first. He had his eye on all the up-and-coming young musicians operating in and around Manhattan; it was his business to know who was good and where they could be reached.

He greeted Robby with a huge grin through which Robby could see the wad of gum being mashed even as he spoke.

"Well, my friend. I hear you really did good—din't cha?"

"Yea, I had a great gig. They liked me."

"Swell, Swell. What can I do for ya now? Lookin' fer more work?"

"Yeah. I was sort of hopin' you could line up somethin' for me."

"Well ya see, kid, I'm not a personal services agent. I don't book jobs or go out lookin'. See, what happens is bands or theaters call me and tell me what they need. That's why you don't hafta pay me no fee or nuttin'. Got it?"

"Oh, I see." Robby felt suddenly deflated, but dared to pursue the quest. "What do you suggest I do now? Get an agent?"

"Well, it ain't my thing, kid, but if I wuz you, I would get some real solid background—like maybe with a network orchestra or somethin'. Know what I mean?"

Robby didn't really understand. "No."

"Well, how old is you anyhow—twenny-tree, twenny-four?"

"Nineteen."

"Nineteen?" Ziggy was incredulous. "Gee kid, I didn't realize you wuz so young. I'll tell you what I t'ink. What you oughta do is hang around New York, get some real experience under your belt with different arrangements and styles—say maybe tree, four years—and den you can call your own shots. Drummers is in big demand, but only wit' a background dat shows you put in your time.

"There's a lot of rock and roll groups starting up too," Robby interjected . . .

" . . . dey ain't goin' nowhere; dey won't last more'n a year or two. You'll see. It'll pass like other fads. Trust me."

Robby was inclined to believe Ziggy, since his reputation was rock solid. It seemed that everyone in the band had heard of 'Lune's Tunes,' and trusted his choices in musical talent. Why else would they have hired Robby after he lost the drum stick during the tryout?

Ziggy gave Robby some names of musical directors at the local television networks—people he knew but could not contact until they called him first. He was sure that Robby would make some meaningful contacts once he began to look in the right places.

At first, he was put off by secretaries and clerks, and he soon became frustrated since he needed work before all his money ran out. "How do you get a break around here if you can't even speak to someone in authority?" he asked himself each day.

Then, one day in July 1955, just one week before his twentieth birthday, Robby broke through. The young secretary recognized him from the show at the Paramount.

"Say, didn't you play drums with the Prima band a while ago?" She was in awe of this 'famous' person standing before her desk. She got all giggly and began to squirm in her chair.

"Yes, but I'd like to see . . . " Before he could finish she interrupted him.

"Of course," she giggled back at him; "You want to see Sammy Stone." She leaned over and half whispered to Robby, "I'll set up an appointment for you. I hear they're looking for a drummer. And you're so cute too."

"Great!" Robby whispered, ignoring her advances but trying to be polite nonetheless. "When?"

"In a day or two." She was staring up at him glassy eyed as though she were about to swoon.

Robby left feeling better than he had in a long time since now, at least, he had some hope of getting a job. He waited patiently, and on the third day, he received a telegram asking him to report for a tryout at the studio. He dressed, took a cab uptown, and wandered his way through the halls until he found the empty sound stage where auditions were being held. He sat, eagerly waiting until his name was called.

"Mr. Ventura."

"Here!" He exploded out of his seat and raced toward the drum stand. His stomach was churning and he felt a nervousness he had never known before. Even when auditioning for the Prima gig, he retained some sense of cockiness and self-assurance. Now, however, something was different and he may have realized that his entire musical career could very well hinge on how well he did today. As he sat nervously waiting for instructions, he toyed with the drumsticks slowly repeating to himself, "Don't drop the sticks . . . don't drop the sticks . . ."

After waiting for what seemed an hour, an unknown person in the back of the orchestra said, "You may begin whenever you're ready." He did his usual warm-up routine and after thirty or forty seconds began a long, slow drum solo that built in intensity and tempo until his fingers were a blur. He performed for seven minutes at which time he finished with the same flourish of bass and cymbals that had brought him cheers at the Paramount.

The same unknown voice said, "Thank you, Mr. Ventura; I'm afraid we can't use you at this time—we appreciate your coming in today."

Robby was incredulous. "What do you mean, can't use me? What's wrong?"

The unknown voice, arrogant and icy, said, "You missed an eighth beat in your fifth measure."

Robby couldn't believe that anyone could have possibly heard what he himself only thought he had missed. "Are you sure?" he pleaded.

"Young man," the icy voice responded, "it is my business to know! Thank you; good day."

Robby was unable to move, stricken by a 'possible' slip of the stick. "Can I do it over again? I'm sure I can please you . . . "

After another few seconds of interminable silence came the testy reply, "Where did you study, young man?".

"Study? I went to Bishop Loughlin High School." There was an immediate undercurrent of laughter that Robby didn't understand.

"What I meant was," retorted the voice now filled with icy venom, "where__ did__ you__ study__ m-u-s-i-c?" The voice emphasized every word and every letter of the word music.

"Study music? I taught myself. Why . . . ?"

"Oh." A different voice added, "Thank you once again, Mr. Ventura. Perhaps you can try once again when you get some formal training. You understand, I'm sure. Who's next?"

Robby was a broken young man, still too immature to be able to relegate this rejection to its rightful place in his young life. Whereas someone older might have viewed this as just one event in a lifetime of events, Robby felt totally inadequate, not having studied music at the right schools or played with the right groups. He was unable to stratify himself properly: a twenty-year old drummer who had already played with a major band at a world-famous theater. He could not see himself as a budding star who needed professional coaching to make him acceptable to the world of serious musicians. No, instead, he saw himself merely as a failure at twenty, unstudied and rejected.

He dreamed of his father, unshaven, overweight and already drunk.

"Hi, Daddy. Daddy! I said, 'Hi,' daddy!"

"Go to sleep; it's late; you should be in bed now."

"Can I sit on your lap Daddy? I miss you."

"Stupid! Look what you did. You spilled my drink!"

"Don't hit me again, Daddy; I love you." ". . . Mom - -EEEEE!"

On his bed alone that night, Robby tried to put things in perspective but was unable. He began to cry, softly at first and then in deep, heavy sobs. This was not the first time that he had been alone and felt so alone. No. He had felt all of these feelings before.

II

July of 1955 was one of the hottest months in New York City's history, with temperatures into the low 100's for sixteen of the thirty-one days. Summers in New York City are always uncomfortable because of the high humidity and the lack of open spaces for ocean breezes to waft through and thus cool the landscape somewhat. But it was especially unbearable for Robby Ventura this particular summer since he lived in the vise-like grip of a congested neighborhood in a one-windowed apartment that held the heat long into the early morning hours at which time the heat renewed its undaunted invasion of the city. Heat warms. Excessive heat melts, and the residents of the city melted into themselves as the oppressive heat continued unrelenting. Only the occasional limousine with its windows rolled up tightly even hinted at the better days that one could merely hope for.

Robby had not worked since his rejection earlier in the month. His ego, which had supported him thus far, had somehow failed him when he needed it most. Too young, too free, too inexperienced . . . yet still too proud to return home and be revived. He stayed in his room for days on end, semiconscious in his desire to shut out the reality of the now moment. He lay on his bed staring at the ceiling from morning till night, rarely eating, never bathing. He had not shaved for three weeks, and looked no different from the denizens of the Bowery just a few blocks away—having remained in the same clothes he wore to his audition. Oblivious to his own body odor, he failed to understand the retreat made by his landlord when he arrived to collect the rent.

"Good grief, what's happened to you?" he asked, reeling first from the odor and then by the wolf-like visage confronting him.

"Nothing . . . nothing." Suddenly embarrassed Robby stroked his face and his hair, then pawed at his clothes.

"I haven't been well, that's all."

"Oh. Well, I've come for the rent . . . ."

"Yeah—well . . . ah. Can you give me a couple of days? I haven't been working . . . I need a few days, please?"

Robby had only a few crumpled dollar bills left in his pocket: all the money he owned in the world; how was he going to pay his rent? He was in no condition to play the drums right now: he needed to practice. After taking a quick shower to refresh himself, he changed into a clean tee shirt and a pair of jeans, but did not take the time to shave. He then went out and, as he walked the streets of the Village, his head began to clear. He then headed uptown to where he thought his chances would be better to get some immediate work though he had no real sense of where he should go or whom he should visit. He wandered aimlessly at first just to feel the blood begin to circulate through his veins, though always heading north toward the action center of the city. When he got to Twenty-Third Street, he was tired and hungry, familiar feelings that helped to make him feel good again: "At least I'm alive," he thought. He crossed from the south side of the street, and spied a familiar pizza stand on the northwest corner of Broadway and Twenty-Third: it was crowded with young people obviously trying to eat fast and do other things while on their short lunch breaks. He ordered a slice of pizza; it was fifteen cents. The slice arrived and Robby spent a few seconds letting the aroma fill his senses. It was hot, so he took a small bite and let the warmth of the crispy slice fill his mouth before he began to chew. As he slowly chewed, his taste buds kicked in and saliva enveloped his pizza and then his entire mouth. It felt marvelous, and he chewed it even more slowly savoring each chew. He took a second bite but made this one a real bite. It was so good that he uttered a long, almost imperceptible moan as he became almost intoxicated with this culinary delight. "Umm - ummmm. . . ," he mumbled just a little bit too loud as he finished the last piece and began licking his fingers clean and wiping his mouth with a too-small paper napkin.

"Good pie, isn't it?" a gentle voice from behind said to him.

Robby turned to notice an attractive young woman, close in age to him, with long, straight blond hair and a bandana around her forehead.

"Yes it is. I've . . . uh . . . eaten here once or twice."

Suddenly, Robby couldn't help feeling self-conscious about his appearance, but as he tried to invent excuses that made sense, he realized that she was smiling at him, apparently oblivious to his still bedraggled appearance.

"You work around here?" she asked him while taking what seemed to him to be extraordinarily tiny, dainty, bites from her slice of pizza.

"No. Actually, I'm looking for work." He hesitated a few seconds before adding, " I'm a drummer and I'm in between jobs."

"A drummer; really?" She glowed with excitement.

"Yes." It seemed like maybe now was a good time to boast as he began to feel his ego begin its resurrection. "I play . . . well, I mean I've played with the Louis Prima band."

"Cool!" she said with admiration and growing excitement.

"Yeah, it was great, but they've gone on tour, and I prefer staying in New York." He tried to create an air about himself that indicated that it was his choice to remain behind.

"I can understand that."

"So I'm looking for some fill-in work until my . . . my agent calls me."

"Why don't you talk to my boss. We always need help. The pay isn't so great but it's a no-pressure job and everybody is real nice. And, if necessary, you can even make your own hours;

they are just happy to have reliable people working there. And the work never ends so you can stay on as long as you like."

Robby was surprised by what she had been saying since it seemed an ideal job for him and others who had unusual schedules. "Where do you work?" he asked her.

"Right around the corner here: the library's newspaper division. We catalog and store newspapers from the 1800's to the present; our reading room is always full of graduate students working on a thesis or something scholarly."

"Do you think they could use me? I sure could use some money right now." He felt the anticipation grow within him as she led him around the corner to the four-story loft where she worked.

As they walked along, Robby could not help notice the slim yet firm body of this delightful young woman who had befriended him. Almost imperceptibly, he felt a familiar stirring in his loins that somehow had been absent for much too long. Standing about five feet four, she was the perfect height—he thought. But his amorous intentions were quickly deferred: getting a job was foremost on his mind now.

It wasn't like any library he had ever seen before: it was grimy and poorly lit, with old and scarred mahogany tables in the reading room. The stacks surrounded the reading room, giving one the impression that this was more a dungeon than a library. Dust hung everywhere: from the books, the bare incandescent bulbs, on the windows—it even smelled strange with a pungent irritation that filled his nostrils with every breath.

"When can you start?" asked the administrator.

"How's tomorrow morning?"

"Fine. Wear your old clothes."

"You're kidding, right?" Robby smiled and was somehow strangely excited as he felt certain that something was happening to him and he had absolutely no control over the outcome. HE HAD A JOB!!

Robby cleaned himself up that evening, savoring the warmth of the stinging needle spray of the shower. When he shaved, he left the right side unshaved for several hours, sneaking glances at himself in whatever mirror he happened to pass. He thought of home momentarily, but dismissed any ideas of calling. He then reflected on that afternoon and the pizza and the girl whose name he didn't know. "God sure deals with me in strange ways," he thought.

As he lay in bed that night, he traveled back to his grammar school days—days that were fun-filled and never serious—days of playing ring-a-leav-e-o, box ball, skelly—days when he would walk along Eastern Parkway with friends and make fun of old people sitting on the park benches. He thought of his first trip to the Brooklyn Museum and how he snickered while he and his friends stared wide eyed in disbelief at statues of nude men and women. He also remembered being brought with his third grade class to the Public Library on Grand Army Plaza and seeing thousands of books on shelves for the first time. "How can I pick a book?" he used to say—"there are so many."

But now he lay alone, practically penniless, in a city that could at once be warm and kind or cold and indifferent. Where was he headed; what lay in store?

His arrival at the library the next morning was greeted by a group of young people already queued up, waiting for the doors to open. The young woman from the day before was sitting on the step, and rose when she saw him approach.

"Hi. Wow, you certainly look different. I almost didn't recognize you." She was beaming at him.

"I like to scare people when I meet them for the first time. This way I can find out what they're really like."

"You're bad," she said feigning a punch, but smiling at him all the while.

Robby's eyes examined her more closely now, and he felt more of that familiar stirring within him. As he catalogued her features, he couldn't help staring at her magnificent blue eyes and perfect, clear skin. When he realized she was aware of his staring, he apologized sheepishly, looking down at his shoes like a little boy caught sneaking cookies before dinner, and said, "I'm sorry—I don't even know your name."

My name is Ellen," she replied with a lilt in her voice and a pixie-like smile on her face. "Ellen Kilkenny."

"Robby. Robby Ventura. I'm Italian." When he said those last two words, he wanted to die on the spot. "Why did I say that," he screamed to himself with his inside voice. "What does she care if I'm Italian?" He paused, looking at her waiting for some response, but she merely smiled at him and made him feel 'gooshy' all over. He felt like a school boy once again, and he had only just met this girl.

Ellen made him feel so totally relaxed that the feeling of sneaking cookies was soon replaced with one of total acceptance and trust. "What a girl this is," he thought; "I never met anyone like her before." And as he continued thinking about how he felt about her, he came up with only one word: comfortable. Yes, that was it; comfortable. She made HIM feel comfortable in the same way that he felt when his mother comforted him after he bruised a knee or when some schoolroom bully made him cry when he was young.

"Comfortable. It's nice to feel comfortable. I like to feel comfortable. I like that Ellen makes me feel this way."

As he pondered the word, he realized that when he thought about Ellen 'comfortable' meant so much more than the word itself connoted. He felt peace when he was with her. He felt totally relaxed and able to be himself without any masks. He . . . he trusted her. Yes! He trusted her in ways he had only trusted his mother and special, close friends. Yet, somehow these feelings were different, better, more intense. Although he couldn't explain precisely what he felt, he liked it a lot. He really liked how he felt . . . about her.

Robby's days soon became filled with hard work and physical labor as he unloaded yellowed, dusty, old newspapers from a never-ending stream of panel trucks, and placed them into the coffin-like bins that he shuttled to the upper floors in the ancient elevator that had no door! Besides not having a door, the elevator didn't have buttons or any type of control handle to start or stop its ascent or descent. The operator, wearing the heaviest leather gloves Robbie had ever seen, pulled on a one-inch-thick steel cable that ran from the basement through the elevator floor and ceiling to a giant electric motor on the roof. He pulled down on the cable to start the elevator in the up direction and pulled up on the cable to halt the elevator. Pull too hard when you want to stop and the elevator immediately reverses direction and may cause the motor on the roof to jam. It was scary at first being in such an ancient machine, watching the cable move inches away from you as the car traveled up and down past large, faded numbers painted on the walls in front to identify the next floor above or below. But the fear left him after a few dozen rides up and down, and he gained confidence in the operator's ability to grab onto the cable and make the elevator do his bidding, stopping almost level with the floor he selected. It always took a few extra tugs on the cable to line up the floor and the elevator precisely so Robby could roll off his heavy cart without too much of a struggle. Then he thought, "I wonder if Mr. Otis installed this elevator himself!"

He couldn't stop thinking of Ellen, and that she had been sent by God to be with him at this time; maybe, perhaps, it was a sign that his life was about to change.

Ellen and Robby took lunch together each day with some of the other library workers. They were becoming good friends though they hadn't formally dated each other. Ellen shared that every penny she earned went for dancing lessons: her dream was to dance on Broadway. She already had some small parts in several plays, but nothing that paid any real money yet. In fact, she hadn't even saved enough money to pay the dues for Actor's Equity.

One evening about a month after beginning work at the library, Robby and Ellen were walking down the steps and out onto Twenty-Third Street. Never one to be embarrassed around women, Robby couldn't understand why he was unable to come right out and ask Ellen for a date. He had wanted to ask her for a long time, but couldn't bring himself to actually say the words. This evening, he promised himself, things would be different.

"Ellen," he said as they strolled along the sidewalk.

"Yes, Robby." She glanced at him momentarily as she responded, while they both headed toward Broadway.

"Do you like Frank Sinatra?"

"Is the Pope Italian? Of course; who doesn't? Why?"

"Well there's a movie I'd like to see, and Frank sings the opening theme. I thought maybe you'd like to go with me."

Ellen laughed to herself at his coyness, hardly believing that he was having such a difficult time asking her out—but she was glad he did.

"Sure. When would you like to go?"

"There's an eight o'clock show at the Majestic; I can pick you up about seven, if that's OK."

"That's fine; I'll be ready."

"Great! See you later." Robby was glad that the ordeal was finally over, and rushed across the street to where his bus would arrive. He heard his name.

"Robby! Robby! Wait!" It was Ellen. She was crossing the street, waving at him. When she got to him, she looked into his eyes wistfully and said, "You don't know where I live; do you??"

Robby, hanging his head in mock despair, looked up with a cocked head and said, "You must think I am some kind of nut. I'm sorry. I . . ."

She interrupted him realizing his awkward feelings and quickly scribbled her address on a piece of paper.

Robby and Ellen saw each other often following their first date, but Robby never made a move on Ellen other than to give her a simple peck on the cheek good night. One Friday evening as Robby prepared to leave his apartment to get Ellen for a date, his doorbell rang. It was Ellen at the bottom of the staircase; she had her arms full of grocery bags that she struggled to carry up the stairs to meet him.

"Here, let me help you," he said as he raced down the stairs.

"Thanks; I almost dropped everything."

"What are you doing here anyway? We're supposed to be going over to Central Plaza tonight."

"I thought I'd cook instead." She began to empty the bags on the table, Robby absentmindedly helping her.

"But, you shouldn't have gone to all this trouble."

"It wasn't trouble." She searched for pots and pans. "Don't you ever cook?"

"Only sometimes; what do you need?"

"I've got to boil some water, make a salad. Got any vinegar?"

"Ellen, listen; you don't have to do this. We can eat out . . . ."

"We always eat out, and I think we should have a home-cooked meal tonight. Are you OK with that?" She smiled at him so lovingly that he almost melted into the floor. His heart must have missed a beat or two.

She looked at him semi-seriously, but concerned that she had hurt his feelings.

"No—of course not." He felt apologetic and a need to express his appreciation for her thoughtfulness. "It's just that you've gone out of your way, and I know you can't afford it any more than I can. I haven't spent any real money on you either . . . and you've gone out shopping and bought all this food . . . and you want to cook for me too. You—you're really special."

While she was unpacking some remaining items, she smiled and said, "I like you too . . . you're a nice guy."

He moved closer to her and took her hands into his. As they looked directly into each other's eyes, Robby felt himself begin to warm to her touch, and though he felt the urge to pursue her, he withdrew.

At a comfortable distance, he found it easier to say, "I like you, Ellen. I mean, I like you a lot. I really do." He was perspiring heavily.

She set down the remaining groceries and ambled across the floor to him, and, taking him by the hand, led him to the threadbare couch that doubled as his bed. They sat at the edge. Reaching for his other hand, she squeezed it gently and placed them both on her lap. Robby's heart was pounding, Ellen persisted in controlling the moment. "We have a good time together, right?" He nodded his assent, his face now fully flushed. "You like it when we're close, don't you?" Again, he nodded. "I like it when we say, 'Good night' and you kiss me gently on my cheek."

"I like that too," he whispered ever so softly but thinking of how much more he wanted from the relationship.

"Do you think we could ever be more than good friends, Rob?"

"Of course; of course! I want us always to be . . . friendly."

"I really care about you . . . and . . . if you care about me as you say you do . . . then . . . well, it's really hard for me to get this out, but . . ." She breathed deeply and said somewhat candidly while averting her eyes, " I like you . . . and you like me . . . so . . . then why haven't we made love yet?"

Robby's heart almost burst through his chest as he heard those words: "Why haven't we made love yet?" No woman had ever said those words to him before; in fact—he didn't believe that any woman had ever said those words to any man. After his immediate reaction of shock and disbelief—Robby felt a sudden disappointment. "This could not be the Ellen I know," he thought. Not knowing how to respond to her query—and to give himself some time to think, he ran from the couch and turned away momentarily. Just as quickly, he turned back to her, and—in an affected, mocking tone—repeated, "Why haven't we made love yet? Why . . . why haven't we made love?" He was struggling for time—time to think. "I'll tell you why we haven't made love. The answer is . . . the answer is BECAUSE . . . ."

He tried to gather himself and return the situation to its former, somewhat more normal, state. He sat down next to her, held her hands in his, and took several really deep breaths.

"What kind of question is that for a nice girl to ask?"

Ellen's reaction was one of rejection and hurt, and Robby sensed it immediately so he continued with a lighter, more jovial attitude. "What kind of boy do you think I am . . . anyway? You think I'm easy or something?"

He saw Ellen relax at his now-obvious humor, and this made Robby relax also.

Acting the clown, he joked, "Do you think you can come up here and cook me a meal and then think that you own my body?" He thrust his fist to his chest in a Shakespearean sort of way and continued, "What kind of a boy do you think my mother raised?"

He had hoped that all his joking would somehow change the original content of what he thought Ellen had desired of him. He wanted to believe that he had misunderstood her. With all his heart he prayed that she was only teasing him.

As Ellen began to laugh at his antics, Robby felt the pressure of the moment ease, and expected her to continue preparing the meal. Somehow Ellen's laughter became contagious, and Robby was soon laughing just as heartily as she, with tears streaming down his cheeks. She walked over to him and put her arms around his neck, but he was laughing so hard he hardly heard her whisper, "Make love to me, Robby."

III

As they lay beside each other, Robby's thoughts were co-mingled with questions and doubts. Ellen was truly someone special—a person who had evoked strange and wondrous feelings within him—a person with whom he thought he could spend the rest of his life. He had often considered marriage to her, but since the moment of his 'seduction' he had become uncertain about what she really felt for him and doubted whether he could ever marry her now. "She certainly isn't like Mom," he thought.

He had supposed that she was a virgin, and had treated her as such up until the first time they made love. The fact that she wasn't surprised him, but not so much as the reaction he felt about someone else having been with her. The "special-ness" of Ellen waned, and Robby found it impossible to reconcile his thoughts and judgments with his feelings. Now, lying next to her, though he felt strangely peaceful and relaxed, he was unsure that he could ever truly love a woman who had previously given herself to someone else. "Why do I have to deal with this," he thought, "I want her; I feel like telling her that I love her; yet can I trust her? Is she easy—can she be faithful to me? I wanted to make love to her, but I didn't; I decided to wait: you're not supposed to touch the girl you might marry. And then she asks me! You can't just come out and ask a guy . . . you can't do that." That's the way it was in the neighborhood. Apparently.

Looking at her dozing beside him, he prayed for the divine gift of wisdom so that he would be able to do what was right. If all he had to deal with now was raw passion, he wouldn't have had a problem: Ellen turned him on right from the first moment he saw her—and now, even more so. If only he could get his head and his heart operating on the same wavelength. He stroked her body and kissed her lightly on her lips, warming to the sensations that began anew; with all his power, he stifled the overwhelming desire to mouth the words, "I love you" which seemed determined to pour forth. He withdrew from her side, and lay back on his pillow, pensive. After a long while, she began to stir. He spoke, "Ellen?"

"Yes, Rob . . . ."

"I enjoyed that a lot."

"I'm glad; so did I."

" . . . Ellen?"

"Umm, what?" She snuggled closer to him, her fingers twirling the few hairs he had on his chest.

"Did you ever go horseback riding?"

"Sure. Why?"

"Did you ever fall off?"

"No, silly. Why?"

"No reason . . . wanna eat?"

She demurred, "Not yet. Do you think we might be able to . . . do it . . . again?" She looked lovingly into his eyes, her face glowing from deep within. She kissed him slowly, with a controlled passion that kept building and building. Robby responded in kind, quickly dismissing any idea of food or horses.

In the days that followed, they spent every spare moment together, sometimes even staying overnight at each other's apartments. Ellen had been selected recently for a small part in the chorus of an off-Broadway musical that was scheduled to open in September, and Robby had booked some pick-up dates with small bands in New York City. The money he made from the library went for music lessons, since he was committed to becoming a skilled musician as well as a fantastic stick man. And he learned his lessons well, soon being able to arrange music and transpose as well as some of his older contemporaries.

Soon, both Ellen and Robby began to make some real money. Ellen thought it best to talk openly about the time when they would move into an uptown apartment and set up a home. Robby purposely avoided the subject of marriage, since he was still troubled about Ellen's former 'liaisons.'

One evening, in a cab heading to Ellen's theater, Robby felt compelled to broach the delicate subject again.

"Have you had many boyfriends, Ellen?"

"No, not at all; just some casual flirtations. Is there some reason you're asking me about this now?"

"I'm curious . . . maybe a little jealous too."

"Jealous? Of what?" Ellen began to bristle, wondering where this conversation was headed.

Robby was entering dangerous territory. "Calm down." It was almost an order. "I just want to know about any other . . . lovers you may have had . . . you know."

Stunned, she retorted, "No, I don't know." She was furious with him. "Haven't you gotten to know me at all these past months?

"Yes, but . . . ."

"But what? Are you disappointed because I wasn't a virgin for you? Is that what this is all about? Did I ask you about how many 'tomatoes' you banged while you were tom-cattin' around?"

" . . . Ellen, I—."

"I thought we had something beautiful between us. I thought you loved me—." She paused as her eyes filled with tears. "Damn . . . .! You're making me ruin my makeup."

"Ellen, please . . . try to understand." She was sobbing now, dabbing at her eyes with a tissue.

"You don't trust me, do you? That's it, isn't it? You think I'm the type that flits around from one person to another each month?" she said emphatically.

" . . . Ah—it's not . . . "

Robby bit his lip not knowing what to say next. He was torn between his own feelings and what he was doing to Ellen's feelings

"It isn't that I don't trust you; it's just that I was totally unprepared for someone like you. Please don't cry, Ellen." Robby fought back tears now as he realized for the first time how foolish he had been. He pulled her to him and kissed her tears. She relaxed at his touch.

"Ellen, I . . . love . . . you. I want to marry you—if you'll have me."

She put her head on his shoulder and wept for a few more minutes before settling back in her seat, trying to fix her spoiled makeup. When the cab pulled up in front of the theater, she held his arm down, indicating that she didn't want him to follow her inside. He tried to force himself out of the cab, but she insisted.

"Don't Rob."

" . . . Ellen—I'm really . . . ."

"Please, Rob; I want to be alone. OK?"

Sheepishly, he asked, "Will you call me?"

She didn't answer as she turned and ran toward the stage entrance.

ROBBY / CARLA

I

Ellen was destroyed by Robby's insensitivity and couldn't bring herself to forgive him. She, like he, had never been in love before, and was disappointed that what they shared didn't result in a lasting relationship. She ached when she thought about him and his magical transformation from the first time she saw him at the pizza stand on Twenty-Third Street. She had seen through that grizzled exterior to the real Robby—the sensitive and caring young man that she had grown so quickly to love. How could he be so base now—to judge her—presume that she was the type of woman who had slept around? That's what he really thought, she believed. Hadn't her actions spoken loudly enough? Apparently not.

Robby longed to hold her once again, sorry for the pain he caused her though certain that it would be unseemly for him to call her—at least until she had time for her feelings to heal. He buried himself in his work—studying by day, working by night—hoping that she would call him. He booked jobs seven days a week now, earning more money than ever though spending none of it except for food and other basic needs. He kept track of Ellen and was pleased when he read that her show had opened to rave reviews. He put on a fake beard one night and sat in the last row of the orchestra just so he could see her dance. She was so beautiful, and yet—her eyes didn't seem to shine the way they once did. She seemed somewhat aloof and just the slightest bit tentative. And still—he yearned passionately to hold her and touch her, wanting to restore within himself the deep inner peace he felt when they were close. But something deep within prevented him from stepping forward. The time was not yet right.

The Macy's Thanksgiving Day Parade was an event Robby had only viewed on television, but this year he determined to stand in the crowd and experience it first hand. He called home on Thanksgiving morning and told Carla to look for him on the TV. She laughed.

"Sure! With fifty-thousand people, you expect me with bifocals to see Robby Ventura on a twelve-inch screen."

He laughed with her, missing the old days in Brooklyn. He had grown up fast—much too fast.

"Ma?"

"Yes?"

"I'm coming home for Christmas. Have ya got room for me? I need a break from work—and other things. I just want to hang out—maybe see some of the old gang."

"Of course I've got room. You're making me cry right now I'm so happy. What do you want to eat? I'll make whatever you want: cioppino, ravioli, manicotti, cavatelli! Everything homemade!"

II

He opened the outside door to his former home and selected the familiar bell on the panel in the vestibule. He rang the bell five or six times in rapid succession, a signal he had used while still in grammar school to let Carla know that it was he. He waited, but there was no familiar buzz at the inside door to let him in. He rang the bell again with his special signal, pushing against the inner door waiting for the buzzer to click the lock and let him in. The outside door was propped open with his suitcase so he heard when the familiar voice called from two stories above.

"Who is it? Is someone ringing my bell?" He walked outside and looked up to Carla's front window to see her proudly hanging out the window, her hair neatly groomed, shouting so that all the neighbors could hear.

"Who is it? Who's there?"

Robby laughed to himself saying, "Things never change, do they?" He shouted loudly from inside the doorway, "Ma! It's me. Your son, Robby."

"Oh! It's my son, Robby. Come right up; I'll buzz you in."

Her brief tour de force completed, she raced into the kitchen to buzz him in and then ran half way down the stairs to greet him, tears flowing freely from the eyes of a loving mother and her aching child.

"Let me take your suitcase . . . ."

"No; I've got it. It's too heavy for you."

"Who do you think carries things when you're not here? Your father?" She tossed her head and muttered a familiar grunt that let Robby know she was—as always—displeased with her husband's performance—as a husband.

"Ma! I can carry it . . . really . . . ." She conceded, happy to let him.

The apartment looked no different from when he left it ten months ago: everything still polished and bright. He walked through the familiar rooms one at a time remembering the pictures, odds and ends, the television set. He felt at home. He felt 'comfortable.' He liked being home. He liked being loved. He also missed Ellen.

Carla helped Robby settle into his old room, proud to see how well he looked—and that his clothes were clean and pressed; she liked how nice his clothes fit him.

"You buy all these clothes yourself?" she asked.

"Who would help me, Ma?"

"Well . . . they look nice. You sure some girl didn't come along to help you pick out colors and get the right size? You never bought your own clothes when you lived here."

"That's because I had you, Ma." He kissed her on the cheek hard.

"Ain't nobody like your mother, you know! Am I right?" She asserted her role as Mom!"

"I know, Ma."

Robby had a large shopping bag that contained a box about fourteen inches square. Carla eased it out of the bag and onto Robby's bed. "Be careful with that, Ma; it's my new phonograph."

"Phonograph? It's too small to play records. C'mon, what is it? You tell me."

Robby opened the box and carefully set it on the dresser. He then opened a bag with phonograph records—tiny ones with large holes in the center.

"What are they?" Carla asked quizzically.

"They're new types of records, Ma. They're called 45 RPM. It's the latest thing!"

"Show me; I don't believe you." She thought he was teasing her, and was happy that she could feel so close to him.

But Carla couldn't believe it when Robby turned on the 45 RPM player and it played real music. She stared at the disk spinning ever so slowly.

"I don't believe it! The world is moving too fast for me." She watched and listened for a few more moments and then left him and went into the kitchen to continue with dinner.

"How's Pop?" he shouted to her a few minutes later from his room.

"Pop is Pop; he's got his good days, and he's got his bad days. You want a big salad?"

"Sure . . . Err, no cucumbers, remember? What time does Pop get home?"

"I remember, all right. I'm still your mother, you know. In about a half hour."

When Vito got home, he rang the bell; it was almost six-fifteen. Robby jumped from his bed and smoothed his hair. He snaked his way into the kitchen and pushed the buzzer that unlocked the front door downstairs. The familiar sound of his father's footsteps on the stairs was unmistakable, and Robby's heartbeat quickened as he thought about the upcoming encounter.

He opened the kitchen door just as Vito reached the top step of the landing, and walked into the hall to greet his father.

"Hi ya, Dad."

"Heh . . . my son has come home . . . finally. You remembered where we live, eh?"

Robby extended his hand, but Vito just looked at it. Then, after what seemed like minutes but in actuality was just a few seconds, he said, "Maybe . . ." He paused. " . . . maybe we need something a bit stronger than a handshake—you and me—eh?" Slowly Vito opened his arms wide and enveloped Robby in a bear hug, taking him totally by surprise.

"I missed you Dad," Robby whispered in his father's ear. "I've missed you a lot."

As they walked into the apartment, arm in arm, Robby thought he detected the slightest trace of a tear in Vito's eyes.

Earlier in the afternoon, Carla made a batch of home-made fettuccini (she called them home-mades), a large salad and pork braciole. This was the first real meal Robby had since . . . since

Ellen cooked for him in September. He missed Ellen more now than he ever had when he was in the city; just being with his family filled him with a desire to have someone of his own to love. That someone was Ellen.

"Robby—eat!" Carla insisted when she saw him staring at his plate.

"Sorry." He ate, but not with the same gusto of days past; his mind was preoccupied. His thoughts were . . . of Ellen.

ROBBY / DONNY

I

Robby's first night home went well; the meal was excellent and the conversation nonthreatening. To Robby, it felt as though he had never left. He decided to join Vito in front of the TV and watch the late movie at 11:30. Somehow watching the lead-in to the film seemed boring, but he noted that Vito's eyes were glued to the screen as he sat zombie-like in his old, well-used, over-stuffed-with-horsehair, all-leather, Morris chair, which was still covered with plastic seat covers. The film, a 'B' movie, was old, fuzzy, and difficult to hear, but it didn't seem to bother Vito at all: tonight he drank high balls made with Carstairs rye whiskey and ginger ale.

After about twenty minutes, Robby got bored with the 'silly' film and excused himself. "G'night Dad," he said as he passed in front of Vito.

"Mmm-mmmph," Vito grunted in response.

Carla, still puttering around in the kitchen, heard the door to Robby's room open, and then the muffled sounds of 'Because of You' playing on his new phonograph. Robby himself appeared moments later in his pajamas, and gave Carla a big hug.

"I love you, Mom; it's good to be home again."

"This will always be your home, you know."

"I know. Good night."

"Sleep tight." And to herself in a prayerful whisper she said, "Figlio mio" (my son) as she made the sign of the cross over his head.

II

The next day, Monday, was four days before Christmas, and the weather was clear and crisp, the temperature well up into the 40's. Carla made Robby a huge breakfast of homemade pork sausage patties (she ground her own pork—twice), pancakes and sunny-side-up, large, right-from-the-chicken-market, eggs. Robby noted how joyful Carla was to be fussing over him using just about every black-iron skillet she had to prepare this morning's feast.

"Mom, your cookin's the best," he said as he devoured the delicious sausage made from 100% prime pork butts. "There ain't no cooking like Mom's cooking," he smiled to himself.

"Eat! Eat!" You got so skinny while you was away. I wanted you would come home so I could take good care of you."

He knew she spoke only out of concern for him, so he let his own feelings fall away.

"You need a woman to take care of you," she continued; "maybe you should get married. You meet any nice Italian girls in New York?"

"Ma! Let's not get into that, OK?" He began to get a little upset, but quickly let it pass. "Nobody makes sausages like you, Mom." He wanted to change the subject, and Carla fully realized what he wanted.

"I still grind my own pork, by hand, ya know."

"It's too much work, Ma."

"Ehh; when I die, you'll never get this again. You think young girls today are gonna do this? You got some case. They don't give a hoot."

He smiled listening and missing hearing her speak her familiar phrases again. "Ma, I'll never marry a girl unless she promises to grind her own pork—by hand, twice—and make me sausages at least once a week. And . . . I'll make sure she gives a hoot!"

"Ha!" she chortled, "You got some case! . . . girls today . . . ehh." Her voice trailed off with the thought hanging.

After breakfast, Robby felt happy and peaceful, having thought of Ellen only a half dozen times since the night before. He showered and shaved and dressed in his Levi jeans, rolled up the too-long pant legs, and pulled on his old 'Loughlin' High School jacket. He strode into the kitchen and hugged Carla tightly. "I'm going to take a long walk—see who's around or home from school. Is Dad off today?"

"He's off until after the first." She looked sad, reflecting on the way things were in the past. "Now he'll sleep late, get up grouchy, have a couple-a shots of whiskey, and walk down to the barber shop and stay there until dinner." She sighed in disgust. "But that's not your problem. Will you be home for lunch? Should I make you something you missed? Hmm?" Oh, how she loved her son; but something was bothering him—she could tell. Mothers always knew.

"I don't think so; I'll probably get something at Otto's or at one of the deli's along Washington Avenue."

She let him go with, "Be careful." Again to herself, she murmured, "Figlio mio," and made the sign of the cross over him as he turned to leave.

III

As Robby left the apartment building, he hesitated for a moment, deciding whether to head south on Classon Avenue, which was his usual route out of the neighborhood, or walk the hundred feet north to Dean Street and double back. With no plan in mind and not knowing why, he headed north and turned west on Dean Street. He remembered the line of twenty locked garages at this end of the street; they housed trucks and nonperishable goods for many of the local merchants. He had to wait a few moments for an ice truck that was backing into Pillechio's ice house. He watched while the workmen removed layers of wet burlap from dozens of cakes of ice that lay on the open-bed trailer that dripped its melting cargo onto the sidewalk. He waved and said, "Hi" when one of the icemen looked up and nodded recognition when he saw Robby standing adjacent to the old, wooden truck body. Although there was still a slight chill in the air, both icemen were sweating profusely after only a few minutes.

He smiled to himself as memories the ice dock flooded his mind. Only the 'big' boys could hang out around the ice dock because of the danger of the trucks coming in and out and the 'adult' talk used among the various workmen. But Robby and some of the more courageous boys managed to sneak in a few minutes now and then. He remembered one time, while sitting off to the side of the ice dock several years before, he overheard a discussion of when Jimmy 'Cigar' Ryan's sister, Betty, did it in the park with Johnny Pegano and Dominick Nicoletti for seventy-five cents each. How naïve he was then, he thought, not even knowing what doing it meant. It wasn't that long before he caught on to what Betty actually did with Johnny and Dominick that night.

The ice men had lots of ice to unload, so Robby walked out into the street and around the truck to hear the unmistakable sound of a Spaulding rubber ball being thrown against a cement wall. Adjacent to the ice house was 920 Dean Street, a six-family apartment house whose front yard was bordered on one side by the projection of Pillechio's ice house. It was against this wall that Robby saw Donny Gargano throwing the Spaulding (always called Spaldeen). Donny smiled broadly as he spied Robby walking around the truck and onto the sidewalk.

"Hey cuz," Donny shouted as he walked quickly toward the low brick wall that enclosed the tiny front yard. He thrust out his hand and asked, "How've you been? Long time no see."

It was a chance meeting of two old friends who had known each other from before grammar school days. "Stay right there," Robby said as he put his hands firmly on the brick wall and attempted to leap-frog over. But he failed and only landed on his shoulder causing both Donny and him to laugh out loud. "I never could do that," he said smiling as he got up and brushed himself off.

"Other than almost breaking my neck," Robby continued, "I've been good, really good," and he began pumping his friend's hand heartily and seating himself on the low brick wall. "The landlady gonna yell if I sit on here?"

Donny raised his eyebrows and said, "Usually, but she spent the weekend on Long Island and hasn't come home yet."

Donny tossed Robby the rubber ball, which he then began to bounce on the ground while the two friends talked about days gone by. Robby noted that Donny had on his heavy TECH jacket, which he had bought while attending Brooklyn Tech. He remembered that he could have gone there too—if . . .

"I guess we both can't give up our high school jackets," Robby said.

"Nah. It's like a trademark. I guess we'll always remember our high school days as some of the best times ever."

"We did have some fun times didn't we?" They both laughed, remembering some of the scrapes they had gotten into together and out of too.

Donny rolled his eyes in a Groucho Marx-like manner and said. "I think you had a bit more fun than I did," alluding to Robby's reputation as a ladies' man.

"Maybe."

Donny couldn't help but drift off for a moment and recall just how different their 'pubesce-ing' years were. Donny was sort of shy and naïve, though in those days the word would probably have been innocent. Yes, Donny was innocent of many of the facts of life that Robby had come to discover so early on. And yet their friendship flourished despite the gap in their worldliness.

Donny recalled how he had shared with Robby about the first party he was invited to by one of the Rossford girls on Underhill Avenue. Robby had laughed when Donny explained about how all the parents were in the kitchen and the boys and girls were three rooms away sitting on the floor in the parlor playing Monopoly. And then one girl finished her bottle of Pepsi and twirled it around in front of her on the floor. When it stopped and pointed to Donny, everyone cheered and the girl stood up and extended her hand to Donny. And he sat there and extended his hand back to her and shook it. Everyone giggled and told Donny that he had to go into the closet with the girl and get a present. So in he went and asked the girl what she had for him. "Don't you like girls?" she asked him in the darkness of the closet. "Of course I like girls; what do you mean?" Frustrated, she reached out with her hand, found his face, and pecked him with a kiss. She left him there in the closet and rejoined the group on the floor saying, "One of you other boys spin now."

Donny chuckled to himself as he remembered that incident and how Robby had to explain to him why they had gone into the closet. "Oh," he remembered saying and how he relived that closet scene in his dreams for many nights after that. The dreams were often better than the peck on the cheek in the closet.

He snapped back to the reality of the present moment as he heard Robby calling his name, "Donny . . .Donny! Hey, man—you off in space somewhere?"

"Naw; I was just daydreaming about that time I was at the Rossford girl's party and they played spin the bottle. Remember?"

"Do I!!' Robby slapped Donny on the back and then playfully started punching him and rubbing his head. "Boy, were you somethin' in those days!"

Donny enjoyed Robby's playful attitude; he missed the many intimate sharings they had had over the years. But now he was more concerned about his hair. "Hey, stop—you'll mess my hair!'

"What hair?? You can't mess up that brush."

Robby stopped and they sort of hugged or came as close as was permitted in those days. Donny's face brightened as he began to laugh out loud: "You know, I may have been naïve in those days, but I wasn't stupid."

"Whadda ya mean?" puzzled Robby.

"Remember the time Ralphie Egan told everybody he felt Gloria's breast?"

Robby recalled the instance immediately and countered, "Yeah; Gloria was her sister's bridesmaid and invited Ralphie along to the wedding as her date."

"And she wore that strapless gown . . ."

" . . . and when Ralphie took her home . . ."

" . . . they were making out in the hallway . . . "

By this time in the story, Donny and Robby were both convulsed in laughter. Donny continued, " And the next day, Ralphie told everybody that he had copped a feel of her right breast.

And when it got back to Gloria, she said the only thing he got a feel of was the wired-up front of her strapless dress and the "iron-maiden" bustier she wore underneath to keep everything from 'falling down!'

"Yeah, Ralphie was a-squeezin' and a-pushin' and the only thing he got wuz blisters from rubbin' on the metal stays holding up Gloria and her dress!!" They both laughed again at the days of innocence gone by that had become memories for these two very young men.

Donny brought them back to the present. "Rob, are you home for a while or just for the holidays?"

"Just till after Christmas; I needed a break from my seven-day-a-week schedule. What about you?"

Donny was a sophomore at CCNY in upper Manhattan and was on a school break that would last well into January. "I've been off since December tenth. You know, study time. We get to study over the holidays for our finals in January. Say, where you headed anyway?"

"Nowhere. Wanna come?"

Donny chuckled knowing that going 'nowhere' with Robby would always be better than going somewhere by himself. "Sure."

Donny turned toward the facade of his building and cupped his hands, shouting up to the empty front window on the second floor. "Ma? Hey Ma, I'm goin' for a walk with Robby. Be back later. OK?"

In an instant, Marie Gargano appeared, waving and mouthing the words, "Be careful."

Robby slid off the wall, while Donny leaped over it onto the sidewalk. As they walked along the street, they passed the many row houses that lined both sides of the street—some with scraggly bushes, others with stunted trees struggling to survive in a 10 x 10-foot front yard. At some curb fronts were scrawny bush-like trees reaching toward sunlight from out of a tiny well in the concrete sidewalk. Strangely, not one house had a single blade of grass growing, other than what grew between the cracked sidewalk cement that erupted wherever a tree root had forced it.

Donny said, "You heard about the Puerto Rican family that moved into 727 didn't you?"

"Into 727?" Robby shook his head. "You're kidding—right?! When?"

Robby's surprise grew from the former, strongly ethnic makeup of this part of Dean Street. For almost forty years, only two ethnic groups lived here: Blacks or Italians. Even more surprisingly, this end of the block had previously been almost exclusively, 100 percent Italian. Mixed in as tenants were one or two Irish or Polish families. Everyone knew everyone else, and there was a welcome sigh of relief when turning into the block coming home late at night. In those days, this was home, and every resident and their guests respected the rights of the people who lived here. It was always a good feeling to come home to Dean Street where 'everybody knew your name.' Even better, everyone knew your mother's name!

Donny continued, "The Palomba's sold their house about three months ago; they moved out to Levittown—on Long Island. The Puerto Ricans who bought it are really nice people. They've got a son, Eugenio; he makes his own kites from wax paper or newspapers. You gotta see 'em!—they are really great. He comes over to my house a lot; he even taught me how to make my own kites. He's also teaching me a few words in Spanish. I don't even know Italian, and now I'm learning Spanish! "

Robby was shaking his head in disbelief. "Wow."

The friends turned south onto Grand Avenue past some idle factories that had turned out machine parts during the war. After another block, they encountered a group of younger boys playing stoop ball—smashing a pink Spaldeen against the rounded steps of their brownstone and hoping it would rebound far enough back into the street to 'make a home run against the opposite sidewalk.' Only very few of the younger boys knew how to smash it to make a home run.

As they continued their walk, Robby couldn't help but notice how much taller and muscular Donny had become. Now a full head taller than Robby, Donny wore his jet black, extremely dense hair in a brush-type crew cut, which, with his horn-rimmed glasses, made him look like a stereotypical Joe College.

"How's school going Don?" Robby inquired. Donny didn't respond immediately, Robby noting the obvious pause. "Everything OK?"

Donny's face reddened a bit as he spoke, " . . . Yeah. Everything's fine. I . . . well, I . . . I sorta switched my major."

Robby chuckled a bit unfazed by Donny's answer. "What do you wanna be now—a nuclear physicist?"

They both laughed, remembering how both of them would play as youngsters pretending to be mad scientists. It was when they both discovered that household bleach was only a five-percent solution of sodium hypochlorite that they had decided to go into business together when they grew up: they were going to manufacture and distribute laundry bleach door to door—just like the salesman for Biancalina Whitening Liquid was doing; they would make a fortune. They often feigned arguing about the name of the business. Robby: "We should call ourselves Ro-Don Enterprises." Donny: "No . . . it should be Don-Ro Industries."

"So what is your new major?" Robby asked.

"Philosophy."

" . . . Philosophy? You can't make money being a philosopher!" Robby was incredulous.

Donny responded very quickly, "I'm going to become a priest."

Robby heard the words, let them sink in for a few seconds before he responded to his friend who had once been as close to him as any brother could be.

"A priest?"

"Yep."

They walked in silence for a few steps, and then Robby spoke again. "Why a priest?"

"You know me," he began. "You know me better than anybody on earth. I think I've got a calling to serve God as a priest. I think I can be a good priest too."

"You can be good at whatever you do," Robby retorted, trying to make some sense out of what his friend was saying, "but you can't get married or . . . ."

Donny smiled, "I know—I know. But that's something I've got to deal with. Hey look—let's not dwell on this now anyway; I've got two years to make up my mind. I want my four-year degree first, and then I'll figure out the rest. Don't sweat."

"Don't sweat? It's not me who's gotta worry about sweatin.' Do you think you can stay celibate?"

Donny began to blush, "We shall see, my friend; we shall see."

IV

They made the left turn up Underhill Avenue past the men's hat factory and the pool hall. Even though it was only ten-thirty in the morning, men were already hanging out, some smoking crooked black Italian cigars or cigarettes and drinking beer. It was much too early to drink wine or whiskey. A few feet further south of the pool hall was Robby's uncle's barber shop.

"Hey, why don't we stop in and say 'Hi' to my uncle Nunzio." He always has a few stories to share."

"Sure." Donny agreed.

Robby's uncle Nunzio was an old-fashioned type of barber who took a good half hour to cut a man's hair. It was nothing like the barber college haircuts that Donny got in the subway stations along the route of the 'A' train in Manhattan. There, for about twenty cents, he got the fastest haircut in America: less than ten minutes start to finish. Sometimes, you even got away without getting your ear snipped by a barber-in-training who was just learning how to use a scissor. And . . . God forbid that Donny should get a shave from a students also learning how to use a straight razor. Arghhh!

Nunzio, on the other hand, made the haircut an experience to be remembered all week long. He used the scissor only, and never used the manual or newly introduced electric trimming machines. He finished up every haircut by shaving the sideburns and nape of the neck after he applied a warm, scented, foam to the area, which relaxed the client. As a special treat, and to ensure a bigger tip, he applied a liberal splash of Bay Rum to the shaved area and then applied a hot towel over the entire face and neck. It WAS an experience. It cost ninety-five cents, but most men who came here gave Nunzio a dollar and a half.

The talk in the barber shop was always completely adult in nature, and, for some of the young boys who came there, it was the first time they heard all the words that remained unspoken at home. In fact, it was here that most of the neighborhood boys learned the sleazy side of the facts of life. Today, however would be a somewhat different.

When Robby entered the shop, his uncle stopped immediately what he was doing and threw open his arms to embrace Robby in a crushing bear hug. "I am so glad to see you! You'll never guess who just left here a few minutes ago." Puzzled, Robby asked, "Who?"

"Gil Hodges!! Gil Hodges just left here and asked me to do him a favor."

"Gil Hodges was here?"

"Yeah, he comes in for a haircut every now and then when it's off season, or the Dodgers are in town."

Gil Hodges was the catcher for the Brooklyn Dodger Baseball Team. He had a palatial home out east on Empire Boulevard in an upscale section of central Brooklyn.

"Did he get his hair cut, Unc?"

"Nah. Just a trim. He really came in to ask me a favor, but now maybe you can help me out."

Robby looked at Nunzio and then at Donny. "You want me to help you out with a favor for Gil Hodges? You kidding me or what!?"

"No kiddin' at all. Listen. He had to leave his car here because he has an award dinner to go to in the city, and his wife needs the car later. He took a cab into Manhattan. He wants me to drive his car back to his house and leave it for her. But I can't do it 'cause I got backed up here all of a sudden. Can you two boys help me out? I'll give ya two bucks each."

Donny and Robby looked at each other almost simultaneously and barely shrieked, "Two bucks? Heck, we'll do that for nothing! Gil Hodges' car? Us? Aw-right!!"

It turned out that Gil Hodges drove a brand new Chrysler Imperial. An upscale limousine-type of sporty car, it had enormous tail fins and wire wheels. It was gorgeous.

Robby and Donny were so excited about driving Gil Hodges' car, that they forgot that only one of them could drive it; the other one had to drive Robby's dad's car so that they could get back home from Gil's house way out near Ebbets Field. It was a dilemma since both boys were aching to drive the Chrysler luxury car. Only after Donny so adroitly pointed out to Robby that Robby's dad would be very upset if Donny got into an accident driving Robby's dad's car . . .

And so it happened. It was a dream that would be talked about for the rest of their lives: Donny and Robby and Gil Hodges' car. It really was of no consequence who actually drove the Chrysler; what really mattered was that it was Gil Hodges' car! Except . . . it did matter. To Donny. Because he got to drive Gil's car!! And for the rest of their lives he would not let Robby forget it.

Later in the day when the boys returned to the neighborhood and safely parked Robby's dad's car in its normal parking space in front of his home, they decided to head over to Otto's ice cream parlor. On the way there, they passed Pete Kelly's garage and noticed a large, illuminated, painted, metallic container outside adjacent to the open mechanic's bay. The box stood about six feet high and about three feet wide. On its front and sides were the words, ICE COLD SODA—10 CENTS. A thick, black, wire seemed to protrude from the right side of the container and over to an electric outlet on the outside wall of the garage.

"What is that? Ice - cold - soda?" Robby asked.

"An automatic soda-bottle dispensing machine. Put in a dime, and out pops a bottle of soda."

"I'll be dipped. I'm gonna try it."

They crossed the busy street, and Robby searched his pockets for some change. He found a dime and hurriedly put it into a thin slot under the words, INSERT TEN CENTS HERE. As the dime clinked down the slot and into a hidden drawer, a light glowed above a button that said, PUSH HERE FOR SODA. After a few mysterious noises and a loud clunk, a bottle magically appeared behind a glass door. Robby slid open the door and extracted the soda bottle. He stared at the bottle incredulously for what seemed like minutes; it was icy cold. He then held it up to Donny.

"Hot stuff," he said. "How do I get this thing open? Donny showed him the large metal bottle-cap opener on the side of the box and watched him pop the cap. "Wow," he said after sipping some; this is a lot cooler that reaching down into the soda chest in Jenny's candy store. Want some?"

"No thanks," Donny grinned. "You remember Nick Toscano?"

"Yeah, why?"

"Well he got involved with a TV producer—some guy from our neighborhood who used to live on Lincoln Place—and they designed and developed this whole idea: refrigerated case—no ice to melt or get you all wet. Put one of these on every corner outside on the sidewalk; no need to find a candy store or a drug store to buy a soda. Once it began to catch on, they sold the idea to some of the local distributors of two of the major soda companies in Brooklyn. I hear it is making lots of money for the two guys."

Nick Toscano? How do you like that. He was hardly more than a grease monkey in a black leather jacket."

"He's in engineering school now."

217

"Nick?? In engineering school??" Robby rolled his eyes and looked heavenward as if to say, "Nick—an engineer? Unbelievable."

They walked up to Otto's and looked in through the large front pane glass window noting that the ice cream parlor was empty except for Otto himself, who was filling syrup dispensers. He nodded to them as they looked in, but continued to work knowing that by eleven thirty his store would be full of people anxious for a sandwich, soda, ice cream cones, or salads. Otto made great salads.

As they turned away, Donny said, "It's only eleven o'clock— still too early for any of the guys to be here yet. Wanna walk up toward Flatbush Avenue?"

"Sure." Robby's face brightened. "We can get a knish and a hot dog with onions at the deli at Flatbush and Church."

They headed up past the Brooklyn Museum, turned left at the library at Grand Army Plaza, and walked along Flatbush Avenue adjacent to the Botanical Gardens and the Zoo.

Donny reminisced, "Remember when we walked those two girls along here a few summers ago and they got so tired from walking in high heels that we had to take the bus back home?"

Robby chuckled and responded, "As I recall, neither one of us even got to make out that night.

Donny stifled a laugh as he said, "Speak for yourself, lover boy!"

Robby started to playfully pound on Donny's arms and back, saying, "Hey! I'm supposed to be the make-out guy—not you.

"Well, I got lucky that night . . ."

"What??" Robby was all over Donny now, playfully mauling him. "C'mon man; tell me what happened."

Shyly, Donny told his friend, "I kissed her a few times, I mean."

"Yeah, I'll bet you're pullin' my chain. Anyway, remember we had to borrow ten cents from them to get home 'cause both of us were broke."

Donny said, "I'm still broke"; he laughed.

"And if you become a priest, you'll always be broke."

"Until I become a pastor . . . ."

V

The walk was invigorating though the winter sun warmed them as they strolled slowly past the seemingly endless rows of trees that lined the four-foot-high stone and cement fencing along the park's perimeter. When most of their idle chatter had subsided, Robby became strangely silent, which caused Donny to wonder why his friend, who was always known to be talkative, had nothing left to say.

"So . . . why did you really come home?" Donny inquired; his deep concern for his friend was obvious from the probing nature of the question.

"What do you mean?" Robby walked along the curbstone attempting to balance himself while pretending not to hear his friend.

"C'mon Rob; what's happenin'?" Donny demanded in a slightly louder tone.

Robby stopped the sham diversion and hung his head for a brief second. "You know me well, don't you, pal?"

"We do know each other; you got a problem? Can I help?"

Robby blurted out, "Now don't laugh; I'm in love, awright?"

Donny's eyes pored into his friend's eyes and allowed a grand smile to develop completely filling his face. "I'm not going to laugh;

it's wonderful. Who is she? Do I know her? Where is she from?" The questions poured out from his bumbling mouth.

"You don't know her. I met her in the city . . . in New York. Her name is Ellen-Mary Kilkenny . . . Ellen."

"Irish, huh?"

"Yeah."

"Figures."

"Hey, c'mon Don; Irish girls are the best; I always told you that!"

"Can't tell by me."

"I know you. You only take out Italian girls."

"Not always, but mostly. Like my Mom says, pal: If you wanna eat good . . ."

They both laughed as they bantered back and forth tossing familiar cliches at each other as they had so many times in the past.

"So you're in love. That's wonderful. Why aren't you jumping for joy?" Donny solicited.

"I should be happy, but I'm not. I screwed everything all up."

Robby was glad for the opportunity to finally unburden himself to someone he could trust. This wouldn't be the first time these two had come together to help resolve each other's problems or figure out solutions to some of the world's weighty problems while walking for hours along any of the familiar avenues in the heart of Brooklyn.

Robby began again, "Lemme go back to the very beginning. I met Ellen at a time when I was really depressed: I had messed up at a network audition for a job playing with a studio orchestra. It was my own fault about losing the gig, but my ego—you know about my ego, right?—my ego was shot to hell. But when I met

Ellen, well, Ellen made me start to feel good about myself again. She singlehandedly pulled me out of the sewer I put myself into. Look. I respected her, Don, like no other girl I ever went out with. She was special. She is special! I mean really special in so many ways. I even thought about marrying her someday."

Donny interrupted, "And . . . the bad news is . . .?"

"We started going out a lot, I mean almost every day. It wasn't really serious at first, you know what I mean, but I knew that I felt good when I was with her, and I wanted to do nice things for her. It was so great to be with her; and I never thought once about being with anyone else. She really messed me up when it came to how I thought about and treated girls—I mean women."

Now even more puzzled, Donny asked, "And . . . ?"

"You know, it was like we didn't have to spend a lot of money going out or eat in restaurants or do anything planned. It was great just being together. Whatever we did or wherever we went was wonderful. And, you know me, right? Well, I never got fresh with her or took advantage. I wanted to, but I held her kind of special, not like a lot of the other girls or some of the Prospect Park girls. She was my special girl and I . . . I . . . I behaved myself. I didn't want her to get the wrong idea about me or why I went out with her. I even saw a different me, and I began to like the new me!"

"Wow." Donny took a deep breath. "This sounds perfect!" Donny was so happy for his friend that he was literally bouncing up and down listening.

Robby paused briefly and then continued softly, almost whispering; Donny had to move closer so that he could hear him. "And then, after about two months or so of going out, we were in my place one afternoon; she had surprised me by coming over wanting to cook supper for us. Then, we sat on the couch and started talking and she told me she liked me, and I told her that I liked her, and . . . then, out of nowhere, she leaned in close and hugged me. She whispered softly into my ear something like, I can't even remember her exact words, 'Robby, don't you want to make love to me?' Do you hear what I am saying!? It wasn't me who asked if we could make love. She did!! I still can't believe it." He expelled the air slowly from his lungs before beginning again, "She asked ME to make love to HER."

Donny was puzzled. The silence between them was uncommon. These two always had something to say to each other. Eventually, Donny interjected, "Are you actually saying that she was some kind of slut all the while and you didn't know it?"

Robby snapped back, "No! She's not a slut!! Don't say that!" His eyes filled with tears.

Donny apologized for his comments once he saw the tears in his friend's eyes. "OK, man. I'm sorry. I just don't get it. What reason do you think prompted her to say that?"

"Well now; that's the heart of the matter. Apparently she hadn't had a real good life, and she liked me a lot, and didn't want to lose me."

"If some girl seduced me, I'd hang around too . . . for a while anyway. Sorry," Donny joked. Seeing that Robby didn't respond to his laughter, he apologized again, saying, "I'm sorry, I'm sorry, I'm sorry. Please continue." Both friends took long, deep breaths.

Robby went on, "Well, my first reaction was, 'No, this can't be Ellen, my Ellen, asking me to take her to bed.' Nothing like this ever happened to me before, and it was happening so fast that I didn't really believe that it was happening at all! I don't know; my mind sort of went blank and I kissed her again . . . and again not really thinking about it. The old Robby surfaced, and I kinda let my hormones have their own way. It was like Ellen wasn't even there with me; it could have been anyone . . . it didn't really matter at first. It had been a long time for me, ya know?

Robby paused for a few minutes to regain his composure before continuing. "So . . . we made love. Eventually as my senses returned, I was able to look into her eyes realizing whom I was with—and I really enjoyed being with her that way; it was special—not like ever before . . . with anyone."

The friends then sat quietly for a long time just watching the world of Brooklyn pass before them. Donny struggled to evaluate all that he had just heard while trying to make sense of the feelings his friend was having. He sensed so much confusion on Robby's part: on the one hand, he had met this wonderful girl; on the other, he seemed unsure about how he should feel because she had asked him to do something that he had asked of innumerable women for years. Donny was stymied. Robby stood and motioned for them to head back home.

As they walked, he continued. "A few days went by and I sensed that Ellen was either madly in love with me or beginning to fall in love with me; I never knew a woman who acted in such a loving way to me before. But I got scared."

"Scared?" Donny inquired.

"Yeah. Really scared. After we did it, and I really liked doing it with her, I began to think: if she was so forward with me, was she also that way with other guys? What kind of woman was she? I had nothing in my experience to make a judgment. And then . . . I thought, I always imagined I would wind up with a virgin. And when I thought about marrying her, I asked myself how could I if she's so casual about lovemaking, and she's not a virgin. I didn't know where I was at or what I was doing."

At that Donny almost stumbled on the sidewalk and cleared his throat, trying to cover his embarrassment at the unbridled frankness that the discussion had suddenly if assumed.

" . . . I didn't know what to think at all. You remember how we used to talk: if a girl does it for one guy, she'll probably do it for anybody who comes along."

Donny interrupted, "That's what we USED to say."

"Well, I still believe it. I wanted our relationship to be something extra special between us. I can't wrap my mind around marrying a girl who has slept around"

Robby then grew silent until Donny broke in, "Do you really believe that Ellen has slept around?"

Robby continued, " I don't really know anything for certain, but I began to get these thoughts; I started to fantasize about the other guys that she might have been with—and I was jealous."

"Jealous? I would have thought you would have been angry."

"No! You don't really know her. She's wonderful—a great lady. That's what's so confusing. Can you help me figure this out!"

"Calm down. Take a minute to relax. Too bad we don't smoke; what we need is a cigarette." Donny continued, "So you were jealous . . . "

"I was jealous that she wasn't mine alone. I wanted her all to myself. But then I thought, I can't marry her. But I never wanted to hurt her either. I just wanted to confront her. I knew it was a bad idea, but I just had to confront her!"

"Then what happened?"

"I really messed everything up. I tried to broach the subject again once while she was getting ready to go to work. We had taken the cab together, but I just made things worse. She was so upset with me that she made me stay in the cab when she got out."

"I called her every day after that trying to tell her how sorry I was, but she hung up on me each time. Then, after, I don't know, four or five days of not seeing each other, she called me; I was so happy that she reached out. I wanted to make things right with her, and now she was giving me a chance."

"She invited me up to her place; she was going to make raviolis for me. She had walked all the way over to Mott Street in Little Italy and bought two pounds of fresh raviolis for me . . . for us. She even made a homemade sauce; it wasn't any good, but I didn't tell her. All during the meal, I felt the urge to bring up my feelings about, you know. So, after the meal, while we were doing the dishes, I said, " . . . "

Donny interrupted, "You mean you dumped on her while you were washing the dishes after she made you a fantastic dinner? What is wrong with you?"

"I know. I know."

"So then what?"

"She broke down, and cried. Again. My heart broke seeing her like that."

"Your heart broke? Don't you have any feelings at all? Are you the least bit human? What about her heart? Her feelings? I don't believe you did that!"

Robby was weeping now, ashamed, it seemed, of what he had done to this woman that he really loved . . . very much. He said, "She told me that she invited me up and cooked the meal so we could talk about what had gone on between us. She knew that we couldn't leave it the way it was and she really wanted to clear the air. I knew how difficult it must have been for her, and she tried to lighten the mood by joking about talking best on a full stomach. The fact is, my stupid pride took over, and I never gave her a chance to speak; I just kept badgering her about her former lovers . . ." Robby was crying unabashedly now.

Donny, again shot back, "Well I just cannot believe what you did."

"Me and my big mouth!! I didn't give her a moment to breathe before I laced into her about her past. All she kept shouting was, 'Robby, you've got it all wrong! You are all wrong.' And then she physically pushed me out the door and almost down the flight of stairs. We haven't spoken since."

"I don't understand. She said you were wrong? You were wrong about what?"

In a whisper, Robby sighed, "Her sleeping around."

Donny was even more confused now. "Phew! Let me try to make some sense of all this. You went out with her for about a month. Then, you began to fall in love with her?"

"Yes. She was marvelous. We had great times together."

"No sex up to that point?"

"No, none. I already told you! I liked her. We did kiss . . . you know; but nothing heavy. We never let it go too far." I tried not to rush things; I wanted her to know that I wanted her for . . . herself and not just for . . . you know."

"Yes, I do know. Then, one magical night she . . . seduced you—asked you to make love to her?"

"Right."

"And you were shocked that your special lady was so forward, but you made love to her? . . . Anyway?"

"Yes."

"And now you're telling me you think she wasn't a virgin?"

"NO! I don't think she wasn't a virgin!! I KNOW she wasn't a virgin."

"Are you sure?"

"What the hell is wrong with you? Are you stupid or something? Of course I'm sure."

Donny put his arm around his friend who was holding his head in his hands; it was clear to Donny that Robby was seriously upset. "Rob, look, I'm sorry. But just think about it for a minute. If she got that upset when you asked her about . . . about sleeping around, then it was obvious that what you said really hurt her deeply. No?"

"I don't know. It was like I asked her if she ever committed murder."

"Whoa! That bad, huh? You know, you made a serious judgment call there. And, if you were wrong, well . . ." Donny mused for a long moment, and then quite offhandedly said, "Look, maybe she fell off a horse . . . or something."

"Don't be ridiculous! You're an idiot, ya know?" Robby stomped off.

Donny trotted after him and together they ambled quietly along until they came to the intersection of Flatbush Avenue and Empire Boulevard. Carefully, they negotiated the journey across to the other side of the park where they could see the lights from the stores that lined both sides of the busy street. They were entering familiar territory.

Donny took a very deep breath, and in the most careful of ways, posed this question, "Rob, just let me ask you this, and don't get upset: is it at all possible that maybe you WERE her first, and she really loves you and wanted her first time to be with you?"

Frustrated beyond belief, Robby shot back, "How in all creation could I have been her first?"

"I don't know; but from what she said; I mean her words don't make sense if you are right. Right? Let's just assume that you are wrong about her . . . just suppose."

Robby burst out, "It's really not that hard to know whether . . ."

Donny interrupted, 'OK, OK. But it just seems like from what you've told me, that she's a wonderful girl. It . . . it really doesn't make any sense she would . . . would . . . SLEEP around." Donny paused again and then, shrugging his shoulders, said, "But what do I know? I'm just trying to see some good in all this because you say that you love her. I don't know much about girls, but I can tell you this, I've met a lot of really nice girls since we were last together, and, you know what? Many of them—most of them—have different ideas about sex and stuff. They want to enjoy the same things we enjoy. You know, the world outside of this neighborhood is not like it is on Dean Street or Classon Avenue."

Donny was not making any headway with Robby, so he tried his best to just ease off. "Ellen seems nice. Sort of wonderful compared with some of the other girls I know you went out with."

"She IS wonderful, Don. I just can't make sense of the whole thing either. I miss her. I really miss how I feel when I'm with her. And yet . . . can I really trust her?"

Donny offered, "Trust her? Are you serious? She cooks for you, she makes you feel good about yourself, she even goes out of her way for you. Who ever did anything for you like that before? You know who? Your mother!"

Donny had begun to rant, starting to understand more about Ellen and how good she is for Robby. He kept telling himself how truly special she must be to have made Robby so happy. Such a gift she is to him.

He went further, "You never really gave her a chance to have any meaningful dialogue with you. You did all the accusing and talking, and she cried! It seems to me that she gave you plenty of opportunities to hear her out, but you had to hear yourself first. Man! You owe her big time. She took the high road each time; she came to you, and you just shut her down! If I were in her shoes, I would never speak to you either. Do you actually believe that you deserve to be with her?"

Robby sighed a deep sigh, "No."

Donny tried another tack. "Look. Do you really love her? Would you still marry her?"

"The funny part is that I do and I would."

"So what's the problem, then?"

"My pride—my stubborn Italian pride. I always figured I'd get a girl who was for me—first."

"Like you were for her? First? You gotta get over this!" Donny was purposely sarcastic as he tried to make a point with his friend.

"You know what I mean," Robby replied sheepishly.

"Yeah. Unfortunately, I do know exactly what you mean! What you mean is : I want you to be perfect for me, but it doesn't matter that I'm not perfect for you!! I had many other women before I met you, but don't judge me the way I am judging you. Right?"

Donny put his arm around Robby's shoulder and gave him a . . . sort of . . . hug, and said, "Boy, Rob—you really messed this one up real good."

They walked along silently for a long time, letting each other's words penetrate as they had done so many times before. The words of a friend can be trusted. The words shared between these two friends can heal.

Many of the stores along Flatbush Avenue had awnings, but they were rolled up now that the winter sun was so low. It was good for the two friends to pass this way together again, since it revived some of the fond memories that had begun to fade. Donny reminded Robby of the time when they were about thirteen years old and they took this same walk. Robby had spotted a well-dressed woman bending down low to look at a pair of shoes on the bottom shelf of a store's window display. He silently approached her from behind—stopping just short of touching her. When he got within inches of her, he let out his loudest Tarzan yell almost causing the lady to drop dead before him. Donny had already scurried half-way down the block, knowing what Robby was up to, embarrassed to death at the antics of his friend.

"We should walk up here at least once a year for as long as we live," Robby said, though fully aware that it would probably never, ever happen again. Suddenly, he forgot Ellen and became deeply saddened.

Donny's words brought him back, "Here's Benny's; we going in?"

"Let's go."

BENNY'S

I

Benny's was one of dozens of generic-type stores designated 'delicatessen' located throughout Brooklyn. It was a good bet that you could find queues of schoolboys and girls in delis all over the city. Deli operating hours tended to mimic the life of the neighborhood; for example, delis near movie houses or theaters stayed open until the last show was over and everyone had a chance to get in a quick 'midnight' snack.' Except for bars, delis were one of the few reliable places to go at midnight on a Friday or Saturday night and grab a hot dog on a nice warm, toasty roll with sauerkraut and mustard for a nickel. Even the knishes were a nickel, but, more often than not, they came with just a smear of heartburn. Deli sandwiches were off limits to most young people because they cost a quarter. Though piled high with pastrami or beef brisket, who could afford twenty-five cents for a sandwich? You needed a job to pay those prices. Or a rich father.

Benny's was a kosher deli, but, being of the genus 'deli,' it conformed to all the proper characteristics of deli—in general. The store windows were clouded (perhaps dirty would be more accurate), the tables held large, open, wide-mouth jars of crusted-over mustard, and the inside was poorly lighted with dusty, bare incandescent bulbs. In all, it was a classic-type of New York City delicatessen where you could eat like a king. Benny made homemade everything—even the knishes—not like some of the larger downtown delis that bought perfectly shaped, ready-made knishes from a local supplier.

"Vat'll it be, boys," Benny asked with his heavily accented voice.

Together, they responded, "Two knishes, sliced, with mustard and two hot dogs with sauerkraut and relish. . . . and a glass of milk."

"Dis is a kosher place, you—." Benny leaned over the counter toward them, feigning slapping their laughing faces.

He laughed along with them when they both said, "Sorry; we meant two grape Nehi's." They loved to tease Benny, and he played along, accustomed to the silly pranks from his many young customers. Benny was always in a good humor.

The boys took a table in the back where they could talk privately without being disturbed.

Robby spoke first, "Don, I'm really serious. What do you think I should do? I really love Ellen and want to marry her."

"You're sure? You're really sure? In spite of everything?"

"Yes. I have never hurt this much before; I'm not happy. it's worse: I'm SAD! Being sad is not good. It's like a part of me died, and I'm walking in the dark all the time. I don't want to eat—don't—want—to—do—anything. That's really why I came home."

Robby paused and sipped his grape Nehi through a straw. "At first, I felt 'comfortable' around her—you know, like when we started to first go out and stuff. Then I started including her in all my plans. I wanted to do things with her and for her; I wanted to be . . . nice to her, make her happy; ya know what I mean? Can you understand what I'm saying?"

"You're in love I guess. If I understand you correctly—and from all that you said about her, I can't believe Ellen is the type of girl who would sleep around; in fact, she seems to have turned you into a celibate since you two split up. Hey, maybe you should be the priest."

"Ha! Seriously, I don't want to be with anyone else. I never knew what it meant to care for someone more than myself. After we dated for a while, I used to ask myself 'what would be best for Ellen?' before I decided on something for us to do. It's like . . . well, sex has become something precious—not a thing to do. She taught me that it's a gift that two people in love give to one another, and that's what makes it so special! I guess love is like choosing to put the other person first, like making a 'decision' to love. I found myself always deciding to put her needs ahead of my own."

Donny sat up straight, and took another deep breath. "I think you just wrote the textbook definition of LOVE! WOW!" Then more silence, until Donny added, " Maybe that's exactly how she felt about you when she . . . ah—when she . . . ."

Robby broke in, "Maybe you're right. Lemme think for a minute. Maybe she 'decided' to give me the most special part of herself. And I threw it in her face."

Then Donny said, "You know, even if she weren't a virgin, it doesn't mean that she wouldn't be a good wife to you; look at how many unhappy marriages we see these days. It's got nothing to do with how many lovers somebody had. Look at yourself: you did it with a lot of girls. Right? And you would be faithful to her, wouldn't you?"

"Of course . . . but guys are different."

"I don't know anymore, Rob. Times are changing. I told you before I met some really great girls, and they do not think like we do. I don't think we can honestly expect women to live up to a different set of standards from us guys."

"I don't know. Maybe you're right. All's I know is I love her, and I want her back!"

They continued eating their meal in silence for a while when Donny broke in. "Suppose you call her and invite her over for Christmas; she lives alone right?"

"Yeah. I don't think she'll come though."

"It wouldn't hurt to call—let her know you still care."

Robby's face lit up! "I'll do it!"

After they finished eating, they headed toward home, back along Flatbush Avenue, stopping momentarily to watch young men tossing a football around the crowded streets. A few blocks further along, they passed a stickball game between some young men in their twenties who apparently worked in the neighborhood and some local youths who looked as though they were still in high school. Stickball games often wound up with the younger men challenging the older, and both sides taunting one another. In the summers, the losers would buy beer for the winners or, if it were an especially important game, the stake would be a half or quarter keg of beer. But not today: it was too cold and it was only a lunch-time game that would last thirty minutes or so.

"When will you call her?" Donny asked.

"I'll call her late tonight after her show. She gets in late."

"You gonna ask her to stay over at your parents' place?"

"Yeah. This way we can spend time relaxing without worrying about catching the subway. Besides, I don't want to be alone with her just yet. If she stays over, Mom and Dad will be around to play chaperone."

"I can't wait to meet her," Donny said.

Robby was wistful, "Neither can I; I just hope she'll come."

"She will; she will." Silently, Donny said a prayer that his friend's dream would turn out OK.

II

Her phone was ringing as she entered the apartment. Ellen ran to it quickly.

"Hello?"

"Ellen? It's me, Rob."

A pause, then, icily, "Yes?"

He could sense the tenseness in her voice. Carefully, he continued, "I'm glad I got you at home. Ellen . . . I miss you, and I wanted to see how you were getting along."

She made no response.

"Ellen? Are you there?"

"Yes . . . I'm here. Robby, but I don't want to speak to you."

"I know. But listen for a moment. Please?"

She remained silent.

"Ah . . . " Perspiration poured down his face and into his eyes. He was so frightened that he was going to make everything worse than it already was. He continued, remembering every word that he had so carefully chosen to say to her. He practically whispered into the mouthpiece, "Christmas is coming, and I don't think it would be good for you to spend it alone."

She interrupted, but he talked over her, "My parents have lots of room here, you'd have your own room, and I thought . . . well maybe you'd like to spend some quiet time and have dinner with us, maybe meet some of my friends . . . Spend the holiday away from the city."

Ellen, still reeling from her last encounter with Robby, had no intention of ever seeing him again. Yet—the softness of his voice, the seeming sincerity, reminded her of their first days together; she felt a renewed desire stirring, and she could almost feel herself in his arms. She said nothing at first, letting his words sink in.

"It's only a feeling," she told herself; "it will subside. If he can't love me for who I am, then our relationship is too fragile to last." Her mind won over her heart.

"I don't think so; sorry." She hung up.

She lay on her bed fully clothed, still wearing all of her stage makeup. She fought unsuccessfully to steel herself against the complex emotions that kept building within. And then the tears came pouring forth: tears that she had promised would not be spent this way ever again gushed from her red-streaked eyes melting her mascara and heavy pancake makeup giving her a clown-like visage. Her pillow became stained as she buried her face in it attempting to soften the sound of her sobbing. To no avail.

Now, completely alone with her pain and sadness, she began to scream out loud and tear at her hair, all the while cursing herself for falling in love . . . with him. She hated herself for what she was feeling, but she hated even more the fact that she actually trusted herself to him. "Love isn't supposed to be like this," she cried. "He's no different," she thought; "he's mean, self-seeking, and egotistical; he wants everything his way. He doesn't care about me; I trusted him and he turned my gift to him back on me! All he cares about is himself. He never let me have a single chance to explain! Damn him!"

Ellen cried until she had no more tears, and then, completely exhausted, found a modicum of comfort in sleep. She slept, but her sleep was not peaceful. Her dreams were filled with images of Robby and herself walking the streets of the city holding hands. She saw them laughing together and having a good time. At about 3 A.M. she woke suddenly and sat upright in bed, her knees drawn to her chest. Softly, ever so softly, she heard herself say, "Oh, Robby, you damn fool! I love you; I do love you."

III

"She hung up on you?" Donny asked as they sat on the front steps of Robby's apartment building early the next morning.

Robby sighed and weakly said, "Yeah."

"So what are you gonna do about it; just let her go? You've gotta go get her, man! You can't let it end this way. You must let her have her say! Give the girl a chance to speak; OK?"

"What are you all worked up about?" Robby couldn't believe how animated Donny had become over this situation. "Hey back off . . . awwright? She's my girl—not yours."

"But you're my friend . . . and . . . I care about you. And besides, she won't be your girl much longer if you don't do something about it. If she is as special as you say, some meathead in show business is gonna snap her right up. You should be the meathead!"

This time it was Robby who put his arm around his friend and gave him a gentle hug. "I know you care; thanks. But I guess I hurt her too deeply for her to ever forgive me."

"If she's half the woman you say she is, she'll forgive you; I know it; I really feel it. Just tell her the truth; tell her how stupid you were; how stupid you are!

Robby chuckled, "Yeah, right."

Donny kept going, "Or, better yet, let her do the talking; girls like to talk. You said you never gave her much of a chance to say anything before she threw you out! "

There was silence for a few moments before Donny spoke again, " Why don't you let me go and talk with her. I'll go and plead your case. Lemme do this for you."

"Whoa! Hold on here. You? You want to go see Ellen?"

"Sure. Why not? I'm harmless. I mean, maybe she'll fall for me, but I'll behave myself, OK?""

Robby smiled again, reflected for a moment, and said, "You're nuts!" and then thought to himself, "I want her back so badly." Deep inside, he ached for a resolution to this seemingly insolvable mess he had gotten himself into. He knew that Ellen was the first girl he had ever fallen in love with and that he yearned to hold her in his arms once again. She was . . . he could not even find the proper words to describe Ellen or how he felt about her. "She is one in a million," he opined; "she is kind and gentle and so self effacing. She cared for me like no other woman before. She really deserves to be with someone worthy of her and all that she brings to a relationship. Oh My Lord, why did you ever let me get involved with her? I just don't deserve her; I am just a big mouth nobody. I'm not even worthy of a 'gimme a buck and I'm your friend' Prospect Park girl . . . no less someone like Ellen."

He tried, but could not conjure up a scene where Donny could be successful interceding for him or pleading his case with her. And yet . . . he almost gagged as he began to speak, so caught up was he in the emotion of the moment. "Donny, look, how would this work? What are you thinking? I mean talk to me."

Robby breathed a bit easier as he prayed that Donny's interaction might ultimately help sway Ellen's mind regarding Robby's monumental insensitivity—or should it be monumental STUPIDITY? Maybe, just maybe, he could undo some of the pain he had brought to her. He could not believe that he actually was thinking more about Ellen's feelings than his own. He was in completely uncharted territory. Maybe this is how a lover should react. And then, maybe Donny has a point. Maybe.

THE PLAN

I

At about ten-thirty, Robby and Donny began another one of their familiar, almost ritualistic, walks, this time south on Classon Avenue then east on Bergen Street. They were headed toward the East New York section of Brooklyn on a journey that would last about four hours: just about enough time to develop a proper strategy to help heal a sad and painful situation between lovers. They hoped.

Their walk completed and upon returning to the neighborhood, they hoped they had devised a seemingly flawless plan whereby Donny would take the subway into the city and meet Ellen outside of the theater, greeting her when the evening show was over. He would try to explain that Robby had acted like the spoiled child he was and that his love for her was unquestioned . . . in Robby's opinion, that is. Donny was to further explain that Ellen was the only woman that Robby had ever connected with; she was the impetus of his long-delayed maturation from selfish gadabout into emerging, sensitive adult. Robby asked Donny not to overwhelm Ellen, but to permit her to say or do whatever she wanted. Recognizing the strangeness of having Donny intercede for him, he was still unsure that he would have another chance with her anyway. But he wanted to risk it if there were the slightest opportunity for a healing or reconciliation. Both friends had agreed that Ellen would decide her own course of action, whether it involved Robby—or not. The only thing that mattered was Ellen's happiness. Period.

Robby and Donny prayed that Ellen would somehow realize the sincerity of Donny's presence, and perhaps agree to let Robby apologize in person or do whatever was necessary to undo the mess he caused. Robby had been brought to his knees by his own attitude and lost the one true love of his life. He knew he did not deserve anyone as special as Ellen, but if there were a chance . . . he prayed. Would she . . . dare she ever see him again? Robby had let go completely and left it to Donny . . . and to God. And that was the plan.

The night of Donny's trek into Manhattan was bitterly cold and windy with temperatures in the twenties, yet Donny, over the objections of his mother, took the 'E' train to Chambers Street and transferred to a cross-town bus to the theater where Ellen was dancing. He arrived close to 10:00 P.M., barely minutes before the show ended. Robby had told him that it usually took Ellen about fifteen minutes to change before she left.

Donny waited outside the stage entrance hoping that he would not miss her; he had only the sketchy description that Robby had given him: blonde, straight hair, five-feet four, beautiful eyes, fantastic figure, great legs, gorgeous. "Sure, it'll be easy; not too many women like that in Manhattan shows," he mocked.

When the cast began to exit, Donny started to perspire, his inner spirit oblivious to the freezing weather. Suddenly she appeared. There was no mistake; she was exactly as Robby had described her—only much more beautiful than Donny had imagined. Still with her stage makeup on, she looked absolutely fantastic. Donny shuddered as he realized that he had never seen or been this close to a girl . . . a woman . . . as . . . mature . . . or as gorgeous . . . as this one. He could only guess at how Robby felt when making love to her. He was quaking in his shoes, but he did approach her and finally speak.

"Excuse me. Are you Ellen?"

She was startled momentarily by the tall young man swaddled in an grey, Alpen-loden, Austrian-type mountain-climber's parka with the hood pulled tightly around his face. The only facial features she could discern were his nose and two eyes peering through the thick lenses of horn-rimmed glasses. He did not appear the least bit threatening.

She said, "Yes, I'm Ellen; do I know you?"

In the bitter chill of the night, he hurriedly explained to her who he was and the general intent of his mission: "Robby wanted me to speak with you. He asked me to say that he really loves you and that he is so sorry for making you unhappy. By the way, I am freezing here. I have more to say . . . if you will let me"

She felt a twitter inside: "Maybe it wasn't over after all," she thought. Maybe, she even hoped.

"Let's go across the street and get some coffee," she said.

"Great; I could use something warm."

"You look frozen! Doesn't that coat keep you warm? You look like a Sherpa."

She gave him a half-smile and very firmly took his arm, actually helping him criss-cross the heavily trafficked avenue. Donny fell immediately in love with this girl himself, and he had only just met her. She was nothing like the Prospect Park girls from the neighborhood. "Wow," he thought, "this is a woman! A real woman."

It was warm inside the coffee shop and fairly crowded with lots of neighborhood people and a few theater goers too; it was getting close to 11 P.M. After a few moments sitting in a booth, Donny stopped shivering and began to warm up; he undid the loop-lock buttons and took off his parka and heavy woolen scarf. He tried to regain his composure though it was really embarrassing for him because he couldn't see Ellen through his steamed-up eyeglasses. He fumbled with them, and reached for a tissue in his coat pocket to wipe them dry.

"This always happens to me in the winter," he explained trying to act casual. Finally, he found the courage to say, "You're very beautiful, Ellen. Robby was right."

Ellen lowered her eyes, unsure of the true intent of Donny's mission, but eager to hear about Robby. Donny ordered coffee and a bagel for both of them, feeling expansive with the five-dollar bill that Robby had given him.

Softly, Ellen, feigning at sarcasm, asked, "So . . . how is the maestro?"

"He misses you, Ellen; really, he misses you like you wouldn't believe. I've known him all his life, and I have never seen him hurting like this. He knows how much he hurt you, and he realizes what a fool he is. He had . . . ideas . . . dumb ideas . . . but his intent was never to cause you pain or hurt of any kind. I would say that he was pig-headed, but that's just me. What I can say for certain is that he would do anything if he could relive his actions and undo the pain and suffering he caused you. He loves you; he really loves you. AND . . . and even if you never get back together, well, he wants to try to make things better . . . for you . . . if he ever could. He is really thinking about you. I've never seen him like this."

Ellen had been listening intently, her eyes focused on this 'boy' from Brooklyn sent out on this freezing night to help a friend. There was unbroken silence for about thirty seconds; Donny was certain she would just get up and leave . . . but instead, she spoke. Slowly and pointedly, she began, "Donny, I don't think your friend knows what love is." Donny was acutely aware that Ellen avoided mentioning Robby by name. She was shaking and flushed, but continued, "He confuses sex with love; passion with romance; he doesn't talk; he reacts. He can't keep his fat mouth shut for half a minute! He rambles on and says whatever he wants to say without thinking or who could get hurt by his words! And he thinks he can just get away with it! I am such a fool!"

II

Donny allowed Ellen to express her feelings in a way Robby could not do. He continued, "Ellen, please. You are not a fool. In the few minutes I have known you I can see how sensitive you are. You trusted him; that is not a bad thing to do for someone in love." He paused, letting his words trail away.

Ellen sipped at her coffee. "It's true, Donny, I trusted in the relationship I thought we had between us, and then gave myself to him. I had never felt that close to any man before in my life. I thought we had something truly special; I did." Her eyes filled with tears.

"Wow," he thought to himself. "Robby has almost destroyed the one woman on earth who loved him selflessly." He cleared his throat before saying, "Maybe he didn't know what true love was before he met you, Ellen. Maybe, like most of us, he just fantasized about what it was and how he should act. You know, Robby never was one of the most selfless people in town. But I tell you this, I think he knows a little bit more about love now . . . thanks to you. If you could believe this, he was like a babe in the woods when he met you; he had been in and out of relationships like one changes shoes or socks. People, jobs, girls—nothing meant anything. He never dreamed about loving someone before or—about having someone love him!"

Donny felt himself rambling, but he was compelled to say what he felt in his heart. "He, like many of us, was always out for No. 1. When he met you, he was hit over the head with an entire new level of emotion and feelings; your soul touched his heart and made him different. He is not the same guy I used to know! He had never before thought of considering anyone else's feelings or of seeking someone else's happiness; he was focussed on himself. But you, Ellen . . . you understand what it means to love someone, to BE IN LOVE with someone: that being in love is all about the beloved . . . isn't it? Loving someone means taking second place. Loving means . . . giving."

Donny hoped he could remember these words that kept pouring out of his mouth so freely; he might be in love with someone sooner or later; you never know. He knew he had to finish up or risk boring Ellen to death; he said, "Love is the greatest gift we humans have to offer each other; it's about giving . . . giving of ourselves to someone else; risking everything for our beloved. When there is no giving—there can never be any love. Unfortunately, Robby was kinda clueless in that regard; that is, until now, I . . . think. I think he really loves you, Ellen, and he is trying to figure out how to be a lover instead of a . . . taker."

Ellen's eyes bored in on Donny's face. He even saw her nod in agreement once or twice.

He went on, "On the one hand he was madly in love with YOU by whatever definition he understood to describe love. He admitted to me that when he was with you—he was very respectful. I think that's how he put it. AND, by his own admission, you are one of the most special women on earth. So . . . here we have Robby from Classon Avenue falling for someone really special, all the while having no clue as to the sensitivity of someone else's feelings or how to engage in a meaningful two-way conversation. Believe me, Ellen, he stepped into a whole new world when you came along." Donny paused briefly before continuing, "I can understand if you still do not want to be with him, but perhaps you might consider giving him a chance to make things right . . . or rather to make things 'better.' He has come to some new place in his life, and . . . if you two 'should' be together, maybe it's worth a shot. And you know what else? You may not believe this about him—but he's lost his appetite; he is skipping homemade meals from his mother. This is really heavy duty, Ellen."

Donny took a deep breath and felt his demeanor brighten. Did he sense something? Or not?

Ellen giggled ever so slightly, knowing how difficult it was for this emissary from Brooklyn to come here and talk to her like this.

Donny laughed when he told her, "He hardly even sleeps anymore—he plays Because of You over and over, and he yells at me!! And he's only been home a couple of days."

Ellen was unable to stifle a smile that made her face appear to glow before Donny's eyes. Inside her heart, though, she was hurt, still unsure of her role in this 're-imagination of Robby and his editorial position on love. Whereas she felt the inner warmth and sincerity that Donny presented, her current state of brokenness precluded her from conceding anything—yet.

"Don, you obviously love your friend, but he treated me as though I were . . ."

She took a breath. "He said mean things to me. He made me . . . he made me . . . feel . . . he made me feel like a whore. A whore! Can you even imagine what that feels like?"

She paused again. "You know, we had some really special times together. I saw how gentle he was with me at first, and I loved him for that. He made me feel like a princess."

Donny interrupted, "Excuse me, Ellen. He talks about you as though you were a . . . queen, not a princess; he tells everyone that you are the most amazing woman that he has ever met, and, and that he feels completely unworthy to have you in his life . . . he believes that he does not deserve you at all. He can't believe that you actually went out with him more than once. I also must tell you that he is completely confused . . . about everything. You may not know it, but he and I grew up under very strict parents. Our lives were well ordered and controlled. Robby was a little wild and broke out early; he was in a hurry to see what the world was like outside of the family. It took me a lot longer. But we still hold onto many of the same values that were drilled into us."

Ellen began to sense where the conversation was headed. "You're talking about my asking him to make love to me, aren't you? He told you didn't he?"

III

It was a few tense minutes before Donny could recover from the previous statements by Ellen. He never experienced such frankness in this regard from anyone. His initial thoughts were that he was in way over his head. Donny had put his head down awkwardly, and it stayed down while he gathered his thoughts and shot a quick prayer to the Lord. "Ah—yes. But . . . ."

Ellen held up her hand mere inches from Donny's face then continued, "Listen carefully, OK? This is really difficult for me, so listen very carefully, because I may not be able to finish this. I fell in love with your friend almost from the first moment that I saw him. There was just something about him; I wanted to be with him exclusively. But he hardly kissed me or snuggled up all during the time that we were going out. We held hands . . . and I was good with that. But as I grew closer to him and began to have feelings for him, I didn't know how he really felt about me."

"Donny interjected, "He respected you . . . You weren't like . . . ""

"Well, that's what I thought . . . at first, but then I wondered whether he was either very shy or . . . maybe not even that much into women, you know? What could I think? I even wondered whether perhaps he was just passing time with me or just wanted some kind of fling; I was confused too about how he felt about a wanting a serious relationship; you know? I had to know whether he was as interested in me as I was in him. So one night after a lot of serious thought on my part, I sort of offhandedly asked him if he wanted to make love to me."

"Offhandedly?" Donny was puzzled.

"You know what I mean, c'mon. I didn't want to come across as being 'needy.' I only wanted to know his true feelings about our relationship and me. But believe me, when I tell you . . ." She paused and took a deep breath that seemed more like a sigh to Donny. " . . . When I said, 'make love to me' I didn't mean 'LET'S GET INTO BED AND DO IT!!' I meant . . . hold me tight, kiss me, cuddle me, make me feel . . . loved . . . tell me how you feel about me—and us. All the songs on the radio are about making love— you know what I mean: like in the movies—passionate kissing! NOT SEX! NOT YET ANYWAY!! Do you understand what I'm saying?

"And Robby—?"

She couldn't hold back; her words gushed out, "It was like I opened the flood gates. Your friend all of a sudden got a real case of the hots—and once he got started; well, it was too much for me to control. He was all over me, groping, squeezing—he was not the Robby I knew a few minutes before, that's for sure. And then he calmed, and I was able to share in his passion. My mind was clear: I loved him and I decided that whatever we did together would be OK. And so I relaxed in his arms; I got so relaxed that we actually did it a few times that night, and it was wonderful. It was a beautiful experience for me, and when we were done I thought he loved me as much as I loved him."

Donny was shocked. "H o l y C o w!" Donny's eyes grew two sizes as he sat there dumbfounded. So that was what happened.

"Holy Cow! is right," Ellen continued. "Everything happened so quickly that—well there were things we should have discussed before . . . before we did IT! I wanted to share some parts of my life with him, but 'hot pants Robby' couldn't wait! And I went along, willingly I must say. It was very special for me. Can you understand?"

Donny reached out and held her fingers lightly. He reddened slightly then shyly said, "Well, I . . . I . . . no, don't actually understand, but I get your drift."

She gazed deeply into Donny's eyes, squeezed his fingers slightly, and smiled the most beautiful smile he ever saw. "I'm sorry; I didn't mean to embarrass you. I guess he's told you everything, hasn't he?" Now it was she who became embarrassed. She looked away, avoiding his look.

"Ellen, please understand. We're like brothers; we have no secrets. Besides—" Donny averted his eyes, then continued. "Besides, I'm going to be a priest."

"Oh great!!" She looked at him squarely and suddenly burst out in loud laughter, finally being able to relax completely with Donny. "I feel like I'm in confession."

"Oh please don't. I just told you that so you would understand the kind of relationship we share. We're not gossips."

"I think I understand. There's still a major problem we have—you know, to get back to what we were talking about."

It was Donny's turn to lower his eyes once again.

Ellen continued, barely speaking above a whisper—her voice quivering as she spoke, "He thinks I've been around—you know—with other men. Doesn't he?"

Donny chewed on his lip for a few brief seconds before he responded, "He said . . . well, he was shocked . . . Ah, I mean . . . well what he really told me was that . . . even if it were true, it doesn't matter . . . it shouldn't matter."

She interrupted him once again. "If it were true? If it were true? So he judges me? He just decides that I am used merchandise?" She cried softly. "Oh boy. That's one of the things I wanted to share with him. I knew he wanted someone . . . special . . . and I wanted to be that someone special for him . . . But we didn't even have time to talk—everything happened so quickly. I could kick him, I swear. I could just kick him hard! Damn him!"

"Ellen, he loves you!"

"Let me finish, please . . . Oh, God this is so difficult . . . when I was fourteen . . ." Her eyes reddened even more, again filled with tears, and Donny fully expected her to relate some ill-conceived romance with a high school classmate. " . . . my father raped me." She was sobbing now.

Donny's mouth drooped, but he quickly reached for her hand. "Ellen . . . ."

"I'm all right—really," she continued. "He was a drunkard, and one night he came home like out of his mind. He burst into my room and went crazy. My mother was screaming at him, but he punched her and knocked her out. Fortunately, the neighbors heard the commotion and called the cops. I tried to fight him off, but he was too strong; I thought he was going to kill me. He's been in jail all this time. My mother filed for divorce, but it takes forever."

"I'm so sorry, Ellen."

"It's just that I wanted to tell Robby so he would know before we got too deeply involved. I never once thought he would think I was a slut; I thought he knew me better. I thought we had something so special between us." She was sobbing heavily now.

"And he judged you . . . ."

She composed herself and continued, "I felt cheated by what my father did to me, and then cheated again when Robby got the wrong idea. I had felt dirty and cheap for so many years; I rarely went out on dates 'cause I was afraid of what might happen—or how I would react. And then . . . when I met Robby, it was different. I wasn't afraid of men anymore. I was in love too. I felt so special. And then it all collapsed." She wiped her tears and forced a smile.

"May I act as a friend of the court for a moment, Ellen?"

"Sure; you're a good person, Donny. Thanks for listening. You're the only one I ever told about this."

Donny spoke softly and slowly, "When two good people get together and through a series of missteps they get separated, the world loses the benefit of their combined love. What we need more of today is for good people to find other good people and move ahead—how else are we going to change the world?"

"I suppose you're right, but it's too late for Robby and me."

"It's never too late, Ellen." And though Donny truly believed what he was saying, he felt totally lost and frustrated as he searched for something more to say. After what seemed like minutes, he finally said, " Say! I've got an idea."

IV

Ellen sat next to Donny as the 'E' train screeched and rumbled along the local tracks stopping every three minutes for stations between Manhattan and Brooklyn.

"I must be nuts," she said throwing her arms up in mock despair. "I'm also glad you reminded me that I still had on my stage makeup and false eyelashes before we left so I could wash everything off in the coffee shop's ladies' room."

Secretly Donny thought that Ellen was just as beautiful without makeup as she was with it. "Trust me, Ellen. You don't have to do or say anything; just meet him. You two have got to come to some kind of resolution, OK? Just one step at a time. You're pretty brave to be doing this, you know. I could never do what you are doing."

"You promised that you wouldn't say anything to him about my father and . . . ."

"I promise; don't worry."

Robby had been so concerned about the outcome of the meeting with Ellen that he had told Donny that he would wait for him by the change booth at the Classon Avenue station starting about midnight. Donny had agreed, since he expected that it would be very late when he returned to Brooklyn, and the two of them could walk home together—sort of like safety in numbers along strange nighttime streets of Brooklyn. When the train pulled into the station, Donny saw Robby scanning the cars as they raced by. Seeing Ellen with Donny, Robby backed away from the turnstile that he had been leaning against, wondering what miracle his friend had wrought; she was here! When the car doors opened, he sort of froze, not knowing what to do next. He never actually believed that Ellen would come along with Donny.

"Come on, Rob," Donny shouted over to him. "Put a nickel in the turnstile and get on the train with us; the conductor's gonna wait."

Confused, but uncharacteristically obedient, Robby searched for a nickel in his pants pocket and, finding one, slammed it into the slot; he raced toward the open door and got onto the train. Shifting his view back and forth from Donny to Ellen, he finally said, "Will one of you tell me what's going on?"

Donny spoke up, "Ellen has agreed to a truce."

"A truce?"

"Yes. Tonight she's my date, so keep your hands off her. She has agreed to see you as long as you both are chaperoned, and I'm it."

Robby was puzzled. "Ellen . . . ."

Donny held up his hands. "Hold it. If you two are ever going to get together again, there must be a healing. Too much has gone on for it to happen instantly, and I have planned a date for the three of us; just three friends out for a good time. OK? Say yes."

Robby acquiesced, "Yes" not knowing why, but trusting in his friend's good judgement. "Where're we going?"

"Coney Island. Nathan's. I'm hungry; I haven't had anything since supper."

"It's freezing out!"

"I know. Shut up."

As the train rumbled along, Robby finally understood what his friend had accomplished by arranging a neutral-type of meeting: it would allow the couple to be together without any pressure to deal with their impasse. Being together would be good for them, and, with Donny there too, it might actually result in the reconciliation desperately hoped for.

They transferred at the next station for the Coney Island train at which time Donny made a call home from a dilapidated phone booth inside the station. Robby heard him say, "Don't worry, I'm with Robby; we'll be careful."

The ride was uneventful with Donny sitting between the two estranged lovers, but there was light conversation, which was what he had prayed for. When they arrived at Surf Avenue, they walked gingerly down the somewhat icy steel steps of the elevated train and down into the street. A few hundred feet from the station was Nathan's, which, even on this wintry night, was as it always was: busy—even now with light sleet falling. The entire corner was lit up like broad daylight with people waiting two deep behind plywood awnings that shielded the cooks from the wintry winds. Everyone waited patiently for their five-cent hot dogs or seven-cent hamburgers (with or without the greasy, but delicious, fried onions) and the world's best tasting, also greasy, crinkle-cut french fries. Donny still had the change from Robby's five dollar bill, so he placed their order, which allowed Ellen and Robby to be alone momentarily. He watched them as he waited for the order to be filled, seeing just how great a couple they made. "Lord, let this work out," he prayed silently.

It was just past 5 A.M.by the time they dropped Ellen off at her apartment in Manhattan and returned to Brooklyn. Both were exhausted as they entered Robby's parents' apartment. Quietly, they both climbed into Robby's bed fully clothed except for their shoes and socks and pulled the covers up over their heads. After a few moments, Donny felt Robby poking him in the ribs.

"What?" he whispered."

"Thanks for all you did."

"I love you, Honey."

This time Donny got a smack to the head and, "Go to sleep; I love you too, pal."

ELLEN

I

Ellen was gratified for Donny's intrusion into her life and the crazy way he arranged for them to meet and spend a few hours together. She was ecstatic that she had an opportunity to spend Christmas Eve and Christmas Day with Robby and his parents. Whereas she hoped for an eventual reconciliation, she could not risk being alone with Robby yet: she needed to surround herself with others as a form of insulation from more hurt. Her show was on hiatus until after the New Year, so Ellen used the day off for some Christmas shopping for Robby and his parents—and for Donny.

She rose early on Christmas Eve, filled with judicious anticipation at meeting Robby once again, and only moderately apprehensive at the thought of meeting his parents. It sounded so formal to her. Nonetheless, she was excited! She arranged her bundles in an oversized shopping bag, picked up the small overnighter that held her clothes, and headed for the cross-town bus. She would be in Brooklyn in less than thirty minutes.

Robby was waiting for her by the Classon Ave change booth as he had done for their previous meeting. She spied him scanning the cars from her seat as the train screeched to a stop. "He looks so nervous," she thought. Then she breathed deeply.

"Hello, Ellen," he called gently, admiring her grace as she eased herself through the exit turnstile with her bundles. "I'm glad you came." He was torn between smiling or—not smiling. He was so confused.

Softly, she responded to his greeting. "Hi Rob, I'm glad too." She had spent many minutes planning how she would react when she met him again: she thought he was stifling a smile, but couldn't be certain. She thought it best just to avert her eyes. She barely pecked him on his cheek.

He took the overnighter from her and carried it up the grimy staircase. They walked the five blocks to his home in silence, each one praying that the other would speak first.

Finally, "This is it," he said once they got within a few steps of the building.

"It's lovely," she replied scanning the tall facade—her heart pounding in anticipation of meeting with his parents.

"You're not nervous about meeting my parents, are you?" he asked.

"Me? No, of course not," she lied.

Robby's mother had been waiting by the window for them to arrive and buzzed them in before they had a chance to ring the bell. As they entered the downstairs vestibule, they could see Carla at the head of the stairs, arms open in welcome.

Ellen reached the top first. "Ellen!" Carla burst out with a broad smile on her face. "Welcome to our home. You're so beautiful—just like Robby says. You're Irish, right? You look Irish. It's OK." Robby cringed. "Come inside!"

Carla threw her arms around Ellen, enveloping her in a bone-crunching embrace.

"Take these bags into the spare room," she ordered Robby. "Ellen, you come in here and relax," leading the way to the kitchen. "You hungry or somethin'?"

"No thank you. I'm fine." Ellen felt the pressure of the moment wane, overjoyed at being so warmly welcomed by Robby's mother; she was especially delighted that it was OK that she was Irish. She did look around though, wondering where his father was.

When Robby returned to the kitchen, he too asked Ellen if she wanted anything, and again she declined. "Maybe you'd like to take a walk?" he finally asked.

"Sure. That'll be fine. Do you mind Mrs. Ventura?"

"No, you go. I show you the house when you come back. But don't be late. OK? We gonna have a nice dinner. You're gonna like it."

"Sure."

They walked south up Classon Avenue and eventually along the foot-worn cobblestone paths of Prospect Park. Robby recalled other times and other girls he had brought here but not for the same purpose that he now walked these paths with Ellen. He cared for Ellen—he knew that for certain; the others, he wanted—for his own selfish purposes—to delight him, to gratify him, to satisfy his warped image of what it meant to be a man. Ellen could never serve such a purpose in his life nor would he permit himself to ever think of her in that way; he never did think of her in that way—then why had he caused her such pain? He still struggled mightily with his feelings, but had begun to understand that he had been driven by a purely selfish motive: he wanted her to be pure for him though he himself was well tainted and hardly pure for her.

Ellen really messed him up. There could be no other woman for him—not since he first met her. Her charm and wit delighted him and filled him with constant anticipation of what joys they would share next. She had become as essential to him as his own breathing, and when they were apart—he diminished.

As he sorted out the events leading up to and following their first night of lovemaking, he realized how unfair he had been. "So what if she had sex with someone before me? It's me she really loves. What's good for me is good for her. I'm not a tramp; neither is she." He felt satisfied with this cavalier attitude.

As he said these words to himself, he wanted to believe them without reservation, but somewhere, still hidden away deep inside, he knew that he harbored the slightest trace of jealousy and doubt. But it wouldn't alter him from his quest.

He reached down for her hand as they walked along, gently entwining the tips of her fingers within his. "You do know I love you, don't you?" he said tentatively.

She held tightly to his fingers, but spoke only after carefully selecting words she thought apt, "I love you, too . . . but . . . I . . . don't . . . think . . . that's . . . enough, Rob."

He didn't respond immediately, still holding fast to her fingers as they carefully avoided each other's eyes and continued to walk.

After a few more moments of silence he said, "Would you like to sit on this bench a while?"

"Yes." Ellen gathered her full skirt with all its many slips around her and carefully sat on the bench and crossed her legs.

In the background somewhere else in the park, a portable radio played music; it sounded like Tony Bennett's version of Because of You.

"You hear that song, Ellen?" He still averted his eyes, playing with a blade of grass.

"Umm."

"Well those words mean a lot to me, you know. I haven't been myself since . . . you know. I just can't put myself together. I . . . I . . . ."

"Rob—please!" She implored. "Please stop." She was suddenly assertive and compelled to say what was on her mind for such a long time. "You judged me, Rob, and made me feel cheap. You thought . . . you still think . . . I had slept around before I met you—and that really hurts . . . "

" . . . But."

"Please! . . . let me say my piece now." She glared at him, her eyes burning deeply into his!

He backed off immediately. "OK, say what you have to say. I'm sorry." She was different now, stronger, more in control.

She continued, "You must believe me when I say that I never loved anyone else in my entire life, Robby. You were the first man I ever longed to be with—the only man I ever allowed to hold me close and touch me that way . . . You were special to me."

Robby's mind raced as she spoke, trying to believe, acknowledging the sincerity in her voice and what he judged to be the truth: "the only man . . . ."

"You were warm and kind; you treated me with respect—I never let anyone get so close to me before; I trusted you." She began to cry gently, reaching for a tissue in her purse.

"Ellen, please don't cry . . . ." He reached over to touch her.

"No! I've got to finish. We went together for about a month, and I can't tell you how excited I was every time we met: you were a perfect gentleman—you wanted me for myself, not for what you could get out of me."

"Then why . . . ?"

Anticipating his question, she shot back, "Why did I ask you to make love to me? In retrospect—that was a mistake—a really huge mistake." She went on to explain to him what she had meant by 'MAKE LOVE' and how he had misinterpreted her openness for . . . lust.

"I allowed it to continue because I really didn't want to lose what we shared, but—even more importantly—I didn't want to deceive you either."

"Deceive me?" He didn't understand.

"You knew that I wasn't a virgin—not the way you mean it, but I really believed that if we loved one another, that it wouldn't matter to you."

"But . . . ." Again he paused, reaching for her hand, but she retreated.

"You know, Robby, there are girls out there who fool their boyfriends every day." Her voice became more forceful as she spoke; she sat up erect and looked fully at him.

"Men are so dumb. Don't you think I could have faked it when we first did it? I could have fooled you easily . . . I could have made you think I was a virgin . . . but it wouldn't have been honest—not for me—not to someone I really loved."

She ached to explain about her father—but she couldn't; it was too painful. Although it had been easy to share with Donny, something prevented her from sharing one more time with this man.

She rose and smoothed her skirt.

"I'd like to go back now; I'm getting a chill."

Robby leaped to his feet, more confused than ever, but wisely let it go.

His mind reeled with her pronouncement: "I'm the first . . . the only " . . . yet she's not a virgin. What am I missing—what am I missing? He racked his brain. He slid his arm around her waist; she did not resist. He was proud of her—though he was hanging on words as yet unspoken. They ambled along the well-worn path, watching the sun set in the winter sky. Out of the corner of his eye, Robby spied the now-still fountain whose spray had showered him often in summers past. Oh how he loved Ellen.

II

They reached the Ventura apartment, and were greeted by youngsters playing in the street and on the sidewalk. Though it was only four-thirty, the day had given way to evening quickly. Robby and Ellen had not spoken since they left the park, nor . . . had they let go of one another either.

Carla greeted them with a huge grin as they walked in the door.

"Hey you two! Don't you know it's too cold to be out this time of day?"

"It was warm up until a little while ago, Mrs. Ventura," Ellen responded softly, forcing a smile. "Ohh! What are these? They smell delicious." Ellen struggled taking off her jacket while sniffing a pan of something covered with steaming red sauce that had just come out of the oven.

"Heh! You never had manicotti?" She pronounced them, 'mah-nee-goat' "You don't know what you missed. You're gonna like it."

"Where's Pop?" Robby interjected.

"Watchin' cowboys on the TV; where else? What-choo 'tink?'"

He thought of going in with his father, but decided to remain in the kitchen with Carla and Ellen.

Carla spoke to Ellen once again with a grand smile that made her entire face light up, "I make-a these special for you 'cause I don't know if you like fish or not. Tonight's a fish dinner—you know. Tradition."

"I love fish, but I think I'm going to love the manicotti too." She pronounced them 'man-eee-cot-ee'.

Ellen was genuinely excited to be a part of something she deemed so very special at this time of year: tradition. She found herself warming to the atmosphere and her spirit being lifted. She felt peace—a peace beyond understanding. She cherished the abundance of pure, unadulterated love that Mrs. Ventura had for her family and for the traditions that she felt so committed to maintaining.

"You're gonna love every t'ing; you'll see."

The evening meal was sumptuous with a vast array of dishes. Vito, conscious of Robby's concern for Ellen and a victim of Carla's never-ending harangue, wore a tie to dinner, something he rarely did, but he, too, was captivated by Ellen and wanted to make a good impression.

Ellen was enjoying herself, not having been with real family for many years. She especially enjoyed the constant references to tradition whenever Carla pointed things out : "These cookies are tradition—my mother teach me how to make these when I was a little girl; this dish is tradition—it's been in my fam-i-ly for a hunn-ret years; these figs, they are tradition too—my mother's town in Italy grows the best in the whole world!" It was all so old-world like, and Ellen loved every moment, admiring Carla for so many reasons, but also loving her for caring for her family so intently.

The time spent during the meal was light hearted and friendly, with Carla insisting that Ellen taste a little bit of "this, and a little bit of this, and, of course, a little bit of this" until Ellen had a little bit of almost everything on the table.

"I'm a dancer, remember," she kept repeating though her mouth was almost constantly munching on something new. "I've got to watch my waistline." Ellen continued her half-hearted protests, though Carla seemed not to hear as she selected a tiny piece of this or a sliver of that for Ellen's approval. "Everything is marvelous, Mrs. Ventura, but you've made so much."

" Don't forget. You gotta save room for dessert, too. We got nice things. And 'spresso. You never have 'spresso?"

"No, but I've heard of it."

"The Irish, they don't have it, eh? Robby cringed again.

Robby's attention was focused on Ellen all through the meal, delighting in her every action and especially grateful at how well she and his mother got along. At about 8:30 the doorbell rang, and Robby leaped up and ran into the front hallway to press the buzzer that would unlock the downstairs inside door.

"It's gotta be Donny and Rita," he announced to everyone.

He opened the kitchen door and looked down the steps as Donny and his girlfriend, Rita Staci, locked the vestibule door behind them.

"C'mon up!" he called down to them.

They hurried up the wooden staircase and eagerly walked into the apartment and removed their coats before entering the dining room that was filled with so many wonderful aromas. As usual, Donny's eyeglasses fogged up immediately as he stepped into the warm and cozy apartment.

"Here, take these presents and put them under the tree," Donny told Robby.

"Hey, you didn't have to bring anything."

"I know; it's just a little something."

Robby ushered Rita into the seat next to Ellen as he introduced them to each other. There was a sharp contrast between the two, since Rita's features were characteristically southern Italian. Standing about five feet seven, Rita was about three inches taller than Ellen and had jet black hair, which she wore in an upsweep.

She had olive skin and large, bright black eyes that welcomed everyone with a knockout of a smile. Her eyebrows were full and arched—a perfect complement to her high cheekbones. Robby always teased Donny about Rita saying, "She's got the face of an angel and looks like Gina Lollobrigida." They laughed, but Donny had thought those same thoughts from the first moment he saw her except he saw a lot of Sophia Loren in her too. In truth, Rita was a gorgeous, statuesque brunette who turned many heads as she walked the streets of the neighborhood. The wonder of it was that up to this point she had had no steady boyfriend. The reality was that she had turned down many potential suitors; she was fussy. Very fussy. Robby was happy that Donny had met this lovely, raven-haired, well-poised, sophisticated, young woman.

Ellen and Rita got along so well that Robby sat back in wonder, wishing that magically he could undo the events of the previous weeks. What good friends they could become, he thought, forgetting momentarily about Donny's intention of becoming a priest.

As all the speculation continued, Carla never ceased being the gracious hostess, serving pies and cakes and three or four kinds of home-baked Christmas cookies, and then setting out tiny cups and saucers for espresso coffee. "May we help you, Mrs. Ventura?" both girls seemed to have said in one voice as they edged off their chairs. But Carla refused any assistance in setting her table. She would let them help cleaning up instead.

The girls got along well, talking animatedly and enjoying each other's company. After coffee, while the girls helped clear the table, Robby signaled for Donny to join him in his room.

"What's up, Rob?"

Robby remained pensive while contemplating how to explain his afternoon with Ellen. "I took her for a walk in the park today, but I I blew it again."

"What?" Donny was visibly upset. "What did you do this time!?" He caught himself shouting before he realized where he was.

Robby sat on his bed and, without looking up, continued, "She did most of the talking; told me how I had misunderstood her. She even told me about not being a virgin—but she also said that I was the first one who ever held her and . . . I just don't understand."

Donny put his hand on his friend's shoulder. "You still don't know then . . . do you?" Donny's heart pounded against his chest wall, remembering his promise to Ellen; his own heart ached seeing such pain in Robby's face.

"Know what?" Robby jumped up from the bed, and looked imploringly at his friend. "What?"

"I promised . . . ."

"Tell me—tell me!" Robby's eyes glared.

Donny's entire body shook as he wept unabashedly—tears filled his eyes; he had to reveal Ellen's secret. "OK . . . OK" He and Robby sat on the bed. Donny's breath was labored—he tried to speak. At first, he couldn't. Then, unable to confront Robby directly, he stared at his shoes, braced himself, and blurted out in one long syllable, "She was raped by her father when she was fourteen." He raised his head only to see Robby gaping awestruck at these words.

Seconds passed before Robby could speak, but all he could say was, "Oh dear Lord".

The two friends embraced, sobbing in each other's arms. At that moment, Robby heard himself mutter through quivering lips, "What a fool I've been—what a damn fool." And then,

Carla called Robby's name. The boys hastily tried to get themselves put together.

Donny tried to be solicitous, whispering, "You couldn't have known . . . ."

"No, but I shouldn't have been so damn arrogant and self-righteous about the whole thing."

"She wanted to tell you."

"What can I ever do to make it up to her? How can I ever get her to trust me again? Or forgive me?" He was still sobbing, filled with more of his own self doubt and hating himself for the unnecessary pain he had caused the first true love of his life. Carla called again.

The two friends sat silently for a few more moments, then Donny told Robby to wash his face and join everyone in the dining room. Robby eased himself out of his bedroom and into the hallway bathroom as quietly as possible, taking several minutes to wash his face and compose himself. On his way back, he sought out the anisette bottle and poured himself a glass, which he swallowed in a single gulp before anyone could see him. It didn't work.

III

Later on, after having rejoined the group, Donny asked, "Say, are we going to midnight mass—or what?"

The girls jumped up, saying, "Yes," but Robby was mute. It was Rita who challenged him, "Don't be such a dead head, Rob. C'mon; it'll be good for all of us to go; besides, Ellen wants to go!"

Robby made no move. Rita, in a mild display of aggression, continued, "So stay home"; and then added, "we can go without you."

Ellen was astonished at Rita's boldness and the self assurance with which she addressed Robby. She actually admired that Rita felt so comfortable in the relationship and could be open and forthright while remaining linked in what seemed to be a mutually solid friendship. She looked over at Robby and wondered about herself and how their relationship would, or could, eventually evolve – if at all.

Reluctantly, Robby agreed to go along with their plans. Someone mocked, mumbling, "Yay!" They finished helping Carla clean up, got dressed, and headed out.

As they walked up the slight hill toward St. Teresa's Church, Robby and Donny led the way, followed closely by Rita and Ellen. The girls got along well, chatting softly about 'girl' things, with Rita predominantly sharing some of the idiosyncrasies of growing up and living in this neighborhood. Ellen laughed incredulously at some of the stories Rita related as normal occurrences.

"You can't be serious," she said when Rita explained how difficult it was to meet boys when one's father was so 'old school'. "Are you really serious?" she asked again.

"Yes, I am. Can you believe that my father shadowed my eldest sister when she went out on her first date? He wore a dark coat and his black hat just to make certain that the boy didn't touch her while they were walking to the movie house."

"What do you mean 'touch' her?" Ellen queried in total disbelief as she puzzled out what 'touch her' meant .

Rita explained, " I mean that he watched to ensure that the boy never held her hand or put his arm around her. The old timers thought it bordered on sinful!"

"Oh my goodness! You girls weren't even allowed to hold hands with a boy?"

"Nope!" Rita chuckled at how almost overnight dating mores and expectations had changed, though she, herself, remained adamant about not kissing a boy until the third date. "You know what else? If a neighbor saw one of the local girls walking down the block holding hands with a boy—well!! The phones would be ringing off the hook within minutes to tell the girl's father."

Ellen shook her head in disbelief, mouthing "Wow!"

That's how it was then, but one must understand the motivation behind the attitude of the neighborhood fathers. They were immigrants: Italian, Irish, German, Scandinavian, Jewish. In their defense, their Old World courting rituals consisted of pre-arranged introductions, fully chaperoned 'dating,' prescribed patterns of behavior, and quick marriages. Coming to America was a monumental culture shock that stunned their sensibilities. Imagine their reaction when a daughter came home from school on a Friday afternoon and announced that she had a 'date' that night. That night? "Who's the boy? When am I going to meet him? Where are his parents from?"

Rita's dad, more progressive than many of his peers, allowed his daughters to select their dating partners (even if it meant that they would see a different boy each week). He didn't adapt overnight; indeed, American-izing took him a while—especially when it involved his first-born daughter. Thus, her tailed her to the movie house on her very first date with an American boy. He did not go in. It cost ten cents plus two cents tax.

The information on other dates is sketchy, but he was totally inflexible on the hand-holding customs of young American boys. In fact, he sternly warned each of his girls that they must not 'shame' him and the family by letting a boy hold their hands while walking in the street. Of course, he would not even hint at what else the boys shouldn't touch that belonged to his daughters; supposedly, they got the message—he hoped. Ellen began to understand the genesis of what made Robby who he was and what may have prompted some of his thinking. Nevertheless, she remained aloof, keenly aware of her feelings and recent hurts.

IV

As they started up the church steps, Rita and Ellen told the boys that they were going to confession before mass, and asked the boys to save them seats. Donny turned to Robby and said in an almost inaudible whisper, "Maybe you should hit the box too."

"Me? You gotta be kidding. I haven't been to confession in years."

"So what? This might be just the thing you need . . . ."

"I'd probably be in there all night," he meekly protested. But then he scanned the perimeter of the church interior, and noticed dozens of persons on line waiting for the sacrament. He knew that the priests would not be spending an undue amount of time with each person, because they had to prepare for the upcoming high mass. Quickly calculating his odds in the confessional, he decided to attend the sacrament. Finally, he said, "Oh! All right. But I'm not going to the same priest as Ellen."

Donny watched as Robby scampered through pews to the other end of the church to put as much distance between himself and the girls. "God forbid," he thought, "that they should hear any of what I should say to the priest."

Robby correctly assumed that tonight, with long lines of persons waiting to make their annual confession, the priests would be more lenient with the penitents. Tonight, it would be,

"Bless me Father for I have sinned, etc," followed by a quick, "Go and sin no more! Your penance is three Hail Marys and two Our Fathers."

Robby waited on a long line but kept his eye on the two girls at the other side of the church feeling as guilty as he had ever felt about anything in his entire life. Confession always made him feel like this—until the priest blessed him and sent him out to make penance.

Donny laughed when Robby scrambled across pews and onto the line, knowing every feeling that Robby was having and just a little bit glad that he felt that way. "Maybe tonight will straighten him out," he silently prayed.

The church filled quickly, and altar boys in long, white cassocks arrived to light the many candles so important to the evening's celebration. The sexton and several women also appeared and began to 'dress' the altar with several dozen poinsettia plants, which they carefully laid out in front the previously bare area surrounding the altar. When the altar was completed, the organist played traditional Christmas music. The church was bright with candle light and red and green live plants everywhere: it was truly festive and beautiful to see.

The organist continued with a medley of liturgical music that helped congregants enter into the spirit of the evening's celebration. Soon, one by one, Ellen, Rita, and Robby rejoined Donny in the pew. Ellen returned first and sat next to Donny; Rita sat to Ellen's left so Robby could sit on her right. When Robby settled, Ellen leaned close to him and whispered, "How was it?" and almost burst out laughing when he said, "As bad as having my teeth pulled!" He was glad to see her laugh; it was her first in a long time; he missed her being happy.

The celebrant, a young priest who asked to be called Father Tom, gave a beautiful homily urging everyone to always seek out the best in others. "When we focus on the faults of others," he began "we make judgments that inhibit our ability to enter into a meaningful relationship with that person. None of us is without sin, otherwise we wouldn't have a need for sacramental confession. The true message of Christmas is that Jesus came to bring peace. And unless we choose to live in peace with one another, we will suffer endless chaos in life. God's spirit dwells deep within each of us and demands that we reach out and love that spirit in our neighbor."

"You'd be surprised," he continued "how often estranged relationships are healed when one party reaches out in love to the other. We humans need to be loved, and unless we receive love, we will ultimately die."

He paused suddenly, took the microphone from it place at the lectern, and walked slowly down from the altar and into the center aisle of the church. "Hey, folks," he said smiling at the congregation as he passed, "do you trust me?" He looked deeply into the eyes of as many persons as he could as he repeated the question.

People were shocked to see a priest act this way at mass. It just wasn't done. But he persisted, "Do you trust me?" Heads began to nod in assent, but no one spoke. "I can't hear you!" he said louder than before and repeated it until he received an oral response from the entire congregation. "Well, now that I know that you trust me," he walked back to the front of the church, "I'm going to ask you to do something for me."

The congregation was still puzzled, but in a good humor as a result of this unorthodox homily. He continued, "I want you to turn to the person next to you and tell them which quality of theirs is most endearing to you. In other words—tell that person what makes them special . . . to you. Go on now—do it!"

Slowly, the congregation responded, but Robby remained . . . mute. His eyes were frozen forward, while he squeezed the seat back in front of him for dear life. After a few seconds, the entire church was buzzing with people talking and hugging—even Donny and Rita. It was Ellen who broke the silence.

"Rob? Isn't there anything about me that you find endearing?"

He twisted his hands, unable to speak at first, but when he turned to look at her, he melted; she was radiant. "Ellen," he began slowly "I am so very sorry for how I acted. You deserve to be with a man so much better than I."

He fumbled for words as Ellen looked at him lovingly waiting for him to answer her question. He did respond. "The most endearing quality that I see in you is your ability to put up with a dumb jerk like me. You are the most wonderful gift that God could have ever given to anyone—and he chose me—He put you smack dab into the middle of my life and I treated you . . . so badly."

She could not restrain her lovely smile; she glowed before him, joyful at his spontaneous, and somehow childlike, love song. Maybe . . . maybe! (She prayed.)

He continued, "You gave such a deep meaning to my life that I could never have imagined. I felt alive like never before; I was reborn, and I do not want to revert to my former self. You gave me a real reason to live, and honestly, I don't know how I could ever get along without you by my side. My dearest, I love you with all my heart, and I'm sorry for all the hurts I've caused you. Can you ever forgive me?"

"Yes! Yes!" She flung herself at him and hugged him with all her strength.

After a few very stirring moments, Robby, though choked with tears streaming down his face, managed to whisper to her softly, "Ellen?"

"Yes my love?" She gazed once more into his eyes, old feelings for him returning, believing and trusting that everything was going to work out as she had hoped and prayed that it would.

He struggled to get words out, "Do I . . . have any . . . endearing qualities?"

Almost immediately she responded, "Yes, of course!" She left it at that.

Completely puzzled by the curtness of her response, he probed, "Well, are you gonna tell me?" Robby cleared his throat and clumsily wiped at the tears that continued falling down his face. A man in love, he stared—and waited anxiously for his lover to reply.

After what seemed like minutes but which was a mere three or four seconds, she held him closely and whispered, "Yes, Rob." And then after another almost imperceptible delay, she kissed him gently on the cheek, and then looking directly into his tear-filled eyes continued, "The most endearing quality you have . . . is . . . that . . . you have wonderful . . ."

Robby could hardly stand still as he waited on Ellen's next words.

She continued, " . . . well, Rob, you have really wonderful . . . friends."

After he fully digested the content of her message, he hung his head in mock despair and began to gently laugh with her.

At that moment, Father Tom called the congregation back to order. Robby sheepishly replied, "I deserved that."

"I'll talk to you later, my dear" she whispered softly into his ear, and gave him a knowing look as she raised one eyebrow. Seconds passed and she squeezed and held his hand tightly during the remainder of the mass.

DONNY

I

Donny was jubilant that after the Christmas Eve Mass, Robby and Ellen's relationship had evolved to where they were able to share openly with one another. Robby knew that the relationship had been healed after Ellen became uncommonly serious when speaking to him one evening. She had previously explained the most intimate details of her earlier life, and made a total commitment to a new life with him. She brought him to his knees once more when she laid bare her feelings about life alone and now with him. "You know," she murmured gently, "you were the one man that I could honestly say took the time to seek out my personal welfare." She ended by adding, "Rob . . . you are my hero! YOU ARE MY HERO! And my love for you will never fail. Promise that you will always be there for me." She glowed with renewed fervor and joy fed by the promises of true love and the confidence in her lover.

Overwhelmed by her words and barely able to speak, he sighed, "I will." And then, once more, almost imperceptibly, "I will."

Now that all seemed right with the rest of the world, all was not right with Donny. For as long as he could remember, he had known the answers to the many problems that confronted him; as a result, he was never plagued with much indecision or doubt. When he received a poor grade, it was simply because he hadn't studied hard enough; when he struck out too frequently playing stickball or baseball, it was because he didn't practice his batting enough; when other boys ran faster than he did, it was because he was slow. Simple. Uncomplicated. Never a dilemma.

But fate began to deal with Donny in new and varied ways following the Christmas of 1955. Now almost nineteen, he was confronted with the reality that answers didn't always come easily—the fact was that the questions were suddenly becoming complex and required extensive thought and sometimes pain. He understood that often there just wasn't one single approach that made total sense or a decision that wouldn't cause someone some degree of pain—and that included himself. Whereas Donny could always resolve the problems of his youth, he was stymied trying to deal with the specific events confronting him. He was, it was obvious, growing up.

II

Donny met Rita at a high school dance in 1953 a few weeks before his seventeenth birthday. Never much of a dancer, he had been forcibly dragged by Robby onto the subway train and out to St. Brendan's High School in Bay Ridge for the weekly Saturday night dance that was sponsored AND chaperoned by the Sisters of Saint Dominick. The last time Donny had been in Bay Ridge was when, as president of the senior class, he had to escort Paula Martin, the president of Bay Ridge High School (an all-girls school and Tech's sister school), to a school dance in the gym. It was, as usual, another of Donny's social disasters. Paula had the social obligation of leading everyone in the evening's first dance. When the music began and the spotlight fell on her table, all eyes turned toward her. She smiled at the crowd and waited for Donny to escort her onto the dance floor. She knew that he was not a 'dancer,' but she also knew him to be gracious and that he would attempt some type of movement that could be recognized as dancing. And, so, with pleading eyes she said, "Donny, it's time. You ready?"

Gracious to a fault, aware that the entire gymnasium was watching, he slowly rose from his chair and approached Paula. She held out her hand to him, but as he reached for it, he tugged a bit too quickly causing Paula to stumble against the side of the table that they were at. When Paula straightened herself, she realized that her poodle skirt was torn across the front, having caught on the table's ragged metal edge. She stood crying as she tried to cover up the many exposed horsehair slips that gave her skirt its billowy look. Someone had a pin and Paula adjusted the skirt as best she could while asking—telling—Donny to take her home immediately! All future conversations between them from that night until graduation were strictly limited to school business.

III

"What am I going to do when we get there?" Donny protested when Robby 'told' him they were going to Saint Brendan's.

"You'll do what everybody else does. Stop worrying for Pete's sake."

"But I don't dance!" Donny pleaded as the memory of the 'Paula Martin incident' loomed clear in his mind, and he was struck with fear at the thought of once again dancing with someone else who wasn't his mother, cousin, Aunt, or the girl next door. He vividly recalled the afternoon of Gloria McCormick's fourteenth birthday party—the day he danced' with a girl for the very first time—and his perspiration increased tenfold. Donny prayed silently that Robby would give up this idea of going to dances!! But deep in his spirit he also understood that young girls loved dancing ,and that many of the 'nice' girls also showed up at these church dances. He was frightened beyond belief about holding a girl in his arms—frightened because of what happened to him when Gloria McCormick asked him to dance with her on her birthday.

When the invitation to Gloria"s party arrived in the mail, Donny immediately rejected the idea of going, but Marie insisted, knowing how shy her son was and how important it was for him to develop some social graces. Marie, herself, tried to teach Donny a few basic dance steps, but that meant that she had to lead, and she was used to following Angelo's lead when dancing. So teaching Donny became a real hardship even after Marie solicited the help of her sister and some of Donny's female cousins. Ultimately, of course, Marie insisted, and Donny went to Gloria's birthday party.

Gloria McCormick attended St. Teresa's School and was in the same grade as Donny though not in his class. She was in the girls' school across the courtyard. She lived on the same block as Donny, about six houses away, but did not play or visit anywhere near Donny's apartment building. Gloria spent most of her time with her own circle of friends; that is, until she began to notice the tall, handsome boy down the block. She noticed him first when the school began rehearsals just before graduation. Donny had been selected as valedictorian, and Gloria told all her girl friends that, "Donny lives right down the block from me!"

It wasn't all that bad, he rationalized, when he walked into the lower level of Gloria's two-story apartment. Almost everyone there was from Saint Teresa's, everyone was about the same age, and he felt at ease being with them. As usual, the girls were doing all the dancing—with each other—so there was never any pressure on Donny—or any of the boys—to dance. UNTIL—Gloria put on a slow Sarah Vaughn record, and walked up to Donny and said, "C'mon. Dance with me for my birthday?"

How could he resist? She was so nice, and he didn't want to disappoint her. BUT . . . though Donny had the right intention in his heart, his face turned from its normally olive color to the ghostliest white of whites and then beet red!! "Dance? Me??" he stammered. "I would really like to, but . . . but." He whispered to her, "You know I don't dance!!"

Gloria reached for his hand anyway and clasped his fingertips ever so gently. His first thought was that her skin was soft, not at all like Marie's or Robby's. She led him slowly into the middle of the basement floor where two other girls were already dancing with each other. The faintest hint of the perfume she wore . . . hit him! He didn't know what happened, but he 'forgot to be nervous.' He was dancing! Donny followed her step by step, his eyes focussed on the back of her head, until she leaned in closer. It felt nice, he thought . . . dancing. Her moves were so subtle that it was effortless for him to keep time; the music continued slow and mellow. She gazed into his eyes for a second or two before resting her head on his shoulder and swaying with the music, moving ever closer to him.

"You're doing great; just relax and try to follow the music," she whispered almost inaudibly, her lips warm and moist against his ear.

Donny was mortified; she couldn't get any closer! He had already gone way beyond his comfort zone. So many new experiences all at once boggled his mind, and he needed time to sort things out. Much later that night, after dwelling on the perfume and her soft hands and being so close to a girl, and her lips on his ear . . . he had to admit , "It was kinda cool being with her like that."

As it turned out, that single incident was a major turning point in transitioning the 'boy' Donny into the 'man' Donny. Life was moving very fast, he discovered, and he had to prepare himself for the ride. The next day, Donny found himself bragging to Robby about the 'great' party he attended at Gloria's house. And about how "everyone was dancing and the lights were low and the music was slow, and there was . . . perfume and . . . well, you know."

IV

Donny eventually snapped back to reality and continued his pleas to Robby, "Listen, I can't go to the dance. I don't really feel all that well anyway."

"Why? What's happened? You sick or something?"

"No. It's my father."

Donny was embarrassed to tell Robby how his father had come home from work really late after spending several hours in Tony's drinking boilermakers—whiskey with beer chasers. He was drunk beyond what Donny had ever experienced up to this point. Marie had already prepared his meal hours before, expecting him home sometime close to the regular time; she kept it warming for hours on the stove waiting for him. But Angelo never came.

When he finally staggered down the block under the watchful eyes of the neighbors, Donny retreated into the apartment to be with Marie. Angelo crawled up the stairs and then burst into the apartment screaming for all to hear, "Marie!! What's to eat? I'm hungry!" Sensing a scene, Donny closed the apartment door. Marie scampered to put the remnants of the food together and place it before her husband. It was obvious that he was not going to eat it; he just poked it around and called the food garbage and other choice words.

Marie cried, but through her tears and sobs, she challenged him that it was ready hours ago, and if he had come home on time, it would have looked and tasted better. This 'confrontation' sent Angelo into a rage; how dare she make excuses to him!! He got up from his chair and threw it across the room and into the ice box. He took the dish laden with food and threw it out the kitchen window smashing the plate and two panes of window glass. Looking for more things to throw, he emptied all the kitchen drawers and threw forks and knives and spoons and anything else in the drawers out the window and into the yard two stories below. Marie was hysterical while Donny stood off in a corner watching this horror with tears in his eyes too—unable to comprehend the madness of the situation unfolding before him.

Angelo, completely enraged, staggered across the room toward Marie and with an open hand began slapping her face and head her while pulling hard on her hair—screaming at her through slurred speech, "You make me good food no matter what time I come home!! I'm the husband; you do what I say you do!!"

At the first instant that Angelo struck Marie, Donny flew from his position near the fire escape across the room to Marie's side, screaming at the top of his voice for Angelo to stop. But Angelo heeded not. Forcing Marie safely behind him, Donny put his left hand on Angelo's chest and readied the right to punch his own father, screaming through tears and sobs, "Leave her alone! I'll kill you if you don't stop!!"

Then . . . only then . . . did Angelo stop. Who was this son of his to tell him what to do? This was his house. He was in charge. He was in charge—once.

Angelo, his mind still controlled by liquor and rage, somehow understood the shocking fierceness before him in the person of his son! Until this moment, no one dared confront Angelo nor would anyone have intervened for Marie. Not in this neighborhood!

Men were supreme even when abusive. Strangely, Angelo's behavior was not uncommon in the neighborhood. Many women suffered at the hands of their besotted husbands, and because divorce was frowned upon, the women just took it.

In the Gargano home, today marked a radical change from the norm. Until now, anytime he stepped through the door to their apartment, Angelo . . . was . . . king . . . the boss! Now, he acknowledged, things are different—today, Marie and Donny became different people. Today heralded a different and more mature relationship between Donny and Marie; it also marked the demise of any respect Donny ever had for his father. It would be decades later—at a time when Marie was dying—that Angelo would feel some slight remorse for what he had done to her for so many years; it would be even longer before Donny would consider forgiving his father and, ultimately, tell him that he loved him.

A few minutes passed before Angelo staggered into the bedroom and flopped onto the bed with his clothes on muttering something under his breath. Marie relaxed somewhat, but noticed that Donny was shaking terribly. She hugged him as they both wiped the tears from each other's faces. Finally, Marie told Donny to go out and get some air, but before he left she told him, "It's the drink, Donny; the drink makes him go crazy." It was 'the drink' that did it to so many contemporaries of Angelo Gargano. To so many others.

Marie slowly removed Angelo's shoes and clothes, being gentle so as not to disturb him; in spite of what just happened, she absolutely loved her man and wanted him comfortable in bed. She knew that tomorrow would be a new day, and that Angelo would want to snuggle and try to make things right. She would, as always, perform her wifely duty—unfeeling, still, and very, very grateful when it was all over. For now, at least.

Years later, as Donny grew older and learned more about the life his parents shared, he evaluated the tales he heard being whispered by aunts and uncles and, sometimes, even neighbors, about Angelo's treatment of Marie and some of the secret liaisons his father was purported to have had. As far as Donny could determine, Marie was a loving and dedicated wife who never shirked her responsibilities even when it meant shopping in all kinds of inclement weather to bring food to the table. She walked so she could save the five-cent trolley fare when the distance wasn't too far. She was a dutiful wife in all the ways that Donny, himself, could attest.

Donny tried to make some sense out of these stories and of his father's insane attitude toward Marie and his desire to always volunteer for the night shift. Perhaps it was the meager pay differential between the day shift and the night shift that attracted Angelo, Donny often rationalized. Having the few dollars more each month merely gave him more money to spend on drinks at Tony's. But then other parts of the story failed to make sense. Donny eventually gave up caring about anything his father did, except as it related to Marie.

V

Angelo had struggled for years trying to get steady work, frequently having to shape-up for a job each day. Shape-up was a process used for job situations where a foreman did not need a steady crew of men for long term; instead, he would hire daily or weekly laborers. It was a common occurrence that men seeking work would arrive at a hiring hall and sit and wait until a hiring boss described the work available and asked who had experience. The flaw in the system was that the work was always manual labor and the hiring boss gave the work to his friends or, sometimes, to those who paid him a percent of their day's wages. The shape-up was fraught with corruption and danger from the gangs of needy men who often resorted to violence if it meant they could put food on their own table that day.

When Marie persuaded Angelo to take the test for United States Postal Letter Carrier, he reluctantly agreed—and passed the test placing No. 6 out of the 1200 men in New York City who took the test. Angelo was proud of his accomplishment and was scheduled to begin work after a short training session—in time for the Christmas rush.

His first few weeks on the job were exciting and fun as he greeted many of his mail customers each day when he delivered letters and packages to small shops and apartment buildings. In those days, letter carriers walked their routes all day for six straight hours. The other two hours were spent sorting their mail for the next day's deliveries.

Angelo was assigned to the Vanderbilt Postal Station on Atlantic Avenue about twelve blocks from home. He would arrive early each day and pick up his load and then walk fourteen blocks to his assigned route carrying a heavy leather mail pouch, which, when fully loaded, weighed almost forty pounds. When the pouch was empty, he retraced his steps part way back to his main office and opened a large iron container placed prominently on the corner of a main thoroughfare—designated a local substation. It contained the remainder of the day's mail that was left there by one of the postal truck drivers.

He did this each day, six days a week. Eventually, the weather turned icy and the temperatures dropped below freezing, but the mail had to be delivered. It rained and sleeted on Angelo Gargano often that winter as he walked his route and then back to the iron box that never emptied of mail and packages. In those days, the letter carriers delivered holiday mail continuously right up to Christmas Eve midnight. It meant long days with mandatory overtime and walking the streets regardless of weather conditions. Some days Angelo walked almost two hundred blocks delivering the U.S. mail.

As Donny pondered this aspect of his father's working experience, he could not but feel somewhat more sympathetic toward his father and the choice he made to leave the Post Office and seek out other employment. But his choice was flawed, because, in retrospect, other fathers who remained with the Post Office eventually received scheduled raises, benefits, and, ultimately, an excellent government pension. Donny wondered whether there could have been some money for his college tuition if Angelo had stayed. Regardless, Angelo opted out of this, and Donny puzzled why. Why did he leave a secure job to return to a life of uncertainty with shape-up and night shifts? Why? Donny never found out.

VI

Robby would hear none of it. "Listen; we're going to the dance, and that's the end of it. Now let's go! Giddy-up!"

Donny protested every step of the way as the young pair walked to the Franklin Avenue 'El' and boarded the train that would inevitably take them to the Bay Ridge section of Brooklyn and St. Brendan's high School. As they bounced along in their seats, Donny was emphatic: "I can't dance! It's not that I won't dance; I CAN'T DANCE!!" But Robby smiled all the while reiterating the same response: "Don't worry; just do what everybody else does. You'll be fine."

The dance was held in the schoolyard adjacent to the high school. Flood lights located on high towers illuminated the entire area, which, by now, contained hundreds of teenagers, half of whom just leaned against the ten-foot high chain link fence that enclosed the yard, the school, and other buildings. The tenants living in the surrounding apartment buildings were apparently oblivious to the loud music and talk, since most windows were dark. Perhaps they were not oblivious; perhaps they capitulated and went out for the evening.

The nun standing at the entrance to the schoolyard collected ten cents from everyone who entered, and levied this pronouncement on all passing through: "No close dancing, no smoking, no leaving and coming back!"

They paid their admission, and Robby led Donny around the perimeter of the huge schoolyard to a group of boys leaning against the fence. Donny recognized some of the boys, but Robby knew them all.

"This is my friend Don," Robby said as he introduced Donny to the group.

Pleasantries were exchanged quickly since everyone's eyes were focussed on those already dancing. It took Donny a few seconds to realize that most of those dancing were girls: girls dancing with girls. The boys, except for a small handful anyway— were leaning against the fence—watching.

"The guys don't dance?" Donny whispered to Robby, relaxing a bit, assuming that tonight's venture would be an exercise in girl watching.

"Later . . . later," he replied.

"What kind of dance is that anyway?" Donny asked aloud. "I never saw anybody dance like that before."

One of the other boys responded, "It's the Irish Lindy—fast and bouncy, designed to wear you out. Keeps the boys and girls apart."

"Looks hard," Donny said casually.

"Nah," someone responded, "the girls do all the work. Watch."

It was true: the leader, whether boy or girl, stood erect, practically rigid, lifting only the left arm to allow their partner to bounce under and around. Donny was mesmerized by the dancers who were mainly female couples engaged in this seemingly endless ritual of bouncing and spinning under and around, dance—after dance—after dance.

"Do they do the Lindy all night long, Rob?"

"Mostly. The nuns don't want us holding the girls close; know what I mean?"

"Yeah, but it's crazy. I'd probably be exhausted if I danced like that all night."

"That's the idea, my man." The entire group chuckled in unison.

After about forty-five minutes of the Irish Lindy, Donny heard the intro to a Perry Como song begin. So did all the boys who were lined up against the fence. It was as though a signal had been given for them to dash madly toward any available girl and began the first slow dance of the night. Donny stood alone, watching, grateful that he wasn't going to be forced to dance with anyone. When the record ended and the next Lindy began, he noted two things: (1) the number of dancers on the floor had diminished . . . significantly and (2) some of the boys did not return to their original spots along the fence. Where did they go? Answer: they went off on their own with the girl with whom they were dancing. And so it was, he discovered, that boy meets girl. The pattern repeated itself every forty-five minutes or so, with only a handful of boys trying the Irish Lindy with their partners.

At St. Brendan's, it was common for a girl who danced with a boy more than once to continue dancing with him the remainder of the evening (or stay by his side if he didn't actually choose to dance every dance). Implicit in this routine was her tacit agreement granting him the privilege of walking or accompanying her home and, once home, giving him, perhaps, he hoped, a good-night kiss. At other Catholic school dances, it was basically the same ritual, with variations.

At St. Francis, for example, where the dance was held indoors in the gym and snacks and soda were sold, there was much more interchange among the boys and girls: the majority of dancers changed partners after almost every dance. There was much more to occupy everyone's time; thus, the 'coupling' ritual didn't occur until the 'next-to-last-dance' was announced over the tinny gym speakers. This announcement was also the de-facto signal for the attendees to couple up to see who was going home with whom—etc, etc.

Robby and Donny continued visiting St. Brendan's for many more Saturdays that summer, observing the same pattern repeating itself inexorably week after week: boys along the fence—girls dancing; a slow dance with boys and girls; pairs off talking; final slow dance, and then the expected (and hoped for) walk home. Donny, quite innocently, suggested that it might be better if a boy picked out a girl to escort home earlier in the evening, rather than wait until the last dance. That way, he could ensure that she were really pretty. Robby laughed at Donny's naïveté, and commented, "The girls all get better looking right after the last dance is announced!"

Donny couldn't wait for the weekly cycle to end, for though he enjoyed girl watching, he never danced, even after one of his female cousins had tried to teach him whenever they were together on Sunday afternoons. On one of Brooklyn's warmest and most humid Saturday nights—a few moments after the second slow dance had ended—Robby walked back to Donny with two girls in tow: one short, one tall, both very attractive.

"Don," he said proudly, "I'd like you to meet Terry McGann and her friend, Rita Staci. They come from our neighborhood, and this is their first time here."

Donny greeted the girls warmly, and didn't feel the least bit shy since he thought they had just come over to say hello. But, strangely, they didn't leave except to dance a Lindy or two with each another after which they came right back to where Donny and Robby were standing. Donny sensed that something was up as he said to Robby, "Why are they staying with us?"

"'Cause we're going to take them home."

"Take them home? I never took a girl home!" To Donny, 'taking a girl home' was a big deal with many expectations; he wasn't ready for all this drama! Donny felt the panic deep within and his heart a-pounding.

"Well then, it's time you began!"

Robby's assertion obviously alluded to the fact that since he had been coming to St. Brendan's with Donny, he had not taken a single girl home. Robby had deferred to his friend's tacit wishes, but Robby's patience had run out: he needed female companionship, and tonight was the night. This ritual demanded that when a girl allowed you to take her home—well, she was amenable to the good-night kiss—it was almost a certainty. It was a departure from the norm that demanded that nice girls never kiss on the first date. And since going stag to a dance was not actually a date—well, rules were meant to be bent, if not broken, anyway.

Donny later overheard a rumor about the possibility that some of the not-so-nice girls at the dances were even a 'bit more' amenable when a boy took them home. "What was it about dancing?" Donny wondered to himself. "It's gotta be a cultural thing to stimulate procreation or something," he mused and promised that when he got to college he would inquire about it from a sociology professor. Most often, though, he wondered, "Why am I the deviant in all of this? Everybody else seems to just go along with all these ritualistic concepts. Take a girl home? Suppose they live in a different neighborhood? Some of the trains stop running after midnight. How will I get home if she lives . . . ?"

Donny paced along the fence, pondering and worrying and worrying and pondering, more afraid of taking a girl home than he had been of anything before. He never realized just how many things made him afraid. Whenever Rita and Terry returned from a dance together, he smiled politely and engaged them in light conversation, but when they went off again to dance together, he battled with Robby.

"You can't do this to me!" he protested.

Robby just smiled back at him slyly and said, "Trust me, my man. Trust me."

When the music for the last dance began—it was, as expected, slow—Robby and Terry scooted onto the dance area hand in hand, leaving Rita and Donny alone—at the fence—neither one making a move: Rita staring out at the dancers; Donny staring down at the floor . . . with his hands in his pockets. As Robby and Terry began to dance, Robby turned to see them both frozen in time and space.

"I don't believe it," he said to Terry, shaking his head in disbelief. "Those two are like peas in a pod—neither one is going to make a move." He excused himself, leaving Terry alone, and ran up to Rita and Donny. "Aren't you two going to dance? This is the last dance, you know!"

Rita had lowered her eyes and began to scan the floor trying to hide her obvious embarrassment. Robby looked Donny squarely in the eyes and said through clenched teeth, "Ask her to dance!" and as he walked away he whispered, "Dummy" to himself and wondered whether he should have put Rita's hand in Donny's and led them both out into the dance area.

It was as though all time had come to a halt, for Donny could hear nothing of the crowd or music—only his heart pounding. He was thoroughly embarrassed that he 'had' to ask Rita to dance; it would be an insult if he didn't.

He raised his eyes to meet hers, and shyly suggested, "Would . . . you . . . ?"

"Yes!" Her voice rang in his ears. At last! Rita was jubilant! She cut him off him before he could finish asking his question, and immediately turned toward him. She gently placed her hand into his and moved in just close enough so that he could feel the soft curves of her body next to his and detect the fragrance of her lingering perfume. "Oh, God," he thought. "More perfume!!"

"I . . . don't . . . dance," he stammered as he began to rock back and forth slowly though in perfect time with the music. But if his dancing was in need of help, his hormones were functioning just perfectly. So this was maybe not such a bad thing after all, he began to think. Maybe not such a bad thing at all.

"You dance very well, Don," Rita said politely as she lowered her head onto his shoulder and moved in just a tad closer.

"I guess . . . you make it easy," he replied, adjusting his right hand to a more comfortable spot at her waist.

"Haven't other girls told you how 'smooth' you dance?"

"No . . . ," he hesitated. "You're the first . . . to tell me—that is."

When the music ended, Donny and Rita continued dancing, unaware that the dance was over or that they had hardly moved from their original spot near the fence. It was only when Robby and Terry joined them that they came to their senses. Robby shook his head in mild disbelief as he grinned and muttered to himself, "First you can't get him to start, and then you can't get him to stop." "Aren't hormones just great!" Robby muttered to himself.

VII

While the Rita and Terry went off to the girls' room to fix their hair and adjust whatever needed adjusting, Donny had an opportunity to talk to Robby.

"So what's the plan, Rob?" he asked, now quite animated. "What's next—maestro—knower of all things?"

"We'll take them home; when we get back to the neighborhood, I'll take Terry to her house and you take Rita to hers."

"And then . . . ?"

"And then what? You walk, you talk, you say nice things to her, and then meet me in front of my house afterwards. If you're nice, maybe she'll let you kiss her."

"Make out? You think so? It's only the first time. Besides, how do I even know that she'll let me take her home?"

"C'mon, Don; relax! If she didn't want you to take her home, she would have left before the last dance. And don't worry about making out; they love to make out—you'll see."

"Hmmm." Donny had always trusted Robby's judgment in matters relating to women, but now, curiously, he wasn't so sure that Robby was correct.

Both girls returned looking refreshed with their hair neatly combed and teased, their makeup freshened, and the gentle fragrance of freshly applied perfume embracing them. Donny took careful note of how beautiful Rita actually was—he couldn't keep his eyes off her as she and Terry strolled gracefully across the vast concrete schoolyard.

"All set?" Robby asked the girls.

"Uh-huh," Terry said with a confident smile.

"Let's go then."

Robby reached down and took Terry's hand as they led the way to the subway station. Donny and Rita followed along—silent for the most part—walking side by side but not close enough to touch.

It was Rita who ultimately broke the boring silence, "Where do you go to school, Don?"

" . . . Tech . . . Brooklyn Tech. Boys' school."

Again, more silence.

"Sophomore?"

"Ah . . . no—Junior . . . Junior."

"Hmm." More silence.

Then, "I go to Catherine McCauley. Girls' school."

"Oh." Followed by . . . silence.

"Freshman."

"Hmm."

The five-minute walk to the station was punctuated by only the faintest sounds that resembled conversation, and had it not been for Rita's initial question, the walk would have taken place in complete silence, with Donny staring at the ground as they walked, fiddling with the loose change for the subway fare in his pants pocket. The boys let the girls enter the turnstile first hoping that they would have the nickel ready for their own fare; and . . . they did! Both boys were relieved since it was too early in a relationship for boys to be paying a girl's 5-cent subway fare.

The ride was swift and the cars were practically empty at this time of night. As the train rumbled into the Eastern Parkway station, Robby and Terry rose, said their "good nights" quickly and left.

"I get off at the next stop; Park Place," Rita said.

"Mine is the one after that; Dean Street," Donny mumbled.

"Oh."

When the train began to slow for Rita's stop, she rose and held onto the back of the seat for balance, as was customary, until the train halted. Donny, too, also rose and reached for an overhead strap.

"You don't have to get off here," Rita said. "I can walk home alone; it's OK."

"No . . . I want to. It's OK; I want to. It's OK, really." Donny kept right on talking.

She said, "It's really not necessary—it's not far. I can almost see my house from the station, anyway."

" . . . I'll feel better if I do."

"OK." Rita smiled at him, secretly pleased that he would be walking with her the block and a half home even though she knew it would be perfectly safe for her to walk it alone. This was her neighborhood.

After the few minutes' walk, she said, "I live here," pointing to the lovely, classic, two-story brownstone on Park Place. As it turned out, it was just a few houses in from Classon Avenue and a brief, five-minute stroll to his own home.

"It's a pretty house."

"Yes; we own it—my parents, that is."

"Nice," he said scanning the building up and down several times. "Nice bricks."

"Yes."

"Nice railing."

"Yes."

"Nice front door. Solid wood?"

"Yes."

After a few more moments of architectural analysis and a few polite "Yes-es", Rita asked, "Do you have the time, Don?"

"Yes; it's eleven twenty-five."

"I'd better go in, then. I'm supposed to be in by eleven thirty."

" . . . Oh—OK." He was disappointed, because the time spent with her had passed so quickly, and he had hardly said anything of substance.

She smiled, turned, and walked up the dozen or so steps to the outside front door. She paused, then turned back toward Donny who remained at the bottom step watching her—his hands still stuck deeply into his pants pockets. Why was his heart pounding now? He would be alone in just a few seconds.

"Don," Rita whispered from the top step.

"Yes?" he whispered back.

"Thanks for walking me home; I had a really nice time."

"You're welcome; and thanks for dancing with me. Good night."

"Good night."

"Thanks, again."

"You're welcome. Good night."

Neither one moved; they just stared at each other, both very much aware that in the preceding thirty seconds they had spoken more substance than they had all night. Rita turned slowly to the door, inserted her key, waved a final good night; She folded her billowing skirt close to her body, and was quickly gone from his view.

"Jerk! Dumb, stupid, jerk!" Donny said to himself as he turned away and headed toward home, kicking any garbage can that happened to be in his way or even near his way.

When he passed Robby's house, he decided to sit on the steps and wait for him, fully expecting him to arrive at any moment since Terry's house was only four short blocks away from Rita's. But after about forty-five minutes, he went home to bed and listened to the "Milkman's Matinee" on the all-night New York City radio station, WNEW. He couldn't sleep. His mind was full of only one thought: Rita.

The next morning the telephone's ringing woke him at about eight-thirty.

"I'll get it," he shouted to Marie who was in the kitchen preparing the tomato sauce for Sunday's dinner. It was Robby, and he sounded wide awake."

"How are you, my man?" he shouted into the receiver.

"Are you nuts? I'm still asleep."

"How'd you make out last night?"

"Make out?" Donny was puzzled, still groggy, and not yet full awake.

"You know. Last night . . . with Rita."

"Yeah—hey! Where were you anyhow? I waited on your steps until after midnight—."

Robby was laughing as he interrupted his friend, "I'm sorry—really. I was sort of tied up, if you know what I mean, and couldn't get away."

"Yeah—I'll bet," Donny replied.

"So did you get a chance to make out yourself?"

"No.—We just talked." Donny's thoughts were of what could have been.

"You like her, don't you?"

"Sure. She's really nice."

"Ya get her number?"

"No; I . . . ah . . . damn! I didn't think of it."

"She probably thinks you don't like her, you meatball."

"Really? I hope not." Donny was fully alert now, hating himself and conscious of the possibility that his awkwardness might cause him never to see Rita again.

"Of course," Robby continued. "Every girl expects you to ask for her number—especially if she lets you walk her home. You gotta learn these things, man."

Donny muttered, "Damn!" again into the receiver.

"Hey—don't worry. She hangs out with Terry, and I'm going to meet Terry at Otto's today. I'll tell her to bring Rita along."

Donny's eyes brightened and he felt relieved, hopeful at getting a second chance. "Look, I gotta go and shower. I'll call for you after mass." Donny raced past Marie with a quick "Good mornin', Ma" and jumped into the shower. In a few moments, she heard her son singing, "It's very clear: our love is here to stay."

"I wonder what's gotten into him?" she asked herself. If she knew, she'd be happy: the hormones were operating normally.

Robby was already outside when Donny came by to pick him up at about eleven-thirty. "Wanna go up to Otto's?" he asked. Donny could only think of Rita, and was so eager to be anywhere that she was that his response was immediate, enthusiastic, and positive: "YEAH!"

When they arrived at Otto's there was the usual Sunday crowd: adults having a late breakfast, teenagers sipping Cokes or having ice cream, excited youngsters looking into the vast showcase of sweets and pointing out the penny candy of their choice to Otto's wife who then ceremoniously picked it up, placed it neatly on a paper doily, and presented it to them. It was only a few minutes after they arrived that Terry walked into the ice cream parlor and spotted Robby and Donny.

"Hi," she said smiling broadly as she walked up to them.

"Hi, yourself," Robby responded, ogling her and reaching out for her hand, which he gallantly kissed.

"Umm—excuse me," Donny interrupted "are you alone?"

"Oh, yes, Don. I stopped by Rita's on my way, but she was going to an aunt's house on Long Island for dinner. She'll be back later tonight; I'll tell her you were asking for her . . . if you like."

"Sure."

Donny's heart sank, and he just slumped in the booth while Terry and Robby talked to each other. After about five minutes, he excused himself and went home.

RITA / DONNY

I

Donny didn't see Robby—or anyone—during the next several weeks while he secluded himself in his room studying for finals. Since these upcoming exams counted toward college admission, it was critical that he do well on the tests. Further, it was imperative that his test scores be well up in the 90's, since it was a foregone conclusion that he could go to college only if he gained admission to one of the highly competitive, free-tuition schools of the City University . Although he preferred to attend either the Brooklyn Polytechnic Institute or Cooper Union, it was not possible for there was no money available for the $1500 annual tuition charge.

Donny had also decided that he would spend this summer working as a bus boy with his friend, Dave Barr, in the Catskills, where he could earn as much as three hundred dollars if he stayed for the entire summer. As much as Marie and Angelo objected, they knew that he had to earn some money because, even though the city colleges were tuition free, money was needed for books, laboratory fees, and clothes. Reluctantly, therefore, they allowed him to go off on his own all summer.

When he returned for the final year at Brooklyn Tech in the Fall of 1953, Donny had already decided to pursue the chemical engineering curriculum if he got accepted into CCNY, the largest of the city colleges. It was a difficult field of study, but with his excellent grades in mathematics and physics, he didn't anticipate any major obstacles in that field of study. He saw Robby only infrequently during this entire school year, since he also held down a part-time job on weekends in Manhattan, and had little

299

free time. When he graduated from high school in 1954, he once again spent the summer in the Catskills, but as a waiter this time. Since Robby had gone off to live in Manhattan in the Spring of 1955, the two boyhood friends had seen each other barely a dozen times since that night in the schoolyard at St. Brendan's High School. When they did get together, it was always a memorable meeting, since both young men had grown to love one another as brothers, though neither would ever admit to that reality. What troubled Robby most about their inability to see more of each other was that he missed the good times they always shared when they went out, either to a movie or cruising through the neighborhood. They would often double date during those times, and Donny always asked about Rita. Unfortunately for Donny, Robby had only gone out with Terry a few times since he first met her; in fact, he hardly remembered Rita.

"Hey, man. If you are interested, why don't you call her up?" Robby inquired.

Donny repeatedly made excuses and tip-toed around the subject whenever it came up.

It wasn't until the Summer of 1955 that Donny saw Rita again: they were both attending the seven-thirty A.M. Sunday mass at St. Teresa's, and he saw her ahead of him on the Communion line.

"She is more beautiful than ever," he murmured to himself, his gaze following her every moment until mass ended. He waited for her outside on the steps of the church; when she saw him, her face erupted into that beautiful smile that remembered; her entire being lit up. His felt his heart skip, he thought. But her smile . . . it was her incredible smile made him somehow feel peaceful . . . strangely peaceful in a way he could not adequately describe. Deep within, he sensed a spiritual connection.

"Wow," he whispered barely loud enough for her to hear, "I forgot just how beautiful you are." He held out his hand to assist her down the steps, staring directly into her eyes.

"Why thank you kind sir," she replied as she performed a mock curtsey to him while removing the mandatory kerchief from her head.

"You certainly have changed, Don," she said. "You never said anything like that to me when we first met. In fact, you hardly said anything at all."

"I know. You must have thought I was a real clod or something."

" YES! . . . or something," she chuckled.

They both laughed, realizing how shy both of them had been on that first night.

"Are you walking home?" he asked her as he took her elbow and helped her down the steep church steps.

"Yes, I am."

"May I walk with you?"

"My, my!" she answered happily, "you REALLY have changed."

"You know," he began, as they walked along, "I've thought of you often since that first night."

"Really?" she demurred. "Why?"

He ignored her question. "You know, I can't get over how great you look." He began to laugh at himself. "I sure missed the boat."

"What kind of boat was that?" she joked. Then, "Well—maybe we both did," she added more solemnly.

"So what have you been up to?" he asked.

"I'm a Senior now—Catherine McCauley."

"I remember."

"What about you?"

"I'm a Sophomore at CCNY, and . . . ." He paused, catching himself before saying anything else.

"That's great," she acknowledged; "it's a hard school to get into."

"It is . . . but . . . ."

"What is it?" she wondered out loud.

"Well, I thought I would have run into you at Otto's one time or another." He had purposely changed the subject . . . again.

"I kinda stayed away for a while. Terry started hanging out with a fast crowd; I didn't want to go up there alone; besides . . . ."

"Yes . . . ?"

"I was away."

"Away? Where?" He stopped walking to look at her, expressing genuine interest.

"Well . . . ." She seemed a bit reluctant to speak at first, but continued, "I entered Our Lady of Mercy Convent in Syosset last spring."

"The convent?" He laughed hysterically. Then stopped.

Rita joined him in his good-natured laughter, but had to ask him why he laughed so.

"I laughed because I've changed my major in college—I've decided to become a priest."

They both paused in the middle of the sidewalk in front of the shops and the passers by and laughed till they cried.

"I don't believe it," she said as she wiped away her tears being careful not to smear the light makeup she wore.

"I don't either. But wait; you said you were a Senior at McCauley. Aren't you still in the convent?"

"No . . . no, I'm not," she told him. "I found out, once I was in, that it wasn't really the kind of life that I wanted. I guess I'm more cut out to be a wife and mother."

"Well, I think it's great that you were able to decide that now rather than ten years from now."

"I know. God has been good to me."

"For sure," Donny added. They walked more slowly now, settling in and enjoying each other's company as though they had been close friends for years. "Are you going steady or anything like that?"

She wondered at his asking that, but simply responded, "No."

The conversation eventually got back to the first night that they met at St. Brendan's.

"I was so scared that night," Donny confided in her. "I had never really danced with anyone except my mother or an aunt. Well, maybe one other girl," he added as his memory zoomed back to the evening with Gloria—and her . . . perfume.

"You looked so frightened," she replied.

"You know," he continued, "I was frightened at first, but then, when I held you in my arms, it was like this peaceful kind of calm enveloped me, and the whole world disappeared. It was just you and me . . . all alone. I remember how soft you felt. It was a very tender moment for me; I felt a real connection . . . like we belonged together." Suddenly, realizing that what he was saying sounded like a love song, he abruptly added, "Well, what I mean is that it was really special for me to hold you like that."

"It was for me too," she added. You were the first boy that ever held me so closely like that; I was comfortable . . . in your arms. You felt strong, in control . . . and I liked that . . . you know what I mean?"

"Ummm, I guess."

After a momentary pause, she continued, "Don—can I ask you a question?"

"Of course. What is it?"

"I always wondered why you never called me . . . ."

"Oh!" He thrust his hands deeply into his pants pockets and struggled to answer. "Robby asked me that same question a hundred times! If you knew how I hated myself after that night . . . I felt so dumb." He paused with his mouth agape. "I . . . the only answer that makes any sense is that I just couldn't get myself to ask you for your number. I lay awake most of that night reliving those last few minutes on your front steps. I didn't know how I was supposed to act. I didn't know the right thing to do. On the one hand, I didn't want to be too forward, and . . . well, I was sort of afraid of what you were thinking too. Ya know, every guy in the neighborhood has a story about what he did when he took a girl home. And they all lie!"

He gained control, paused, and smiled. "I really liked you, and I wanted you to like me. I didn't have any experience then, you know." He turned to her at that moment and took her hand in his saying, "I did go to Otto's the next day—I thought maybe you'd come."

"I don't recall what happened that day . . . " she reflected back.

"You went to your aunt's house on Long Island."

"Oh! Well, I wondered if maybe I had done something wrong or . . . or you didn't like me, or . . . it was so confusing for me too because some of my friends say to act one way and . . . I didn't know whether you expected me to kiss you—or what . . . ?"

He interrupted her, "Oh no! Don't think that. It was me! It was all me. I was just too bashful . . . . Besides, I didn't think nice girls kissed on first dates; do they? Do you? Did you? Did you want me to? I wouldn't even try. I couldn't." Realizing that he was ranting, he paused again and took a breath. "Phew, someone should write a book on first dates."

They both took deep breaths. She smiled at him, and, wanting to put him at ease, interjected, "Some girls do. I don't. But I wouldn't have minded if you did. Anyway . . . that was a long time ago, and I'm really glad to see you. Maybe we could start over."

"I'd like that," he smiled at her as they continued around the corner onto her block. "Rita?" he asked.

"Yes?"

"Can I have your phone number . . . ?"

She turned to him with a supercilious glare and said, "And what do you have in mind . . . priest -to -be?"

They both chuckled, but he said, "Just a movie . . . just a movie. OK? My treat. I can go out with girls, you know."

"Sure—I'd love to. It'll be fun. Can we go to Otto's after? What time?"

II

Rita and Donny saw each other often in the months following their re-acquaintance. She invited him to high school dances and her Senior Prom, and he invited her to every college dance or social during the fall semester. They became extremely close as their relationship developed, and they spent a great deal of their free time together or on the telephone. Since changing his major from Chemical Engineering to Philosophy, Donny found that he frequently had several hours each week that he could spend away from his studies, and invariably, he spent these hours with

Rita either at her house or walking the length of Eastern Parkway with her.

Their relationship, while not platonic, was not torrid. They engaged in the typical hug-and-kiss rituals, but Donny took care never to allow himself to proceed too far. He also knew that he was occupying Rita's time in what many of her friends warned was a dead-end romance. He didn't consider their friendship a romance, though he did occasionally debate the wisdom of his decision to join the priesthood.

During the weeks preceding Christmas of 1955 when he and Robby had become involved with Ellen, he seriously questioned the validity of his vocation or even whether he actually had any vocation at all. At his weakest moments, he wondered why the thought of a married priesthood hadn't surfaced in the Catholic Church long before this. Nevertheless, it wasn't until the Christmas Eve Mass, when Father Tom urged the congregation to turn to their respective partners and share some endearing quality, that Donny felt an incredible stirring deep within him—a movement heretofore unknown to him and for which, therefore, no response had previously been cataloged. Puzzlement—fear— doubt—dilemma: all of these feelings were present, and Donny was totally unprepared for them when they burst forth into his life. Was this a turning point . . . a crossroads of decision? It began the moment he turned to Rita and caressed her hands in his.

"This may sound silly," he began, "but Father Tom is an all-right guy, so let's go along with it."

She held his hands gently, cherishing the moment (he was unaware how special it really was). While the organist played in the background, she gazed intently into Donny's soft, brown eyes as he spoke.

"You have many endearing qualities, Rita, so it's hard to know where to begin. But—I suppose—your most endearing quality—is your genuine goodness and gentle nature. You always seek out the best in people and are always ready to forgive someone who wrongs you. Your smile welcomes people and puts them at ease. You put others first; I see that so often. And, you may think I'm crazy, but honestly, if I weren't going into the seminary soon, I'd ask you to be my steady girl." Her face brightened, shocked by his pronouncement and very much embarrassed. She took a moment, looked casually around the church, and saw that most of the congregation were also sharing endearing qualities. "OK," he said, "your turn."

"He had no trouble doing his," she thought. "Why am I having such a hard time saying what I want to say." Her words eventually came. "You have many endearing qualities, too, Don, but there is one special quality that I admire most."

He looked intently at her now, sensing that she was not having an easy time of it.

She continued deliberately; he waited. "You are one of the most loving and giving persons I know. You seek ways to help others and bring them to the same level of awareness as you. What you did for Robby and Ellen! Just look at them—it's marvelous." She paused momentarily, gathering her thoughts. Her demeanor softened, and her eyes glistened as her smile returned. "And . . . I can't tell you how special it's been for me to spend time with you all these months. I know it's been difficult for you too—going out with me while planning your future with the church. Yet, that, too, is admirable: You want to participate in life as much as possible so that you can become a better priest—a real priest for real people."

And then, her already moist eyes lovingly filled as she whispered so that he strained to hear, "And if you weren't going to become a priest, I would want to be your steady girl. I would be proud to have your children—I know that they would be as beautiful—and as special as you." Drained and perspiring, she was on the brink of tears, hoping that he understood clearly the full intent of her words.

Just as she finished, Father Tom began to call the congregation to order, but Rita, boldly, surprisingly, embraced him. He felt the caress of her cheek against his, and thought he heard sobbing. She continued in her embrace, her voice tremulous, barely able to speak, but he heard her. Words, her words, barely whispered, resounded in his ear; clearly, he heard all that she said: "I - like - you, Donny; I - like - you - very - much, and I'm so happy that we've had this time together." The moment did not pass quickly.

The mass resumed, and the choir sang carols while the congregation followed along. Donny, though, perplexed by what happened between Rita and him, was lost, completely bewildered, and rudely inattentive for the remainder of the mass. So lost in himself, he was oblivious that Rita had quietly slipped out of the pew followed by Ellen. He barely responded when Robby tugged at his sleeve to join the crowd leaving the church. "C'mon, the girls are waiting." Outside, Rita and Ellen were engaged with one of Rita's classmates; Robby and Donny stood by.

Later, on their way to Otto's, Rita hardly spoke to Donny; she seemed fine, he guessed, but preoccupied. He thought he understood. He didn't. They joined their usual group of friends at Otto's, which remained open late especially for the younger crowd. As Otto's Christmas present to the group, he offered complimentary punch and cookies. But for Donny, life was spinning out of control; he was caught unaware by the rapid pace of the evening's events and what was happening to him; indeed, between him and Rita. WHAT WAS GOING ON??

After Otto's, Donny escorted Rita home, silent, rehashing the earlier events during mass. Still reeling, he was relieved to spend a few private moments inside the warm and cozy vestibule of her home, sheltered from the cold, wintry night outside. In here, they were always comfortable, able to 'talk' with one another away from the idle chatter and pressures of friends and parents. The vestibule had become their special place, a place where they were free to learn and discover so many things about each other in an open and honest way. It would always remain special to them.

Rita was leaving for Long Island in the morning with her parents for five days, and neither she nor Donny found it easy to conclude their evening. The attraction they had for one another suddenly intensified releasing feelings that bonded them deeply. Their time together had become precious beyond expectation.

After a few moments recounting the night at Otto's, Donny sought to query her about what happened in church; but Rita, aware of her own amorous stirrings, sought to calm the moment. She interjected, "Tomorrow is an early day. I really must go up now." Though his disappointment was evident, her path was clear; she said quietly, "It's awfully late, and my father is a light sleeper."

"I know . . . except . . . well, I thought we should talk . . . ahh, ya know, I'm really going to miss you."

Donny was struggling to say more of what was in his heart, but could only manage to speak with his eyes—words that Rita easily interpreted. Deep within, she felt the full impact of his unspoken words, and it touched her profoundly. Feelings heretofore alien to both had abruptly and unexpectedly evolved to where their spirits became one: she had become so much a part of him that he ached at the thought of them being apart. The warmth within his being, continuously, happily, nourished in her presence, was evolving, rapidly, into desire . . . for her. What did it really mean? Was he barreling headlong toward the inevitable crossroad where the signs, typically, are shrouded by confusion and doubt? Only time would reveal that answer.

Their eyes locked, allowing her heart to speak directly to his: hardly audible, she whispered, "Me too". The moistness in her eyes conveyed an unmistakable message to him; nevertheless, he bristled as she let his hand slip slowly from hers when she turned reluctantly toward the staircase.

Before her foot touched the first stair tread, he barely whispered, "Rita!". She paused, anticipating, anxious, one foot in mid-stride. Motionless for a few seconds, she turned to find him at her side. His eyes, moist as hers, touched her inner depths such that she welcomed the open arms that drew her slowly to him. She responded happily. They embraced silently for a few seconds, conscious of the hearts pounding within their chests.

They kissed, but it was different now. His lips, gentle, as always, harbored a raw, unknown passion that drew an unexpected, though proportionate, response from her as she released herself to his advances. Her reaction, usually measured and controlled, surprised her as she shunned all caution and went with her feelings, unwilling, unable to break it off.

He held her more tightly now, kissing her neck and ears while running his hands through her hair, holding her ever-more tightly. She sensed him edging toward a precipice where she would not go, and she stopped. His breathing labored, then he felt her easing him away. He understood. The moment passed. He accepted.

Rita spoke, "Are you OK?" He nodded, yes. Moments of silence passed. Then, caressing his cheek, she continued, "Don, I really must go; I'll get in trouble". She whispered her words, almost pleading as she pretended fiddling with her hair, attempting to take control of the situation and herself.

"I . . . I'm—."

Before he could utter the words, she placed a finger on his lips and said, "I know—I really do." She kissed him lightly once more on the lips, and raced up the stairs as he watched longingly.

When she put the key in her door, she turned, looked down at him, smiled, and softly mouthed, "Good night." But she never did add the words "My love" that she so longed to say. How could she? It was he who would have to say those two words to her before she could ever let herself reciprocate in kind. That's the way it was in this neighborhood.

ROBBY & ELLEN / DONNY & RITA

I

Robby and Ellen were married in May 1956 in a quiet ceremony in the side sanctuary of Saint Teresa's church. A miraculous change had taken place in Robby immediately following the Christmas Eve Mass: it seemed he had miraculously matured and become the most avowed proponent of marriage and fidelity that one could imagine. He and Ellen agreed that since Ellen's apartment was in a slightly better section of Manhattan, they would relocate Robby's meager belongings there.

Ellen's play had gained much notoriety, and it was fully expected to move onto Broadway for the new season in the fall. Ellen's expectations were high since a move to Broadway and a larger theater would include a substantial increase in her salary for probably two or more years. Robby determined that he would continue working the small club dates for a while longer, since the money was good, and it kept him busy while Ellen was out of the house performing in the show. He also signed up with a prominent music instructor who told him that he had the potential to be an outstanding musician and arranger. All things considered, Robby and Ellen were pleased with what was happening to them in their personal lives as well as with their careers. And why not? They loved their work—and they were good at it. They were doubly blessed.

A few weeks after they were married, the telephone woke them early one Saturday morning. It was Donny.

"How are you pal?" Robby said sleepily into the receiver.

"Rob—we gotta talk. I need to talk to you."

313

"Sure. When do you want to get together?"

"As soon as possible." He sounded nervous.

"Come on over; I don't go to work until seven-thirty tonight—we can spend the day. Ellen's got a matinee, so she'll be gone."

"OK. Bye." And he hung up.

As he hung up the receiver, Robby turned to Ellen who was smiling up at him from her pillow. "He sounds troubled, Ellen. I know him. Something's wrong."

Donny arrived at their apartment about an hour later with a look of seemingly total despair: his hair was unkempt, he looked as though he hadn't slept in days, and his beard appeared to be about a week old. He was unprepared when he was greeted with a sumptuous breakfast of pancakes, sausages, and hot coffee.

"Gee Ellen," he said. "You shouldn't have gone to all this trouble—really."

"It's no trouble at all. Besides—we haven't seen you for several weeks; we miss you."

Robby sat at the table across from him and said, "I hope you don't mind me telling you, but you look terrible."

Donny poked at his breakfast. "That's what's driving me crazy, guys! I am terrible. I just finished taking exams, I'm supposed to enter the seminary in the fall, and all I can think about is . . . Rita Staci!" He jumped up from the table and began to pace the room, oblivious of the animated look on the faces of Robby and Ellen.

"It wasn't so bad during the semester—I was caught up in workshops that kept me almost totally occupied." He paced the apartment, speaking openly but never making eye contact with Robby or Ellen: he just spoke.

"We saw each other, but most of the time it was for an early movie or an evening watching TV at her house. On the weekends, she was usually busy, so we went out alone only once or twice. It was like she didn't want to be with me—and that was OK—I guess. But when classes ended and I began to prepare for exams, I would open up a book and all I could see was her face. I couldn't study!"

"I called her up, and she'd cut me off and tell me to study. Well, I'm finished studying!" He was almost shouting now. "And I'm finished with exams, and I'm going nuts! I'm trying to see her—and she seems to avoid me. I pray for guidance and I only get more confused. I don't know what I want anymore!"

Donny began to cry, but Robby and Ellen were at his side in an instant comforting him. Ellen apologized, for she had to shower and get ready for the matinee; she left the two friends alone.

Donny composed himself somewhat when Robby spoke to him. "Listen Don, it's not easy you know—I mean you got caught up in something that sort of snowballed."

"I know that now, but what am I going to do? I can't go off to the seminary and be thinking about her all the time. I mean—how do you resolve all this? You should know!" Donny looked hopefully into Robby's eyes, fully expecting some magical answer as in days long gone.

"What do you want to be when you grow up?" Robby said in a semi-serious way.

"I want to be a priest!" He was emphatic. "I've always thought about it. You know that."

"Yes I do, but . . . ."

"Well, if I'm supposed to be a priest, why am I so confused about everything—and why can't I get her out of my mind?"

"Do you love her?"

" . . . Love . . . her? I . . . don't . . . I mean . . . I never thought about . . . love. I know I want to be with her. But marriage?

I don't know!" After a few moments of reflection, Donny continued, "I love the Lord, Rob. I really do. I'm sure that I'm supposed to be a priest—it's not a question of . . . ."

"Do you love her?" Robby interrupted more emphatically.

Donny flailed his arms and searched for words. "The question isn't whether I love her or not. The question is: why am I in such a pickle about how I feel? I AM TOTALLY CONFUSED!"

"Do you love her?" Robby asked once again with a tone that signified finality.

"I don't know! I don't know! "Donny was perspiring now. "How do I know what it is to love a woman? I've never let myself be free enough to explore the real meaning of loving a woman. I've always held myself in check. How am I supposed to know the answers to these things? Why isn't it easy?"

Robby put his arm around his friend and spoke very slowly and softly. "Do you remember when I shared with you what was going on with Ellen and me? Well there was nothing I wanted except to be with her. I could only focus on her. I loved her; that was it."

Donny shrugged matter-of-factly. "But, even if I love her—and I'm not sure I don't—I love the Lord too and want to serve him as a priest." He threw his hands up in despair. "I don't know anything anymore. Am I just a sex-starved guy who wants to make it with a girl or am I really in love with her? Who knows the answers to all these questions?"

"Not I Don . . . not I. But I can tell you one thing."

"Please."

"God is not a God of confusion and turmoil. He is supposed to bring us peace—right? Isn't that what you always told me?"

"Yes."

"Well then—assume for the moment that you could choose the priesthood OR Rita. Which choice do you think would render you greater peace of mind?"

"But a priest is supposed to serve God and his people."

"What kind of priest could you be wondering whether you made the right decision or not?"

"Well . . . ."

"And remember Don, each of us has a vocation—not just the clergy—right?"

"Of course . . . yes."

"Well maybe—just maybe—your confusion stems from your inability to decipher what vocation God has selected for you."

"But I don't want to be selfish . . . "

Robby laughed, "Selfish? Do you think being married and raising a family is a picnic? Being celibate may be difficult, but remember what our parents have gone through all their lives. NO . . . giving up the priesthood is not being selfish my friend, not at all. It just may be doing God's will. And for whether or not you love Rita, remember what Father Tom said that night at mass: Love is a decision—a decision we make to serve someone other than ourselves. Love is NOT a feeling or an emotion. It is a decision, a free-will choice we make—a promise to make someone else more important than we are. Love is giving all we have to make someone else happy."

II

Donny got up from the chair and paced the room slowly, muttering to himself. "Maybe I do love Rita. I know that she makes me happy, and I certainly want to make her happy. I miss her when I don't see her. I'm sad when she hurts.

Maybe . . . maybe I could postpone my decision to enter the seminary for another year. It isn't smart to decide this when so many questions still remain. Then I could date other girls and see how I feel about Rita and the priesthood. That would take the pressure off—."

"Whoa! Slow down there. You really need time to sort out things, buddy!" Robby smiled at his friend who grinned back sheepishly. "You look terrible!"

"But I feel better. Thanks." He hugged his friend just as Ellen returned to the room.

"Hey! What's going on here? Did I miss something?"

Donny went over to her and gave her a big hug too. "I love you guys—I really do! She stopped in her tracks. "What? Did you say love?? I . . . love . . . Love? Oh boy!"

The next day, Donny conferred with Father Tom who fully supported his decision to delay admission to the seminary. He told him his feelings were not uncommon; rather, it was quite ordinary: that he should question one vocation versus another. It was healthy and should not be a cause of stress. Admission to the priesthood—or the married life—should be decided based on adequate reflection and made without reservation or duress. And then, once the decision is made, it should be entered into joyfully—with God's blessings.

Donny felt a strange peace now, and decided to call at Rita's home for her. It was about six-thirty P.M. when he found Rita sitting on the front steps of her building. She smiled as he approached, but Donny thought that it lacked some of the exuberance that it once had.

"Hi Rita. Can I sit with you?"

"Sure; I just came out."

"How've you been?"

"Good. You?"

"OK. I saw Ellen and Robby yesterday."

"Oh?"

"Yeah. They were asking for you."

He could see that this conversation was heading nowhere, so he asked her if she wanted to walk up to the park. She hesitated at first, but conceded when he insisted. They walked up to Eastern Parkway and into the Botanical Gardens, a favorite spot of their's. They walked past the Japanese Gardens and the greenhouse and toward the lily pool where they sat on the slate ledge that overhung the water.

"I've decided to continue at CCNY this year . . . take some post-graduate courses."

Rita's heart skipped several beats, and she sat erect and faced him squarely. "Oh?"

" . . . I'm going to defer my decision for the priesthood for another year—and I wanted to tell you about it."

Her heart sank; this was not exactly what she had hoped to hear. "It's OK; you don't . . . ."

"No! It's important to me." His pulse quickened as he gazed at her, and the thought of becoming a priest quickly faded. "I am really struggling with this decision, and I've got to give myself more time. Also, I wanted to let you know that I think I've been grossly unfair to you—and to myself as well—"

"Oh no . . . ."

" . . . Wait! Listen. Please. I have very strong feelings for you: very strong. I don't know if you feel the same about me, but I've got to sort all these things out."

"What is it you want to sort out?" she asked quizzically.

"Rita, I don't know what it means to love a woman—I mean really love, not just sex. And I'm having an impossible time understanding what's going on inside me."

"And?" She felt herself becoming agitated, wondering where this was going.

"And I need your help."

"How can I help you?" Somehow Rita began to feel like a pawn in a chess game: help Donny regardless of what happens to Rita. She didn't like the feelings she was having.

"Well . . . I thought maybe we could continue dating—even see other people—and see what happens after a few months."

"You mean you want to date me and other girls, and after a few months, you'll decide whether you want me, some other girl—or the priesthood !?! Do I understand you correctly?" She was approaching anger now, an emotion he had never seen her exhibit before.

"Rita! Hold on, please. I don't want to hurt you. I care about you. It's just that I've got a problem that I can't resolve."

"And what about my problem that I can't resolve!?" She stood looking him right in the eye waiting for a response.

"What problem? You have a problem?" he said innocently.

"What problem?" She began to cry, but struggled to speak forcefully. "Don't you know?"

"Know what? Have I done something?" Donny stood in total awe of what he was seeing in Rita. He continued, "Tell me, please."

"Listen Don. When we first started seeing each other, it was fine. No commitment, no promises, just good friends." Her eyes were wet and red, and her mascara had begun to run. She continued, "And that was OK. But after a while . . . well . . . ."

320

"What?" Donny was truly solicitous as he attempted to derive the truth.

"I fell in love with you!! You idiot!"

"You fell in love . . . with ME . . . ? When?"

"You are such a meathead! You know that?!" She turned her back on him and walked a few steps, and let out a deep sigh, glad she had finally said it.

Donny walked up behind her and put his arms around her waist, carefully resting his cheek next to hers.

"Don't," she said half-heartedly, attempting to move away. "Please don't."

Ignoring her plea, Donny held tightly to her sensing her trembling, and determined not to let this moment pass.

"I had no idea," he whispered softly to her." He put his lips close to her ear. "I had no idea that something like this could ever happen to me . . . to us. I didn't plan on anything like this."

"I know." Her voice was barely audible. She sighed again and wiped another tear that had raced down her cheek.

He turned her to himself and scanned every part of her face with his eyes. "Rita . . . my love . . . I don't ever . . . want to hurt you again. It's clear now what I must do. It's all very clear. Thank God, it's finally clear!" He was grinning broadly now feeling an indwelling peace settle in throughout his body. "I love you! It's been like that all along, and I didn't know it."

"Are you sure? You're not just saying this . . ." Her voice trailed off as he kissed her so very softly but with a deep sense of passion that caused her to almost swoon in his arms.

"Rita, let me be very clear about this: I LOVE YOU! I have had so many feelings—Oh Lord, so many feelings. I thought—well—I—well, . . . I couldn't make sense of anything. I looked at you, but I never really saw who you are . . . the real beauty you bring into this world. My precious!! I saw you only with my eyes, and now I see you with my heart! I thought my feelings for you were selfish. Forgive me; I was too confused, so foolish. Stupid."

He paused, just gazing into her jet black eyes which were glistening and seemed even larger than they actually were. "I . . . love . . . you! No doubt about it. I couldn't be any more certain about anything. WOW!"

He picked her up and twirled her around and around. "How could I have been so blinded?" He was like a little child rejoicing in the moment.

Suddenly he stopped and put her down.

"What's wrong, Don?"

"I've gotta call Robby and let him know!"

They both laughed and headed for the nearest pay phone.

DONNY / RITA

I

Donny loved Rita. He could not stop saying it. To acknowledge his love for her did more for him than any other single event in his life. Whereas he had thought that the career choice of "being a philosopher" was impractical unless someone were becoming a priest, he now viewed his chosen course of study as his destiny, and he pursued it with increased vigor. "I'll teach! It's what I always wanted to do anyway," he told himself. And so when he graduated cum laude from CCNY in May 1957, it was with a clear-cut goal of teaching at the university level. Rita was overjoyed at his decision to pursue an academic career, since she knew that Donny could then continue his pursuit of other scholarly ventures as well. Although he sometimes expressed concern that he could initially make more money going into sales or some technical field, he seemed satisfied now—especially since he had applied for and been accepted into the Master's program at Fordham University in the Bronx. They would smile, happily, when they thought of the time, in just a few short years, when they would be introduced as Professor and Missus Gargano—or, as Rita privately joked: Missus and Professor . . .!

Donny's enrollment in Fordham's Bronx campus was uneventful, and didn't bring about any significant changes in his routine. And though Donny rode the subway almost two hours each day, he found that he was able to spend most of the time reading assignments for his next day's classes. It was an exciting time for both Donny and Rita; that is, until Rita's family decided to move out to Long Island—a move scheduled for sometime in the

323

spring of 1958. It was early on a brisk morning in the preceding October as they walked along Eastern Parkway that she told him.

"Long Island?" Donny asked her. "I'll never see you anymore. What town anyway?"

"Huntington."

"Huntington? How far out is that? A hundred miles?" Donny was visibly upset at the thought of not being able to see Rita on a regular basis anymore.

"What made your father want to sell so suddenly anyway?"

"You know what's been going on in the neighborhood," she said, trying to soften the moment. "Our neighborhood is like one huge extended family where everyone knows everyone else; everybody feels safe walking here even late at night. Right? You remember how we didn't dare do anything wrong for fear one of the neighbors would yell at us or tell our parents. It's like an enclave where almost everyone shares similar beliefs and ideology. Most of us go to the same church, shop in the same bakery and butcher, even use the same insurance man and undertaker. Well, it's changing now. My father said that brokers have been buying up houses all over the neighborhood for the past six months, and he wants to get out while he can still get the best price for our home. It's all so sudden and so crazy! "

Donny struggled to accept the inevitable. "Did he sell already?" He seemed so disappointed.

"Yes—a broker wrote a contract for $17,000. Dad is scheduled to sign it tomorrow, and we should be moving in April."

"Ouch! April? When will we get to see each other? I don't have a car . . . ."

"There's always the train . . . ."

"Train?" Donny raised his voice so that others turned to look at him. "All I DO is take the train—five days a week, sometimes six—and now I have to take the train on weekends too? When will I study if I'm running back and forth to Huntington all the time? How far is your house from the station? I suppose I'll have to walk from the station to the house if your father isn't home!"

"Well, when we get married . . . ."

"Married?" Donny looked grave now.

"You know we didn't plan to get engaged until I got my Master's degree and got a job! That's about a year and a half; that's the soonest we could think about getting married. How will we live? Where would we live?"

She sighed, loving him as she watched him wrestle with the idea of providing for a wife and maybe a family. "What I meant was that after we get married, it wouldn't be so bad. We would be together . . . ."

"Rita, listen to me." Donny sat down next to her on one of the cedar-wood park benches that lined Eastern Parkway. "I get my Master's and then I get a job. I can always go for my Ph.D. nights; that's not really an issue for us. Ideally, though, we shouldn't begin seriously thinking of getting married for another three or four years. That is the best plan for us. We would have a few dollars in the bank . . . ."

She interrupted, "Three or four years?" Rita was shocked; in her mind's eye she had them getting engaged within the next six months and had already set a wedding date in her own mind within the next year. "Three or four years? You can't be serious; I'll be an old maid—I'm already almost nineteen! All of my close girlfriends are engaged, and one of them is getting married right after Easter." It was Rita's turn to be visibly upset.

As Donny prepared to respond, he noticed that people had begun to stare. He took Rita by the arm and ushered her along, away from the eyes and ears of the others. He understood her concerns and how supportive she had been of him and his education. He wanted to calm her and assure her that, 'things would work out.' But how? "How are we supposed to live if we get married before? You said you wanted to finish college, too, so you could teach after our children grow up."

"Well . . . I do want to finish college."

"If we get married right away," he retorted, "we won't be able to afford your tuition and mine . . . ."

"Then I'll quit and get a job! Now! That's a plan!" She spoke with finality. At that moment he loved her more than ever. He took hold of her and caressed her gently.

"Listen to us," he whispered. "We're shouting at each other like we were strangers. Why don't we just wait a few weeks and see how things develop. I don't want this to come between us."

Rita concurred saying, "Oh, Donny, we've come so far together; nothing must ever come between us. We'll work it all out; I know we will."

II

Rita's father's decision to move was merely a response to what had become obvious to every homeowner in the neighborhood: the Italians and Irish were moving out, and Blacks and Puerto Ricans were moving in. Oddly, though, hardly any Jews were selling. Rita's father reasoned that if he delayed selling his home much longer, he wouldn't be able to command the premium price he was being offered by the realtor that had begun buying up most of the block on which the Stacis and their friends lived.

"If we don't go now, he won't even offer us ten thousand," he warned his family over their constant protests. No one initially wanted to leave the neighborhood, but when the economic pressures became so critical, people saw only the money and sold.

Donny understood that Rita's father's thinking was probably correct; his own landlady sold the building two weeks ago and two new families had already moved into the top floor apartments.

"Change is inevitable," he told Rita.

"I understand that," she responded, "but why must it have such a devastating impact on us?"

The next few weeks were spent by Donny and Rita checking the timetables of the Long Island Rail Road for service to and from Huntington on weekdays, weekends, and holidays. Together, they had devised a scheme whereby Donny could take the subway from school on Friday nights directly to the Long Island Rail Road depot at the Flatbush Avenue Extension. He could then travel to Jamaica and change to the Huntington train. In all, it wouldn't take more than three hours if all the proper connections were made. Suddenly, the situation didn't seem as grave as it had before they had done all the research. Actually, the situation remained exactly the same; now, they merely understood it better.

Meanwhile, the neighborhood continued to experience an increasingly rapid rate of change where old, established families were moving out being replaced by new ones of different ethnic backgrounds. The Italians, Donny saw, were a cliquish group; they felt most comfortable living close to families whose ancestors came from familiar towns in Italy. That's precisely how his neighborhood was mostly populated. Donny also surmised that since many of his mother's contemporaries did not speak fluent English, it made sense for them to live among neighbors with whom they could easily converse. Why, at least half a dozen of the local shop owners learned to speak one or two of the more popular dialects in the neighborhood; it made good business sense, but also made 'the little old ladies' feel comfortable in their shops. Everyone agreed: 'It is really nice living in this neighborhood.'

And then one day . . . Marie Gargano explained to Donny that even though they couldn't afford to move, they would be moving to a 'more Italian' neighborhood 'way out' in Flatbush right after Christmas. She had already lined up a part-time job as a babysitter.

And so it was: the metamorphosis of an enclave out of which came television producers, business people, teachers, engineers, entrepreneurs. What had seemed to be the essential ingredient in the raising of one's family: a stable neighborhood—was changing forever, never to be the same. And, as it swept up Rita Staci and Donny Gargano, it swept up many others.

AL'S FEAST—THE FIESTA

I

Al Zito became a well-respected television producer and achieved a great deal of success as an innovator in an industry that seemed narrowly focused on situation comedies. Joe Weintrauben particularly liked Al's ideas about family shows and themes that explored the roots upon which the early days of our society were founded. He had charged Al with the task of doing a major special to air during the following fall season. Weintrauben told him to find something fresh—something that hadn't been done before. Al agreed, but had not an inkling of what he would do.

"Well, what does he really want?" Donna-Marie asked him one evening while they were dining alone.

"He didn't really specify—he never does. But I suppose what he's looking for is basic Americana: the people who make up the country and who make it—or made it—great."

"Sounds like a huge undertaking, if you ask me."

"It is if you think on such a grand scale."

"So think smaller—don't be so ambitious."

"You mean . . . limit it to New York . . . ?"

"Maybe not even New York," she came back. "New York is so complex in and of itself. How about . . . Brooklyn?"

"Brooklyn!" He sat back on his chair and closed his eyes, his mind racing. "Maybe not even . . . all of Brooklyn," he mused.

She picked up on his train of thought. "Why not a neighborhood—maybe the old neighborhood?"

"Yeah! The old neighborhood!"

For the next couple of days Al toyed with ideas for a program that would showcase the people and places of his old neighborhood. His mind reeled with thoughts of using the local residents in key parts of the TV show. He was excited about the concept, and when he shared specifics with Donna-Marie, she got caught up in his enthusiasm.

"When will the show air?" she asked him.

"Late summer - early fall; probably right after Labor Day.

"Maybe you could do a spot on the Feast . . . ."

"Oh Donna—! What a great idea. I could have interviews with the committee people and the vendors, and . . . and the teams for the greased pole . . . ."

Donna-Marie saw the glint in his eye and knew that Al was on the right track. "I've got another idea," she offered.

"What is it?"

"Why don't you donate some money to the feast committee; they might make you a major sponsor of the feast. You know how they're always looking for financial donors. They might even let you have a voice in how things are run."

"I've got to think about that one, hon. I don't want the show to look fabricated or put on. For the show to be a success, it has got to be real—not contrived."

"You could work it out; I know you can." She smiled at him proudly.

"I'll think about it for sure; thanks for your help."

"You are very welcome."

Al rested his chin on his hands and looked across the table at Donna-Marie; once again this woman of his had brought peace into his life. Now he had a general direction in which to move. "Have I told you that I love you today?"

"No, not yet," she replied, anticipating a further dialogue.

"Oh," he said and then continued eating without further response until he was hit in the head by a piece of Italian bread that Donna-Marie threw at him with a precision aim. Al could hardly contain his laughter for he loved to taunt her like this.

"So you wanna get rough, eh?" he growled at her. In an instant he was at her side of the table pretending biting her all over her neck and face.

This continued until Donna-Marie began to kiss him lightly on any part of his face that she could touch.

"You keep doing that and you'll get me all excited," he warned her, but to no avail.

"I'm warning YOU," she teased back. "You'd better stop this—I'm a married lady, you know!" She toyed with him.

"Well, I'm a married man!" he rejoined and then kissed her passionately on the lips. She reciprocated willingly. He lifted her off the chair, overwhelmed by her inner strength and beauty. How happy he was to have her in his life; truly, she was the greatest thing that had ever happened to him. Then, "And now we're going to do what married people do." He stalked off toward the bedroom with her cradled in his arms.

"Save me . . . someone save me . . . " she mocked, her words soon replaced with feigned giggles and then nothing as they melted into each other's embrace.

II

The first official committee meeting of the 'Society of Saint Sebastian in Brooklyn, New York' wasn't scheduled until mid-February, so Al was not surprised when Bruno Gallo was reluctant to speak with him about plans for the feast before that time.

Bruno Gallo was the current president of the Society, having been elected by acclamation at the conclusion of the previous feast. Gallo was forty-seven years old, sported a walrus-like, greying mustache, and weighed just under two hundred pounds. At five-foot seven, he was considered obese by some, portly by others, and jovial by all. He was a generally happy person who worked hard at the local shoe-repair shop that he bought from its former owner ten years before. Considered well off by his neighbors, Gallo was proud of the fact that he had become an independent American businessman after being in this country only eleven years.

"But Mister Gallo, it's important that we begin as soon as possible," Al pleaded into the telephone when he first called to set up a meeting.

"Com-pa-re," Gallo replied, using the familiar term that native-born Americans pronounced goom-ba, "we just can't-a-call a meeting because you say so. We have a schedule that we must-a-live with—people have lotsa things to do besides get ready for the feast." Gallo's thick Italian accent did not hide the strength and determination with which he spoke.

"But Mister Gallo, this could mean a great deal of publicity for the neighborhood and the society."

"I'm-a-sorry! You wait until next month, and I see that you get invited to our first meeting." It sounded final to Al.

"Suppose," he countered, "I donate five hundred dollars to the society—no strings attached?"

"Five hundred dollars? Heh, that's a lotta money; you sure? No strings?" Gallo asked.

"Yes, five hundred dollars—no strings—to the society." Al held his breath while waiting for Gallo's reply.

"You know, com-pa-re, you must be a good-a man. I think maybe we can do some-a business after all. Gimme your number and I call-a you back when I fix em all up."

Al wondered who was more shrewd: Gallo or him. He decided in Gallo's favor.

The first meeting with the entire committee was held two weeks after Al Zito's initial call to Bruno Gallo. "Money still works wonders," Al grinned.

The meeting was scheduled to convene on Saturday morning at 10 A.M. at the society's headquarters, which was located mid-block in a storefront amid the many apartments and shops located on Grand Avenue in the area just south of the Crown Heights section of Brooklyn (actually, most of it began one block into the Park Slope section). Al meandered through the familiar streets, noting how congested this area had become. Was it always like this? Most of the apartment buildings were four or five stories high and contained as many as twenty separate apartments, some facing the street in front, others facing a back yard. Fire escapes were located either in the front of the building or the rear, depending on the physical configuration of the apartments within.

In this section of the neighborhood, each building was designed to accommodate ground-level storefronts—businesses such as tailor, shoemaker, candy store, poolroom or tavern, among others. At the corner, facing two streets, was the largest storefront: the drug store with a eighteen-foot-long soda fountain. Seeing all this now, today, was reminder of how so many people and so many businesses were able to co-locate in such a compact area. His excitement built as he confirmed in his own mind the wisdom of his choice of the feast as the vehicle for the fall special!

As he neared his destination, he noticed that there was a cafe-style curtain half-way up inside the store-front window, in front of which, facing the street, stood a four-foot high statue of Saint Sebastian. He walked through the open front door and was confronted by another, larger-than-life-size statue of the saint at the back wall surrounded by a semi-circle of three-foot high carts upon which flickered dozens of tiny candles in red and white glass containers. The members of the committee, who had obviously already gathered, were seated in a semi-circle facing the saint's statue, according him the honor of presiding, in absentia, over their activity.

Al entered and quickly scanned the area, noting a full-length curtain strung across the width of the room toward the rear. He knew that the back half of the room had a kitchen and was used for many 'diverse' activities including card games and light meals, all of which was hidden from the view of anyone who might come looking for a husband, father or son. He had heard that on some occasions, very late at night, one or more female figures could be seen entering or leaving . . . alone.

Al was introduced to the group, sixteen members, by Bruno Gallo, who explained that Al was indeed a welcome benefactor of the Society, and he that he was a man to be treated with RESPECT. Al was pleased with what Gallo said, though he was surprised to discover that each member of the committee—all men—was foreign born. Even the youngest member, who was about twenty-five, spoke with a heavy, southern Italian accent. Having been a life-long resident of this neighborhood until he moved to Manhattan, Al had no insight into just how cliquish this group was.

"Why aren't there any American-born members? Or women?" he thought as he carefully studied each man in the room. As Gallo called the meeting to order, Al felt like an outsider—an A-MERRY-GAN—as he often heard the old timers call those of non-Italian birth. "So now I, too have become an A-MERRY-GAN!" He smiled thinking of what Donna-Marie would say when he told her.

The meeting progressed well, with Gallo maintaining loose, but constant, control over the proceedings. Al was surprised to learn that every man in the room had his own specific ideas about how the feast should be run, but when all had spoken, he understood that everything would be just as it had been from its inception years ago. The primary question that Al had come to resolve was the way in which the camera crew could film the events preceding the first day of the feast and then the actual feast itself with all its individual components. It was readily apparent to Al after about an hour that he would inevitably have to 'make do' with the situation as it ultimately evolved, for he could not glean a consensus as to a filming schedule or a relocation of some of the major attractions of the feast from the committee members. He had been especially concerned with such major events as the procession, the greased pole, and the pie-eating contest. The only concession of any consequence that he received was that all planning meetings would be scheduled in sufficient time to permit a camera crew to set up for the filming; oddly, the committee was eager to have themselves photographed for television. A lesser concession was that they would schedule meetings with prospective concessionaires well in advance of the feast itself to permit the studio editing crew time to design the best footage. The actual filming of the feast itself remained a monumental problem, and Al decided to trust the wisdom of his chief photographer and art director as how best to gather the footage he wanted.

When the meeting was over, Gallo signaled, and each man knelt down in his place facing the statue. Al followed their lead, and heard Gallo pray that the results of this meeting would ultimately bring glory to Saint Sebastian and then to God. Al was pleased with the spirituality exhibited by these men, and made a mental note to include their sensitive display as a prominent part of the show. He thanked them for their time, exited, and strolled through the neighborhood, choosing to take an alternative route to his Manhattan apartment.

Although still late January, the weather was warm and sunny with temperatures up into the high 50's. As he passed the pool hall, he smiled at a familiar face frozen in the doorway, a sentry guarding the gamers and gamblers inside. He nodded at unfamiliar persons whose eyes bored in upon him whenever disturbed their field of vision. He felt judged, an alien, a squatter come to disturb their solace. An odd feeling vexed him as he ambled along these old, familiar streets; he understood, believed, and accepted the truth in the old maxim: "You can never, ever, go back home." The profusion of eyes peering down from windows high above and the army of onlookers standing on elevated stoops or in street-level doorways struck him like a thunderbolt! He, a former denizen of these byways, was an intruder. Waxing nostalgic, he mourned—home is no longer here; indeed, he knew he was as much a foreigner on these streets as though he were in Europe. Surprising also was the intermingling of an Asian child among those running and playing in the streets. He made a mental note to include a segment on the changing nature of the inhabitants of the area. Al would encounter other surprises as the preparations for the feast evolved.

On his way home, he decided to stop at the offices of ADISCO to visit with Nick Toscano who had some thoughts on a new project.

ADISCO

I

Al left the IRT subway at the West Fourth Street station and walked west two blocks to the ADISCO offices. Since 1955, he had expanded the original business concept developed with Nick Toscano to include cigar-vending machines, a forty-five RPM juke box design, and the revolutionary concept now being marketed for combining syrup and seltzer in a single-dispenser nozzle. This latest concept, also the brainchild of Nick, evolved from watching Otto pump syrup—or syrups—into a glass and then take the glass to the seltzer dispenser nozzle. This new product replaced the existing fountain with pressurized containers of seltzer and syrup located in the basement where they were combined with tee connections to facilitate delivery to the fountain, via hoses, as one product. Otto himself had agreed to test the prototype unit for several weeks, and shouted out loud, "ya—it vorks!" when Nick finally came by to seek his assessment.

Al was pleased with Nick's rapid development into a businessman, but was more pleased that Nick had just completed his third year of engineering school at Cooper Union. He couldn't help wondering why Nick, now twenty-four, was still single. But as he thought a bit more, he realized that the poor fellow had little enough time to do the work he was doing let alone date.

Nick rose from his chair when Al entered the room, and walked over to greet him warmly.

"What are you doing here on Saturday?" Al asked, seeing how tired Nick seemed.

"I'm here every Saturday, boss. How else do you think we make all this money?"

Al nodded his head and put up his hands as if in defense and said, "Oh spare me! Here it comes again." And then seriously he said, "What's up?"

Nick bubbled with excitement. "Listen," he said, as he ushered Al into a chair and then sat on the desk facing him. "I've been working on an idea that I think will go over big. And if I'm right, we can expand it all through the city and . . . and even out to Long Island."

"Go on." Al sat fully attentive, focused on Nick's spontaneous presentation.

"Well this is 1958, and people are making major purchases in television sets and hi-fi's. It's the coming thing—will you grant me that?"

"Of course." Al conceded the obvious point, aware of Nick's clever method of moving him along logically from one point to another. It was like sitting before Socrates himself.

Nick continued, "The only places where people can purchase name brands of TV's, radio's, or hi-fi's are at major department stores or specialty shops like Lafayette Radio—which is really for enthusiasts."

Al nodded his assent once more.

"What I propose," Nick continued in his slow and methodical way, "is that we open a retail store—and then, perhaps, a small chain of retail stores—that will sell only TV's, tape recorders and other electronic entertainment products. Consider it an ELECTRONICS SUPERMARKET, if you will. I believe that people will prefer to shop our stores, where, incidentally, we will offer one-on-one technical service and advice AND sell each product at a slight discount over the department stores I plan to market all major brands and models. We'll have the selection, the inventory, AND the expert sales help to make the customers happy and keep coming back."

"What kind of sales projections have you made?" Al asked.

"The numbers are phenomenal! Everybody wants a TV set; some people already have two. Hi-fi buffs are building their own sets because they can't get the quality they want in commercial units sold by the big stores. I've made calls to some importers uptown who tell me that Japan is about to unload at least a half dozen new models of TV sets, compact tape recorders, and stereo components." Nick was pacing the room, which filled with the excitement that spontaneously overflowed from him. "You've heard the names Sony and Panasonic—right?"

Again Al assented.

"I have a professor at school who just returned from Japan and told me that an entire new world of entertainment is under development by them. There are color TV's, hand-held video cameras, video recorders, car stereos—it's unbelievable! He also told me that these firms are currently able to market electronic devices for far less than we can here. If we can capture some of their distribution network, we can be among the first to introduce not only the new product innovations but other lower-priced, higher-quality equipment to the public." Nick seemed exhausted, took a deep breath, and said, "So-what do you think . . . boss?"

Al looked at him admiringly and responded," It all sounds exciting . . . and when I look at the start up figures and proposed first-year inventory, I'll be better able to comment, but for now—I say it's a go!"

"Great! Now for the best part," Nick added.

"More? What's that?" Al wondered.

"Location. Guess where I've decided to open our first store? . . . with your approval, of course."

"OUR store? Our store? OK. I give up—where?" Al smiled curiously, waiting for Nick to follow through with what was sure to be a blockbuster of a surprise.

"On Washington Avenue, right opposite the National Theater . . . ."

"In the old neighborhood?" Al wrinkled his nose as he chafed at what Nick said, and then relaxed and let him continue.

"Sure—it's got practically a captive audience with lots of middle-aged people, tons of teenagers, and plenty of local businesses that will give us the draw for our initial customer base."

"I see," Al concurred. "People go shopping in the neighborhood anyway—and many shop practically every day—so we'll have a natural base of customer support already in place." Al now sat at the edge of his chair, his business man's mind racing. "And with the low rental costs in that area, we won't be risking a great deal initially." He thought for a moment and then continued, "if it works . . . ."

"It will!" Nick interrupted.

" . . . if it works," Al continued emphatically and suddenly serious, "we could open another store downtown."

I thought about that already," Nick interrupted again, a Cheshire-like grin growing on his face. "Most people around here don't have cars; they have no way of carrying things home—except on the bus. The department stores charge extra for home delivery, and for items like a TV set, the cost could be huge! We will deliver FREE! It won't cost us much anyway—once we work it out."

Al smiled broadly nodding his head in affirmation, again proud of his protege's perception and business acumen, and said, "You seem to have everything laid out—as usual. You've done a good job, a really good job."

He looked at his watch and said, "I've got to go now. Would you like to come home for dinner?—You know you're always welcome."

"No thanks. I've got a date."

Al nodded again, happy to know that Nick now had other activities with which to entertain himself. He rose to leave, saying goodbye to his friend and business associate, but was called back the instant his hand touched the door knob.

"Al!"

"Yeah, Nick?" Al said turning back. "Something else you need?"

"We . . . ah . . . we . . . ." Nick had that same Cheshire-like smile on his face, signaling to Al that something was up.

"OK—what is it?"

"We . . . need to pick a . . . a name for our store."

"You can handle that, Nick." Al turned once again to leave, but paused, offering a suggestion. "How about ADISCO Electronics."

"I was thinking of something a bit more catchy."

"Catchy? Like what?" Al waited for the apparent shoe to drop.

"Remember MAD-MAN MUNTZ? His advertising was responsible for more TV sales than RCA and Dumont between 1949 and 1953."

"So?"

"So, our name should be catchy too if we're going to break people's mind set about purchasing major items from well-established retailers such as Macy's or Bamberger's."

"Agreed. Have you got a name in mind? Wait. I'm sure that you've got something in mind or you wouldn't be looking at me with that sneaky look of yours. OK. Let's have it."

"You're right. I do have a name."

"Well?"

"Don't laugh. Promise?"

"Awright already! What is it?"

Nick took a deep breath and blurted out, "Naughty Nicky's."

"Naughty Nicky's?" Al roared with laughter. "Naughty Nicky's? You must be nuts!."

"You said you wouldn't laugh."

"I'm not laughing!" But Al could hardly breathe as he roared out loud. "Maybe we should call it, Awful Al's. Or Dopey Donna's."

He continued laughing at and then with Nick who had joined him in loud guffaws. He sat down again trying to compose himself. After a few moments, he wiped the tears from his eyes, rose, and walked over to Nick and gave him a bear hug.

"Nick, I love you! And if you think 'Naughty Nicky's is the way to go, then I'm with you all the way. Really—I am." Then, raising his hand in a mock toast, he cheered, " Here's to Naughty Nicky's. Long may it thrive!"

"Thanks." Nick could not bring himself to tell Al that he had initially wanted to use the name "Crazy Nicky" but discarded it as being too sensational and in poor taste.

Once again, Al turned to leave, muttering just loudly enough for Nick to hear, "Wait till Donna-Marie hears about this."

Nick was pleased with the results of the meeting; he knew that if Al had any real problems with the deal—or the name—he would have said so immediately. Nick picked up the phone and quickly dialed a number. When the other party responded, Nick said, "Hello? Carmine? Listen up!"

NAUGHTY NICKY'S

I

Carmine Della Rocca was a survivor of the first order, having managed to support himself in many varied and different ways since his high school days. Now twenty-eight years old, Carmine had undergone a very slow but consistent metamorphosis over the past few years that resulted in a new, cleaner-cut look. His mustache was gone as was his greasy, slicked-down hair style. Other changes resulted in him altering his preferences in female companions, which previously had been limited to only the most undesirable of the easy-access, Prospect Park types. During the summer of 1957, while employed as a salesman in Rosen's hardware store on Washington Avenue just north of Bergen Street, he found himself suddenly enamored of a young woman who appeared to be in her mid-to-late twenties. He first noticed her in June when she bought a pair of pliers at Rosen's, and then only occasionally after that as he cruised the neighborhood or spent his lunch breaks at one of the many local luncheonettes, delis, or diners along the avenue.

His most recent glimpse of her was when she hurried across the hectic traffic on Washington Avenue; He especially enjoyed how her bust bounced and jiggled when she maneuvered to evade an oncoming trolley car. Her skimpy tank top did little to camouflage her ample bosoms, a highly pleasing distraction to men and many women who joined with Carmine's covert appraisal. On other occasions when the frequent ogling was less veiled, she seemed oblivious. Carmine admired her ability to be herself. She seemed tough and sure of actions. He liked her.

Carmine, in some ways, still operated on a different set of rules from most men, and, therefore, considered it quite normal to follow her one day during his lunch-time break. He made his decision to embark on this undercover mission when he spotted her as she turned the corner of Bergen Street and headed toward Louie's Luncheonette. Louie's had a walk-up window, at which she stopped and ordered a hot dog and a soda. Carmine, meanwhile, secreted himself behind a telephone pole on the opposite side of the street where he could admire, undetected, every facet of her, noting, especially, her delightful protuberances, which he considered to be the most wonderful set ever to adorn any female body.

After several weeks of trailing her, he noticed that there were other parts of her anatomy that attracted him as well. One day, he decided, she looked especially lovely, seeming a bit taller and even a bit more sophisticated than before. Perhaps it's her high heels, he mused, and continued his secret surveillance. Another day, he noted how lovely her hair looked, though it was, in fact, not the least bit unique in its color, style, or cut. Though only about five feet two inches tall, she had, Carmine asserted to himself, one of the nicest pair of legs in the neighborhood. Her face, though somewhat ordinary in structure, had a forceful look about it that stimulated him when he thought about her and him together; he would gladly become a slave to her every demand.

One particularly hot day, he discovered her standing at Louie's window eating a hot dog and sipping a coke. What surprised Carmine as he observed her was that he had taken little note of her flimsy outfit, but admired, instead, the petite way that she was eating. Not known for his own excellent table manners, or any other forms of social grace for that matter, he marveled at how she was able to make eating a hot dog appear genteel.

He decided to follow her as long as necessary today to determine where she worked; he was committed to asking this woman out. He was unprepared for her sudden retreat when he saw her glance at her wristwatch and walk rapidly away. Carmine reacted instinctively, and raced across the street and followed only a few paces behind her. When she entered Cooper's dry goods store on Washington Avenue, he followed her in a few moments later, and was upset when he saw her slip behind the counter and through the curtained doorway into the back room. Mister Cooper was occupied with a customer, so Carmine browsed, hopeful that she would reappear momentarily before he, too, had to return to work in the hardware store next door. As he feigned examining socks and ties that lay on one counter, he was unaware of the person who had come up behind him.

"Hello, may I help you?" the voice softly inquired.

Carmine, daydreaming about his 'lady fair,' was momentarily caught unaware by this offer of help. When he turned to respond, it was she. He fumbled for words, "Oh . . . I . . . Mmmph."

But she thoughtfully smiled at him, and then simply asked, "Is there something I can do for you? Something in particular you need?"

"Ah . . . yes . . . will you go out with me?" And then he almost collapsed not believing that he spoke the words he heard pouring from his mouth.

"Go out with you?" She was stunned, and turned to walk away but paused when she hear him whisper, "I'm sorry." She turned back, and waited on his follow-up, but Carmine was frozen in time. He did not respond to her until she put her hand on his shoulder and asked solemnly, "Are you OK?"

He came to his senses consumed in perspiration. All he could say was, "I'm sorry—I'm really sorry; please forgive me," before he bounded out of the store.

She watched as he made a right turn and disappeared from her view. "Some kind of nut," she muttered to herself. "Not bad looking, though," she chuckled.

II

The next day, Carmine arranged to be outside the store when she came out for her usual lunch-time break. He waited by the curb directly in line with the store entrance to ensure their meeting. When she exited the store shortly after noon, she bristled momentarily when she spotted him, before deciding to walk quickly away and toward the nearby hardware store. He followed her, several steps behind, and called softly, "Excuse me, Miss."

She paused again, turned angrily, and said emphatically, "What is it now?"

Carmine looked forlorn and sheepish as he spoke, "I really want to apologize—I mean after yesterday. I'm really sorry if I frightened you—or anything—I didn't mean to."

She sensed his sincerity immediately and just shrugged and said, "OK" and began to turn away when he spoke again.

"My name is Carmine . . . Della Rocca; I work in the hardware store here."

She could see that he wanted to pursue the matter further, and attempted to cut him short. "Look, I've only got a half hour . . . my father will be angry if I'm back late; I really must go!"

"Your father?" Carmine smiled at her. "You mean you're Cooper's daughter? How about that! How come I've never seen you before?"

Her response was immediate though unintentional, "I've been away at college, and now I'm helping out for the summer."

"Hey . . . that's great! What's your name, anyway?"

Frustrated with herself at not being able to abort this meeting, she said, "Iris."

"Hey, hey. That's a beautiful name—like the flower, right?"

Irritated, she shot back, "Yes. Just like the flower." Again she turned to leave, but halted when he called after her once again.

"Iris?"

Turning toward him, frustrated still, she said, "Yes? What!"

"Can I buy you lunch? . . . I mean—sort of to make up for my rudeness of yesterday?"

"You want to buy me lunch? I don't even know you, and . . . it's not necessary anyway; you didn't do anything."

"Yes I did; and I'm sorry—I really am. I'm really a nice person. I must have frightened you, and that wasn't right. I . . . I . . . only wanted to . . . to make your acquaintance."

Carmine was proud that he had been able to deliver his carefully prepared and much-rehearsed monologue. Iris felt sorry for him, and pondered saying no primarily because her father discouraged her from dating boys who aren't Jewish. But, there was something about this Carmine guy . . . . She simply said, "Yes—OK."

Whatever magic she wrought that day had instant results, for Carmine's demeanor improved dramatically—magically—monumentally—thereafter. He and Iris eventually became good friends and even went out on occasional movie dates when she came home for college break. Carmine also cultivated a new sense of responsibility from her when he discovered that he could put away a few dollars each week if he worked a couple of nights and Sunday at Rosen's. This change in Carmine was evident to practically everyone who knew him, and was responsible for Nick Toscano's call to him this Saturday evening.

"Yo Nicky! What's happenin' babe," he shouted into the receiver.

"I thought you had decided not to speak like that any more."

"Yeah—I mean . . . yes. It ain't easy, you know; what's up?"

"Al gave me the OK to move ahead with the shop."

"That's great!"

"It sure is. Now what I want you to do is set up a meeting with Iris and us for early next week. Can you do that?"

"I don't see any problem. She'll be in for the mid-winter recess, but I'll call her tonight to confirm it."

Carmine was jubilant that Nick had the confidence in him to include him as a key participant in this new business venture.

"Hey Nick," he said.

"Yes?"

"I'm really grateful that you've asked me to work with you—I really am. And for Iris too."

"You'll earn your money and so will she. Besides, it's best if we keep things among friends. There's too many thieves out there who'll steal you blind if you give them a chance."

"Anyway—thanks again." "Call me when you set it up with Iris . . . OK!"

"Right!" This was a new Carmine.

Nick had devised a scheme whereby Carmine would function as the Customer Relations Director for the inaugural Naughty Nicky's store that was to open soon. Nick was aware that Carmine knew his way in and out of every corner of this neighborhood and practically every other neighborhood in Brooklyn as well. His plan was to develop various promotional schemes involving

Naughty Nicky's either as a financial sponsor or the offeror of a prize at selected group functions. His concept included sponsoring a PAL Little League baseball team and providing free uniforms and equipment—all of which would carry the Naughty Nicky's logo. He also planned to offer television sets or tape recorders as prizes for some of the more popular fund-raising campaigns conducted by the churches, Knights of Columbus, PTA's, etc. His entire marketing strategy was based on saturating the immediate area with the Naughty Nicky's concept of high quality, broad selection, and top-notch service at discount prices.

Carmine's role in this venture was clear: he was the spokesman, at the local level, for this new marketing strategy. He would visit shop owners, meet with local groups, and, in general, infiltrate organizations from whom Naughty Nicky's could gain maximum exposure. Iris, on the other hand, being the daughter of a local merchant and formally educated in modern marketing strategies and concepts, was to become the store manager and, for ADISCO headquarters, marketing manager/purchasing agent. Her role was therefore defined as making the first Naughty Nicky's successful by selling the inventory that she determined was most lucrative and salable. His choices of Carmine and Iris were not made indiscriminately, for Nick believed that both were "hungry" to get ahead and would dedicate themselves to making it work. In addition, since they were both well known locally, it was in their own best interest to succeed.

III

The Grand Opening celebration of the flagship Naughty Nicky's was scheduled to coincide with the Memorial Day holiday on May 30. When that day came, the streets were literally jammed with people and cars, and everyone was in a festive mood since the holiday itself fell on a Friday, and the entire nation was ready to enjoy a long three-day weekend. It was a fabulous break for Nick who planned an on-going sale for the entire weekend. With Al's concurrence, he was also going to stay open until 8 P.M. on Friday and Saturday and a half day on Sunday flaunting the blue laws, which were not, incidentally, honored by Jewish shopkeepers in New York City.

Carmine had arranged with Milo Pappagallos, owner of Milo's Diner, to offer five free dinners for two for the winners of door prizes awarded during the Grand Opening. Milo had negotiated with Carmine that he would pay for two of the dinners whereas Naughty Nicky's would pay for the other three. What Carmine offered as an incentive to Pappagallo's and to others who chose to offer door prizes was a below-cost price on any single purchase they made over the next month. This concept spurred Marty Sheehan, owner of the Shamrock Bar and Grill, to offer a Basket of Cheer as another of the door prizes. Cooper's offered six pairs of socks (any color), and Rosen's offered a set of wrenches (American made). Soon, the entire neighborhood was caught up in the mood initiated by Nick Toscano—the progenitor of Naughty Nicky's, an entirely new concept in neighborhood marketing strategy.

When Friday, May 30 arrived, Nick, Al, Donna-Marie, Carmine and Iris were at the store at 5 A.M., at which time they began to string banners, colored flags, and streamers all over the store interior and out onto the sidewalk. When the sales help arrived at 7 A.M., Carmine issued them red, white, and blue smocks in keeping with the nature of the holiday. Nick had privately arranged with the commander of the 80th precinct house for permission to display console television sets on the sidewalk in front of the store. It was understood that Naughty Nicky's would donate a new TV set to the PBA within the next week.

Iris had called in several local housewives to come in to distribute free coffee and cake from Ebinger's, the best bakery in Brooklyn at that time. She had also contracted with technical personnel from the various equipment manufacturers to conduct demonstrations and answer questions. In concert with a local high-fidelity magazine publisher, she designed and set up sound-proof booths in the rear of the store where customers could listen to high-fidelity music from any mix of components and speakers they chose, selectable from the vast inventory available. It was the first such set up in the city, and was responsible for the bulk of their first day's sales. Iris had done her research well, and was only just beginning to realize the potential market for electronics in the home-entertainment field.

Al was unprepared for the magnitude of the response by people to Naughty Nicky's, but was even more surprised when Iris tallied up the day's receipts at the end of the day. He confirmed in his mind that Nick's concept was, indeed, viable and should be expanded to the populated areas of Flatbush, Bensonhurst, East New York and, ultimately, Long Island.

He congratulated everyone and personally handed each sales person a twenty dollar bill when they left that night. He then went up to Carmine and Iris and handed them each a one-hundred dollar bill and said, "I want you to know that I understand the measure of your contribution to the success of this operation. I'm instructing Nick to put you both on salary PLUS one-half percent of the gross sales each month. You deserve a reward as much as anyone here."

He then turned to Carmine and asked, "Did you deliver the console set to the Feast Committee, as I asked?"

Carmine responded simply, "Yes, sir; I did."

Al looked at him and said, "Thanks. I'll be needing your help again a few weeks before the feast. OK?"

"Sure! I'll help any way I can."

Iris studied Carmine's demeanor in Al's presence, and smiled to herself as she felt a hunger for him develop within her. "He really is something else!" She thought carefully about her long-anticipated seduction, planned . . . for tonight.

LA FESTA SAINT SEBASTIAN

I

Robby and Ellen got caught up in the excitement of the Feast and decided to offer their combined services to the Feast Committee. Bruno Gallo, aware of Robby's musical connections, asked him to coordinate the entertainment for the four nights of the Feast, from Thursday to Sunday during the second week of September. On Friday, Saturday, and Sunday evenings, it was usual for well-known Italian performers to sing folk songs, tell jokes, and dance in the old-world, nostalgic style familiar to inhabitants of this area. The neighborhood folks awaited each evening's performance, when a singer or comedian climbed up a makeshift ladder onto the rickety stage and performed in Italian, backed up by the rag-tag band composed of old men and boys who played their instruments well, though they sometimes failed to start or finish together.

Residents of buildings immediately surrounding the Feast venue had first choice of the two or three hundred wooden folding chairs provided free by Pucci's Funeral Home, whose name was prominently silk-screened on each chair back. The chairs, neatly set in rows in the street directly in front of the elevated bandstand, were coveted as prized possessions each night. When Robby and Ellen suggested clearing the street so that the entertainers could also perform in the street, Bruno Gallo overruled them, citing the TRADITION of the preceding feasts.

"We can't be too innovative," he said. "Our people expect to have this feast run just like all the others before it; so keep that in mind."

353

Robby and Ellen were frustrated by Gallo's edict, but accepted the importance he placed on the need to follow 'tradition'.

"I suppose we should just contact the same old performers as in previous years," he groaned in frustration.

"They expect continuity, Rob. We can't disappoint them."

"But what about the rest of the people who come here to spend their money and have some fun? Shouldn't they be entertained too?"

"I suppose so," she replied, "but much of what they come for is to see the Italian people and the culture they share."

"You're probably right, but there are so many popular Italian-American performers today—not just the unknowns from Italian theater and films. Maybe we can get some of them to come here for one night."

"Now that's an idea!" she said enthusiastically. Robby knew that no matter what other ideas he came up with, the Committee would ultimately decide which performers should be invited to entertain. He consciously decided to stifle his frustration and work hard for the overall good of the Feast itself, but would not delude himself into thinking he could change their already-made-up minds—that is, unless he could get Perry Como or Tony Bennett to appear—for free!

II

Al's job had begun many months before when he met with the committee. They were extremely cooperative, and had made him most welcome, not only at meetings, but also at their apartments where he met their families and shared meals with them. Since early June when Carmine personally delivered a new television set to the club room, they were even more gracious to him even though he kept them busy with dozens of requests for help. Al had been developing the concept of 'community' as the primary theme for the TV special. It was his intent to portray this microcosm of Italian culture as one of the few remaining bastions of unchanging heritage from our European forebears.

The film crew had rented empty storage garages on Dean Street a few blocks away, and stored their equipment there each night, taking only the exposed film with them for immediate overnight processing. Each day, the art director established a different priority for the shooting, hoping to meld each day's segment into a homogeneous entity. He would, for example, photograph the local people as they lived out their normal daily activities of shopping, standing on corners talking or leaning out upper story windows propped up on pillows or folded arms. One scene repeated consistently and certainly destined for the show was of a mother shouting down into the busy street below for her son:

"Anthony! Anthony!"

And if Anthony didn't respond immediately, it was likely that someone else's mother would get his attention: "Anthony! Don't you hear your mother calling? Hurry up and answer her."

And no matter what Anthony was doing, everyone with him would wait until Anthony responded to his mother's cries and returned from whatever errand she had for him to run.

"Whadda you want, Ma?" he might dutifully shout up at her.

"Go to the store and get me a half-pound of ricotta," she might say—followed by, "here's the money!" which she tied in a handkerchief and tossed out the window to him. And all the Anthony's of the neighborhood would scurry off to do their mothers' biddings—because that's the way it was. And that's the way it was captured on film along with many other daily activities in the neighborhood.

On Monday of the week of the Feast, Al had film crews stationed throughout the neighborhood shooting scenes that might have public appeal, consistent with the overall theme of the feast as a community celebration. This day, the first of the street vendors arrived at about noon in an old Ford station wagon loaded down with two by fours that had seen many years of prior use at this feast and others in the Northeast. The driver and an assistant sought out their designated spot, which had been marked on the pavement in yellow chalk; they set out immediately erecting the booth from which they would hawk their wares beginning Thursday night. During the day, more vendors arrived, and followed the same ritual of locating, unloading, hammering, and applying multi-colored canvas to the frame.

As one of Al's staff acted as an interviewer, each vendor was asked to describe the particular product or game that they would feature. This Feast, as with many others like it throughout the Northeast, was part of a series of feasts populated by a roaming band of vendors that filled voids created by local vendors. As an example, it was usual for the San Sebastian Feast to have six vendors that sold freshly cooked-on-the-spot sausage and peppers. If only two or three local merchants were interested in opening a stand of this type, Bruno Gallo would call the tour coordinator and request three additional vendors.

It was therefore important for each vendor to be interviewed as they erected their respective stands to ensure that the film footage would cover the variety of food vendors and game merchants. What was surprising to Al as he reviewed each preceding day's footage in the studio was the large number of non-Italians participating in this year's feast. It seemed incredulous to Al, who just a few short years ago lived in this neighborhood, that such a change could have come about seemingly overnight. It was also preposterous to note that someone had obtained a permit to open a stand at the feast vending socks, sunglasses, and various paper products; it used to be that the feast highlighted food, games, a little bit of gambling, Italian records, imported gifts, and the greased pole.

This Feast, which previously embodied the essence of Italian culture in this corner of New York City, seemed to have morphed into something much more cosmopolitan in nature, no longer staffed solely by Italian vendors, but others offering foods and wares unrelated to Italy, Italian culture, or Saint Sebastian.

Whereas Al was expecting food vendors to offer Italian staples such as sausage and peppers, dried figs, Torrone nougat candy, calzones, and zeppoli, he was further unnerved when Louie Wong obtained a permit to sell chow mein, egg rolls and wonton soup. When he spoke to Donna-Marie on the Wednesday of the Feast, she sensed his melancholy at what he feared was the ending of an era.

"I don't believe it, Hon," he said to her. "It's not really an Italian feast anymore: It's more of a neighborhood street fair. And it isn't even a neighborhood fair; there are vendors from all over the East coast looking to participate."

"Perhaps that's what we're coming to, Al. Maybe the mobility of our society has brought us to this point in time, and, perhaps, your TV special should focus on that." She couldn't help notice his sadness; it was as though a part of him had died . . . .

"Things never stay the same, do they, Hon?" he mused.

"I guess not, Al." She tried to console him, for his hurt was deep. "I guess that's what they mean when they say you can never go home."

"It's like our heritage is decaying right in front of us," he shared. "I'm sad that the only thing we'll have soon will be the memories. What will our children have to remind them of their roots? The things we did when we were kids? They'll all be gone. Maybe someday I'll write a book about the old neighborhood and the way it used to be." He was only half joking.

Al was committed to presenting the Feast as historically unfolding from its roots in remote, southern Italian villages to this specific Brooklyn neighborhood. What ties remained? Why this saint? This show must avoid depicting the feast as a static event isolated in time.

His approach to the feast would present it primarily as an apostolic celebration where the community of believers gathered to eat, sing, and party—a New Testament concept promoting communal support and the common good. The feast mimicked the principles inherent in building 'church'—people united in the common goal of sharing in the gifts that God had given.

Al wondered whether the feast officials understood the historical provenance of their own undertaking. "Oh well, it didn't matter any more. There probably won't be many of these isolated local gatherings in a few years. People will have multinational street fairs in Manhattan where everybody can come and celebrate."

Al resolved to dedicate the conclusion of the TV special to the dynamic cultural changes in the neighborhood and to the successful amalgamation of the various ethnic groups into the newly evolving community. But, he insisted, the Feast must be portrayed primarily as a celebration—a true celebration of the ongoing American experiment with immigrant culture and the miracles born of ethnic fusion in the new world. Once upon a time, the Feast was America emergent; today, the Feast is American.

III

Donny met Rita Thursday evening at about 5 P.M. at the Long Island Rail Road depot in downtown Brooklyn; from there they walked the twenty-two blocks to the site of the Feast. When they got there, the entire area was aglow, brightly lit with flood lights and colored lanterns everywhere. They saw the telephone company truck leaving, having completed digging the hole for the greased pole, which was now being lowered by volunteers from the fire department. As Donny and Rita walked among the vendors, they were overcome by the delightful aromas emanating from the food stands.

"Want something to eat?" Donny asked Rita.

"Are you kidding? Of course! We don't get this in Huntington."

They walked up to the nearest vendor selling sausage and pepper heroes, and watched as the giant rings of pork sausage sizzled in their own fat on the gas-fired grill.

"Don't you just love the way it smells?"

"Absolutely! Pork rules!"

They resumed their stroll while savoring the huge sandwiches encased in wonderful, crusty Italian bread. Both well versed in the dangers implicit in eating while walking with these types of sandwiches, they laughed at each other's futile attempts at keeping oil from dripping down their chins and onto their clothes. They realized it was silly to keep walking and eating, so they paused . . . and ate.

They were adjacent to a stall where a half-dozen children were tossing pennies into the center of a large table holding tiny glass bowls of water and small goldfish. Every now and then a shriek of joy filled the air as a penny landed in a bowl and the child claimed that bowl and its prize. Donny wondered how these vendors could make any real money selling the cheap trinkets or collecting coins that children tossed at fishbowls.

Rita mentioned that tonight, one of her cousins was at the feast, having walked his pushcart across the Manhattan Bridge to be here at the feast. He did not occupy a stall; rather, he roamed the feast peddling his wares. Later tonight, near 11 P.M., he would retrace his steps and wheel his cart back across the bridge to the small garage he rents on The Bowery, where he stores his inventory of colored beads, tin horns, yo-yos, paper hats, snow globes, fish bowls, and other trinkets. He works feasts in The Bronx, Manhattan, Staten Island and Brooklyn. In truth, he would become a millionaire before he reached fifty and own the largest independent toy business in the entire city.

This all happened because he collected the pennies, nickels and dimes from children at feasts and fairs, and on street corners in the city. Of special note is that he attained his wealth long before he owned a car or truck; he lived the American dream, escorting his business (pushcart) everywhere he went. Occasionally, he paid five cents to a street urchin from lower Manhattan to assist him navigating down the treacherous subway steps onto the platform of the 'A' train's stop at The Bowery. It was here he often worked, waiting out a storm or blizzard. He worked twelve hours a day, seven days each week.

Just about the time they finished their sandwiches, Donny spotted a stand where the proprietor was holding a large, shiny meat cleaver over a two-foot-square wedge of almond-nougat candy that was cement-like in structure. She deftly placed the cleaver in a carefully selected spot, and whacked it with a single blow from a heavy, ball peen hammer. The candy split, not cleanly, sending shards of nougat flying. Once placed within a mouth, a piece of this candy rivaled any modern adhesive with a special affinity for teeth . . . with fillings.

"Want a piece?" Donny asked Rita.

"It's no good for my fillings . . . but, sure!"

Donny bought ten cents worth of the brick-like nougat candy and gave her a large piece.

"This is great isn't it?" he smiled as he chewed into it, praying that his fillings remained intact.

"Mmmph," is all she could utter, her jaws nearly glued shut.

IV

Robby and Ellen were already up on the bandstand discussing the entertainment for the evening. Tonight, it would consist of the band and community dancers. Robby, with Ellen, had selected several elderly couples to lead in the familiar folk dances, highlighted by the Tarantella. Tonight only, the wooden folding chairs would be set in a semicircle to permit dancing in the street. As in previous feasts, specific patriarchs would have the final say as to which songs the band would play, relegating Robby once again to a minor role; yet, he was strangely proud of the old-timers that wanted, and retained, some power within the community. It was the respect they commanded that he admired more than anything else—yes, he thought, the "RESPECT".

When they climbed down from the bandstand, it was about seven-thirty and beginning to get dark. The individual vendors had begun to turn on their own lights. The crowds were coming.

V

Al had previously established a command post atop the roof of 533 Underhill Avenue, and from it he could view every activity below. Nick's suggestion of using war-surplus walkie-talkies proved helpful to Al when he wished to communicate with the film crew or art director.

It was about 9:30 P.M. when Robby Ventura stood before the microphone and called for a drum roll. As cameras and eyes focused on him, he announced the beginning of the Tarantella, the most festive of Italian folk dances. On his cue, four elderly couples tottered, arm in arm, to the center of the open semi-circle and began gesturing among themselves and to the good-natured hecklers in the crowd.

"Get some shots of every couple," Al directed via his walkie-talkie. "Get some extra shots of that really old gent—the one seriously bent over."

As the strains of familiar music began along with the necessary rhythmic clapping, each couple sprang to life to the joy of the crowd, and began to sway as they had done for years past. Broad smiles graced the faces of each couple, and though each perspired heavily, none dared stop. Indeed, they seemed to grow stronger as the music continued.

In the midst of this happy exhibition, two teenage males suddenly forced their way into the center of the group of dancing couples, and mimicked their actions, shouting and then gyrating erotically. When one of the elderly gentlemen stopped dancing and asked them to return to the crowd, he was pushed back, and fell down onto the pavement. Instantly, the interlopers were surrounded by men from the crowd who pinned their arms against their sides and escorted them away from the Feast. As the shouts and curses from the intruding teenagers trailed away, Robby urged the music on, this time inviting other couples to join in. The interlopers never returned.

"Did you get all that?" Al shouted into his walkie-talkie. Then to himself, "What is going on around here?"

"Yes, chief," was the somber reply.

VI

"I sure wouldn't want to be one of those hooligans tonight; they're gonna be sorry they came here," Donny lamented, shaking his head. Then to Rita, "Do you recall things like that happening here at the Feast before? Or seeing the streets so dirty?"

"No . . . never. Just look around . . . kind of turns your stomach seeing people disgorging half-eaten sandwiches and dirty napkins onto the street."

They walked past a remote alley that reeked of vendors' garbage left for 'someone else' to pick up.

" . . . broken soda bottles . . . ."

" . . . looks like a pig pen . . . ."

" . . . didn't used to be like this." And then, someone from the crowd shoving and shouting "Hey buddy, get outta my way, will ya?!"

"They aren't even neighborhood people, and they act like they own the street."

"Let's go watch the dancers."

"OK. At least that will be fun. The old timers are so cute."

VII

The film crew wrapped about midnight, and a runner took the film directly to the studio in Manhattan as he had done after every shoot. Al sensed that something amiss when he gathered everyone to conduct his usual debriefing with the crew.

"What's up, guys," he queried.

One of the cameramen replied, "Well, let me be honest, Al . . . I got the impression that the Feast was an ethnic event—a kind of celebration."

"And?"

"And . . . it turns out it's just a flea market for vendors . . . a sideshow where somebody sells you junk you don't want at ridiculous prices . . . ."

"But it is an ethnic . . . ."

"Maybe it WAS, Al," another crewman interjected. "Maybe that's what it used to be, but look around—those ruffians? The garbage in the street? It isn't the same anymore!"

Al ached, accepting the hard truth: "The glory days of this feast are no more; no longer will visitors from remote parts of the city converge on this neighborhood to share in the joy of the Feast. No longer will happy couples arrive to partake of the fun and food and music and show RESPECT because they are in someone else's neighborhood. The crew is right: the king is dead: God help us all."

At home early the next morning, Donna-Marie was sensitive to Al's plight; she had known about, but never acknowledged, the ongoing changes occurring 'back home.' "You know, Al, what Manny said to us one Christmas is true: the only things that we have . . . the only things that endure . . . are love—and the family."

Al remembered Manny's tender words and his toast, "Alla Famiglia!—to the Family"; he knew Donna-Marie was right. Thinking about Manny's words reminded him of a philosophy teacher who often lectured on the importance of 'words'.

The prof, an older gentleman, exhorted the class one day: "Some philosophers teach that the spoken word dies once uttered; I say, instead, that words can never begin to live unless they are spoken. Think about that!" Today, Al thought about that admonition; he remembered that it was scriptural as well: In the beginning was The Word, and The Word was God. He reminded himself to thank Manny.

Al's reflections persisted. Neighborhoods change, people age, buildings decay and collapse. But love . . . love continues to grow—given a fair chance. He took his wife into his arms filled with hope that her spirit could help heal his. With a look only lovers can know, he sought Donna-Marie's eyes and whispered, "I love you so much; you give me a reason to press on and not quit."

"I love you too, Al; you are my whole life!"

Her words, now more than ever before, scorched his soul; her love, pure, unadulterated, and unaffected sustained him. She loved him beyond all reason. He could feel the tears in his eyes, and wished—prayed—that soon, now, finally and forever, he could expunge the once-again intrusive image of . . . Laine Powers August.

VIII

"Take me to your house, Donny; I'm frightened," Rita said clinging tightly to Donny's arm.

"Don't be afraid; everything's all right."

"I don't like the crowd—it's rough and rowdy. People are shouting."

"OK. Let's say good night to Robby and Ellen, then we'll go."

"Fine, as long as we can make it quick," she conceded reluctantly.

As they walked toward the bandstand, Donny was certain that he saw anger in Robby's face; maybe he remembered what the Feast used to be; maybe he was saddened at what it had become.

IX

The humid night air swirled its way through the open windows of the Flatbush Avenue bus as it rumbled along the bumpy city streets, carrying with it dust and the heavy, sweet, pungent smell of diesel fuel. Donny squeezed Rita's hand, fearing that if he loosened his grip, she, like the glory days of the Feast, might flee. He had averted his face from her several times since entering the bus, lest she see his moist eyes. He ushered Rita toward the back of the bus where he sat by the open window.

"Are you all right, Don?" she asked, resting her head on his shoulder.

Still staring out the window, he said, "I'm . . . fine. I'm . . . OK." But his thoughts were of 920 Dean Street, and Brother Artemus, and the ice dock, and the kid with the nice face, and Jenny's, and Otto's, and . . . that nothing seems to last . . . nothing endures.

After spending a few moments in deep reflection, he took his always-present pen and began writing on his always-present notepad. Rita sensed his concentration, and waited until he finished then asked, "What did you write?"

He handed her his notepad; these words were scribbled across its pages:

DONNY'S LAMENT

I wonder where the days have gone
when kids would run and play in streets,
And parents sat on stoops to share the news
in shirtsleeves or curlers.

I wonder where the days have gone
when 'clean' was good,
and stoops were scrubbed by landladies
who said, "Don't chalk up my sidewalk!"
I wonder where the days have gone
when trolley cars clanged along cobblestone expressways.
And only 'they' had cars for transport . . .
outside 'the neighborhood.'
And where, I ask, can one go
where streets are safe at night,
to walk your girl home hand-in-hand
and maybe steal a kiss . . . or two?
And when did we become so smart
that 'ethnic' means rejection, or more—
and avant-garde—with no respect
for those who led the way?
And why, I cry, did I stand by?
My enclave—it collapsed!
We fled so fast and dinna think
or care 'bout how it made me . . . ME!
"Oh sure," you cry, "it's all the way:
the world must hasten forth—
'else how's our land to prosper
if we just stagnate here?"
One never—ever—can go back
'cause crumble fills the void . . .
and—like the tide—it levels
all castles of the mind.

And you, great Saint! . . . can you perceive
the loss of what once was: a Prayer,
a tribute from your brood?
Shall we just move on?

When Rita finished reading, she put his pad and pencil into her purse, and urged his face toward hers; she sensed his hurt. Looking deeply into his teary eyes she smiled lovingly at him and gently whispered, "Don't be afraid, my love. Everything will be fine . . . you'll see." She paused, reflecting further on the sadness they both experienced this night. Then, after a brief moment, she spoke, "Don?"

"Yeah?"

"I've been thinking about the feast and how different it all seemed—you know, those rowdy teenagers and some of the mess we saw."

"Hmm."

"I remembered a poem by Emily Dickinson. She wrote about honoring the simple days of old that led us to where we are today. She described a scene where someone enters a forest and stumbles onto an overgrown path strewn with leaves and acorns amid fallen trees, dead branches and wind-blown debris. Evaluating this moribund and apparently infertile scene, the person pauses to question his own mortality and purpose in life. Dickinson posits that the expanse of decomposing materials simply heralds the expectant glories that await: some acorns are sustenance for small animals; other acorns shallow-root and mature rapidly to nurture deer that feed off the tender, young saplings; and lingering everywhere amid this disarray are the eggs of the next generation of forestation, ready to continue the process ad infinitum." Donny listened intently while she concluded, "The Creator planned it this way . . . unless a seed dies . . . . It all depends on how we choose to interpret what lies before us. "

"Wow, I didn't realize what a deep thinker you've become. But, you're right. For certain. My grandmother always got after me when I worried about 'stuff'. She would say, 'Donny, remember to take time to smell the roses; they bloom just for you!' "

He sat silently beside her for a few brief seconds before adding, "Rita, do you know what separates you from most people in this world . . . what makes you so very special?" She must have blushed, but he couldn't tell; his eyes were still moist. "I'll tell you. No matter what kind of adversity comes along, you can put a positive spin on it; you seek out the good in things. And then . . . and then, you manage to smile your glorious smile—it puts everyone at ease and . . . it just melts my heart. I love you so much, and I thank you for being you!"

Rita sighed, thankful she had eased some of the strain of the evening for him; she loved him so, and hated when he was sad. She snuggled and cuddled, acutely aware of all that her beloved was feeling.

In that moment, Donny recalled Saint Paul's scripture: There are only three things that endure—faith, hope, and love; and the greatest of these is love.

He felt at peace; her words, her radiant smile salved his spirit. Mostly, though, he cherished moments like this with her nestled by his side; they completed each other. The bus rumbled along, then later, as they neared his home, he questioned, "Rita?"

"Umm?" she murmured.

"What is that Italian toast your father says at meals when everyone gets together for the holidays? He's always so proud when he says it. Is it Alla . . . Alla . . . something?"

"It's Alla Famiglia . . . To the family."

"Family. Family is very important to him, isn't it?"

"Yes. Very much." She snuggled even closer than before, wrapping her arm around his and holding tightly to both of his hands. She continued, "To him the toast is more than just the words. To him, it is a confirmation of how vital and enduring the family unit is—and must remain. The toast itself calls for a strong response from all family members to ensure the survival of the family as the central core of the community. The family teaches us and nurtures our ability to love."

Donny pondered what Rita was saying, reflecting on the times he had heard her father forcefully pronounce, "Alla Famiglia!" and everyone respond equally as forcefully. He began, finally, to grasp some of the deeper mysteries of life, mysteries that, for some, can never be solved.

"Alla Famiglia," he thought, and brushed away a tear.

Rita saw him and asked, "Are you all right, Hon?"

"Sure . . . the wind just blew a speck of dust into my eye."

"Oh." She let it pass, but was certain she heard him murmur again softly to himself, "Alla Famiglia—Alla Famiglia!"

Finis

THE NEIGHBORHOOD: ITS CHARACTERS

Marie Gargano
Donny Gargano
Angelo Gargano
Namm's Dept Store
Loeser's Dept Store
Sidney's grocer: Gone with the times
St. Teresa Avila School: Best around
P.S. 42
Uncle Jim: butcher
Gemeiner's butcher
Sleven Bros fruit and vegetable
Ft. Greene Meat Market: Busy place
BTHS: Best around
Brother Artemus, Principal
Sr Mary Steven
Tony's Bar & Grill
Timmy - no shower yet
Robby Ventura: Cool cat
Mr Lowe, Tailor
Vincent Speranza: The Bull
Frankie Famiglietti: The Boy
Buster Sperato
Carla Ventura
Vito Ventura
Jenny's
Eileen
Sally Benson
Arlene D'Arcy: Lovely young miss
Nick Toscano: Tough guy made good
Rocco Toscano: Nick's Dad
Salvatore & Rose Toscano. Nick's G-Parents
Carmine Della Rocca: It's only tea!
Anna , Carmine's sister
Al Zito. Beretta. 22

Sevvi Carducci: Hood
Charles Atlas: Godson, Compare'
Donna-Marie Capasso: Best Around
Viteri's bakery: Yummy
Eileen McGill: Donna's girlfriend: Pretty to look at
Joe Weintrauben: Nice guy, big boss
Al's mom, Rosa
D-M's sisters Marcella & Elena & Joe and Lou
Rafaela & Sal Capasso
Manny Zito & Cathy
Johnny Wenofski: Worker w/ Carmine
Robert Jarvis' Soda supply
Jabbo: Vito's brother
Ziggy Lune: Agent
Sammy Stone: Musician
Dorman's Bar: Hangout
Ellen-Mary Kilkenny: Gorgeous
Jimmy Cigar Ryan
Betty: Sister
Johnny Pegano
Dominick Nicoletti
Rossford girl
Ralph Egan & Gloria
Palomba's
Eugenio
Uncle Nunzio: Barber
Pete Kelly's garage & Ben Harris
Benny's: Very yummy
St Brendan's dances
Paula Martin: So sorry
Gloria Buonavito: Perfume
Terry McGann: Nice
Rita Staci: Sweetheart
Dave Barr: Catskills
Catherine McCauley HS
OLMercy Convent
Bruno Gallo: Capo, local

Rosen's hardware
Cooper Dry Goods
Louie's Luncheonette
Iris Cooper: Smart AND pretty
Gloria McCormick
Milo Pappagallos: Diner
Marty Sheehan's Shamrock Grill
Ebinger Bakery: Best around
Pucci Funeral Home: Around the corner
Louie Wong at Feast
Tony's Bar & Grill